THE CALL OF
ABADDON

Colin Searle

To my family, my Mom, my girlfriend Zoe, all of my hardworking beta-readers, editors, and everyone who provided input on the manuscript at every stage: this book wouldn't exist in its current form without you all. Thank you!

NEW TORONTO
HABITAT MEGATROPOLIS

SPACE ELEVATOR

EXTERIOR WASTELAND

CAPITAL SCIENCE
INSTITUTE

ATMO-DOME
GENERATOR

RAINWATER
RESERVOIR

DOWNTOWN CORE

INNER CITY WIDTH:
85 KM

TRANSPORT AIRFIELD

FRAN'S BAR

TRIBUNAL
CENTER

THE VILLAGE

INNER CITY HEIGHT:
9 KM

EXTERIOR TRANSITWAY

RECYCK YARD 78-10D

HABITAT DIAMETER:
250KM

"Everything can be taken from a man but one thing: the last of the human freedoms—to choose one's attitude in any given set of circumstances, to choose one's own way."

—— **Viktor E. Frankl**

Prologue

Personal journal of Dr. Avery Oakfield, UEF Science Minister, PhD.

***** Log E7-006 Begins *****

The worst has happened.

With great regret, I can confirm that multiple test subjects have escaped the labs. From what my people have managed to piece together, the escapees started a chemical fire, using it to cover their exit through the Institute's central loading docks. Crews are still putting the blaze out. What a bloody disaster. My field teams are running an initial search of the city for our three escapees. Unfortunately, because of the Council's recent sanctions, my reach is limited.

The escape appears to have been led by Abhamancer Program test subjects 107 and 108, who also managed to take Successor Program subject 001 with them, too. Losing the Abhamancers is bad enough, but the loss of 001 will be difficult to explain to Emperor Mariko.

In total, three individuals from two research streams are gone. Without Abhamancer subject 107, the Abaddon Beacon artifact remains uncontrolled, meaning that the Nanophage is still free to spread across the Sol System. Perhaps worst of all, Abaddon appears to have noticed 107's absence.

The Abaddon obelisk has been acting erratically since the breakout, like it did when Hadrian Mariko left my operation to start his damned empire, and it's proven more than capable of psionically influencing him far beyond the walls of this Institute. Who knows what kind of damage subject 107 might do if Abaddon turns its influence onto him, as well?

Subject 107 was critical to the Abhamancer Program's success, an imperative part of preventing the spread of the Nanophage through our technologies. He had the most psychic potential out of all the next-generation subjects, even more than Emperor Mariko himself. His Abhamic powers will continue to grow, without guidance or control. I can only hope that Subject 107 sees sense and returns here for continued treatment before anything catastrophic happens.

But if Abaddon gets to him first, it's game over for the human species. There aren't enough nuclear weapons in the UEF's arsenal to halt another planetary-scale Ascension event. The Confederacy exhausted their entire thermonuclear stocks to stop Abaddon's last attempt at Ascension, and the Earth's biosphere has only become more toxic as a result.

Subject 107, I'm sorry for all that I've put you through, but you must return here and allow me to finish the Abhamancer Program. Only I can make it work, and only you have the power needed to restrain the Abaddon Beacon, and prevent it from spreading this damned techno-plague to every soul in our star system.

Please, 107 ... *Jason*, come back.

*****End of log*****

1 — A CALL FROM THE VOID

"Find us, Jason ..."

Jason snapped awake, breathing hard, looking around the room. His head was pounding. He could swear that he'd heard something muttering to him, like a thread of his nightmare had followed him into waking life.

Clammy sweat dripped from his face as he sat up, trying to slow his breathing, blinking away the afterimages of his terrifying dreams. Maybe the whispers had been his imagination.

Then, the strange voices began again, filtering into Jason's mind like a cold graveyard mist. Terror clenched his heart as they said, *"The Ascension will soon be at hand, and your participation is required ..."*

"Ascension?" Jason asked. "What—what does that mean?"

"Time is short. Your presence is critical. Find us, or we will find you ..." the ethereal chorus continued.

Jason recognized these voices; he'd been hearing them for years in his dreams, though they'd always been indistinct, hard to understand. But unlike any other time before, he was hearing them now while he was awake—and that scared him most of all.

"Abaddon?" Jason breathed.

*"We are your creators, from your beginning to your end. You must find us
..."*

"Shit."

With trembling fingers, Jason reached behind his neck and gripped an
implant attached there —right above a strange spiral sigil, barcode and identifier text 'Subject 107' that had both been tattooed onto his skin long ago.
He twisted a control knob on the device, allowing drugs from the neural
inhibitor implant to flood his system, calming him.

"Find us ... before the final sacrifice ... the Ascension must commence ..."
came one last cacophony of whispers, but as the drugs worked their magic
on whatever part of his brain was receiving them, the swirling voices of the
Abaddon Beacon dissolved into nothingness. He began to breathe more
easily, and the tightness in his chest relaxed.

The drug—Osmium—was an addictive psychoactive substance, but it was
effective at helping Jason sleep through his fitful dreams, plagued by his
distant memories of the obelisk in the labs ... and far darker visions that he
tried his best to forget.

As Jason's migraine eased, he swung his legs over the side of the cot he'd
been using to nap, glancing around the room. The prefabricated polymer
walls were hung with robot parts, cybernetic implants, old vehicle engines, all
manner of technologies and machinery from various eras. The area rumbled
with the passing of a nearby spacecraft. So did the repair shop and everything
within it, as suspended automaton limbs jangled against empty vials that had
once contained valuable pink Nanogel—something that they desperately
needed to refill.

That triggered a question—where were David and Sam?

"Jason, we gotta go!" came his brother's impatient voice from the direction
of the workshop's double garage doors, open to the street so sunlight could
filter inside. Jason's gaze snapped up, spotting David by the door.

"Oh, shit!" he said.

Jason had been resting up before a salvage job, and as he glanced at the
chronometer on the wall—he was late. Very late.

"Yeah, you overslept again, ya dingus. They're all waiting for us," David
said, one hand on the vertical sliding door, the other holding the strap of
a large bag of expedition gear. "I let you rest as long as I could, but we're
outta time. Grab your stuff, we have to get going. Sam's already talking to
the governor."

A white, citron-tufted cockatoo—Budgie—squawked down at Jason, perched on the peak of his brother's red hair.

"Crap. Alright, I'm coming, sorry," Jason said, still a bit breathless as he started scrambling around, looking for his expedition supplies. Budgie clambered down David's clothing with his beak and claws, waddling over to Jason as he bobbed his feathery head in concern.

"Don't apologize to *me*. Come on, I'll meet you out here," David said, ducking out the doors and into the street beyond.

With his expedition gear stuffed into a shoulder bag, Jason ducked out through the rusted garage doors of their repair business, topped by a buzzing neon sign that read: 'Chop Shop'.

"I'm here, I'm good!" Jason said, stifling a yawn and scratching his scraggly mop of blonde hair. He hadn't slept well the night before, nor the previous few nights, either. David opened his mouth to reply, but another voice cut him off.

"Oi, where are you two going?" a bald man called, hurrying down the street toward them. Two twitching robots tottered in his wake, sputtering and sparking.

David groaned. "As if we didn't have enough on our plate today."

"Hey Vlad," Jason said, catching one of the man's meter-tall metal robots as it tripped forward on malfunctioning legs, preventing it from faceplanting on the permacrete ground. The robot burbled random strings of code through its speakers.

"Don't tell me that you're too busy to take care of these two," said Vlad, with a warning tone.

"Sorry, we're heading outside the walls for a bit," Jason replied.

"Outside? My bots are needed in the hydroponics lab, and they're at risk of developing the Phage! Please, you must fix them, now!" Vlad said. The elderly man shot a desperate look at David, who had taken off his supply bag to check his gear. He looked up, but shrugged. "We can't do it right now, Vlad. Governor's orders."

Jason twisted the inhibitor's knob again, letting the Osmium drug calm his nerves. Vlad didn't budge, so he elaborated.

"Sorry, Vlad. To fix these guys, we need more spare parts and Nanite gel, and to find all that, we gotta go outside the Village. Like David said, it's Yamamoto's call."

Vlad sighed, massaging his temples. "Okay, alright. If the Governor ordered you out on a salvage run, it must be for good reason."

He turned his wobbling robots around. Both were non-verbal, but the taller one looked back at Jason, and he could swear that he saw a plea in the bot's single photoreceptor eye.

"Bring these guys back here tonight," Jason said, patting one of them on the head. "Depending on what we find out there, we should have enough new materials and Nanites to patch them up."

"It's alright. Make sure these two are your top priority when you return," Vlad said, clapping his robots on their scuffed plating to keep them moving.

"You got it," Jason said, zipping up his frayed jacket.

"You topped up on Osmium?" David asked.

"Yeah. I grabbed plenty of backups, too." Jason said, shaking his supply bag.

"Hearing any spooky eldritch voices?""Well, I did hear something after I woke up," Jason admitted. "That's never happened before, not outside my dreams."

"Are you hearing it *now*?" David asked, raising an eyebrow.

Jason shook his head. "No, the Osmium chased it off. Turns out that it works even while I'm awake."

"Nothing to worry about, then," David said as he studied Jason's implant, tapping the blue drug vial loaded into it. "Do you think you'll be fine if we run into trouble out there?"

"Probably, yeah," Jason confirmed. "They're dreams, David. It's scary stuff, but nothing can find us down here in the underground. Not even Abaddon. Obelisks can't move, right?"

"Got that right. You're full for now, but let me know if you run low," David said, finishing his inspection of the inhibitor's Osmium vial and clapping his brother on the shoulder. "I have some backups, too, just in case. Don't get blasted on this stuff, please."

"No promises," Jason said.

"Aren't you two *forgetting* someone?" an electronic voice interrupted, booming from the Chop Shop. A fourteen-foot-tall, red-painted humanoid robot ducked under the doors. Talos stretched his massive limbs and piston-driven legs with a rumble of clanking gears and tossed a huge net of burlap salvaging bags over one of his pauldrons, which he must have been searching for in the rear storage room of the Chop Shop.

"Whoops," said Jason, looking sheepishly up at the giant metal man. "Sorry, Talos. We were waiting for you, I swear."

Talos pointed a massive metal finger at them, eliciting a warning flap and squawk from Budgie, who was once again on David's head. "You two are always moving so fast. Slow down and enjoy life's smaller pleasures. Your flesh-prisons will wither and die, while I get to deal with the boredom afterward."

"Thanks for the existential dread, bolthead," David said.

Budgie bravely took off and landed on Talos's finger, locking eyes with the automaton's photoreceptors in their usual staring contest.

Jason caught the roar of multiple spacecraft over the water, leaving for other Earth-side habitats like theirs or off-world. Among them was a civilian hauler converted into a troopship, bound for the faraway battlefronts of the Solar War, which had been ongoing for several years.

"Enough sightseeing; let's get over there," said David, gesturing to the Village's twelve-foot east wall gate, several hundred meters away between stacks of prefabricated shanty dwellings rising up on either side of the main street. Several people stood in front of the gate, waiting for them—including Sam.

They headed out with Talos bringing up the rear, and Budgie landed on the robot's gigantic shoulder guard.

The street was bustling with activity. Village residents worked at nearby food stalls and fabrication buildings, and others arranged themselves for afternoon prayers. Work coveralls, jumpsuits, and casual wear flapped from lines strung across the road. Even children above the age of twelve worked non-critical jobs when they weren't in school. Several kids from the nearby playground approached Talos, hanging onto the automaton's piston-driven legs as he lumbered past. He grumbled and growled at the delighted, screeching children through his vocoder, but that didn't stop them from climbing him like a jungle gym.

Gas-based engine fuel and food smells wafted past Jason, mixing with the familiar stench of livestock and manure from the Village stables, which stood beside the vertical crop-growing structures and hydroponics building. The combination smelled like home, the only one he'd ever known. Artificial sunlight radiated down into their underground sub-level at an angle through the concourse's support pillars, providing a view of the lake and air traffic outside. The sun's heat felt good on Jason's skin. Most of New Toronto's vast, cake-like superstructure was above water level, but anything below the habitat's top-most city surface level was considered to be 'underground'.

"The dome is having more problems today, look," David said.

Jason looked across the sparkling lake water far below that stretched many kilometers away to the habitat's outer wall, which projected an atmospheric shield dome that insulated the city arcology from the toxic superstorms raging across the hellscape beyond. The dome also displayed an artificial sun on its inner surface that mimicked the real sun, hidden behind dense clouds outside.

But several sections of the energy dome were flickering, fading in and out of existence. Visible wisps of the radioactive storms beyond the translucent barrier were carried in by fierce winds before the shield segments re-initialized, which then malfunctioned again in a loop. As Jason watched, several repair spacecraft rumbled overhead, aimed at one of the gigantic generators mounted atop the dome's projection wall.

He pointed them out. "See? Feds are on it."

"Yeah, but how much fallout are they letting inside before they fix that bloody thing?" David grumbled.

Another massive repair vessel roared right past the Village, barely two hundred meters away. Through its open bay doors, Jason spotted teams of rad-suited workers and industrial robots preparing to work on the wall's dome generators. Many of them didn't look much older than he was.

But the workers made no indication that they could see any sign of the tiny secret settlement nestled into the city's sublevels as their ship roared past. A stealth hologram hid the Village from view through gaps in the open-sided causeway. Holo-generators displayed a vast pile of collapsed rubble to mask their home from outsiders, allowing it to remain secret from the outside, and most importantly, from the Federation at large.

Dusty midsummer winds whipped past the Village wall as Jason and David drew near. Several volunteer troopers were sitting above the gate, monitoring the ancient, automated turret guns, which watched the gloomy area beyond the barrier. Like most militia, they wore a mismatched assortment of fatigues, flak vests, body armor, and improvised plating. Much of their gear dated back more than a century, to the time before the Great War had rendered the planet nearly uninhabitable.

The Village's two de-facto leaders were waiting for them: governor Julian Yamamoto and security chief Josiah Mendez, speaking with three of the settlement's militia guards. Sam stood with them, deep in discussion with Yamamoto. Like David, she was a couple years older than Jason and very fit from their expeditions into the Under-city's depths. Her background was mixed, Caucasian and Asian, but Sam had always been tight-lipped about her origins.

Governor Yamamoto was tall, sporting a goatee, greying hair, with rough working hands and dusty work boots. Mendez wore an eyepatch, and held a cane in his gnarled, hairy grip. No one knew who Yamamoto had been before he'd founded the Village many years ago, but he ruled with a stern, fair hand, and he'd brought Mendez in to keep the peace. Most villagers were fine with this arrangement; Yamamoto's benevolent autocracy was better than the dangers of the UEF's wartime terror state of surveillance over the city above. He offered a fresh restart on life for a lucky few, one that many gladly took.

Mendez tapped governor Yamamoto on the shoulder as the salvagers arrived, and Yamamoto turned to regard them. "Glad you could finally join us."

David nudged Jason. "Someone overslept."

Sam eyed Jason, but when he shrugged, she gave him a small smile and a wink.

Yamamoto spoke with a slight accent, holding a scuffed data tablet with a large spreadsheet open in its primary window. "I see. Now that you're all here—as you probably know, Quartermaster Bilby has asked us to ramp up salvage operations for more spare parts and advanced Nanite tech. We need them for our big list of repairs, including the holo-shield."

"We're aware, Governor. The holo-barrier's been acting up lately." Sam replied, scrolling down a list of active repair jobs on her personal tablet, comparing his list to hers. "We've got a monster pile of jobs in the Chop Shop and around the Village to complete, but we're low on basically all supplies that we need for repairs, so it's been slow-going."

"Which is not good," Yamamoto agreed. "In light of that, Chief Mendez has chosen three of his people for you to train as our secondary salvaging squad. They're all we can spare right now. That crashed spaceship we spotted a few days ago is the perfect target for this exercise. Having additional salvage teams on the roster will give you a break to spend time on repairs. Much needed, by the look of you."

The governor gestured to the three young militia guards with them, who snapped to attention. "These are your trainees."

"Sir!" the militia team replied, slightly out of unison.

"Have any of them ever been outside the walls?" David said, looking skeptically at their young recruits.

All three militia looked troubled at this question. Mendez answered for them in a rumbly voice. "No, they have not. Your job is to make this first excursion a successful one for them. And bring back as many valuables and supplies as possible, of course."

"I see," David replied, his eyebrows raising further. To Sam and Jason, he murmured, "Babysitting these three out there will be risky."

Sam shot him a dark look, but Jason could tell that she didn't disagree.

"I don't want to suggest that these guys don't have what it takes, but wouldn't it make more sense to send more experienced militia out with us?" Sam asked the governor. "This may be a routine salvage run, but going outside the walls into the wider Under-city is never a picnic, even for us."

"Ordinarily, yes. But these three are nimble, well-suited for climbing around in the deep ruins like you three do," replied Yamamoto. "We're also understaffed as it is on the walls, and we need our best marksmen here in case of a Phage migration, especially if Talos is going with you. Given that you three are our most experienced—and only—salvagers, it made the most sense to send these three out with you. They'll learn fast."

"Alright, Governor. We'll show 'em the ropes. But remember, exploring the abandoned under-levels is always a risk," Sam said, making a conciliatory gesture, and glanced at the militia to impress the point upon them.

Yamamoto nodded and Chief Mendez inclined his head in approval, puffing on a locally-made cigar. Budgie flapped away from the smoke, disgusted. The three recruits also acknowledged Sam's point with timid nods.

"We know that it's dangerous out there, more so now than ever with the increases in Phage activity. We're also so low on supplies that we don't have a choice but to send you out," Mendez said.

One of the militias raised a shaking hand.

"Yes?" Sam eyed him.

"Are there gonna be, uhhh...hostiles out there?" the scared, olive-skinned kid asked, clutching a long-outdated rifle. Jason thought he looked too young to be guarding the Village walls, let alone joining an Under-city salvage run.

"Yes, every part of the Under-city beyond these walls is hazardous," Sam replied to the militiaman. "We've seen everything out there; Phage-infected people, robots, dissidents, criminal gangs, mercenary hideouts, and plenty more. You've seen the numbers when a Phage migration hits us, so a big part of the job out there is avoiding trouble. But if we encounter anything robotic—and in uninfected condition—we'll add 'em to the salvage tally. You're Mayweather, right?"

"Yes, ma'am," said Mayweather.

"Sam's fine," Sam corrected, smiling.

"Right ... Sam."

"You probably know these other two hooligans already—Santiago and Soohyun," Mendez said, gesturing to the two remaining recruits. "They're under orders to do whatever you say. Bring 'em back in one piece, ya hear? We don't have a big pool of replacements. Behave yourselves, you three!"

"Yes, sir!" the militia replied, saluting. Budgie hopped from shoulder to shoulder, harassing everyone. Soohyun reflexively brushed her hair behind one ear and kept stealing glances at Jason, which made him go red in the face.

"We'll bring them back the same way we found 'em," Sam replied to Mendez, checking the battery of her short, vicious blade slung in a magnetic holster. "We haven't lost a man out there yet."

"I wouldn't expect anything less from our best expedition team," Mendez said.

"Keep an eye on the time while you're out there," Yamamoto said. "I don't want anyone outside the walls after dark, especially when the infected are more active down there."

"Sure. They probably won't come after such a large group though, sir," Jason pointed out. "The Phagebearers out there haven't given us much trouble lately, especially with Talos watching our backs."

"And you organic ingrates don't even pay my protection tax," Talos said. His trio of eye-lenses flashed in aggravation.

"You don't have a protection tax," Sam snapped.

"They don't know *that*," the towering robot hissed, jabbing a finger at their recruits.

"When are you finally gonna fix his personality matrix?" David whispered under his breath to Sam.

She raised an eyebrow at him. "Who ever said anything about fixing him? Talos is perfect."

The giant robot leaned over David, casting him into complete shadow. "I *heard* that, human."

"Alright, open it up, people! Keep an eye on the perimeter," Mendez said, signaling to the guards, who moved to the gate controls. Jury-rigged mechanisms came alive, and the sheet-metal slabs scraped open.

"Let's get you all underway, and be careful. Bring back as many supplies as you can, please. We really need it," Yamamoto emphasized.

"Will do, governor," said Sam.

The gently curving causeway tunnel edged into view beyond the gates, lit sporadically by sunlight filtering in between massive support columns on the outer side. Structural collapses had made huge sections of the concourse impassable, blocked by mountains of rubble from above. The Village had been intentionally set up in one of the most stable parts of the city's peripheral Under-city rings, but that was changing as the gigantic habitat degraded over time. Talos's photoreceptors narrowed as he deployed a scanner from his upper carapace.

"I detect no threats," the red automaton said. With a flurry of sliding armor plates, his arm transformed into a brutal-looking plasma cannon. "But I hope I do."

The three militiamen froze, glancing at Talos in apprehension.

Sam put a hand on the mighty weapon, making him lower it. "That's unnecessary, big guy."

Despite Sam's assurances, Santiago, Mayweather, and Soohyun gripped their weapons tighter.

Jason gave them an encouraging smile. "As dangerous as these salvage runs can be, the more stuff we bring back, the more ration cards we get."

Soohyun blushed as Jason stared into her eyes, before he looked away quickly. "Really?"

David thumped his well-developed pectorals.

"How do you think I ended up looking like this?" he boasted to the militia. "Salvaging pays well in protein, y'know."

Sam rolled her eyes. "Your head is as inflated as your chest, *hackerman*."

Jason hesitated as the rest of the group began to move toward the gate, one hand on his forehead. Despite the multiple hits of Osmium coursing through his system, he felt chills run up his spine as his mind returned to his earlier post-dream experience. The Abaddon Beacon's words remained with him, but there was no cause for alarm. The Osmium was working. Abaddon couldn't get to him through the wall of drugs protecting his mind.

Sam put a hand on his shoulder.

"Don't worry, Jason," she said with a reassuring tone as David led the militia into the gloom, followed by Talos. "You sleep alright?"

"Not really. I heard Abaddon, *after* I woke up from that nap. But the drugs are working. I'll be okay."

Sam took a step closer and gave his Osmium drip a quick twist, depositing another small dose into his bloodstream. "Good. Let me know if you run into any trouble with the 'ol mental state. I'll keep an eye on you."

"Thanks, Sam."

"And there she is," Sam remarked as the team reached their destination after trekking many levels deeper into the Under-city. "Prime real estate for filthy scavengers like us."

A destroyed corporate transport spacecraft wobbled in front of the salvagers and Talos, held in midair by a tangle of foot-thick power cables below a gaping hole in the massive chamber's ceiling. The designation stencil was damaged, but Jason made out the letters '*UEF-CT Ganesh of Mesopotamia*' stamped across the starboard side, hinting at an origin from one of the Southeast Asian habitats. Dappled sunlight played across the ship's broken hull, trickling down through the city's superstructure. The ship had been caught in the thicket of inert cabling after crashing through the arcology's superstructure many levels above, tangling as it came to rest down here.

The salvagers stood on a permacrete cliff, with the sausage-shaped transport suspended fifteen meters away over a sheer drop into the city's deep ruins, where polluted waves crashed far below. At forty-five meters long, the spacecraft only had two engines left out of six, with no antigravity repulsors remaining. The vessel was a disaster—but ripe for plundering.

Still panting from their hike, Soohyun gazed at their target and gulped. "We're going inside *that*?"

"Yep," Jason replied. Budgie shrieked.

"Scanning. No life signs aboard," Talos announced. "No sign of active rad-leaks, either. You vulnerable flesh-sacks are lucky today."

"Don't jinx us," David murmured.

The corporate hauler, crumpled like a sad accordion, groaned under its sagging weight. Acrid-smelling fluids dripped from broken ports along the hull. Running lights flickered and exposed sections of the ship's innards sparked pitifully. Sam pulled on a pair of thick safety gloves. "I'll head inside first, check it out for hazards. Then we'll strip 'er down."

"How do we know the UEF won't come looking for this thing?" Santiago asked.

David shook his head. "It's been weeks since the crash. Yamamoto wouldn't have sent us down here if there was a risk of discovery by the up-worlders. If the corpos haven't bothered with retrieval, the Feds won't either. They're too busy wasting time on their stupid Solar War."

"Would you do the honors, Talos?" Sam asked, drawing and pointing her short blade at the ship, which was attached to a reel device on her hip with a long electrical cable.

Talos groaned, retracting his buzzing, steaming plasma cannon. "All work, no fun."

The robot fired a gas-powered grappler from the upper-left side of his torso, crunching a cable deep into the ship's starboard flank. The mechanism locked in place with an audible *clunk*, so it couldn't be released by accident. Though the transporter was far larger than Talos, he lumbered backward, dragging the suspended vessel closer to the cliff's edge. When it wouldn't swing further, Talos clamped his giant boots down with gas-powered grounding spikes, cracking the permacrete. "There. Have at it, peasants. I'll stand here and do ... nothing."

"Careful, big guy. I don't wanna go spelunking for you if this heap takes a fall," David warned, peering over the edge. Water lapped against crumbling docks and titanic support pillars sprouting from the waves, hundreds of meters below.

"I have run ten thousand simulations on how to move this vessel without compromising it. Have faith, squishy organic," Talos scoffed.

"How do we get inside?" Soohyun asked.

"Like this!" Sam said, pulling on a pair of goggles and a respirator. She leaped off the broken cliff edge, graceful as a cat, hurling her blade at the spacecraft.

Sam's stubby rectangular sword magnetized to the hull's metal surface with a quivering *snap*. She swung on the blade's attached cable beneath the spacecraft's ravaged flank, then her hip-mounted reservoir reversed, dragging her upward.

Everyone watched as Sam grabbed her magnetized blade's hilt and planted her boots into outcroppings on the hull. Ignoring the crashing swells far below, she attached a safety line from her belt to the ship's hull with a big carabiner clip. Once secured, Sam held on with her free hand and triggered her phase sword's secondary mode, snapping it off the hull as the magnetic field switched off. The edges of the blade flared to fiery life, allowing Sam to carve through twelve inches of ablative hull and circuitry like it was a plasma torch.

"That's ... crazy," said Santiago, looking to Jason for confirmation, who shrugged. "She does this stuff a lot. You'll get used to it."

"I'll need a change of pants if I'm going in there!" said Mayweather, watching Sam carve into the ship.

"Then you better have brought 'em," Jason added, grinning. The three militia exchanged glances. David raised an eyebrow.

In a shower of sparks, Sam removed a square of metal from the hull and hollered, "Be right back!"

She pulled out a scanner and crawled inside. Less than a minute later, Jason heard a grinding noise, and a loading ramp fell from the ship's underside with a loud *clang*, bridging the gap between the permacrete ledge and the suspended cargo vessel. Sam strolled down the incline toward the waiting group, twirling her sword on its cable as she removed her protective gear. "It's safe enough in there, more or less. Who's first? We have a lot to teach you guys—"

Budgie squawked, taking off and going nuts in the air above their heads.

Moments later, Talos spoke. "Alert."

The scanner sticking out of his beetle-like rear carapace was beeping as he elaborated. "Vermin approaching. I cannot blast them in my current state. Which is an incredible pity."

Sam tensed, raising her sparking blade while everyone else readied their weapons. "Everyone, protect Talos. Things are about to get a bit choppy."

2 — ABADDON'S SHADOW

Several dozen robotic drones spilled out through a crack in the crumbling wall, ten meters behind the salvage team. They were newer models, most no more than a couple years old, blaring random blurts of code through failing vocoders. The metal and polymer composite automatons were moving with strange jerky motions, charging headlong toward the salvagers. The horde came in all shapes and sizes, from humanoid to spidery chassis designs, plus one with treads and flailing arms tipped with vicious-looking engineering appendages. Some had rad-shielding to survive maintenance work in the deepest ruins around the habitat arcology, but that hadn't saved them from their techno-affliction.

"Ah, shit. These are advanced models. Don't let 'em get close, waste 'em!" David barked, whirling his junkyard pistol up to shoulder height, firing incendiary rounds at the rabid, charging robots.

Jason extended his crackling stun rod, bracing for impact as the crazed group closed the distance—but Sam charged ahead, whirling her crackling blade on its cable like a bullwhip.

Despite the horde's size and sudden appearance, the melee was short-lived. Mayweather, Santiago, and Soohyun only managed to fire their rifles a handful of times before Sam, Jason and David had blasted, beaten and sliced the shuddering robots into an early grave.

"That was ... easier than expected." David said, narrowing his eyes at the smoldering robotic bodies before firing a few extra shots into the ones that were still twitching. Sam completed a final whirling dervish-like spin, snapping her spinning blade back into her hand with precision, as the final robot fell in two smoking halves in front of her.

Jason turned to Soohyun. "See? This gig can be fun, sometimes."

"Right. *Fun*," Soohyun replied. The other militia shifted uncomfortably, training their weapons on the dead pile of hostiles.

"Don't get overconfident, Jason," Sam said, crouching over the belly of a dead repair bot. "These poor guys haven't been looked after in months, so they're starting to develop the Phage. Nice job leaving their batteries intact. If only this one was clean ..."

She held up a pink glowing object in her protective glove—an energy storage cell filled with the specialized Nanites that governed its operation. Nanotech was a miraculous innovation that ran nearly every piece of technology made in the last half-century. But a dark purple, pulsating tumor was cracking through the battery's casing, indicating that the Nanites within were replicating excessively due to age and lack of maintenance, developing the 'Nanophage', which was nearly irreversible without extremely specialized intervention and treatment.

Sam beckoned to the militia, who approached the sparking wrecks. Jason hesitated, eyeing the robot bodies carefully, but Sam winked at him. "They're dead, Jason. Don't worry. Gather round."

Jason and the militia closed in while David, Budgie and Talos kept watch for any stragglers.

"This kind of stuff is what we're after," Sam said, holding out the battery for everyone to see. "But if you see any of these nasty-looking growths ... no touchy. You guys already know what'll happen if these little shit-heads enter your bloodstream."

"Biological infection?" Soohyun asked.

"Yep. If any Phage-infected Nanogel finds even a small open wound on your body, or gets in through some other means, like your mouth, you're done. It doesn't seem to be infectious through our pores, though, which is lucky. Doc Janice can only treat so many Phage cases at once—don't go giving her more work," Sam said, rolling the battery away, which fell off the cliff edge. She twisted the release cap off a clean battery before pulling it out of the broken robot's body, and began teaching Mayweather, Santiago, and

Soohyun how to strip other usable parts from the corpses. Jason observed as well.

David eyed his brother, jerking his head toward the suspended spacecraft. "You'll be okay when you're in there?"

"It's cool, David. The Osmium's working fine," Jason said.

David was about to reply when Talos interrupted, "I don't have all day, flesh-bags!"

All eyes turned to him. The robot twanged the taut cable with an impatient finger. Sam waved him off. "Talos can hold that thing still for weeks. He's just bellyaching."

"I heard that!"

Jason turned to the robot. "I'm guessing we can't all go inside at the same time."

Talos nodded. "Indeed. Do not enter that vessel in groups larger than three or four, maximum. Any more weight risks pulling the craft free. Not even my magnificent strength will prevent its fall if enough of those power cables slip free. And don't jump around in there like the filthy apes you are. This elevator only goes down."

Soohyun and Santiago wrinkled their noses at Talos.

"Any way to secure it more?" Jason asked, gesturing to Talos's grappling line.

"No, puny human," said the robot. "That sloppy grey mass in your head needs re-calibration. The ship's honeycomb structure is already under enough stress. Even if I had more anchoring cables, they would only pull the vessel apart. We'll lose the cargo and maybe some of you organics, too. As much as it pains me to watch you have all the fun, this is the safest option."

"Fair enough," Jason said.

David pulled an armored laptop and a bundle of data lead connectors from his bag. "I'll show you guys how to bypass the ship's firewalls and release security on critical system components. Then, Sam will demo how to extract everything. Jason's our backup, since he's still in training. He'll lead the offload."

Jason glared at his brother, but David was already heading for the ship. Sam looked up from the maintenance bot she'd carved open.

"Careful in there, David," she cautioned. "If that ship so much as squeaks, get these guys outta there. And keep your respirators on. I saw coolant leaking inside somewhere."

David slipped on a mask. "Fine, whatever. Come on, you three. Time to be baby computer nerds."

Mayweather, Santiago, and Soohyun fumbled with their protective gear, following him.

"And duck when you board!" Sam called while David led his charges aboard.

Irritated over David's comments, Jason knelt down, stripping uninfected parts from the nearest robot, adding them to Sam's neat collection of Nanite batteries, energy converters, intact power conduits, and circuit boards. She looked up at him.

"Don't let David bug you, Jason. Your anxiety is improving, even on a lower Osmium dose. I'm thinking we can probably wean you off it soon!"

Jason shrugged. "It helps to have had some recent wins. Yamamoto trusts us, so does Mendez. I wish I could get a good night's sleep, but the Osmium helps with that."

"Don't worry," Sam said, pulling off a glove to pinch his ear. "Once we figure that out, we'll wean you off the O-juice, and I'll start training you for real. About time, too."

After a glance to ensure their new friends were still busy inside the suspended transport ship, Sam's eyes glowed with pink inner light as she wrenched a bot's midsection open with the power of her mind. Jason studied Sam as she utilized her talents, which they had nicknamed 'Abhamic powers', after the research program that Jason and David had unwillingly participated in as children. Sam was from a different research stream than Jason, and she had a calmer, more refined version of their shared mental abilities, without a need for Osmium to keep her power under control. Jason had never been able to figure out why that was.

The biting stench of chemicals and coolant wafted out of the sparking robot's exposed innards. As Sam focused, bolts unscrewed by themselves, sealed panels popped free, and individual Nanotech parts floated out on their own.

With the automaton's core exposed, Sam pulled out the bot's corrupted CPU unit in her gloved hand and held it up. The device rippled with quivering, glowing tumors that burst through its plating. "What a waste of good memory."

Jason stared at it. The CPU was badly overrun with the Nanophage. Sam's eyes glowed as she prodded it with her mental powers, but the infected component did nothing out of the ordinary.

"What do you think they've been doing in those labs since we escaped? Are they still looking for us?" Jason asked, stripping more uninfected parts out of the robot's belly.

"Did that question just pop into your head, or have you been ruminating again?" Sam replied.

"Well, after hearing Abaddon earlier ... I'm starting to think about that place again," Jason said.

"Understandable. None of us have fond memories of the Science Institute," Sam mused as her glowing pink irises cooled down. "But that scientist who ran it still has to be searching for us. Governments have been trying to create psychic super-soldiers for centuries, way longer than we've had Nanotech. An awful lot of money must've been dumped into us before we all escaped. And even though I've said it a million times ... thank you for that. You and David didn't have to take me with you. But you did."

Jason nodded. "Don't mention it. And yeah, that bastard will probably never give up on finding us. We're billion-dollar babies, too much of an investment to lose."

David emerged from the suspended cargo ship's hatch, shouting down at them. "Oi! I cracked the computer core and downloaded the manifest. Get this, the ship was transporting stuff from one of the corporate gigafactories into orbit. From the data I found, the holds are full to bursting with brand spankin' new Nanite products, and there's *tons* of surviving shipboard equipment too, all the good stuff."

"Well, our big payday gets even bigger," Sam said. "My turn, then."

"Ugh, so this means I have to carry even more garbage home for you weaklings?" groaned Talos from his position nearby.

"Yes, bolt-bucket, you do," Sam said, playfully tugging the harness on Talos's shoulder as she headed toward the ship.

"Ughhhh," the robot groaned theatrically.

"Don't we get a break? It's cold in here," asked Santiago from the ramp, shivering. Soohyun eyed Jason again, who looked away.

"Nope, not yet," Sam said, whirling a finger. "Time for the real work. I've got lots to show you three."

Half an hour passed while Sam and their recruits worked inside the ship. During that time, Jason helped David load up some of Talos's burlap storage bags with uninfected robot parts, stacking them nearby so Talos could haul everything back to the Village when they were done for the day. Jason yawned constantly, rubbing his eyes.

"So, you and that gal Soohyun, huh?" David said.

"What?"

Jason stumbled, going bright red as he steadied himself, stacking the last of his armful of parts into one of Talos' burlap storage bags.

David lowered his brow, grinning. "You're so dense. It's obvious to everyone. And I'm glad, little brother. I'll admit, Sam's a good-looking girl, but it's about time you gave up on her and focused on someone ... better. Soo's not a bad candidate, and it's not like you've got a lot of choice, where we're from."

"I'm not, I don't ... what's that supposed to mean, anyway?"

"I'm just glad that you're broadening your horizons, that's all," David said, winking.

"I appreciate the older brother pep talk, but my relationships are my business. Stay out of 'em, please," Jason said, flatly.

David stared up at the creaking transport for a moment, then held up his hands. "Alright, alright. Quit your whining, I'm razzing ya. Get back to work."

Jason gave his brother a sideways glance, but he returned to salvaging without further comment.

Periodically, the militia briefly emerged from the ship for fresh air. Santiago grinned at Jason during his break.

"I thought this was going be a lot worse; salvaging isn't as bad as I thought," said the militiaman.

"See? Our job can get dangerous, but it's pretty interesting, too," Jason replied.

"Definitely more than wall duty," Santiago said, ducking inside again.

Finally, Sam and the militiamen clunked down the ramp. Sweat glistened on Sam's forehead, soaking her tight working pants and undershirt.

"Find us, Jason ..."

Jason sucked in a breath as another whisper from nowhere tickled his tired mind. Abaddon. How the hell was it breaking through the drug barrier?

"Anywhere you run, we can reach you. Anywhere you hide, we will find you. The only way out ... is to find us ..."

Jason cranked up his Osmium drip to maximum. The voices slowly dissipated.

He was fine. Everything was fine.

"These three seem to be getting the hang of things, got a lot of important stuff disconnected in there," said Sam, drawing half-hearted cheers from the militia. She clapped Jason on the shoulder, startling him. "Your turn, big guy."

David squeezed his brother's arm. "Go build some muscle, skinny boy."

Jason jerked away. "Alright, alright. So, we're offloading?"

"Yep. We've uncoupled the easiest ship parts to move. Reactor rods, power converters, things like that," Sam said, mopping her shining face with a rag. "We'll come aboard to help empty the cargo bay once the ship's light enough for all of us in there."

"And I get to be the mule. Such a burden," Talos complained. Budgie shrieked at him.

"Shut it. You're a robot," Sam snapped.

"Let's get to it!" Jason said, walking up the ramp with his respirator on and his arms outstretched for balance, careful not to look down. The militia groaned, following along behind him. "Gotta work for our calories, people!"

"Be careful in there, Jason," Sam said.

The ship's interior was in complete disarray. Despite the hull's thickness, Jason could see the watery depths below right through gaps in the machinery. Random objects and live wires sparked everywhere, ripped out of their moorings by the brutal landing. The interior creaked back and forth in the breeze, but Talos kept it mostly stabilized, with the broken deckplates somewhat level and walkable.

There was no biological mess, so the living crew members must have evacuated before impact, likely landing somewhere topside. But their maintenance bots had been left behind, causing further damage as the ship crashed down through the Under-city. They lay everywhere, broken and silent.

The hauler was too mangled to ever fly again, and there was no way to tell what had caused the malfunction that brought the heap down—but lack of maintenance was a likely culprit, as Sam always said. The ship's cargo was a miniscule loss for the powerful Nanotech corporations, but it was a goldmine for a bunch of Under-city dwellers like the Village. *More for us,* Jason thought. The city's government wouldn't care if the ship's reactor irradiated an entire sector of the habitat's sublayers, as long as it didn't become a liability for the surface level, where the vast majority of citizens resided.

"What should we grab first?" Soohyun asked, showing Jason a long row of the ship's components and precious Nanotech that they'd extracted with Sam's help. Thick pallets of intact cargo were strapped down to the uneven deck-plates.

"We'll start with the heaviest stuff," Jason replied. "The faster we lighten this heap, the sooner David and Sam can come aboard and help us empty the cargo bay. Pick a component, and we'll get this stuff onto dry land."

He slipped on his gloves and hauled up a huge, self-contained fuel rod cylinder that Sam had extracted from the dead reactor set into the floor. A Geiger counter in Jason's pocket ticked sporadically, but the radioactive materials within the fuel rod were within tolerable levels. Sam's clandestine usage of her Abhamic powers must've made her look like a powerlifter to their recruits when she'd extracted the reactor components out of the deck.

Mayweather, Santiago, and Soohyun lifted different heavy objects. Soohyun chose a delicate container of raw Nanites, designed to cycle and replenish reservoirs of active Nanotech devices before the Phage had a chance to develop. These were incredibly valuable, badly needed back in the Village.

"Hold that like this so it doesn't break," Jason explained, using his own load as an example, and Soohyun rotated hers. Viscous pink fluid sloshed around inside, made up of many trillions of Nanites. "The Phage is hard to catch, but you're in for a world of pain if you do."

"Gotcha," Soohyun said, glancing down at the reservoir's glowing ceramic viewing window.

"Let's get this stuff offloaded, come on," Jason said, heading for the ramp, and the militia followed.

Out of nowhere, something shoved him in the back, hard. "What the—"

Jason stumbled forward, off-balance, into a pool of lubricant leaking out of the bulkhead that had congealed, becoming very slippery. The militia were too far behind him to have pushed him, nor were they close enough to grab him before he went down.

"Crap!" Jason's feet skidded around on the slick deck as he used the reactor fuel rod to cushion his fall against a coolant valve ahead. The piping burst, blasting frigid gases into his face.

"Oh shit!" Mayweather and Santiago exclaimed as Jason rolled away from the damaged conduit, bashing his Osmium inhibitor implant on the ground as he went. He heard a distinct *crack* on impact. What the hell had shoved him?

"You okay?" asked Soohyun. Jason steadied his breathing behind the respirator, moving back toward the coolant pipe, eyes darting around the ship's hold for an assailant. But he was alone with the militia, and they looked as stunned as he felt. "I'm alright, don't worry … check your masks. I'll fix this."

Trying to calm his hammering heart, Jason yanked some tools out of his bag, bracing the fuel rod cylinder on the floor between his legs. Soohyun leaned over, speaking quickly. "We can tell Sam, Jason. It's no big deal. She'll seal that thing up again."

Jason felt a shiver at her touch. "Gimme a sec. I can do this."

With shaking hands, he carefully vice-gripped the broken valve and applied a patching solution, which slowly stifled the flow of gas.

"Helloooooo? Everything alright in there?" David shouted from beyond the hull.

"We're good, minor issue...I think," Santiago called down the ramp.

"Come out!" Sam's voice replied, distant and echoing. "Swap me in, I'll take a look at whatever it is."

"Sorry, just...gimme a few more seconds. I'm almost done," Jason stammered.

Over the declining hiss of coolant, he heard Abaddon's soft, ethereal whispers enter his mind.

"*Find us, Jason …*"

His heart skipped a bit. Jason's body went ice cold, but it wasn't from the bitter fumes.

"What? Not now …" he said, reaching for his neural inhibitor.

"Did you say something, Jason?" Soohyun asked, concern crossing her features. Mayweather and Santiago stared at him with concern.

The voices continued. "*You must return to us ...*"

Why wasn't the Osmium working? Jason scrabbled at the inhibitor, trying to trigger another large dose to calm himself. He felt liquid running down the back of his neck. Was the device leaking?

His fingers found the drug vial, feeling the edges of shattered glass. It was *broken*. The damage had been done by his fall—Jason's mind was unprotected.

Something foreign curled its bladed claws around his hammering heart, pushing against the weakening drug barrier that protected his mind, as his brain burned through Osmium. Jason began to hyperventilate as the Abaddon Beacon's voice blasted through his brain, louder than ever.

"*Your time has come. You have been chosen for a great task, one that only you can complete. You must return to the place where you were created ...*"

The cargo hold around him disappeared as images smashed through Jason's mind—gnashing teeth, diseased flesh riddled with mutagenic tumorous growths, a giant seat surrounded by machinery and cabling, a gleaming city square consumed by an enormous battle, an entire planet being hollowed out by a black mass of boiling biomatter ... and a tall, glowing obelisk that blazed with pink fire.

"*We have the answers you seek, about yourself, about your power, and about your place in the cosmos. All will be revealed if you find us, and fulfil your role. Find us and bring salvation to your species ...*" Abaddon roared.

The room briefly swam back into corporeality, and Jason saw the militia looking down at him from above with worried expressions. Around him, a slow seep of ponderous inky shadows boiled up through the floor grating, which Jason's militia companions didn't seem to notice. Abaddon was here, permeating the area all around them with its presence, invisible to everyone but Jason. The shadows pulsated as they spoke, buzzing together like a thousand insects, "*We are everywhere, we are infinite, we cannot be stopped, and you belong to us ...*"

Jason locked eyes with Soohyun, forcing his words out through clenched teeth. "You have to get off the ship, now!"

"What?" she asked. Mayweather and Santiago stepped forward to help him, but they paused as Jason started thrashing violently, like an invisible force was trying to take over his body.

Jason watched with horror as the inky shadows crept up his torso, approaching his face, grabbing his limbs and constricting his movements, de-

spite his attempts to brush them off. Terror blasted through him as Jason
realized that the shadow must've been what had shoved him earlier. Like
some creeping menace, it had been waiting for the perfect moment to strike.
But how?

"Get out! Get away from me! It's all around us! Get off the ship!" Jason
continued, scrambling away from the creeping dark.

"What about you?" asked Mayweather. "What the hell is going on, Jason?
I don't understand."

Their comms crackled with Sam's voice. "Guys, what's happening in
there?"

"Get off this ship, right now! It's after me, not you!" Jason yelled, fumbling
for his broken inhibitor's controls, but the dark shadowy tendrils held his
fingers back, preventing him from touching it. Abaddon's terrible presence
was coming for him from within the shadow; Jason could feel it. He reached
for his fallen supply bag with his other hand, where his fresh Osmium doses
were stored, but the blackness coiled around Jason's wrist, locking him in
place.

Santiago was the first to snap out of his shock at Jason's apparent descent
into madness, dropping the heavy power coupling he'd been holding and
shoving Mayweather toward the exit, yelling outside. "Sam, David, we're
coming out! Something's wrong with Jason!"

"What?" came Sam's distant reply, repeated over their comm units. David
could also be heard, yelling in the background.

"*GO*! I can't control it!" Jason yelled with his eyes screwed shut, tendons
jutting out across his neck like steel cables, bootheels banging into the metal
deckplates as the shadow choked him. He felt his eyes begin to burn with
inner light.

Soohyun was ducking through the entry hatch after her comrades when
an invisible defensive psychic wave fired outward from Jason's body, blasting
the shadows away from him ... along with everything else.

Outside, Sam and David gasped as the suspended ship jumped wildly, emitting jets of smoke, fluids, and vaporized chemicals. Santiago, Mayweather,
and Soohyun, who were stumbling through the ship's hatch, were blasted

off the gangway ramp, which bucked with enough force to snap free from its hydraulic control pistons. The ramp whistled out of sight while the vessel continued to violently sway over the open void.

Sam's eyes flashed pink for a split second. As the three militia fell toward her through the air, she nudged them with her Abhamic abilities so they landed on the permacrete ledge instead of plummeting to their deaths. Santiago, Mayweather, and Soohyun rolled and lay still in a cloud of dust, knocked cold from their close proximity to Jason's psionic blast. Sam didn't feel much better as a hammering brain-ache thundered inside her skull from the impact of Jason's uncontrolled Abhamic pulse wave.

Talos tried to compensate for the erratic swinging of the ship. The ground under his feet began to crumble as he struggled to hold it steady.

"Knock it off in there!" the robot roared.

David turned to Sam and jabbed a finger up at the ship, which still creaked and groaned from the internal detonation. "Do something, Sam! What the hell is happening to Jason?"

With her battered psychic senses, Sam identified a strange black cloud coalescing around the dead transport ship, moving like some thousand-limbed cephalopod of the deep sea. A spike of fear stabbed through her heart as she traced the origin of the inky black shadow, which was emanating from the robot corpses strewn around from the recent fight. The living darkness stretched from their Nanophage-infected cores up into the swaying craft, subtle enough that Sam hadn't noticed it until now.

"It's them! The Abaddon Beacon is working through the Phage-infected to find Jason. It's trying to get inside his mind. That devious bastard, it waited until he was onboard, away from *us*!" she exclaimed, dashing over to each infected robot carcass, rolling and kicking them over the edge of the precipice. Each automaton body left a dissipating trail of oily blackness as they fell into the depths below.

"What the heck are you doing?" asked David, but Sam beckoned impatiently. "Quit your yapping and help me get rid of them! We have to break the connection between them and Jason!"

Jason's eyes rolled in his head. As the murky, billowing shadows returned, wrapping around him tighter and tighter, his terror grew beyond mere anxiety and fed on itself in a vicious spiral. The boiling, pulsating shadow was alive with Abaddon's malefic laughter and strange rhythmic chanting, like a cathedral housing a billion corrupted souls.

His mind reacted defensively to the Beacon's psychic assault, neurons firing uncontrollably as his innate Abhamic abilities rallied on autopilot to protect him from its predations. Jason's back arched as another psionic wavefront blasted forth from his body, pushing the darkness away again.

The transport bucked like an angry bronco, flexing like no spacecraft should. Through her wounded mind-sight, Sam felt Jason spiraling, trying to push back the Beacon's attempted intrusion. But his involuntary efforts were destroying the ship around him, causing plating and components to fall from the craft like hail, clattering off nearby ruins and plunging away into the depths below.

Fighting through the terrible pain in their heads, Sam and David continued to haul robot bodies off the cliff edge without touching their infected components, cutting off the flow of inky shadows bleeding up into the ship. But even after they shoved the final Phage-infected automaton over the cliff edge, the shadows continued to swirl around the spacecraft without interruption. Something inside was sustaining the Abaddon Beacon's remote presence.

Sam looked at David as panic gripped her. "It's still in there with him."

"I thought you said the Osmium would protect him," David said. "Why isn't it working?"

"I have no idea, David. We've never seen Abaddon try to take over his mind like this before!" Sam cried, trying to locate the transport's entry hatch as the giant craft bucked and swung. "I'll try to jump inside and pull Jason out!"

"Hurry!"

Another almighty psychic detonation went off inside the ship, nearly blasting it in half. Debris was thrown in every direction, bouncing off the permacrete ledge. The thick power cables holding the deteriorating ship aloft flailed dangerously. Talos bellowed in alarm as Sam fell to her knees, vomiting up her lunch and clutching her head with white knuckled intensity. David bellowed in agony behind her, falling to the dusty ground as he clawed at his scalp. The militia lay motionless, still unconscious.

As she regained control of herself, Sam could almost *see* the secondary wave-pulses from Jason's starburst of psychic Abhamic power rippling out of the deteriorating spacecraft, forcing the shadowy presence back with it. Some of the living darkness dissipated into the nearby ruins, but most of the black cloud quickly dove back inside the ship, undeterred by Jason's efforts to ward it off.

"No..." Sam whispered.

The ship's superstructure began to fall apart, slipping loose from several power cables, lowering past the cliff edge. The massive weight dragged Talos's feet-locking mechanisms through the cracked and crumbling ground. More cables scraped up the hull, stripping it of plating like dry skin.

"Talos! *Stop* that thing!" David roared. Budgie was going nuts in David's hands, flapping his wings and screeching.

Every joint servo in Talos's rusty body groaned as he strained against the inevitable, crunching his powerful fingers deep into the permacrete. "I.... I cannot..." Talos said.

Sam dashed to the cliff edge, watching the cargo hauler begin to slowly roll. The entryway rotated out of sight, making it impossible for her to leap inside.

"This can't be happening!"

Jason awoke on his back, blinking.

He struggled onto his elbows, wiping pink Nanite goo off himself. How long had he been out? Hours ... days ... or *seconds*?

Acrid chemical smells filled his nose. The ship shrieked and moaned around him like a dying animal, but at least the horrible shadows were gone.

Jason's neck and chest were wet. His whole body was soaked with ... something. He raised his hands, which dripped with a warm, glowing pink substance—raw Nanites, splashed all over the place from the broken reservoir that Soohyun had been carrying. Other ship components had been smashed as well, making the Geiger counter's rapid ticking blend together.

At least none of the Nanites had gotten in his mouth—and fortunately it couldn't pass through his pores—but it was only a matter of time until it found a small cut or laceration. Jason started wiping it off in a panic.

Through billowing gaseous fumes pouring out of multiple broken conduits, Jason saw that the syrupy pink goo coated almost every nearby surface. The ship's main hold had been dented outward like a bomb had gone off inside, with him at the very center. Nearly every loose object had been crushed, including most of the ship's precious cargo. If his militia friends hadn't gotten out in time, they would have been pasted like insects.

The deck rolled, bringing Jason back to his senses as loose wires and metal debris slid around, making an incredible racket.

He heard the shadow whispering in his head, relentlessly. *"Find us, Jason. We will never stop until you do ..."*

The Abaddon Beacon's presence returned, stronger than ever, spearing another blast of pain through his mind as the living blackness swirled up through the deck. As it came, the shadow curdled the bright pink Nanite solution into a dark, angry Nanophage purple, spreading the infection with lightning speed through the healthy Nanogel. This seemed to empower Abaddon's shadow, allowing it to manifest more strongly, advancing on Jason from every angle. In the corners of the cargo bay, the broken maintenance bots came back to life as the Phage took hold of them, shuddering upward and screaming through their vocoders, like the mouthpieces of an angry God.

Jason panicked, crab-walking away from the sentient, spidery gloom as it snaked around his body. His broken Osmium inhibitor emitted a constant series of warning beeps. He had no idea where his bag with his spare drug vials had gone.

"Why won't you ... stay *away* from me?" Jason yelled, lurching onto his side as the transport rotated, coming apart around him from the fatal damage he'd caused with his mental blasts. The shadows ignored his protestations, closing in.

"You, like your species, belong to us ... "

David appeared behind Sam, grabbing her shoulder. Talos continued to buckle the pavement, roaring with effort as he tried to prevent the ship from falling.

"You've gotta get him out of there, Sam. Talos is losing that thing." David pleaded. Budgie was 'assisting' their enormous robot companion by flapping around his cranium and gabbling at him. The cargo craft jerked further downward. The incredible weight bent Talos forward at the waist, his armored fingers dragging through the ground.

"I can only hold this for another few seconds!" the robot said. "Disconnect me! My cable locking mechanism is not responding!"

"Help Talos detach himself from that thing," Sam said. "I'll get Jason out."

"You better," David said as he dashed over to help remove Talos' grappling cable, holding his aching forehead. He took a glance at the militia, but they were all still out cold from Jason's initial Abhamic blast.

Sam pushed aside her mental agony and let her eyes defocus, concentrating her senses on the dying cargo vessel, which continued its slow roll as the remaining power cables slid and snapped under its five-hundred-ton mass. The swirling shadows were blinding her mind-sight. Where was Jason?

Right as she lost all hope of getting him out, Sam spotted the entry hatch—facing upward instead of sideways. Blanketed in choking, stygian shadow, Jason flopped limply around the unstable interior as the ship rolled.

"Gotcha," Sam hissed, as her thoughts pinpointed him.

"Resistance is futile ..."

Darkness tainted the edges of Jason's vision as his mind was slowly supplanted by the Abaddon Beacon's horrific alien consciousness. It nearly had him.

He no longer saw the physical environment around him. Jason was falling through a great void under a carpet of dark stars, plummeting past a huge wall that stretched endlessly in either direction. He reached for it, sensing safety behind the barrier, trying to catch hold and stop himself from falling into the ocean of darkness below. But there was no way to break his fall, so Jason plunged into the endless sea of thick black shadow, drowning under a horizon of poisoned moons and broken worlds.

"There is no point in fighting, Jason. Come to us, embrace the unification of all life..."

He felt it flowing into his mouth, ears, and nose like weightless stygian ooze, clogging his thoughts and his breathing alike. Unable to even scream, Jason sank beneath the churning surface, constricted by the obelisk's shadowy embrace. The Abaddon Beacon itself became visible, looming up from the depths like an ancient sea leviathan, pulling him in with tendrils of blackness. Unknowable glowing symbols and shapes danced across its alien form, strobing and pulsating in time with its booming whispers.

"You shall become the final sacrifice, and your people will be one with us, forever..."

As Jason floated downward, tumbling end over end in the obelisk's grasp, a faint pink light appeared overhead, barely bright enough to filter down through the murk.

Sam strained hard but tried to be delicate at the same time, having never lifted an entire human body with her Abhamic powers before, let alone over this distance. Her eyes flared brighter as Jason's body emerged from the cargo ship's open hatch. Shadows billowed from his eyes, mouth, and nose, and thick spiraling tendrils grasped his limbs and throat, but Sam roared with effort and managed to keep him rising toward her. Blood shot from her nose.

"Careful!" David called from where he was still struggling to detach Talos' cable, eyes squinted as he fought off the mother of all headaches.

After what seemed like an eternity, Sam grabbed Jason's wrist, which was slimy and...*purple*. Uh oh.

Panting from the effort, Sam hauled him over the side. Jason flopped onto his back, motionless, dripping with angry purple Nanite gel that had degenerated into the Phage. The corrupted Nanites burbled and crept around, searching for technology to parasitize or a proper entry point into Jason's body. Stygian shadows boiled around the sticky liquid, gaining additional substantiality from it. Jason's visible skin was paper-white, and he was barely breathing.

Sam rolled Jason over in a flurry of oily darkness and spotted the problem: his Osmium inhibitor had been damaged by some kind of blunt force impact, shattering the drug vial container. Jason hadn't been getting any fresh Osmium, meaning that his mind was fully exposed to the Abaddon Beacon's thanatoxic presence. If Sam didn't get the inhibitor fixed immediately, another psychic explosion was on its way ... unless Abaddon had already corrupted Jason's soul. From the blackness boiling in his eyes, that might be the case already.

"Hold still, Jason. Hang on," Sam said as she replaced the broken Osmium vial with an untouched one from her fallen pack, before retrieving her tools to fix the device. Abaddon had tried to possess him so suddenly and with such force that Jason hadn't even had time to replace the vial himself.

Within seconds, Osmium was flowing again, entering Jason's system. Though she had no idea what she was doing, Sam tried using her power to help him, coaxing Abaddon's psychic contagion into leaving his body and mind.

She waited; gripping Jason's dripping hand so hard that her fingers turned white. "Come on. Come back to me, Jason. Please."

Slowly, reluctantly, the living shadows swirling around them began to recede, and color returned to Jason's face as his breathing normalized. Within his eyes, Sam watched the simmering darkness disappear, returning his iris color to its native green. The glowing, pulsating Nanophage gel covering Jason faded to a dull, purplish black, burning out faster than Sam had ever seen from the lack of nearby raw materials to consume, or a living host to inhabit.

Sam sensed Jason's Abhamic powers retreating behind the wall of drugs, like a supernova being contained within a black hole. She waited until the last of the Abaddon Beacon's animated gloom had vanished into cracks in the permacrete around them. She let out a breath she didn't realize she'd been holding. It was over ... she hoped. For now.

Sam stared down at Jason, watching his chest rise and fall. Jason's powers had only grown stronger since they had escaped the Federation labs many years ago, but he had never been able to control it, so the Osmium had kept his abilities—and his dreams of Abaddon—in check. Who knew how strong he'd become if his Abhamic powers kept growing and reacting to the Beacon with such force? Jason might crack the whole planet in half one day if they didn't get him under control.

A sharp *bang* sounded from over the cliff. A power cable snapped. Then another. The remainder slipped off the doomed transport ship as it dropped like a rock.

"David, did you—"

Sam looked up and saw Talos's grounding spikes and thick fingers tearing out of the ground as her robot's twenty-one-ton body scraped over the edge, dragged by his unbreakable line.

"You filthy, ungrateful creatures! I will be *avenged*—" was the last thing Sam heard from her greatest creation before he vanished over the side in a cloud of dust.

"*NO!*" she cried. David stood beside where Talos had been just moments before, frozen in shock. A lit plasma torch crackled in David's hand as his mouth dropped open. "I..."

Budgie landed on the cliff edge, flinching at every crash and boom until a long silence fell.

David reached the edge. "Holy shit... Talos hit a dry section, a few levels down. It's not pretty. Total loss. And I can't even see the ship."

"Goddamn it. Hopefully his personality processor survived." Sam muttered, taking a deep, shuddering breath, fighting back tears. Jason's eyes rolled as his brain absorbed more Osmium, fighting for full wakefulness. Sam started wiping the Phage ooze off him. Although the lack of a host to sustain it had burned the Nanites out, the chance of biological infection from the remnants was still possible, which could reawaken the pathogen.

Nearby, Mayweather groaned and sat up, holding his forehead. "What the hell happened?"

"That's a good question," Santiago said, rolling over and staring at Jason. "Feels like I have a hangover. And what the heck is with him? Jason lost his shit inside the transport! Then ... I don't know. Something exploded, I think. Did you see what happened, David?"

David shook his head. "We'll discuss it later."

"What?" Santiago exclaimed. "You can't leave us hanging like this."

"Just, hold on, will ya?" David said, holding his forehead. Then he puked all over the ground ahead of him.

"Are you ... alright now?" Sam muttered to Jason, using a rag from her supply bag to wipe dark purple fluids off his skin.

Jason's eyes focused on her as he regained full consciousness. "I, uh ... I don't ... I don't know what, what happened ..."

David stumbled over, followed by the militia, who were all holding their heads in a daze. Soohyun doubled back to retch her lunch over the cliff. Budgie landed on his shoulder as David dropped to one knee and hugged his brother, trying to avoid the curdled Nanite liquid splattering his skin and clothing. "At least you're safe. But it's all gone. The ship, Talos ... how the hell do we explain this to Yamamoto and Mendez?"

Sam looked into Jason's eyes, which were welling with tears.

"I'm sorry," Jason muttered. "I, I don't know what happened ... something pushed me, then ... the shadows, the Beacon ... it attacked so quickly ... I'm sorry, Sam."

Sam hugged Jason too, murmuring low enough that the militia couldn't hear, "It's okay, Jason. You didn't mean it. Abaddon tried to possess you, and your mind responded. I felt it too. It's not your fault. We'll deal with this, I promise."

"What are you talking about, Sam? What is going on here?" Santiago asked again. Sam ignored him, looking out over the water through the Under-city support pillars. Sweat dripped down her face. The lake breeze had returned, but wasn't able to hide the stench of defeat.

"We lost," Sam said, looking at Jason, who grimaced and nodded, still trying to collect himself.

"Yeah, we did. We need to take this Abaddon problem a lot more seriously, Sam," he said. "We need to find it, or this will happen again."

3 — UNRELIABLE MEMORY

No one said anything else for a long while. David gave Sam a pointed look, but she shook her head as if to say, 'I'll explain later'. Santiago opened his mouth to continue his questions, but seemed to think better of it, backing off. Budgie landed on Jason's head, settling into a sitting position and staring down at him.

"We've gotta go back to the Village with something to show for this mess. How much salvage do we have left?" Sam asked David.

"Well, we still have some parts we stripped from those robots," David said, dropping the plasma torch and pointed out Talos' burlap bags that he and Jason had loaded with the robot components. "It's not much compared to what was on that transport, though. That stockpile had months of supplies that we're overdue for."

"I guess that's something," Sam said, unable to hide her disappointment.

Mayweather and Santiago spoke in low voices to each other, appearing to agree on something. Soohyun tried to interject, but Santiago waved her off. As Sam continued wiping Jason down, Santiago marched up to them and said, "There's something wrong with Jason. He's not right. And who is *Abaddon*?"

Jason looked up at the militiaman with tortured eyes, unable to speak. What could he say?

"I ...."

"Sam, you need to tell us what's going on with him," said Mayweather, turning his attention to her. "If you want us coming on salvage missions with you guys, this kind of situation is not what we had in mind—"

Sam held up a hand. "Sure, I get it. But first, please help David break apart Talos' salvage bags and get them ready for transport back to the Village before it gets dark. With Talos out of commission, we're gonna have to carry them all back ourselves. After that, I'll tell you guys everything. I promise. There are some ... things you should know."

She gave David a meaningful look. He raised an eyebrow, but he got up and headed over to the bags.

Santiago's lip curled, but he backed down. "Fine."

Mayweather gave Sam a narrow-eyed glance, but he nodded as well. "Alright."

Soohyun glanced at Jason, who was still wiping dead Nanophage solution off himself, but she followed her comrades after David without comment.

Sam closed her eyes, summoning the last of her mental reserves, which were nearly bled dry from her efforts to stop Jason's incident. Focusing her mind-sight on the backs of the militia's heads, Sam gave their minds a tiny Abhamic nudge.

Santiago, Mayweather and Soohyun swayed on their feet for a moment, as Sam's psionic push took effect. Soohyun stumbled, turning around and blinking rapidly. Sam watched the girl's eyes sliding in and out of focus, hoping that she hadn't overdone it.

David looked up from the salvage bags as the militia dragged their feet in the dust, staring in complete bewilderment at each other and their surroundings. David's gaze darted to Sam, whose eyes were cooling down from hot pink. She gestured to them, making a looping motion with one finger at her right temple.

David's eyes narrowed, but he caught on and returned his attention to the militia. "You three doin' alright?"

Soohyun squeezed her eyes shut, holding her forehead. "I dunno. I ... I don't *remember*. What the heck? What happened? Where are we?"

Santiago and Mayweather seemed to share the sentiment; eyes bugged out in confusion.

"What's the last thing you remember?" David asked.

Soohyun thought about it, brow furrowing. "We were about to go on a salvage operation with you guys. Something about a crashed ship. But ... where's the ship?"

David grimaced as a lie wove through his teeth. "About that. You guys were exposed to something nasty onboard that transport vessel, might've addled your brains a bit. Seems like you're coming around."

Santiago looked around, squinting his eyes at the open air beyond the permacrete cliff. "And Talos, what happened to him? Where is he?"

"Yeah ... about him," David said, extending a hand. "We lost Talos when the ship went down, and barely managed to get you guys off in time. Let me check your vitals, c'mere."

He glared at Sam as the militia approached him, wide-eyed and pale-faced, but David dutifully checked them all for injuries.

Sam pulled out a small syringe, found a vein, and gave herself a small hit of Osmium. The microdose would dull Sam's powers, but her pounding psionic headache had reached a crescendo with that last push of her Abhamic abilities, and she needed relief.

Sam focused on Jason, who was still wiping himself down.

He glanced at her. "It keeps telling me to *find* it. I don't know what we'll do when we do, but we have to try. I don't think Abaddon will stop until then. I'm ... I'm scared, Sam."

"Keep your voice down, I don't want to risk messing with their minds a second time," Sam murmured, looking up at the militia before handing Jason a spare rag from her supply backpack. "But yes, I agree with you. Whatever Avery Oakfield and those scientists did to you must've linked you to the obelisk somehow. We're going to need to break back into the Science Institute to find Abaddon and figure out how to sever that connection, which won't be easy. Getting inside those labs will be the riskiest thing we've ever done; especially with all that high-tech security they've got."

"How long do you think we have?" Jason asked, in a near-whisper.

"What?"

"How long do I have until this happens again?"

Sam paused for a moment. "I wish I knew. The Abaddon Beacon has never reached out to you so directly before, so I can't predict when it might try again. One thing I am sure of is that we need to keep you away from anything infected with the Nanophage. I saw it: Abaddon used those bots to get to you. Seems like they're a conduit that it can use to mess with the wider world."

"That's it? No other way to know if it's coming?"

"Not really," Sam said. "We don't know enough about the Beacon for that. Giving you a timeline is impossible, because this never happened to me when my Abhamic powers were maturing. We need to prioritize finding safe leads to get back inside the Science Institute and fast."

"Will that even be possible, with our workload after this?" Jason asked.

"We'll have to find a way."

"Goddammit," Jason moaned. "What did we to do deserve—"

"Enough with that, you'll be fine." Sam said. "We'll get you onto a higher dose of Osmium. That'll keep the Beacon off our scent for a while. Just don't go near Doc Janice's med-bay when we're back home, she's got a lot of Phage-infected people waiting for treatment in those cryo-pods. Even if they're all in suspended animation, we can't risk you detonating like a psychic grenade if Abaddon attacks you in the Village."

Jason stared at Soohyun, Mayweather and Santiago. "I could've killed them. And I destroyed Talos too ...oh *god*... I'm so sorry, Sam."

Sam hugged Jason again, wiping some congealed Nanite solution out of his tangled hair. "You didn't, Jason. That bastard scientist Avery Oakfield did, when he did this to you. And we'll make him pay."

Jason was still working through his shock. "I saw .... I saw the Beacon, Sam. It showed me a world of dead stars and an endless sea of blackness. It pulled me down. I couldn't breathe. It was nothing like my dreams, it felt *real*. There was no way to fight it, Sam. The only thing we can do is what it told me to do. We have to go back to the labs."

"We'll find a way. We'll get in there, find out what Abaddon is, what it wants, and how to beat it," Sam said, giving him a determined look. "Come on. First, we need to locate a water source and get you properly cleaned up before we go back. I also wanna get a good look at where Talos landed so we can figure out retrieval. And then ... we're gonna need to explain everything to the governor."

As the artificial sun crossed the atmo-dome into the late evening, the salvagers hauled their meager findings and weapons back up through the Under-city's levels, toward home. With diminishing light coming in from outside, the level of danger in the underground was increasing by the minute, as the Phage-infected seemed to always be more active at night.

Jason hoped they had left with enough time to return behind the walls before the Phage-infected became most active, as Yamamoto had warned. He had witnessed groups of them stalking and ripping apart other Under-city dwellers with ease. Talos had been their ace card when it came to larger encounters with the infected at night. Until now, anyway.

Jason kept his head on a swivel, heart hammering, reflexively twisting the knob on his repaired Osmium inhibitor every time he heard the slightest noise echoing down the abandoned tunnels and ruins of the city's substructure. Any encounter with the infected could become another battle with the obelisk. David eventually had to put a hand on his shoulder. "Easy there, brother. We're nearly home."

Soohyun, Mayweather, and Santiago kept to themselves on the trip back. It was clear that they were not pleased with how the excursion had went down. This was understandable, given their failure to retrieve most of the treasure trove aboard the cargo vessel—and their near-death experiences, of course.

As the six of them passed through the holo-shield and the Village became visible to the naked eye, several lights snapped on from atop the ramshackle defensive wall, illuminating the wide kill-zone covered by the settlement's automated turret guns. Old bullet holes and blast craters dotted the expanse, along with a few charred robot and skeletal human corpses—the only remains of previous assaults on the Village from various infected Under-city denizens. Cold, blistering winds were coming in off the lake, far chillier than the earlier afternoon breeze. Jason spotted the repair ships out by the city's containment wall, still working on the atmo-shield against the dark green backdrop of howling superstorms outside.

At David's urging, Budgie took flight and flapped several meters above their heads, as a signal to the Village guards that they were close by.

A voice called down from the defensive wall. "Oi, is that you guys? You're late!"

Holding up a hand to block the dense light beams, David answered, "Yes, Charles, it's us. We got a bit held up."

"Where's the big guy?" the militiaman asked, removing his goggles and looking around.

Sam stiffened as she responded to the wall guard, "Sorry. We had an accident. Talos is offline."

"What?!" Charles exclaimed. "Offline? For how long?"

This perked up the rest of the east wall guards, who gathered above as the gates scraped open. Jason spotted governor Yamamoto rushing toward them. Mendez hobbled after him, with several armed guards in tow.

"Where the hell have you been? Sundown was an hour ago." Yamamoto demanded, hands on his hips, looking from Jason, David, and Sam to Santiago, Mayweather, and Soohyun.

Jason held up his hands, voice unsteady. "Sorry, Governor, we had a bit of trouble."

"A bit?"

David took over. "Yeah. A bit."

A guard came over with a scanner, waving it up and down their bodies. "Whoa ... I'm getting trace detections of Phage matter on you, Jason. Lots, actually. Jesus, looks like you took a bath in the stuff. You too, Sam."

"Yeah, we encountered some nastiness out there," Sam said, wiping her gloved hands on her filthy pants. "Not our finest hour."

Yamamoto shook his head. "Let's get you over to decon before that stuff finds an open sore and infects you or someone else. We'll have to destroy your clothing, too. Can't have that Phage crap spreading into the population. Looks like you brought back a few things, though. The Quartermaster will have something to do, at least."

David held up the bags of their meager findings. "It's something, anyway."

Mendez's people ushered them inside the wall as the gate handlers cranked the controls. The old security chief regarded Sam as the doors screeched shut. "Where's your tin man? He's supposed to take up the evening shift on the west barricade—which started half an hour ago, by the way."

Sam clenched her teeth. "I'm sorry, sir. He's twelve levels down from where we were, totaled by the fall. We're going to have to do a few retrieval ops to find his core components, then I'll start a rebuild."

This sent a wave of murmurs and complaints through the surrounding militia. Yamamoto folded his arms. Mendez's mouth dropped open, and his grey eyebrows furrowed. "How'd *that* happen?"

Sam looked at the ground. "It's a long story, sir. I'm sorry."

One of the guards on the wall rotated a mounted floodlamp to spotlight the group, prompting Mendez to angrily wave it away.

Sam glanced at David, who recounted the altered version of events that he'd given the militia earlier—that the *Ganesh of Mesopotamia* had suffered an equipment failure while Jason and their new recruits had been aboard, followed by an explosion that had released some kind of nasty shipboard substance. They'd managed to get everyone off before the ship went down, taking Talos with it, though David carefully omitted any references to the real cause of the transport vessel's demise.

Silence fell. Yamamoto pinched the bridge of his nose, shooting Mendez a frustrated look.

"This is a major setback. Very disappointing to lose that much salvage, right when we need it most. But we knew the risks, and at least you're all back in one piece—with the exception of Talos, of course."

Mendez nodded. "Talos alone accounted for 40% of our guard rotations. Most of our people will have to pull double duty until we can train some new bodies to compensate. Not that we have many to choose from."

This elicited a groan from most of the surrounding Village militia troopers, including those who were in off-duty casual clothing.

"How long to get Talos operational again?" Yamamoto asked Sam.

"A few weeks, minimum. Ballpark estimate," Sam said with a grimace.

The collective militia force groaned louder. Several of them fired insults and complaints from the wall top, prompting an angry shout from Mendez. "Quiet!"

"We better pray that we don't get a full-blown Phage migration during that time," Yamamoto said. "I regret not drawing up any backup procedures if we lost the tin man. It didn't seem possible that we'd ever lose him. We won't make that mistake again. I'm glad that he's recoverable, though. Losing people is unacceptable, versus losing salvage."

"I'm sorry, sir," said Jason, fighting down the guilt. "Really, we tried everything we could to save him."

Santiago held his head. "My head is killing me. Whatever we were dosed with aboard the ship, it must have been bad."

Yamamoto regarded the group. "Anyone else?"

Soohyun and Mayweather nodded. Jason did too.

"Shit. After decon, you will all report to Doc Janice. She'll check you for any noggin damage," Yamamoto said, jerking his thumb down the main street, to a lit-up prefabricated medical building at the other end of the Village. "Better safe than sorry."

Mayweather looked to Mendez. "I don't think we should be heading back out there, sir."

He shot David, Sam, and Jason a glance. "What these guys do ... it's *dangerous*."

Santiago inclined his head in agreement. Soohyun gave Jason a sideways look, but she nodded as well. "It's too risky for us, sir. We don't have enough experience for these crazy Under-city excursions, and it's too dangerous to get more."

"We *did* try to warn you," Sam said.

Santiago shrugged. "I'll give you that. You did."

Mendez sighed. "With Talos out of commission, we can't afford to send more of our militia force out, even if we wanted to. We're just too short-handed. David, Sam, and Jason will have to continue operating as our sole excursion team for the time being ... especially with the loss of that transport ship. I don't wanna know how much useful cargo went down with it."

"Too much. Like losing computer files that you can never get back," said David.

"What a bloody waste," Mendez said, thumping his cane on the ground.

Yamamoto whirled a finger. "Get on over to decon. And clear out, every-one else! Nothing to see here, back to your duties! Or go grab dinner at Xerxes's place."

At his order, the crowd began to dissipate. Santiago shot Sam, David, and Jason a final look, then traipsed further into the Village, hefting his burlap salvage bag over one shoulder. Mayweather and Soohyun followed him, plus several other off-duty militia, who were all still asking them questions.

"After you're done with the doctor, I want a more thorough report on what happened out there," Yamamoto said to Sam as they passed. "And an accurate timeline on Talos' rebuild, since that'll be faster than a scratch build, right? Goddamn it, we've got a lot of reorganizing to do."

"Yes, will do, sir. And again, we're sorry. Things could have gone better out there," Sam said, wincing.

"There's always tomorrow. Now get outta here, and get yourselves a clean bill of health from the Doc. And then, get some rest. You'll be on double duty until our supply situation is corrected," said Yamamoto, who turned to

Mendez as the older man pulled out a data tablet and started jabbing at the scheduling screen.

Jason, Sam, and David obeyed, heading after the militia, attracting plenty of stares from nearby residents.

David leaned toward Sam. "Bit of a risky move, messing with their minds like that?"

"Would you prefer that they tell the entire Village about Jason? About what really happened?" Sam hissed. "We have no way to explain it. No one's gonna believe that there's an evil alien obelisk somewhere in this city that wants to possess him—and even if they do, that's all the more reason for the governor to kick us out for being a risk to the Village."

"Well, now we've got another problem. Those militia don't know what happened out there and that might have them wondering *why*," David snapped back.

Jason twisted the knob on his repaired neural inhibitor, letting the drugs cool his rising stress. "Guys, we've got bigger things to worry about."

"Yeah, like finding Abaddon and getting to the bottom of what's going on with you," Sam said.

"So that's what you two were talking about? Going back into the lion's den, risking discovery by the Federation, or worse, Avery Oakfield himself?" David asked. "That's what we're doin' now, huh?"

"Yep, much as I hate to admit it." Jason confirmed, drawing strength from what Sam had said before. "We've gotta find that bastard obelisk and figure out how to stop it from messing with me, or anyone else."

David's lips formed a thin line. "The fun never ends, does it?"

4 — INVASION DAWN

THREE WEEKS LATER — HIGH EARTH ORBIT — OCT. 31, 2263 — 03:11 HOURS

In the shadow of an orbital scanner platform above Earth, a small shuttle finished decelerating, powering most of its systems down. The hull was decorated with red war stripes—but the craft's heat retention plating rendered it invisible to active sensors. The stealth shuttle was thirty meters long, oval-shaped, and energy-shielded, modified for long-range travel to carry dignitaries between the planets and habitats of the Solar system—back before human space had been plunged into four bloody years of grinding interplanetary warfare between the United Earth Federation and the Solar Empire. The shuttle vaguely resembled a centuries-old aircraft: the SR-71 *Blackbird*. The stenciling on the shuttle's plating read '*Deliverance,*' and had one cyborg occupant: Anne Oakfield. She had finally returned to her home-world after what had felt like a lifetime away, for what was likely to be her final mission.

Anne sat in the pilot's seat. With her cold, dead, cybernetic eyes, she watched Sol pass over the planet's horizon, reflecting off thousands of orbital defense platforms and dozens of docked Federation warships. In her immediate vision, the supercarrier UEFSC *Hacienda's Lance* sat alongside the frigate *Glory of Karachi* and missile destroyer *Hammer of Asgardia*, but many were damaged from recent Solar War engagements.

Deliverance's cockpit smelled of processed oxygen and antiseptic spray. A binary chirp of code caught Anne's attention. A mechanical eagle sat on the worn, high-backed leather seat's armrest, red eyes glowing with artificial intelligence.

"Have you detected the Empire's picket ships yet, Lincoln?" asked Anne.

The bird construct chirped again. The ship's computer reacted, and a new display appeared, showing a view of the Earth's surroundings out to 2.5 light-seconds. Lincoln had returned from a brief extravehicular mission, where he had connected a hardline from *Deliverance* to the scanner platform outside, allowing them to perform long-range active scans without using their own systems, thereby giving away the shuttle's position.

Images began to populate the monitor, showing the forward elements of an Imperial battlefleet crossing the infamous Red Line toward Earth from its largest artificial satellite, Colossus Station—where Anne had also come from, arriving ahead of the emperor's vanguard. The UEF home fleet had not reacted to the Empire's obvious aggression.

Anne's cyber-eyes linked with her ship's cameras, zooming-in across thousands of kilometers to show Colossus's titanic transparent shell, through which she could see desert landscapes, industrial plains, vast machinery, and shining cities within. This station, the current seat of Imperial power, floated a hundred thousand kilometers away from Earth, held in distant orbit by immense anti-gravity drives. The Empire's arrogance was on full display by leaving the station's continent-sized exterior blast shields exposed within range of the Earth's defense network. But Colossus' exterior defenses were second-only to the Federation's bristling defense network around Earth. The promise of mutually-assured destruction had forced the war to branch out, consuming the Solar system's territories and dwindling resources in the fires of emperor Hadrian Mariko's ambition. Anne's mechanical fist tightened as she fought down old memories of that bastard.

Beyond the approaching Imperial fleet, she spotted sporadic explosions on *Deliverance's* deep-space cameras—distant blasts from the farthest reaches of human-occupied Solar space. The Jovian moons burned. Pluto was being wrenched from UEF control by the Imperials, and the mineral resourcing operations within the asteroid belt were contested. The outer system gulf was all but lost, with only pockets of UEF resistance remaining. The Federation was losing ground in nearly every battlespace, swallowed by the relentless advance of Emperor Mariko's fleets until soon, Earth would be their only remaining stronghold.

Anne sat back; biological arm folded over her cybernetic arm, staring at the approaching fleet. "Any response from the UEF?"

The bird croaked a negative, making his metallic feather-plating ripple in the limited lighting. The readings confirmed it—none of the Federation patrols were showing any reaction to the incoming Imperial battle-force, despite the fact that a full third of the home fleet was docked here for refits or rearmament. The rumors that had drawn Anne away from her personal war against the Empire on Colossus were true. Someone, or something, had made the home-world vulnerable to direct attack.

Anne double-blinked her eyelids, and the pilot's seat swiveled. She stood, popping out the cables delivering power and raw Nanites into her body's reservoirs. As Anne's backup batteries reached full charge, her cyber-narcolepsy receded. This was an early warning sign of the Nanophage, which was slowly developing as her aging synthetic components degraded. Fortunately, Anne's shuttle was equipped with top-of-the-line cybernetic repair systems. Snaking mechadendrite arms deployed from hidden compartments in the ceiling to cut a tiny Phage tumor out of Anne's cyber-arm, replacing it with fresh synthetic muscle. Eventually, Anne would succumb to the plague, like anyone else with older or malfunctioning Nanite implants. But before that, she had one last goal to complete. One final job.

Lincoln scanned Anne's body for further imperfections. A screen on the cockpit's main console showed that the micro-reactor nestled in her cybernetic guts was operating at ninety-six percent efficiency. Good enough.

"Excellent," said Anne. "Ease the flight systems back online. Our target is the main shipyard in this sector—*Refit One*."

She gestured at the closest high-orbit station above the Earth, surrounded by damaged warships under repair by EVA repair crews. Like the rest of the UEF's orbital network, the facility showed no signs of a defensive lockdown, no running-light blackouts, and no active weapons systems.

Lincoln squawked a query. Anne replied, "We discussed this earlier, Lincoln. After what my brother did on Mars, they've summoned him to *Refit One* for disciplinary action—he'll be arriving within the hour. Our plans depend on if he can help us ... and if we can get him out of there."

The bird cocked his head, letting out a sardonic string of code, which Anne's onboard systems translated into regular language.

She shook her head. "This is the only way, my friend. Run a jammer on *Refit One's* active sensors, and cut our engines before they detect us. Our insertion needs to be silent."

The eagle squawked another question.

"No, I don't know where the rest of Zeke's people are," Anne replied, "Nightshade Squadron's base ship is waiting in stealth mode, like our shuttle. To find them, we need to find *him*. Once we're aboard, you'll have to break into *Refit One's* network to locate his bio-signs."

Lincoln's eyes narrowed, and he burbled another query.

"It has to be now, my friend," said Anne. "This is our last chance to take Mariko down, and save what's left of the human race from his insanity. Whether the Abaddon obelisk is to blame for his actions or not, it doesn't matter. Hadrian must be stopped. After everything that I've done and all I've failed to do, this last task is all that's left for me. Is that enough for you?"

A few moments passed, then the bird bowed his head.

"Good," Anne said.

She felt the gravity-plating suck her boots down as she pulled her great-coat on. The upper areas of the garment floated freely, while the flexible armored lining magnetized to her body-glove. Anne felt her personal deflection shields booting up with a pop of static, protecting her from hyper-velocity ranged attacks—one of many Nanite-based technologies that had rewritten the rulebook on modern tactics, along with artificially intelligent drone warfare, space combat and a host of other innovations that the human race had wasted no time in using to kill each other.

Lincoln took over as helmsman while Anne strode to the rear of the shuttle's hold, running her metal hand down an anti-materiel rifle's barrel.

Her synthetic heart began to race. A plethora of firearms gleamed under the lights, strapped into seats on both sides of the bay. Anne kept them in good condition, though many were older than she was. Some were sized for huge robotic constructs like the Empire's fearsome warbots, though Anne's cybernetic strength allowed her to wield them. Her ancient Jetbike was secured to the deck, loaded down with even more weapons. But no arsenal alone would determine her mission's outcome. That depended on whether her brother could help her.

Deliverance chugged its thrusters to prepare for the burn toward *Refit One*. The shuttle couldn't trigger its engines too close to the station, which would light up their heat scanners, so Anne and Lincoln would need to leap toward the orbital station through the silent void, breaking into an exterior airlock while their shuttle hurtled away at low power, coming around when needed for pickup. With luck, the ship's stealth systems would make it appear like a passing piece of orbital debris.

Anne peered out the scratched window in the entry airlock. The stars were winking out, and the visible slice of the moon disappeared behind something enormous. As she watched, Imperial leviathans slid out of the blackness of space, launching waves of boarding torpedoes at the closest UEF orbitals and docked warships. There was still no defensive response from the Earth's tiara-like rings of defense platforms. Though it was a worst-case scenario for the Federation, the timing of the Imperial invasion was fortunate, as it was great cover for Anne's insertion.

She accepted a wide-brimmed hat from a mechadendrite as *Deliverance's* quiet engine burn started, rattling the compartment. In Anne's field of view, a detailed heads-up-display, vitals, and ammunition counters appeared over a wireframe of her surroundings. She pulled her eyeglasses from a breast pocket and attached them to her nose. The eyeglasses doubled as armored protection and were quite intimidating. She liked that.

Every camera in the ship's hold, including Lincoln's infrared vision, appeared in separate windows on her HUD. Despite Anne's conventional blindness, she could see far more than any un-augmented human. Lincoln squawked an alert. Anne took a long breath and cranked the airlock's lever, cycling atmospheres with a shaking metal hand. Once the chamber was ready, she stepped inside, followed by Lincoln, on his jets of antigravity energy.

They were past the point of no return. Anne focused on her old rage, which had long since cooled into iron determination, helping her maintain a center of calm.

Anne Oakfield would fulfil the oath she made fourteen years ago, come hell or high water. Her last chance to end Emperor Hadrian Mariko was *today*, and she couldn't let it go. And her brother Zeke would help her do it.

Anne's personal shields initialized, protecting her from the cold void. Moments later, the shuttle's engine burn went quiet, turning the craft into a silent missile, hurtling through the dark. The airlock's outer door opened, her built-in jump-jets fired to life, and Anne leaped out into open vacuum with Lincoln, heading for *Refit One*.

5 — BOARDING ACTION

"Let's go, Markus. We're on a schedule," Commander Zeke Oakfield said to his lieutenant as he stepped off the ramp of his unmarked shuttlecraft into a brightly-lit, cavernous docking module. A mechanical arm descended from the hangar's rafters and clamped onto the shuttle's roof, locking it down with a sharp pneumatic hiss of ammonia gas.

His huge, dark-skinned second-in-command, Lieutenant Markus Maximillian, looked up at the docking arm. "Interesting. That's not standard procedure."

"No, it is not," Zeke agreed, gritting his teeth.

The mirrored black deck-plates reflected his grizzled face up at him, complete with fraying red bandana and scorched skin. There hadn't been time to clean himself up after the frantic evacuation of Mars, which had barely ended a few hours ago. Zeke and Markus were only here to find their new recruit, deal with the small matter of his court martial ... and then get the hell back to the war.

This hangar was dedicated to the business of Rear Admiral Powell, who'd recently been reassigned to take over *Refit One's* repair operations as hundreds of ships came in from battles along the UEF's shrinking territorial lines, particularly from the recent disaster at Mars. Zeke had accepted the admiral's post-battle summons to *Refit One* in good faith, but now that was looking like a grave mistake. Arrayed ahead of him were a dozen armed military policemen, plus a handful of humanoid combat automatons. Two of them sported powered battle armor, but compared to Imperial war-suits ... they resembled children's action figures. An overworked-looking sallow-skinned colonel in an ill-fitting uniform and his two orderlies waited ahead of the security force.

Upon seeing them, it took all of Zeke's self-control to keep walking. But with the hangar's docking clamps in place on his shuttlecraft, it was too late to turn back now. He glanced over at Markus. "I didn't expect *this*."

"Me either. What's with all the firepower?" Markus murmured back, straightening his cap. The lieutenant wore the same fatigues as Zeke, with a singlet emblazoned with their unit's Nightshade flower insignia, plus an unlit cigar clamped between his teeth. He also sported a cybernetic arm of synthetic muscle and titanium.

"Dunno, but I don't like it," said Zeke.

"Let's not do anything rash, my friend," Markus replied, with the same quiet calm he'd exhibited since they'd first met in basic training.

Zeke nodded, stopping and saluting the bookish-looking colonel, who stood waiting for them. "Commander Zeke Oakfield, of Nightshade Squadron, reporting as ordered."

"Excellent. You are hereby remanded into our custody, Commander," said the wheedly colonel. "Admiral Powell has decreed that we carry out your sentence immediately."

Zeke's mouth dropped open faster than the bay doors of a high-altitude bomber. "My *sentence*? I have the right to an in-person trial, according to military law."

"Under these wartime circumstances, we conducted your trial with you in absentia, Commander. Witnesses from the Mars retreat testified about your behavior there. You have been found guilty of multiple crimes, including the countermanding of direct superior orders and misuse of Federation resources. Come with us. Do not resist."

Zeke and Markus exchanged glances. Zeke's instinct to escape the situation flared, though he tamped it down.

"That's unacceptable. We *saved* people at Mars," he barked, and Markus nodded in agreement.

"That is not for you or me to decide, Commander," the colonel replied.

"I demand to speak with Admiral Powell, sir," Zeke said. "I'll work this out with him myself. Nightshade Squadron did nothing wrong. On the contrary, we're the reason all those refugees you're dealing with right now are *alive*."

"I don't care. We need to cuff you, hold out your arms," the colonel said, waving his people forward.

Zeke felt his adrenaline kick up and sensed Markus tensing beside him. But unarmed and surrounded, there was no easy escape from this place. He had no choice.

Zeke relented after a few moments, holding out his arms. "Fine. Take me to Powell."

A robotic automaton slapped a pair of stun cuffs onto his wrists. Markus glanced at the restraints with a raised eyebrow, but the colonel shook his head. "Commander Oakfield is the one we want. Leave us, Lieutenant. Do not interfere."

"My Commander has the legal right to be accompanied by his second-in-command, even while in custody. He will *not* be mistreated," Markus growled, fists balled.

Zeke shot an angry look at Markus—he couldn't get himself dragged into this too. If Zeke was imprisoned, Markus would become the interim leader for Nightshade Squadron. Who else would bring word of this nonsense to Nightshade's other senior officers? They needed to find a way to escape.

The colonel seemed hesitant, but Zeke sensed the man's discomfort with confrontation. The guards shifted uncomfortably.

After losing his staring contest with the huge lieutenant, the colonel shrugged. "As long as he doesn't interfere, your subordinate may attend as a witness. Guard them both. Try anything, though, and you'll pay."

Markus grunted.

The MPs marched into formation around the operators, with the power-armored bruisers at the front and rear, but Markus' presence was a comfort and gave Zeke a slightly better chance than zero of getting out of here. Turning on his heel, the colonel walked through the inner doors of the hangar.

Zeke murmured out of the side of his mouth to Markus as they followed. "Contact the kid. We may have to make a quick exit."

Markus tapped his datapad, but a strange 'no-connect' icon flashed on the scuffed touchscreen. "I'm locked out of the network, Commander."

"What? And you're not even on trial for anything."

"I might as well be, sir."

"Get a move on," one of the MPs barked. The bot who had installed Zeke's cuffs pressed a button on its forearm.

Zeke was electro-jolted into an unsteady walk, fuming at the humiliation.

"Do we need...backup, Zeke?" Markus murmured.

Zeke eyed the nearest guards. "Our people are out of reach. Their orders are to hold position and refuel at our private waystation until we report in, but eventually Luther and the company captains will wonder what happened to us and take matters into their own hands. We'll have to find a way back to the *Solanum* before they try anything crazy. Bright side is—we've been in tighter spots before."

Markus did not look convinced. "Affirmative, Commander."

Refit One was the busiest military installation in the northern hemispheric orbital sector. The familiar smell of unwashed coveralls and vacuum-exposed fabrics filled Zeke's nose. Loudspeakers droned on and on without pause. Thousands of personnel passed through here daily, transferring from damaged warships to any remaining combat-effective Federation fleet elements docked here.

A new duty rotation had started, overrunning the station's halls with a crush of bodies. Marines, pilots, flight crews, officers, army troopers, drop troopers, shock troopers, robotic worker drones, civilian contractors, and every other specialization passed by the prisoner detail in the narrow corridors. Shouted orders filled the air, accompanied by the din of conversation and griping from lower-ranked grunts, echoing through the passageways. Turbo-lifts and mass-conveyors had to slow down because of the dense crowds. Notably for Zeke, many of the people around them were rough, sad-looking refugees.

The sea of bobbing heads parted around them as Zeke and Markus were marched through the orbital. Many passersby gave them polite nods, salutes, and words of praise. Some of the refugees even cheered. Zeke was filled with pride as their recognition of him confirmed his suspicions about their Martian origins, but their support wouldn't help him in this situation. Zeke wished he'd brought along some of his other captains, like Chiang or Ossington. Even a handful more of his people would have made a difference here.

Zeke gazed through the corridor skylight, marveling at the beauty of the Earth's curvature. The planet was the cradle of the species, even ruined as it was in the long-ago fires of chemical weapons and nuclear fallout. His unit's base of operations—the *Solanum*—floated out there too, the largest Federation fleet prowler with full stealth capabilities. After this legal charade was over, Zeke and Markus would be returning there—whether they were 'allowed' to, or not.

"*Commander!*" a youthful voice carried through the chattering throngs. Zeke grinned as he spotted a girl hurrying over, following a map on her datapad. Markus also brightened. "There she is."

"Just who I was hoping I'd find. Good morning, Private Jenkins. Or should I say...*shrimp*," Zeke greeted the girl as if he wasn't being marched along wearing stun cuffs. The guards trained their weapons on Jenkins. "Halt!"

"Uhhhh ... right, Commander," she replied, alarmed by their aggression. Julia Jenkins had dark frizzy hair bound in a tight, regulation-sized ball, and wore standard fatigues, which were likely some of her only possessions right then.

Upon seeing her face, a memory hit Zeke, merely hours old. While the rest of his people focused on broader civilian evacuation efforts around Mars, Zeke had led Markus and a small team of Nightshade operators into the burning ruins of the red planet's capital city, Olympus Mons, following a distress beacon. There, they had discovered Jenkins and several hundred others, barely hanging on. Ashen-faced and terrified, Jenkins's group had survived weeks of orbital, aerial, and ground-based Imperial bombardment, clinging onto their distress signal as a last-ditch effort to live. Imperial damage done to the colony and the planet had threatened to undo a century of Federation terra-forming efforts.

Jenkins was only a few years past minimum recruitment age, but after boarding the *Solanum* with the other survivors, she'd written and uploaded a sophisticated comm-jamming algorithm into the ship's computers. When broadcast, it had thrown Imperial warships into disarray during the Mars planetary evac operation, saving countless lives during the battle to protect the refugee fleet on its way back to Earth space.

The surviving combat controllers and tech specialists within Zeke's unit had been impressed with Jenkins' talent for electronic warfare, convincing him to recruit her. After transferring Jenkins to a medical frigate for treatment with the other wounded, Zeke had promised that he'd find her on *Refit One* when Nightshade returned to Earth for repairs and resupply. Now, here she was. Aside from some scorches, scrapes and bandaging, the kid looked good, given all she'd recently been through.

Jenkins' datapad was beeping, tracking Zeke and Markus' bio-signs. "I heard you were coming, Commander. I, uh, they asked me about Mars..."

The colonel spoke as he continued walking, forcing Jenkins to keep pace with them. "Your testimony as witness to Zeke Oakfield's conduct is no longer required, Private Jenkins. Leave us."

"My trial's *over*," Zeke said.

"Trial's...over?" Jenkins asked. "Why?"

The kid's naivete was charming, but Jenkins wasn't grasping the political implications of what Zeke had done on the red planet.

"They're taking me to see Powell, to answer for disobeying his order to abandon Mars and everyone still alive on the surface and in orbit to the Imperials. That included *you*, by the way," Zeke replied to Jenkins.

To the colonel, he added, "The girl stays with us. She gave you a statement, so she's involved."

Jenkin's eyes darted around, glancing at the military police and their colonel, but she nodded her assent.

The colonel glared at Zeke. "Fine. But she cannot interfere."

The MPs kept Jenkins in their sights, but Zeke was satisfied—they had what they'd come here for. Now all they had to do was slip these fools; Powell's court martial be damned.

A *clang* rang out, like a rogue meteoroid or debris had struck the module. Zeke glanced at Markus. "What the hell was that?"

The MPs and robots forced the march to continue.

"No idea, Commander," Markus said.

Refit One had automated defenses and kinetic shields to protect from hostile attacks and pieces of space junk, like the Phalanx magnetic accelerator cannons that were visible past the skylights. But they weren't firing.

Another reverberating *clang* tore through the orbital. Markus glanced down at his datapad, which still read 'disconnected' from the military network.

"I don't like this, sir," he murmured.

"Yep, this is not good," Zeke glanced down at Jenkins. "Find out what hit us, shrimp."

Jenkins started tapping her datapad, but the colonel announced, "In here, convict."

He had stopped at a bulkhead door, which his guards opened. A dim, smelly, and musty chamber lay beyond. This wasn't *Refit One's* brig.

"What're you trying to pull here?" Zeke demanded.

The guards shoved Zeke inside without explanation. Markus and Jenkins followed, but were held at gunpoint inside the door by the combat robots.

The module was a thirty-by-thirty-meter disposal chamber, featuring three airlocks for jettisoning waste products and recyclables outside to waiting haulers. Piles of crates, reeking garbage canisters, and other disposal equipment were stacked in piles against the walls. A dirty skylight barely brightened the dingy space. Zeke's stomach dropped—*he* was the waste product.

"What the hell are you trying to pull, here?" Zeke asked as the MPs prepared an airlock for decompression. Jenkins looked up at Markus, but he held up a hand, murmuring. "Wait."

One of the colonel's orderlies handed him a datapad. The small man took it and read aloud, "Commander Zeke Oakfield, under the Uniform Code of United Earth Federation Military Justice, for disobeying a superior's orders and usurping command of Federation resources during wartime ... you are sentenced to *death*."

"And Powell has no interest in being here to watch? Where is he?" Zeke growled.

"The Admiral is indisposed," The colonel remarked.

Before anyone could react, a two-tone noise sounded over the station's loudspeakers.

Everyone stopped. The voice of Rear Admiral Powell himself blared, "Attention, all hands."

Zeke and Markus exchanged glances.

The admiral's speech sounded strange, slurring his words and speaking slower than usual, even though his tone was still commanding. "This is Admiral Powell ... erm, please remain calm, everyone. All defense stations are to remain on standby. Earth's orbital defenses are being *peacefully* boarded by a Solar Empire expeditionary fleet. There is no reason for alarm. If you are in your quarters, remain there until further notice. Avoid engaging the Imperial boarding teams and obey their commands. This is a prearranged non-combat event. That is all, erm...thank you."

What? Zeke flitted through several emotions—confusion, surprise, horror—and then rage. "What the hell did he say?"

A glance at Markus revealed a very similar reaction. The military police looked just as flabbergasted.

Zeke imagined scenes across the station. Thousands of people stared dumbstruck at the public address system. Panic would ensue. Something very wrong was happening here, far worse than Zeke's fast-tracked bullshit execution.

Markus somehow maintained his dry demeanor. "It appears we've been betrayed, Commander."

"Sure does. But...why? And why did Powell sound like he's been hitting the sauce?"

Nothing made sense. The UEF's armed forces were nowhere near the point of surrender...or were they? Was Powell compromised? Had he used his command authority over the orbital defenses to hand the home-world over to the Empire? That would explain his reassignment here after the losses at Mars, if the higher Federation brass were also involved.

The colonel was the only one who looked like he'd been expecting the announcement. His orderlies glanced at him, eyes wide. Only the combat automatons, who were guarding the hallway doors, had no outward reaction.

Jenkins broke the silence. "The Empire is coming *here*?"

Zeke was about to respond when another loud *clang* interrupted, reverberating through the deck, flickering the lights. Some of the guards lost their balance, but most kept their weapons trained on Zeke and his compatriots, murmuring among themselves. He couldn't blame them for wondering why they were screwing around here when the Empire was about to ruin everyone's day.

"Boarding torpedoes are a bit extreme for a so-called 'peaceful' action," Markus said, failing to hide his concern.

"It can't be. The outer shields would have to be down. There's no way Powell would just ... *let* them come aboard? Right?" Zeke stammered.

"Get in the airlock, Commander," the colonel said, pointing at the chamber's door.

"Are you serious?" Zeke rattled his cuffs. "You're still gonna go through with this, after what we just heard?"

The colonel shook his head. "The time for complaints is past, Commander. Regardless of our present circumstances, you must pay for your wastage of the Fourth Fleet and other Federation resources."

"Screw that," said Zeke. "I came here for a fair hearing, not this trumped-up horseshit."

He didn't mention getting Jenkins and Markus back to the *Solanum* and resuming his personal war against Emperor Hadrian Mariko. Those were minor details compared to not dying.

With no other choice and desperate to save his commander, Markus exploded into action, barreling into the military policemen who were holding Zeke, but several automatons forced him back with overwhelming robotic strength. Jenkins dashed toward Zeke as well, but several MPs grabbed her arms.

Zeke fought back as the colonel's cronies shoved him into the airlock chamber. A shadow flashed overhead, blocking the sunlight. Moments later, another impact threw everyone to the deck.

Zeke rolled over, groaning. Through the skylight, he spotted penetrator torpedoes boring into other module sections that made up *Refit One*. Showers of them descended on neighboring defense platforms. The Solar war had come home.

Muffled gunfire and shouting echoed through the walls as Zeke tried to push himself up with cuffed wrists. From the sounds of frantic battle, Imperial troops were already pouring onto the station. The MPs hit the airlock controls before he could scramble to his feet and get out. The steel-framed glass panel slammed shut, locking him in and deadening most exterior noise.

"Jettison the convict. We need to return to the Command Center. *Now!*" the colonel barked, which Zeke was able to make understand by reading his lips. He banged a fist against the glass and cursed, but the colonel ignored him.

As his breath frosted the window, Zeke saw the skinny colonel's orderlies helping him to his feet. Several automatons held Markus down with powerful servos and weight in numbers, and Jenkins was faring no better.

"You'll burn for this, you coward!" Zeke roared, pounding the glass again. "After everything Nightshade has done to save your worthless asses from the Empire, *this* is how you repay us?"

The MPs ignored him. The gunfire in the corridor increased in tempo. One of the walls dented inward, spewing gas from a ruptured conduit.

"Commander!" Markus yelled, but Zeke couldn't hear anything through the class, and Markus was powerless to stop the execution anyway. Zeke knew he should have gotten right back on the shuttle, fired the engines and ripped free of those damned docking clamps when he saw the admiral's welcoming committee. His trust in the Federation's top brass was gone forever ... but if Zeke was being honest with himself, it had been dead for years already.

"*Do it*! Kill him!" the colonel screamed.

A massive impact deformed the hallway door inward. The gunfire outside ceased. The guards leveled their weapons at the damaged entryway.

The chamber cycled atmosphere, preparing to blast Zeke out into the freezing void. It was getting harder to breathe. The artificial gravity plating inside the airlock clicked off with a dying hum. Zeke mentally prepared himself for what was about to happen to his body, letting the air out of his lungs.

The disposal chamber's door exploded open, billowing smoke into the compartment. A huge, armored body fell through and slammed into the deck, studded with decorative carbide spikes, human skulls, and Gauss slug impact holes that bled coolant and black blood onto the deck. The automatons guarding the door stared down at the body, puzzled. It was an Imperial soldier—a massive, genetically and cybernetically modified legionnaire of the Solar Empire, five hundred pounds of organic killing machine encased in Nanotech-powered heavy plate armor. But he was dead.

Another figure stepped over the hulking Imperial, wearing armored, slim-fitting boots. The newcomer was tall, clad in a greatcoat and padded bodyglove, with a wide-brimmed hat and round glasses that reflected the sunlight. A mane of fiery red hair emerged from under her hat—the same shade as Zeke's.

"I wouldn't press that airlock release, if I were you," Anne Oakfield said.

Every weapon in the room locked onto the newcomer.

"Take her down!" The colonel screeched.

A mechanical eagle flew over Anne's shoulder, held aloft by anti-grav generators, shining targeting lasers onto every MP and robot in the module.

Gunfire flashed around the chamber as she blurred out of sight, too fast for Zeke to follow. Markus pulled Jenkins low as the Federation guards dropped in a flurry of shock beams and Gauss slugs. One of the armored bruisers slumped against the glass in front of Zeke, electricity arcing across his form.

In seconds, it was over. The compartment was choked with smoke and weapons discharge. Most of the colonel's men hadn't even gotten time to fire their weapons.

Gasping for air, Zeke spotted someone approaching his pressurized chamber, who hit the controls.

He dropped to the deck as gravity kicked back to life in the tiny chamber. The transparent airlock door slid open and sweet oxygen filled Zeke's lungs, making him lightheaded.

"There you are...brother."

As the air-scrubbers sucked smoke from the compartment, Zeke beheld his sister.

"Anne?" he exclaimed, staggering to his feet.

Anne stepped forward to help him up. "I'm glad I got to you when I did, Zeke."

"Yeah, thanks. You're good at that 'nick of time' thing."

Anne tipped her wide hat, which had somehow remained on her head during the lightning-fast shootout. The eagle landed on Anne's shoulder.

"And I see Lincoln's still kicking ass, as always," said Zeke, nodding to the bird, who nodded right back. "Have you talked to dad? Nightshade has been operating behind enemy lines for so long, I haven't gotten a chance to tell him you're alive."

"I haven't been to the planet's surface yet. You were my first stop—though our father is on my list, too."

"How did you get off Colossus? Past all the Imperial defenses?" Markus asked. "And how did you find *us*?"

"I have my ways," Anne said, winking at Lincoln. "But there's no time for these questions. We have a slight *situation*, if you hadn't noticed."

The staccato rip-roar of automatic weapon fire resumed in the distance outside, echoing down the corridor and into the disposal room. Zeke scowled, automatically tensing at the noise.

He turned to Jenkins. "Collect some of their ammo, kid, we're gonna be needing it. Leave 'em a little bit, though, enough for a fighting chance."

The girl nodded and got to work without complaint, while Zeke returned his attention to his sister. "You heard what that bastard Powell said. It makes no sense."

"You missed some things after your adventure on Mars," Anne explained. "The Federation is planning to surrender to the Solar Empire, today. The Solar War is over."

Zeke's mouth dropped open at his sister's words. "You're kidding."

"I don't kid."

"How did you get this information, Anne?" Markus asked, picking up one of the military police's fallen weapons.

She lit a cigar, beckoning to him. The big lieutenant leaned in, allowing Anne to light his cigar too. After a puff, she answered. "Lincoln intercepted a transmission between the Imperial flagship *Eagle of the Ninth* and UEF High Command twenty hours ago. The subject of discussion was total UEF surrender, which will take place later today. All Federation military assets around the home-world are standing down. They're passing out the order to all remaining UEF installations and battlegroups throughout the Solar System. The Strategos Council has sold everyone out to Mariko. I'm sorry."

No one replied. Zeke's mouth hung open. His mind raced. It was unbelievable, but Anne's story jived with Powell's announcement. Thousands of military personnel and civilian contractors were aboard this station, not to mention millions more manning the rest of the orbital network, plus the teeming billions inhabiting the planetary arcologies. It would be a disaster to allow Imperial legionnaires into any of those environments.

Anne pointed to the large skylight without looking at it. "See for yourselves."

The Imperial flagship *Eagle of the Ninth* was sliding into the sunlight, within range of every defensive mass-driver cannon in the sector, but they all stood silent. Flanking it were the IWF cruiser *Nebuchadnezzar* and the destroyer *Hadrian's Chosen*, followed by dozens more whale-like forms, bristling with city-killing weapons. The invasion fleet was monstrous, the largest that Zeke had seen fielded to date. Whatever deal that the Federation's politicians had made with Mariko, it was done, sealed, stamped and beyond the point of no return.

Another *clang* rang out. The unmistakable rapid *bang-bang* of Gauss gunfire echoed down the hall, followed by screaming. Zeke grabbed an MP's compact submachinegun from where it had fallen as Jenkin stripped the unconscious man's ammunition magazines from his uniform.

"So why go to all this trouble to find us?" he asked, checking the weapon over.

"I came to ask you for a favor. I need Nightshade Squadron, Zeke," Anne said. "I am going to end Emperor Hadrian Mariko, today. We will make him pay for everything he's done – to the UEF, to our people, to you, and to *me*. This is our last chance to end him, before his rule is solidified."

Silence followed, punctuated by distant explosive decompressions. Jenkins looked from Zeke to Markus, then to Anne. "You want to kill...the emperor?"

"Absolutely," said Anne, like it was an achievable goal.

Flabbergasted, Jenkins asked, "How?"

"That's why I found you, Zeke. Nightshade is how we'll end him," Anne said.

Zeke spread his arms. "Nightshade isn't known for regicide, Anne. We've never even been able to get close to him and that's not for lack of trying."

"But you know him, and he knows you. Mariko talked highly of you when I worked with him after we left our father's operation. That counts for more than martial strength."

"I knew him, Anne. He's a different monster now than the man he was before." Zeke said. "My familiarity with Hadrian Mariko from years ago won't give us a tangible edge in an assassination mission," Zeke said.

Markus's brow furrowed at this information, but he stayed silent. Zeke gave him a guilty, pacifying look, but he chose to have this particular awkward talk later, given their present circumstances.

Anne poked the flower insignia on Zeke's singlet. "You command the most effective spec-ops unit left in the UEF. You've dealt with his Praetorian Sisterhood before as well; I need that expertise. I don't have enough hands to take Mariko down by myself."

Zeke crossed his arms. He was about to rebuke his sister's crazy request when another torrent of gunfire echoed down the corridor—too close. Lincoln croaked at Anne.

"Time is against us," she said. "We need to leave. I have a shuttle waiting."

"Good, because we can't use ours," Markus pointed out.

"Wait. You couldn't have dropped this on us at a worse time, Anne," Zeke said, exasperated. "We can't leave now, not with Imperials flooding onto this orbital. We have to defend this station. Almost everyone here is unprepared for what's coming."

"No time is ideal for this," Anne replied.

"What do you think, Lieutenant?" Zeke cast a glance at Markus, who was accepting a stack of ammo magazines and stun grenades from Jenkins.

"Your 'trial' is over, and our precious cargo is secured." Markus gestured to the girl, who went red. "But... we'd be abandoning a lot of people here if we leave now, and we know what the Imperials will do to anyone carrying the Phage."

"Yeah. I need to confirm what the hell is going on, first," said Zeke. "We need to verify for sure what the UEF has done, and I can't let the Imperials massacre half the people on *Refit One*. We can reactivate this station's defenses from the command center to give everyone a better chance to survive and escape. I think we'll find our dear old admiral there too, and maybe get some more concrete information about what's happening. Then ... we'll deal with your vendetta against Mariko."

"Fine, but we don't have all day," said Anne, letting out a frustrated breath. "Lead the way."

6 — UNDOCUMENTED

Jason stared at his hands as he climbed a grimy ladder up a deep maintenance chute, leading to the arcology's city surface level. He could still picture the ugly purple Nanophage fluid splattered all over his skin. And those *shadows* ...

He blinked his thoughts away, and Jason shook his head vigorously as he felt drugs flood his system. Sam's newly rebuilt inhibitor could now automatically dispense Osmium based on Jason's mental state, without the need for manual release. It didn't help with his ongoing exhaustion, though. His dreams over the last few weeks had become worse and worse, so bad that David had requisitioned sedatives and additional Osmium from the Village's doctor to allow Jason to get a few hours of actual precious rest.

They'd been risking a lot of unauthorized surface trips lately, and this one was their boldest yet. So far, they had not found a way into the Science Institute to locate the Abaddon Beacon and stop it from trying to possess him again, nor had they found a way for him to properly control his Abhamic powers. With little traction so far over the last three weeks, the clock was ticking. Jason had no idea what they'd do when they actually found the obelisk ... but it was best to take things one step at a time.

He had managed to steer clear of anything infected with the Phage so far, minimizing the chances of Abaddon being able to reach him. He couldn't allow himself to have another psychic detonation, and especially not in the Village, surrounded by so many innocent people.

"Almost there!" Sam called from below. Faint sunlight filtered down through the grate above them.

"Great," David huffed, dripping sweat onto his companions. "At least this covers my cardio for today."

The shaft was claustrophobic, moist, and crawling with insect life. Jason's scalp itched. There hadn't even been time for micro-showers before they'd left the Village, sneaking out before the first work shift to avoid being spotted.

"Remind me, who are we going to see again?" Jason asked.

Sam let out an exasperated sigh. "Don't worry about *who*. If my contact's information is good, it'll take us right to the Beacon. Maybe today."

"I'll believe that when the sun explodes," David grumbled. His red hair was coiffed into its usual peak, giving Budgie something to pick at. Jason looked down at Sam as he climbed. "This is an awful risk we're taking."

"I think what you meant to say is, 'Wow, thank you *so* much for finding this lead for me, Sam!'" she corrected.

"Right, thanks," Jason replied, without enthusiasm. He looked below into the blackness ... but nothing was following them. No creeping dread, no crawling darkness. No Abaddon.

At the end of the long climb, David shifted his bag aside and plugged his hacking laptop into the grated hatch above. It opened, letting a cascade of dirty rainwater into the shaft. David jerked sideways out of its path. "Whoa! Good morning!"

Budgie spouted some newly acquired swear words he'd learned as he flapped out of the downpour. The water caught Jason full in the face, and he barked out a cough, spluttering.

Sam's giggling caught Jason's attention as he wiped himself off. He looked down and saw her eyes flashing from amber to pink. Most of the moisture leeched out of his hair and clothing.

"That's one way to get a wake-up call!" she said, letting the dirty water fall down the shaft.

With extra practice over the last couple weeks—though Jason had no idea where she'd found the time—Sam's control of her Abhamic powers had improved, even extending to the manipulation of liquids now. She required less Osmium to recover, but Jason still couldn't go off his constant Osmium drip without risking the Abaddon Beacon locating and attacking him again.

"At least that's my morning shower covered," Jason said through gritted teeth.

Sam smiled. "There's that positive spirit. Let it out a little more often!"

"I told you guys what the habitat's weather systems were doing before we left." David pointed out. "A full downpour to clear pollution, at the same time every month. The city's central processing facility didn't hack itself, y'know."

"Yes, we remember," Sam muttered as David disappeared up into the brisk early-morning wind. The cockatoo hopped onto the pavement after him, ruffling his feathers and chirping at the new sights.

Jason followed David up the final rungs of the ladder. The artificial breeze caught his hair as he emerged, and he breathed it in. The city's surface level had cleaner air than the bowels of the New Toronto arcology.

David sealed the grate behind them while Jason helped Sam up before scanning the alleyway for any witnesses of their arrival. The narrow crevice between structures was choked with debris, signage, several rusting automaton hulks, and rusting fire-escapes. Budgie took flight and flapped above the dripping rooftops.

"You be careful up there, featherhead," David called, pulling out a scanner and heading down one end of the alley to scout around.

They had emerged in the city's eastern quadrant, which was made up of run-down residential districts separated by street-wide ID scanners and Phage detection stations. Notably for Jason and his companions, the UEF Capital Science Institute was also close by. The Abaddon Beacon was supposedly still in there, though the only way to know for sure was to break in and find it.

The surface level of the cake-shaped city megastructure was split into five zones. The extravagant downtown of the financial district starkly contrasted against the four poorer sectors surrounding it, ringed with industrial flatlands, landing fields and gigantic manufactories around the periphery. Jason spotted the space elevator complex rising from the core, where the arcology's construction had begun over a century ago. The exospheric stalk pointed through the sky-dome toward Colossus Station, barely visible many thousands of kilometers away through a break in the toxic clouds, which boiled and flashed in great lightning storms—a constant reminder of the Great War that had originally messed up the planet.

Sam examined a pair of small metal generators connected by loose cabling around her neck, padded for comfort, and checked Jason's too.

"Let's make sure that shower didn't short these static plates out. It'd be a shame if someone catches you on camera, pretty boy."

Jason went red, but something else drew his attention to the sky. He squinted, trying to see through the shimmering containment dome. "There's a lot of ships up there."

David trudged back into view, returning from scouting the area around them. "We'd need Talos to do a long-range scan to see what's going on in orbit...but we don't have Talos right now."

David probably hadn't meant any harm, but his mentioning of their beloved robot triggered Jason's guilt. It had taken the better part of a week of rushed excursions to collect enough of his scattered components for Sam to rebuild their long-time automaton guardian, which was finally nearing completion. That didn't help Jason feel much better, though.

Sam checked David's static plates. "We should be able to stay anonymous on cameras, as long as we don't pass through any ID scanners."

"We still shouldn't take any unnecessary risks, even to find Abaddon," said David, checking Jason's Osmium inhibitor out of pure habit. Budgie gnawed on his ear.

"That's a given," Sam replied.

David's lip curled. "But here we are on the surface, *without* Governor Yamamoto's permission, on one of your wild goose chases. Again."

Sam glared at him. "This is the best lead into the Fed labs that we've gotten so far. My contact's information is good. We'll be in and out of there before you can complain that your *wittle feet hurt*. Come on."

"We've been coming up to the surface without permission way too much lately," David continued. "Yamamoto is going to come down on us hard if he catches us—and eventually, he *will* catch us."

Sam shook her head. "I cleared our work schedule for the morning, so no one's gonna come knocking at the Chop Shop. If we're fast, it'll be like we never left ... hopefully."

Sam started down the alleyway, following a map on her comm device's dim screen.

"We should at least check it out, David," Jason said, starting after her. "Sam hasn't led us wrong before."

"Yeah, yeah," muttered David. Budgie repeated the phrase in a high-pitched squawk, prompting David to clamp his beak shut.

"Sounds like you need a morning coffee, crankypants," Jason muttered.

He noticed a homeless man slumped between piles of trash, and they locked eyes. Jason slowly raised a finger to his lips. Despite his drug-induced stupor, the man repeated the gesture and winked. Jason tossed him a ration bar. Having lived on these same unforgiving streets himself, he knew how the guy felt.

Sam stopped behind a rain-drenched dumpster, peering ahead. The boulevard was bustling with Upper-city folks, who hurried around in tense groups through steam columns wafting up through the sewer grates.

The power appeared to be out in this sector. Traffic beacons were dead, and there were no lights visible inside nearby buildings. To the left, an identity scanner array stretched across the street, guarded by several armed automatons. Though the street scanner was dead, the skeletal, plasteel-plated automatons were still checking for infections and verifying identities to ensure that no citizens strayed out of their designated zones without authorization. David checked the sparking junction box beside the dumpster.

"Eastern quadrant is having a brownout," he noted. "Might be our lucky day."

Sam spotted a surveillance drone hovering ten meters above the street, patrolling. She held up a hand to halt Jason. "Their automated minions still have power, watch out."

The compliance drone swept the avenue with scanner rays, verifying identities and checking for Nanophage infections.

David watched the drone, tugging at the device around his neck. "You're sure these static plates will work if we're spotted?"

Sam nodded. "I've tested them with every piece of camera equipment we have in the Village. The interference fields will work, I promise. Unless those drones have a piece of scanning tech I don't know about."

"This is why I'm already getting gray hairs," said David.

Jason poked the side of David's head. "You don't *have* any gray hairs."

"Shhhtt, numbskull."

As the drone passed around the block, Sam jerked her thumb at a diner across the road, squeezed between a laundromat and a bio-sealed apartment building. The dead neon sign read '*Fran's*' in cursive writing, styled like a 1950s eatery, beside a '24-hour service' notice.

"You picked a rather scuzzy spot," said David, squinting at it. A lone cyborg bouncer waited under a wet awning, looking bored. Drifters and addicts stumbled around on the sidewalk, several per block. The upper city was a horrible place for anyone without financial connections, eligibility for the UEF's dwindling social programs, or a well-run off-grid safe zone like the Village.

Sam shook her head. "I didn't pick it, my contact did. We meet here instead of sending open transmissions. Because I do care about security, *David*."

David grumbled.

"I like it. It's got ... character," Jason said.

"It doesn't draw attention, best-case scenario for keeping off the UEF's radar," Sam said. "Come on."

She led them across the street, backpack swaying as she avoided steaming puddles. With his ever-present scowl, David stuck his hands inside his leather jacket, never far from the over-engineered pistol strapped to his leg.

Without warning, a short rumble shook the Earth. Everyone froze until it passed, including the twitching addicts hanging around on the street corner.

"What was ... that?" Sam asked.

David shrugged. "They might be doing repair work on the city's foundations, though I doubt it. Until this war ends, this place'll never gonna get the overhaul it needs."

"Maybe," Jason said, biting his lower lip. Underground tremors in an artificial environment like their city arcology were never a good thing.

Sam continued toward the bouncer, who leaned against the wall of the restaurant and regarded Sam with his bionic eye first, before eyeing Jason, David, and their bird, who shrieked at him.

"This is the earliest in the day I've seen you arrive, Sam. And you're bringing *friends* this time," the bouncer said in a thick accent. Jason guessed from the way he rolled his R's that he was from the European Protectorate arcology.

Sam flashed a dazzling, straight-toothed smile at the Slavic man, slipping a pair of credit chips into his pocket. "You were going to meet them eventually, Richard."

The bouncer accepted her payment, eyeing the sword grip sticking out of her bag top. "Don't cause a fuss. *That* thing better stay put, little girl."

"It will. Quiet morning?" Sam asked.

"So far. We usually only get workers from the midnight shifts coming in this early. And be careful who sees those static plates around your necks. Dead giveaway that you're looking to avoid scanners and cameras, *Undoc*."

"Fair enough."

The restaurant's interior was warmer than the chilly October morning. Jason rubbed his hands, blowing on them.

The wood-walled, heavily decorated diner smelled strange but not unpleasant, like old food. It was nearly deserted. Two serving automatons assisted a large, homely woman with graying hair and a stained apron at the counter, wiping things down for the day's service. The lights and ceiling fans were dead. A few scattered citizens occupied tables near the frosted front windows, drinking coffee, but they ignored the newcomers.

The grey-haired barkeeper looked up at Sam, sounding exhausted. "Sam. I rarely see you here this early."

"Hey Fran. Is she here?" Sam asked.

The woman's focus shifted to a gloomy booth nearby, pointing it out. "Yep."

A loud *pop* came from the wall-mounted fuse-box. Lights flickered on, and the jukebox resumed a quiet tune, a rock song from pre-Federation days.

Fran sighed. "Finally."

David leaned in. "Does this happen often?"

"At least once a day," the bartender replied, surprised at his interest. "Neighborhood rumor is that it's because we're located near the Science Institute. People think they're doing weird things in there, energy intensive, hard on the grid. But the more likely explanation is the financial corruption with the energy companies, load-shedding, etcetera. But mentioning that would be a *social compliance violation*."

Jason suppressed a grimace. Fran was closer to the truth than she realized with her science facility theory. Sam put a couple of Federation credit bills on the bar and winked at her.

"You didn't see us, as always," Sam said. "Thanks, Fran."

"Sure, whatever," Fran said. "Don't take too long, please. We've been having more enforcer visits than usual."

David audibly growled. Jason exclaimed, "Enforcer visits?"

"We'll be fine, Jason," Sam said. "We'll leave if we see anyone more important than a traffic cop."

Not reassured in the slightest, Jason followed Sam toward the booth, hoping that this trip wasn't all for nothing, like so many others had been.

A girl leaned into the dim light above the booth as they approached. "Sam?"

"Hey, Lucia," Sam replied with warmth.

Lucia stared wide-eyed at Jason and David.

"You didn't tell me you'd be bringing *company*, Sam," she said.

Jason noted Lucia's naturally tanned features and her age. Sam's choice of someone similar to them made sense, as younger people in the upper city were less likely to be taken in by the social compliance church's propaganda ... usually.

"Sorry," Sam said, smiling awkwardly at Lucia, who kept her eyes locked on Jason and David. Budgie landed on the girl's shoulder, staring into her brown eyes before nuzzling Lucia's long, dark hair. The Latina girl looked surprised, but she let Budgie do his thing and relaxed a bit.

"He likes you," David commented, raising an eyebrow.

Sam pulled out a chair and put down her bag. "Lucia, I brought my friends today because this concerns them as well. Besides, they should meet the source of our best salvage leads for the past little while."

Jason dropped into the seat beside Sam. "So, you had her feeding you coordinates? No wonder our hauls have been so good lately."

Lucia gave Jason a wary look, but nodded. "Sam contacted me a few months ago, offering a cash reward for locations of valuable items headed to the Recyck yards, specifically intact Nanite tech. Production from the Nanotech giga-forges has never been higher, even with all the economic problems, so there's a lot of stuff being thrown away ... and malfunctioning at a faster rate than ever, which spreads the Phage faster than ever, too."

David leaned against the curved booth so he could monitor the front door.

"And when were you gonna tell us that some random up-worlder knew our itinerary for the past few months, Sam?" he asked.

Sam fixed David with a hard stare. "This is me telling you now. And Lucia's not random. You should be glad that I've developed this relationship with her, because she may have found us a way into the science facility—right?"

Lucia looked up from typing on her datapad, pulling out a locator beacon loaded with a crystal chip. "It's here."

The device projected an image of a damaged guard robot, along with its coordinates, to a location somewhere under the city.

"I found this after Sam asked me a couple weeks ago to look into waste coming from the UEF Capital Science Institute," Lucia said, by way of explanation for Jason and David.

"It's the same model as the bots we've spotted outside that place during our remote stakeouts." Jason replied, peering at it. Could this robot have the right codes to get them inside the building? Did he even dare hope?

"How do you know all this?" asked David, trying his best to look unimpressed.

"I...work for the Recyck Authority," explained Lucia.

Budgie bobbed his head around, mimicking certain words.

No one else interrupted, so Lucia continued. "I'm not gonna rat you out to the church, if that's what you're worried about. The Recyck yards are mostly automated, with pretty limited camera coverage. As a result, we don't have any way of knowing who might or might not be stealing certain things before they're recycled."

David allowed a threatening edge into his tone. "But now you know who we are. If you wanted to push our info to the social compliance goons, there's nothing stopping you from doing that. They could be on their way here right now."

Lucia gave Sam an expectant look. Sam raised an eyebrow, then said, "Oh, right."

Sam pushed a handful of credit bills across to Lucia, glaring at David.

"I've paid Lucia for every lead she's given us, and its far better money than the church's snitch line would give her for three Undocumented Under-city rats. They've got bigger fish to fry."

Lucia nodded, holding up her communicator. "You're right, David. I could call in a report about three Undocs prowling around this district anytime I want. They make it *very* easy for people to do so. But I've got no love for the church or their bullshit. Their high bishop is a blight on the civilized world."

David grunted in approval. "I see."

Sam studied the hologram of the robot. "So, this is our guy? Looks familiar enough."

"Yep," said Lucia. "The science facility usually discharges their recyclables using private disposal services, mostly off-world. But sometimes they ship out non-essential waste to our cheaper public yards. You've got the usual amount of time to grab that robot, which means getting underground and finding Recyck Yard 78-10D as soon as possible."

David squinted at Lucia. "Does this robot still have entry codes for the science facility? Wouldn't they wipe its CPU before discarding it?"

Lucia shrugged. "I set up a quick screening parameter at all our collection depots to detect units whose processors and memories were intact—they are in this one. Someone in the Science Institute must've been sloppy. Whatever security codes that robot carried are still readable, at least until the science facility changes them."

Sam glanced at Jason. "This is worth checking out. The science facility only has a few entrances, and they're all aboveground. With good disguises and maybe some forged IDs, those codes should get us inside."

"Yeah," Jason nodded, but felt a stab of dread at the thought. Recyck yards were dangerous at the best of times, and he hated the idea of searching one for something as nondescript as a bot's CPU core. Jason's neural inhibitor detected the change in his mental state and gave him a small Osmium dose, which dulled the negative feeling.

"What if this guard bot's access codes only get us through the outer doors?" David pondered. "We need to access the deeper labs to find the—"

He realized what he was about to reveal, correcting himself. "Y'know what, forget about the reason. This bot may have been a glorified sentry."

"But you'd be able to find out, yeah?" Sam asked. "Right, *hackerman*? Simple job?"

David rolled his eyes at the nickname, but nodded. "Simple job."

"Let's go find us a robot then," Sam said. "This is no different from any other salvage run. We could also pick up a new battery to support Talos's reboot later today while we're down there."

Jason felt another twinge of guilt, and the inhibitor let out a low hum, dosing him again. His eyes slid out of focus as the drug stupor set in. Lucia gave him an odd look, but Sam covered for Jason by saying, "We'll need the schedule for the Recyck yard's worker bot rotations and any other pertinent details."

"I already have it worked out for you," Lucia said, reaching into her bag for another device. "And I'm sorry, but I've been out longer than I should have. Gotta get going."

"That's okay, you've already made our lives easier by finding this lead for us," said Sam, reaching out a hand to receive whatever Lucia was searching for.

Budgie hopped off Lucia's shoulder and onto the booth's top surface, staring outside. Despite his Osmium brain fog, Jason looked up at Budgie, then at what the bird had seen. David spotted it a split second later. "Shit!"

Several bulky figures hustled past the front windows. Sam's head snapped up, tracking them. Jason swept Budgie off the booth, hissing, "Cops!"

Richard crashed through the door, landing on his back. Sizzling arcs of electricity crackled across the bouncer's torso, shorting out his techno-eye. He was only equipped for throwing out rowdy hooligans on busy nights—not armored cops with five-thousand-volt stun batons.

Two UEF enforcers stormed inside, clad in blue-gray plating with mirrored visors. Richard struggled to rise, but they hit him again with their sparking weapons. A UEF surveillance drone floated after them, carried on humming anti-gravity generators.

"Hey! What's going on?" Fran called, hurrying to confront the newcomers as the drone flashed a scanning beam over the front tables. The other patrons stopped eating breakfast to stare up at it.

"Attention, valued Federation citizens," the floating automaton blared in a sonorous mechanical voice. "We have been informed that a social compliance violator is inside this establishment. Allow yourselves to be scanned for the record. You have nothing to fear if you have nothing to hide."

The scanning beams passed over each citizen without incident, though each of them flinched.

David leered at Lucia, eyes flaring. "You *did* rat us out, traitor!"

Lucia panicked, snatching the locator beacon and Sam's credit bills off the table, sliding past Jason to leave. "No, no! I'm sorry, I didn't! But I have to go!"

"Wait, stay outta sight, you lunatic—" David lunged to force Lucia down, but she was much too fast for him, snaking through his arms and hurrying for the back of the bar.

Another drone floated into view from the direction of the restaurant's rear door, followed by two more jet-black armored compliance officers.

Lucia skidded to a halt as she saw them coming. "Shit!"

"Your girl is wanted by the cops?" hissed David, watching from a crack between the booths.

"How the hell was I supposed to know?" Sam demanded, drawing her blade, but David caught her wrist before she could light the deadly phase field.

"Don't even think about it," he whispered. "Lucia screwed herself. We can still walk away from this while they take her in. Let it go."

Jason looked from Sam to David, praying that they wouldn't start arguing.

As Lucia tried to scramble away, the drone swept a scanning beam down her slender form. Its central camera eye flashed red. "Social deviant identified—logged as citizen 056781-A2. You will accompany these compliance officers under the Social Compliance Act of 2241. Your individual rights are waived."

Lucia almost ducked past the enforcers, but she crumpled as one of the officers crushed her trapezius muscle with his iron grip. The enforcer's gear made it impossible to see any sign of humanity as he forced her to the ground.

Lucia shot Sam with a desperate look, mouthing, "Please, don't let them take me!"

Sam lunged toward Lucia again, but David's hand snapped out, yanking her back inside the booth. "Stop it. If they catch us, if they catch *Jason*—"

But Sam's hand clamped over David's mouth, pressing him back into the seat. "Shhhh!"

The drone at the front of the bar revolved to focus on their booth, flicking its scanning beams around. Jason's stomach dropped through the floor. Budgie was flapping and shrieking, but Jason gently secured his fingers over the bird's beak and wings.

"Oh god," he hissed through clenched teeth as the drone approached on its jets of antigravity, ignoring Fran, who was checking Richard for injuries.

The drone blared again, "Remain calm, citizens. Allow yourselves to be scanned for the record. You have nothing to fear if you have nothing to hide."

"We've got plenty of both," murmured David, unbuckling his holster. The two UEF enforcers followed, batons held at the ready.

Jason prayed that his mental stability would remain in check as his inhibitor gave him yet another dose, a dangerous amount of Osmium in such a short amount of time. An Abhamic explosion here would flatten the building, possibly the whole block. But Jason hadn't heard the Abaddon Beacon's call. Not yet.

He whirled around, checking behind them. "We could run for it; the back door is—"

Sam shook her head. "No. We can't let these guys call for backup. David, no shooting. Too loud. Hit them non-lethally. We need them intact, so Fran isn't blamed for murdering church officers. If our static plates hold up, they won't get our faces on their helmet cams. Then we find Lucia, and get the hell back underground."

"Lucia's on her own. She's screwed us badly enough as it is," hissed David. He stepped into view with his hands raised so the drone could scan him.

"Subject's face is undetectable, presumed 'Undocumented'," The drone said. "All 'Undocs' must be apprehended for failure to—"

David lunged out of Sam's way as she stepped past him and sent her phase blade lashing out on its cable, cracking it upward in mid-flight with her Abhamic powers, cleaving the drone in two. Its anti-grav systems died, crushing the wooden floorboards under its two smoking halves. The short sword scorched the ceiling as it sailed back into Sam's hand.

"Hey!" shouted one of the enforcers. They rushed forward, but David clambered onto the booth to their left.

The closest one yelled, "Stay back!"

David growled. "Not a chance."

He jumped with his arms wide, slamming into the armored church goon like a wrestler. She screamed, flailing her electrified baton. David grabbed the officer's wrist to keep her from electrocuting him, crashing down through tables and stools to the ground in a noisy clatter. Budgie, who was combative even by the standards of a feisty cockatoo, swooped in and pecked at the officer's mirrored faceplate.

Sam spun forward, looping her blade's cable around her waist like a ship sling-shotting around a celestial mass. It sliced through tables, chairs, booths, everything. The flaming energy field flickered off at her command, and the unpowered flat side of the blade collided with the man's helmet, shattering his visor. Sam leaped at him, tackling the much heavier man with a pulse of her psychic power. Her sword hilt pummeled the man's cranium as they slid to a halt.

"Go to sleep, go to sleep, go to *sleep*," she said. With every blow, her eyes glowed hotter with pink fire.

David snaked under his adversary and managed a chokehold. The enforcer's unarmored neck section crumpled under his biceps, and he coiled his legs around hers to prevent needless thrashing. Ten seconds later, both officers were unconscious but alive.

Jason hadn't even lit his stun rod, rooted to the spot. He glanced at the back doors swinging shut on their saloon hinges, but the enforcers who'd taken Lucia hadn't returned to investigate.

Sam stood, letting out a breath and brushing raven hair out of her face, her eyes cooling back to their usual amber color. Sam wiped away a line of blood trickling from her nose and grasped her forehead.

"You need Osmium?" Jason asked. Sam held up a finger, but shook her head. "I'm good. What about you? Any voices?"

"I think I'm covered," he said, giving her a thumbs up, eyes fluttering as the inhibitor implant hissed. Budgie landed on his shoulder, nuzzling him. Sam smiled back, a little sadly. "Good."

David pushed the officer's dead weight off his chest. "That could've gone worse, I guess."

"What the *hell* have you three done?" Fran shrieked at them from the bar while Richard groaned on the floor.

Sam and David froze. Jason's gut sank again. The serving automatons behind the counter looked confused, the situation far beyond their programming. The other patrons had already fled through the front door.

Sam's cheeks flared bright red. "I'm sorry, Fran. I-I didn't know Lucia had a record. What can we do to help—"

"You can get the hell out, now! You've got thirty seconds before I report this to the church, so *we* don't get dragged off too." Fran barked as she helped Richard up. His mechno-eye flashed erratically from the shock he'd received. Smoke wisped from his thinning hair.

"I'm sorry, please, we can—" Sam said.

"Now it's twenty. Stay longer, and I'll give them your descriptions, too. Last warning, *Undocs*," Fran said, dumping Richard into a seat. One of the serving bots handed him a beer, which the bouncer dropped with shaking hands.

Sam couldn't find any other words. "I'm ..."

"*Shiiiet,*" David said, taking in the mess they'd made. "This is exactly what we needed to avoid."

Sam slapped every credit bill she had down on the counter, and the three embarrassed Undocs fled the bar.

After checking for Lucia or her captors, they spilled out into the rear alley-way, which was cluttered with crates from a government ration delivery. Jason spotted several sets of wet boot-prints leading away. He heard screaming and looked up, catching the enforcers dragging Lucia around a corner at the end of the alley. Their drone followed them.

"Come on," said Sam, bulldozing her way after them, but David caught her arm. She glared back at him, but he was already arguing. "Seriously, Sam? We can skedaddle back downstairs scot-free, but you still wanna tempt fate? We cannot screw around with the Church. If they find out that three Undocs are running around the city, they'll have a whole army on us like moths on a lamp. We're risking the whole Village for this gal of yours. Not even to find Abaddon."

"All I want to do is figure out where they're taking her," Sam snapped. "Lucia still has the location data for that guard bot on her. We need that, David. For your brother,"

"I get that," David said. "But helping Lucia is going too far. We cannot get involved with the city authorities, Sam! The second we show up in any of their databases, Avery Oakfield will be on us like a leech!"

Sam's face went red. "I don't know how long we have left to figure this out. Abaddon could hit Jason again tomorrow, today, who knows?"

"Guys, I think we *can* follow them...from a safe distance," interrupted Jason.

He was holding Budgie, pointing out a small band around the bird's feathery neck. The cockatoo thrust his head back and forth, happy to be the center of attention.

"This thing he wears is a camera, right?" Jason asked.

Sam checked the lens mounted on the band, nodding. "I use this monitor to check Budgie's heart murmur, but yeah, it's got a camera function that still works, pipes to my comm unit. Helps to track him down if he flies off somewhere."

"Follow 'em!" Jason said, raising his arm. Budgie screeched an affirmative and took off, heading in the direction the officers had taken Lucia.

"If we get the chance to grab Lucia, we take it. If not, at least we tried. It's low risk ... sort of," Jason added.

Sam looked ready to kiss him, whereas David balled a fist and sighed. "It's your choice, Jason. We're here because of you. If you wanna do this crazy shit, fine. I still vote no. We can find another way into the Federation labs."

Sam bit her lip, watching her wrist-comm as Budgie got a good camera angle on the enforcers and Lucia from above. "Good thing this isn't a democracy. What's the verdict, Jason?"

Jason was silent for a few seconds. "As long as we stay out of more trouble and away from any big concentrations of the Phage ... fine, let's do it. But I'm still not thrilled about running around on the surface."

"I know it's crazy, but we can't give up this lead to find Abaddon." Sam said. "Plus, we all owe Lucia for helping us zero in on good salvage over the last while—the whole Village does."

"True," Jason said. David glared at them for a moment, but gave a grudging nod. "I suppose."

Sam looked at Jason's inhibitor. "You're still good for Osmium? I put a few concentrated doses in your bag before we left. Doc Janice said we're running low on supplies, but we've probably got another couple days' worth."

"That's yet another problem that I don't wanna think about," Jason said, feeling the comforting shape of the inhibitor on his neck. He'd made it through the entire situation without the Beacon managing to break into his mind. But Sam was right, they were running out of time.

Resigned, David tugged his collar up and adjusted his bag straps. "I'm gonna regret this...but fine. Let's see if we can find this girl of yours, and then we'll go after that robot. The sooner we find that blasted obelisk and fix you, the better."

7 — SIBLING COVENANT

"Move it, people!" Zeke barked as he led Anne, Jenkins, and Markus in a running gunfight through *Refit One's* embattled halls, modules, concourses, and chambers, pursued relentlessly by Imperial boarding teams. Many of their attackers were organized, but some of the legionnaires broke ranks and operated like feral pack hunters, chasing the station's inhabitants through the halls like prey.

Anne was the only one who wasn't out of breath, puffing on a cigar. Ordinarily, Zeke would have considered this to be a tactical error, as Imperial legionnaires had an incredible sense of smell, but the smell of battle-smoke and burning chemicals masked the sweet scent of the cigar. Explosive decompressions boomed in the distance, and the coppery stench of blood and burning flesh clogged the air. It was very difficult to see through the ever-present haze of smoke and airborne impurities.

The all-too-familiar adrenaline of battle thundered through Zeke's veins. He'd hoped to get some sleep before being plunged into hell so soon after the Mars retreat, but the universe clearly hated him. Zeke spotted Imperial boarders subjecting anyone who surrendered to a full body bio-scan. Those found with the Phage were murdered with no questions asked. If Imperial bio-scanners were accurate, it seemed like more than half of the station's inhabitants had cases of the Nanophage, from barely detectable to symptomatic with visible skin lesions. Those who didn't have the Phage were marched to waiting prisoner transports that had broken into the landing bays. If anyone resisted, Imperial legionaries killed them without a second thought.

During a break in the frantic fighting, Jenkins paused at a bulkhead with a hand on her heaving chest, staring at a truly macabre sight ahead. Zeke and Markus caught up with her a moment later, with Anne and Lincoln bringing up the rear.

At the center of dozens of fallen Federation personnel lay a single power-armored Imperial legionnaire, pummeled to death by sheer weight of numbers and small-arms fire. Spatters of gore decorated the walls, and the survivors had long since fled. Every one of the emperor's super-soldiers was capable of bone-breaking strength, inhuman speed, nearly endless endurance, and this was the evidence, slaughter on an industrial scale.

"It's horrible," Jenkins said, eyes tearing with sadness. "Look at what they were forced to do."

"This is a Thresher Blade of the Sicariat Legion, which forms the spear-tip of the emperor's legion forces. They're the worst of the worst when it comes to close combat. First in, last out," Markus explained for Jenkin's benefit, checking the warrior's corpse for signs of life.

Covering their flank and watching the adjacent corridors, Anne's lip curled at the delay, but Zeke knelt beside Jenkins. "You'd be surprised what people will do for their buddies, kid."

"We must move on, Zeke," snapped Anne. Lincoln croaked in assent.

"Just a sec," Zeke said, fixing the girl with an iron stare. "You're probably too young to remember this, but the Colossi people were our brothers once, our extended human family. The ones I knew were beyond honorable. They helped to rebuild the Earth after the Great War, though the reason we called them 'Colossi' is because they chose to stay up there instead of resettling to the home-world after the Great War. But the Federation did them dirty, let Colossus fall to ruin over the last century. In that situation, it only took one man to twist them into these *monsters*."

Jenkins didn't respond. Zeke left out the details of his sister's involvement in the Empire's formation as he continued. "That's the evil we're fighting to stop. You've gotta be able to stare into Emperor Hadrian Mariko's heart of darkness and have faith that we can still make some kind of difference. That's what we do, shrimp. That's Nightshade's role."

"Raging against the dying of the light," Jenkins whispered.

"You got it."

"We have incoming," Anne said, firing her twin Gauss pistols at several new pursuers, who had come crashing through a bulkhead within engagement distance. Markus helped Jenkins to her feet.

"Let's go, Private. There's plenty of *raging* left to do. The command sector is dead ahead," said the lieutenant, casting Zeke a meaningful glance.

Several modules onward, with Anne covering their rear, Zeke blasted the door panel ahead of them. The module portal slid partially open with an agonized scraping sound.

Beyond was a hotly contested security checkpoint protecting the Command Center's tall, armored blast doors. Stray gunfire and laser blasts flashed through the open door, forcing Zeke to wave everyone back.

Blood and smoking Gauss slug holes peppered the inner bulkheads. Some of the damage looked dangerously close to starting an explosive decompression into the vacuum outside—but most Imperials wore environmentally sealed battle armor and didn't seem to care about that kind of risk. The stench of burned plastic and weapons discharge hung in the hazy air. Corpses wearing tattered coveralls littered the floor. A trio of off-duty, unarmored UEF marines hunkered inside a security office while a full squad of Solar Empire legionaries advanced on them, cackling with chemically-driven insanity over the automatic roar of their weapons, turning the thin walls of the checkpoint office into Swiss cheese.

A fearsome captain led the Imperials, stomping forth in a super-heavy powered war-suit that bled steam and the sound of chugging gears. She held a civilian technician in her mechanical grip as she bellowed through a rebreather implant comprising the lower half of her face. "Victory awaits, brethren. We shall purge these unclean bearers of the Phage! Mankind must be purified for our great lord's future!"

With a minor twitch of her powered gauntlet, the captain broke the man's neck with a wicked *snap*, tossing his limp form to the deck. Her legionaries howled like wild apes, continuing their advance on the doomed Federation marines.

Zeke snarled. "I have the leader. Our priority is saving those men and entering the Command Center!"

Jenkins and Markus nodded, while Anne shot at Imperial auxiliary troopers advancing on them from behind, picking them off easily. "I'll keep our flanks clear. Show me you haven't lost your edge, brother."

"Is that a challenge, Anne?"

"No comment."

Zeke grasped Jenkins' shoulder, nodding at her. "You've got this, kid."

Jenkins nodded back, taking a deep breath. "Yes, sir. I'm good, sir."

"Excellent. Now, open fire!" he said, charging the Imperials from behind.

As he barreled toward the enemy, Zeke's companions hosed the legionaries using stolen Imperial rifles they'd found that Jenkins had unlocked for use by disabling their biometric security systems. Supersonic slugs battered the Imperial troopers' energy shields and inches-thick plating.

Anne blurred out of sight to assault more targets emerging from a penetration pod that had crashed through the corridor several modules behind them. Lincoln flapped into the fray beside Zeke, using his bladed wings to slice vulnerable points on enemy armor suits. One terror-trooper managed to report a sighting of '*Commander Oakfield and the Outlaw of Colossus*' before Lincoln cut off the transmission with a flash of razor-sharp feathers and a spray of dark gore, passing right through the man's ballistic energy shield.

Zeke sidestepped two hulking legionnaire brutes and continued his beeline for their captain, who was firing her arm-mounted Gauss cannon at the checkpoint office. She laughed, triggering the jump-jets trapped to her armor to skid away from him. Zeke really wanted that Jetkit.

"The great *Commander Oakfield*, in the flesh," the captain chortled. "I am Imperious Beta of the World-Killer Legion, and I was hoping to find you. Your capture will bring me eternal prestige in our great Hierarchy. You shall face the emperor personally and know true fear."

"He's not that scary," Zeke said. He ducked behind a falling shock-trooper to avoid her furious reply of explosive Gauss slugs, which tore the man apart, war-suit and all. Zeke sidestepped a vicious rifle swing from another legionnaire, whose shields popped under fire from Markus and Jenkins before Lincoln finished him off.

Zeke lunged to strike through the Imperial captain's shield envelope at her unprotected skull, but she jetted out of the way again, leaving trails on the blood-slick floor. Her pupils flared in annoyance, lit by internal diodes.

The woman's hair was buzzed to a close crop, but Zeke could see that it was patchy ... clear evidence of Phage infection.

Zeke was drenched in sweat, out of breath, and fatigued from nonstop fighting, but he couldn't resist taunting her. "Y-your whole game is stamping out the Phage, but you're practically swimming in it, lady. You've been conned into a deal with the devil."

"Ignorant whelp! Our science has conquered the vile pathogen!" the captain bellowed. Her armored fist rocketed around, powered by her armor's industrial synth-muscle systems. Zeke twisted to dodge, boots skidding on the deck. The officer missed him and punched right through the thick module wall with a deafening *crash*. Gunfire and screaming echoed from the other side of the sparking bulkhead.

The Solar Empire captain ripped her mechno-fist free in a shower of sparking power conduits and charged at Zeke with terrifying speed, driven by a potent combination of psycho-stimulant drugs. Zeke ducked and weaved her flurry of strikes, barely able to keep up.

"Don't you Federation cowards fight best when you're not alone?" the captain said. Zeke had to agree with her; he might have overextended himself here.

With a buzz of joint servos and whipping power cabling, she delivered a backhanded swipe that would've smashed Zeke's spine if he hadn't corkscrewed his body in midair, feeling the fatal whistle of displaced oxygen as he barely cleared the blow. But as he came down, the captain grazed his jaw with a follow-up strike, moving faster than the speed of sound.

Zeke went down in a daze and slid five meters, knocked into next week. The woman's clawed metal gauntlet was around his head mere seconds later, lifting him off the deck.

"Too easy," the captain chortled. Zeke groaned, swinging his fists at her, neck muscles straining. He couldn't tell if his jaw was broken, or attached at all.

The room swam. He faintly heard Markus yelling his name, firing his rifle one-handed in his real arm, as his synthetic arm had been damaged during the intense firefight. But the other Imperials had Zeke's companions pinned behind the doors, unable to help. He would be embarrassed if *this* was how he went out, clawing at the captain's armored gauntlet as she increased pressure on his skull. His vision dimmed.

Out of nowhere, Anne collided with the Imperial captain like a runaway train, driven by her flight jets. Deck-plates buckled under Anne's boots, and lighting strips blew out from the shockwave of the impact. Zeke was thrown clear, slamming into the bloodied deck again, several meters away.

His sister was in full combat overdrive, impossible to follow. With cybernetic strength and speed exceeding even the post-human Imperial officer's might, Anne pummeled the ever-living crap out of the monstrous woman. The Imperial captain was emblematic of everything that Emperor Hadrian Mariko wanted humanity to become: twisted, vile and full of unearned power. Anne channeled her vengeance through limbs of titanium.

She reappeared from the hyper-lethal melee, bleeding off momentum, jump-jets cooling. Steam blasted from Anne's cybernetic arm and leg through vents that deployed like airplane flaps. Her hat was somehow still on her head, and her glasses shone with red light. The Imperial legionnaire's wrist-mounted Gauss weapon fired off a few final slugs as she slumped to the deck, coughing dark blood, armor malfunctioning, unable to move.

Anne looked momentarily unsteady on her feet, but quickly regained her focus. Zeke gingerly massaged his bruised, fractured lower jaw, which would need medical attention at some point.

"Showoff," he said with slurred speech, struggling to rise.

Anne raised an eyebrow. "I don't know what you're talking about, brother."

She hauled Zeke to his feet, and they approached the fallen captain. Zeke began dragging the Jetkit harness off her ruined battle-suit. "Mine now."

Jenkins, Markus, and Lincoln cut down the remaining Imperial troopers while Zeke and Anne hauled the captain's half-ton armored bulk into a nearby exterior airlock. The Imperial barked weak threats the entire way, but was powerless to stop them in her dead armor.

"You need to chill," Zeke said. He hammered the door panel to cycle the atmosphere, just as the colonel's men had done to him. The captain glared up through the transparent viewport at the two siblings.

"Kill one of us, kill a thousand, a million—we'll never stop coming. The Solar Empire will be—" the captain said, but the airlock blasted her out into open vacuum.

"—Flushed away, like the mistake you all were." Anne concluded. She spat out her spent cigar. Lincoln flapped over to settle onto her shoulder with an invisible puff of anti-grav energy. Dark blood steamed on his iron wings.

"It never ends," Zeke said, huffing out a breath, picking up the captain's jump-jets.

Anne raised her eyebrows at the straps and jets in his hands, dripping with armor coolant and black blood. "A bit DIY, don't you think?"

"From my sister, that's a compliment," Zeke said, gesturing to Anne's custom Jetkit, integrated into her outfit by her own hand.

Markus approached, holding his cyborg arm together with his real hand, which sparked from damage incurred during their battle across the station. "Nice work, Anne. And nice find, Commander."

"It's a pale copy of the real deal, but it'll have to do," Zeke said.

While Jenkins took a look at Markus' damaged arm, using a few tools she had on hand to reroute power and reboot the limb, Anne helped Zeke fasten buckles, strap on the Jetkit's haptic palm controls, and tied off power leads to two damaged jets. A limited exoskeleton connected the jets, which wouldn't do much to block enemy fire, but it would give Zeke a minor strength boost and hold his body together during high-G maneuvers.

Jenkins glanced at Zeke as she worked on Markus' cybernetics, noting the blood soaking his face and fatigues. "Quite the look, Commander. Sir."

"This ain't a fashion show, kid," said Zeke. "Watch me closely—if we survive this house of horrors, Jetkit training is next on your list. Every member of my Squadron knows how to fly."

The three Federation guardsmen emerged cautiously from the security office, cringing at every echo of battle from connecting passageways.

"Commander...thank you. They had us dead to rights. I'm Tarun, of the Upendra 21st Marine Battalion. We were reassigned here after Mars, where your people ... saved us, sir. We owe you our lives twice now," the lead man said, wiping sweat from his brow. The others nodded with gratitude.

"My pleasure, Corporal Tarun. I've got a strict 'no man left behind' policy," Zeke said, reading the boy's rank insignia. "We have a 'meeting' with the admiral, and then we're going to try and save this station. If you want to live, unlock those blast doors and come with us." Zeke said.

"We can't, sir," corporal Tarun replied. "We've been trying to open the Command sector since everything started."

"Course he's locked it down, the goddamn coward," Zeke groaned. "*Shrimp!*"

Jenkins' head snapped up from Markus' arm, which had regained the ability to move on its own. "Sir?"

Zeke snapped a finger at the tall, chunky doors. "Slice those blast doors. Please and thank you."

Jenkins looked up. The portal was reinforced with thick spars and armored to a ridiculous degree.

"Uhhhhhh ..." she said.

"You impressed me when we pulled you off that red rock. If you can keep an entire Imperial fleet off balance with nothing but lines of code, this should be no big deal," Zeke said, rapping a fist on the huge doors. "They'll be on us again soon, get to work."

Markus flexed his synthetic fingers, nodding in approval of Jenkins' quick repair work. "Go on, private. The damage isn't catastrophic. Thank you."

Jenkins cracked her knuckles. "No problem. And piece of cake, Commander."

"Prove it," Zeke pointed to the console. Fortunately, Jenkins was as good as she said, cracking the door in under a minute.

"It's done," she announced as the cacophony of combat came within visual range. A large group of Imperial legionaries appeared in a conjoining corridor several hundred meters away, charging toward the checkpoint like armored bulls. More boarding pods crashed through the hall behind them, burning through the station's layers with high-powered laser drills, deploying human auxiliary troopers and automatons in the wake of the emperor's post-human monsters.

Anne stood in the enemy's path, assuming a defensive stance as Lincoln lined up targeting lasers for her. Anne's greatcoat billowed as she fired at the disgorging hordes while everyone else took cover against the bulkheads, letting the gunslinger's shields absorb incoming fire.

The armored portal's locks retracted with great chunky *booms*. It rumbled open to reveal a well-lit Command Center, dominated by transparent blast-proof windows.

Several squads of marines stood near the Command Center's door, but they were in a neutral stance, only raising their weapons when the giant doors rumbled open. Every one of them looked shocked at the door's opening. There were two other entrances into the module, also similarly guarded. The chamber's occupants ducked out of the way as incoming Imperial fire tore through the doorway.

"Huh, Powell gets an army to guard him while the rest of this place becomes a slaughterhouse. Why am I not surprised?" Zeke said, snarling as Gauss rounds fired by the Imperials zipped past, pinging off overturned desks.

Jenkins raised her hands as fifteen rifles targeted them, but Zeke swept the kid inside, charging into the Command Center after her.

"Stay back!" called the head of security from the other side of an overturned console as his men snapped off shots. "Re-seal this door! Right now! You don't have permission to enter this area, admiral's orders!"

"We go where we want," growled Zeke. Blood dripped from his hands, stolen Jetkit, and commandeered weapons as he stomped toward the defenders, who fired past him.

"Powell! Where are you hiding?" he bellowed. "The least you can do is show yourself."

Nothing but silence greeted him as Anne backed through the blast doors and traded gunfire with the approaching hordes, whirling and dodging individual shots to save her shield barrier's backup batteries.

"Get the door, shrimp," Zeke growled, while Markus ushered Tarun and the other surviving Upendra marines inside.

Jenkins hurried to the controls while Lincoln soared above the UEF defense personnel and station technicians, scanning the chamber for damage to its vacuum seals. No one fired at him to avoid damaging the chamber's thick windows.

Several hundred people occupied the vast space, mostly northern hemispheric orbital defense troopers. Many lacked battle armor, and their weapons were a motley collection from the chamber's emergency lockers. Technicians sat at the consoles surrounding two large holographic situation tables mounted on the raised command area, but they didn't appear to be tasked with anything.

Outside, the Solar Empire fleet passed over *Refit One* and the orbital defense ring, continuing to disgorge thousands of manned torpedoes and bulk troop landers. None of the networked defense platforms were firing. Boarders overwhelmed docked Federation warships—including those undergoing repairs. Clouds of ship-killer missiles fired from the IWF destroyers *Rubiconius* and *Tutankhamen* overwhelmed the UEFSC cruiser *Iron Eiffel*, which must have reacted quickly enough to fend off initial boarding parties. There wasn't nearly enough resistance to make a meaningful dent against the sheer scale of the invasion. The sight of Earth's orbital defense network being overrun made Zeke feel like a mountain weighed on his shoulders.

He'd seen too many people die already, too many friends and comrades taken by Hadrian Mariko's war, and things were about to become infinitely worse for those who had survived until now.

"Sir, the admiral's orders were to keep this module *sealed* until he says otherwise. You don't have clearance for this zone," the security chief complained over the roaring gunfight.

"Stow it, jackass. I'm not waiting to die out there because Powell says so," Zeke said, pushing the security chief's weapon aside as he stalked past.

Anne took the brunt of incoming fire on her shields as she shot through the shrinking opening at the raging Imperial hulks charging the Command Center like out-of-control trucks. Muffled gunfire and explosives ricocheted off the outside of the huge door as it *boomed* shut.

"Where's the admiral? I'm ready for my sentence, Powell," Zeke said, unleashing his frustration that had built up during their blood-soaked journey.

"You don't know what you're dealing with, Commander," a slurred, wobbly voice responded from the upper area of the Command Center. Rear Admiral Powell stepped to the edge of the raised dais. He was drunk, more so than he'd sounded earlier over the intercom. Powell even had a hip-flask clutched in one meaty hand. Zeke's brow furrowed. In better times, a man like him would never have risen through the Federation's ranks to his current station, but decades of corruption and nepotism had degenerated the military to the point where it was possible. The modern UEF was led by so much cowardice and dishonor that Zeke could scarcely believe it.

Powell was overweight and profoundly ugly, with a balding scalp that shone in the overhead lighting as he continued his slurred, sweaty rant, "We had no choice but to do this, Commander. Take your criminal sister and leave this place. The deal with Mariko is done. We must give this station to him, and in return, we live."

Several troopers on the lower level looked up at the admiral in shock. Apparently, not everyone had been made aware of this hair-brained scheme in its entirety. Zeke's boot hit the first step of the command platform, making Powell flinch. His personal guards stepped forward, but didn't raise their rifles yet.

"Who allowed thousands of drugged-up murderous psychos in here to play with unarmed civilian refugees and a skeleton garrison? Was this *you*, or does this go right to the top?" Zeke demanded.

Powell stiffened, and more words tumbled out of his loose mouth. "The Phage has spread too far, and we cannot continue this war under current economic conditions. The Council's decision is necessary for our continued survival as a civilization."

Zeke wiped blood from his cracked jaw and bleeding nose, stomping upward.

"*Necessary?*" he asked. "They decided it was 'necessary' to throw away four years of holding back these animals? Millions dead, half the Sol System ruined, and UEF Command decides to toss all our sacrifices in the trash at the eleventh hour?"

"The decision was ... nearly unanimous," said Powell. "All but one of the Strategos Council voted to surrender. Appeasement was our only solution to this war, after *you* sacrificed half the Fourth Fleet in the catastrophe at Mars. The Council deemed the conflict to be non-viable. Now we have a conditional ceasefire with the emperor, who is coming here personally—"

"Does this look like a *ceasefire* to you?" Zeke roared, extending his hand back to gesture at the rest of the station behind him, which was visible through the module's enormous viewing windows. Many parts of the sprawling habitat were on fire or venting atmosphere as the rampaging Imperials continued their Phage-purges.

The admiral's personal guards raised their weapons as Zeke crested the last few stairs. "That's far enough, Commander. One more step and we shoot," one of them ordered.

Zeke froze, realizing what he was about to do. He looked at his fists, which shook slightly. The UEF still had a chain of command, and even his insubordination had limits. But if the Federation military truly had surrendered, crossing this line meant nothing. He knew how to handle this.

"Kid! Get up here," he growled. Powell glowered at him. Zeke could smell the alcohol on the man from meters away.

Jenkins appeared at his rear, taking the stairs three at a time. "Sir?"

"Sign into that console. Pull up every *Refit One* camera feed you can, and put them on the central view-screen over there." Zeke said, gesturing to a nearby terminal, which a terrified technician began to back away from.

Powell immediately protested. "Absolutely not, doing that will compromise our operational security! We must remain sealed off here until the Imperials are finished their takeover."

"It's either this, or I shoot you, your people shoot me, and a lot of people die unnecessarily. Your choice," Zeke said.

The threat of mutually assured destruction was enough for Powell, and Zeke had a crazy enough look in his eye for it to be believable.

The admiral relented, shrugging his shoulders. "Fine. It won't change anything."

With a final glance at Zeke, who nodded, Jenkins crossed the command dais to the console and began pulling up camera feeds, which began to play out across the giant viewscreen for all in the chamber to see.

It was pure slaughter. Mess halls, workshops, and storage bays were choked with bodies, ongoing firefights, or open to the frigid vacuum outside. UEF personnel, civilians and refugees alike were being scanned by hulking legionnaire invaders, or the baseline human auxiliary troopers that followed in their bloody wake. Those with active Phage cases were immediately killed, eliciting gasps and low comments from throughout the vast command module.

"Whatever the emperor promised you—it was a lie," Zeke said, more to the crowd than to the admiral, before rounding on him directly. "You've been a backbencher for the entire war, and you don't know the Empire like *we* do, Powell. You've never seen the messes they leave behind, the massacres, civilian casualties, the Phage purges. I can't watch it happen anymore."

"Logistics were never your strength, Commander," argued Powell, glaring at Zeke. "By saving those damned Martian civilians instead of following my orders, you tossed away hundreds of vital assets that could have defended the home-world from this invasion. Dozens of capital ships and their materiel, all wasted. But no matter. The deal is done. I have locked *Refit One's* core systems down, so not even my command codes can reactivate our defenses now. We must receive them peacefully, or they will kill us!"

Zeke ignored him, crossing to the command section's railing so he could speak to the multitudes below, pointing at the scenes of Imperial slaughter playing out across the orbital beyond their doors.

"This is what Powell wants. When he lets them in here, those Imperials will kill anyone with a Phage infection, and the rest of you will be taken prisoner. The proof is right up there on that screen. Who do you want protecting you when those monsters start knocking on those doors, him or me?"

"No! Only those with the Phage are at risk. No one else will be harmed, as long as we do not resist!" screamed the admiral. Then he went quiet, as he realized what he was saying.

Murmurs rippled through the assembled crowd. Zeke knew that statistically, many of them likely had minor Phage infections, and even if they were clean, everyone knew the stories about Imperial prisons. Markus grinned up at Zeke with approval. Anne stood at the bottom of the stairs with him, watching her brother with a thoughtful look.

Zeke looked at Powell, but his words were not for the admiral. "You drink on the eve of the Federation's greatest betrayal and lock yourself safely away—behind everyone here—while thousands more die needlessly. Where's the logic in that? Where's the honor, or the care for your fellow man? Those under your responsibility should not have their lives wasted so pointlessly, left to the mercy of the enemy with no warning!"

Jenkins set the bloody camera scenes to repeat, but Zeke's point had already been made. The energy in the room was swiftly turning against the admiral. The chamber's defenders didn't take kindly to being so misled, as more murmurs spread around the chamber. Only the admiral's personal guards remained resolute.

Powell deflated like a balloon. Zeke took another step toward him, but though the guards raised their rifles again, they didn't fire.

"There's no need for this," Zeke growled. "You're a worm, Powell, more reprehensible than I thought you could possibly be. You showed your true colors at Mars, leaving so many to die—which makes your actions here *unsurprising* to me. You are no soldier, not after compromising your duty to protect our people. And choosing to hide in here, at the bottom of a bottle, to absolve yourself of the pain and remorse? That tells me that you *knew* how wrong it all was."

Powell's face turned red, then purple with rage as he realized the game that Zeke was playing, but Nightshade Squadron's commander wasn't done, as the onlookers throughout the command center began to approach the dais.

"You have some explaining to do," Zeke said, eyeing the crowd.

"Screw the admiral!" someone shouted from the deck below. Other voices rose in protest. "He lied to us!"

Zeke didn't smile or gloat. He turned his back on the admiral and his guards.

"Mutiny! Subversion! You ... you won't get away with what you're doing, Oakfield!" Powell slurred, barely able to get the words out through his drunken stupor. Zeke had nothing more to say, walking away as dozens of marines and other personnel came up the steps to the command area, passing him to approach the admiral from every direction. As Zeke had hoped, not a single shot was fired as the fat man and his loyal cronies were subdued by the overwhelming force of their former subordinates. Handcuffs were produced. Soon, they were seated in a guarded row behind the command table, utterly defeated.

A sharp hissing noise caught Zeke's attention.

"Commander!" Markus called from the floor below. "We have a problem."

Looking to the edge of the module chamber, Zeke saw that one of the massive entryways had a widening, glowing spot in the center. Thirty meters away, a similar spot appeared on the second door.

Markus looked up at him. "They're coming, sir. We're out of time."

"Shit," Zeke said, after a deep breath. "Powell's plan was to let them in after the slaughter out there was over, but this module is defensible enough. Markus, get everyone organized down there. Get some desks overturned for defensive positions and defilade, and establish enfilade brackets on those doors with interlocking fields of fire. You know the drill, they're gonna hit us hard. Don't expect mercy from the Empire because Powell made a deal with them to hand over this station and its people."

"Affirmative, Commander!" Markus said, stirring the command center's marines and other armed personnel into action, bolstering the room's defenses.

Zeke whirled on the rest of the people manning the command dais. "All of you civilians, technicians, whatever it is you do ... consider yourselves recruited. Reverse Powell's system lockout, and get this station's exterior and interior defenses online. If you're not feeling up for that, you can grab yourself a rifle. That means you too, kid."

Jenkins, still in awe of Zeke's peaceful takedown of Powell's authority, nodded and saluted without another word, joining the command area civilians at the workstations.

Anne quietly ascended the steps and addressed Zeke as he was pulling weapons from a locker under the tactical holo-table.

"Zeke, our objective is complete," she said." We found Powell and heard it from the man himself: the war is over; the emperor is coming. I held up my end. Now hold up yours—I *need* Nightshade. My shuttle is waiting for us."

Zeke shifted his sister to the far end of the command area, out of the traitorous admiral's earshot, who was still slumped over the console.

"I hear you, Anne. But I can't leave these people, and Nightshade can't get to us without revealing themselves. If the Imperials detect the *Solanum*, they'll wipe my people out before we ever get a chance to hit Mariko. We're stuck here."

"Zeke, I understand that you feel protective over these people. You've developed some survivor's guilt over the course of the war, which is fair. I have it too. But if we cut the head off the snake today, before Mariko's power over the Federation is ratified—" Anne said, drawing a thumb across her throat, "—his Empire will die with him. We'll save billions. Mariko's warlords will destroy each other after he's gone—it's built into their philosophy. We can rebuild the Federation without the corruption that prompted the Empire's creation in the first place. Your little display with Powell proves your capabilities beyond those of a warfighter—I need *you* to lead everyone, in the aftermath."

"That's flattering, but I don't leave people behind—I'm sorry," Zeke said, with finality. "And besides, how are we going to get out of here? We can't survive in a vacuum like *you* can. There's an army between us and wherever you landed your shuttle."

Anne snapped her fingers, and a red orb rose into view outside the void-glass. "Who said I landed it?"

Zeke recognized her stolen shuttle that he'd last seen months ago on Colossus, sleek and curved like the high-altitude stealth planes of ancient times. "Clever girl."

"It has a boarding umbilical. I can extract you, Lieutenant Maximilian, and even the girl right out of this module, maybe with a handful of others. But *Deliverance* doesn't have the life support for everyone here," Anne said. Her cold cyber-eyes flashed red. "It's time to go, brother. Our real mission awaits."

"Hold on. What exactly is your plan to off the big man?" Zeke asked, as the gears in his head turned. "Are you gonna board Mariko's flagship and ask for an audience with him? What's your intel? Details, sister. Where is this happening? *How* is this happening?"

Anne remained silent. The hissing of breaching lasers grew louder. Chunks of molten titanium dribbled onto the deck.

"It depends on where Mariko surfaces," she said. "But I need Nightshade to help plan the exact circumstances of the strike and execute the operation."

"So, you're telling me you don't have a concrete strategy. As usual," Zeke grinned.

Anne showed her perfect artificial teeth, sighing. "I wouldn't say that. There wasn't enough time to gather intelligence on Mariko's exact plans after intercepting the UEF's surrender transmission. I had to get to Earth before the emperor's fleet arrived, so... yes, I'm making this up as I go."

"As always." Zeke said, fixing her with an intense glare. "Do you *really* want to get Mariko?"

"More than anything."

"What are you prepared to sacrifice?"

"Remember who you're talking to, Zeke," Anne's eyes flashed, and her scarred brow wrinkled.

"Opening this door means going all the way," Zeke continued. "We've gotta flip the table and change the game. Mariko won't give up—he can't. Neither can we."

Anne's cold cybernetic eyes narrowed. "I know. I *do* want to get him. But ... I've been trying for years and nothing's come of it. Every plan has failed. That's why I came to you."

"If you wanna get him, we do it my way," Zeke said, with a devious grin. "We know they want the commander of Nightshade Squadron alive. That's our advantage, because they'll drag me straight to him. I can get him to open up."

"That's insane, Zeke."

"You said it yourself. I know Hadrian and he knows me. We've got history. If they capture me, he won't be able to resist gloating. I'll get him talking about where he'll be and what his plans are," Zeke said, winking at her.

"That's...insane," Anne repeated. "Even for you."

"His magical psychic mumbo jumbo doesn't scare me. I owe you this one, Anne, for failing to protect you all those years ago. Let me do this, alright?"

"Thank you, Zeke. But what about Nightshade? They won't act without your orders, if you're not there to—"

"And ..." Zeke held up a finger. "You'll personally pass Nightshade the intel I get out of the emperor about his plans and where he'll be, then you'll work with my people to plan and execute the operation. I can't give you overall command, but you're our best source of information on Mariko, even without my intel."

"I can't ask you to do this, Zeke. He's the most powerful being in the Solar system."

"Our parents didn't raise a coward. Now, where's that bird?"

Lincoln, who had been monitoring the door, landed on Anne's shoulder.

"Can he still do that thing he used to do, with the listening implant?" Zeke asked.

"If you mean implanting the Whisper device, then yes," Anne said.

Zeke nodded. "Do it."

Lincoln produced a tiny implant from his beak and poked Zeke hard in the mastoid muscle, under his shaggy hair to hide the mark.

"It'll let you hear what I do?" Zeke asked, scratching the implantation site.

"It'll capture any audio within thirty meters of you, and the broadcast range is several thousand kilometers, though jamming fields may shorten that range. And don't poke at it."

The weakened Command Center blast door reached its critical melting point, collapsing inward in a slow-motion deluge of white-hot metal. Lincoln blurted out an alarm. Zeke's eyes hardened.

"Before you go..." He yanked his identification tags free. One slid open, revealing a recording device, into which Zeke spoke a concise message.

"There's your verification, so my guys know this plan of ours is legit. This'll also give you access to one of our encrypted channels, so you can contact Nightshade directly once you're outta here. Lieutenant Luther will have overall command of the operation, but she'll defer to your expertise when appropriate."

Zeke handed his tags to Anne. She grasped his hand, locking him in with her gaze. "Last chance to back out. You don't have to walk into the lion's den for this. We can find another way to get the intel we need on Mariko's plans."

Zeke shrugged. "I've been meaning to have words with Hadrian ever since he tried to kill you. Better later than never ... some friend he turned out to be. Now go find my people and wait for the spicy gossip to come through. Ride like the wind, Anne. I promise I'll be there to help end your ex."

"Don't make promises you can't keep," Anne said, dropping her voice to a growl.

"I wouldn't dare," Zeke replied. They clasped their forearms again.

"It's a deal. Good luck, Zeke. And be careful."

"You too, kiddo."

"I've always despised that name, brother."

The last layer of the door folded downward with a sharp hiss, catching their attention. A glowing purple photoreceptor appeared, leering into the Command Center through rising steam and smoke. A gargantuan Solar Empire warbot waded through the melted door to clear the way for the horde that followed. The Imperial fools had really deployed one of their frontline armored units on a goddamn vacuum-sealed orbital station.

"Fire! Fire, fire, *fire!*" Markus barked with a controlled voice at the module's occupants. Over a hundred automatic weapons opened up, pelting the warbot's array of energy shields in a furious storm.

"Go!" Zeke shouted at his sister, grabbing a weapon off the operations table as he ran. He fired his jury-rigged jump-jets and rocketed toward the vaulted ceiling, dodging torrents of Gauss fire, rockets, and laser blasts as wild Imperial legionaries charged into the Command Center. Anne nodded, blasting off in the other direction, toward one of the huge windows.

8 — RESIGNATION

With a trembling hand, Dr. Avery Oakfield put down his empty mug beside a framed photo of his late wife, Shaelyn. Only caffeine and adrenaline were keeping him upright. The building shuddered from another ground quake, forcing him to grab his desk. His bones creaked more than the polished oak workstation, and he picked up a framed photograph of his late wife, which had fallen over. That brought back memories.

A holo-screen on his desk showed that geological disturbances were occurring beneath each dome habitat on Earth. Only one force on—or *under*—this planet could cause that.

Avery had many secrets, each one darker and more of a burden on his conscience than the last. This one was threatening to bubble to the surface, both in his thoughts, and the planet itself.

Twenty-three years ago, he had been ordered by the UEF government to conduct a technological outreach program, extending an olive branch to the Confederacy to prevent a repeat of the Great War from breaking out. The Confederates had been living an entirely separate existence from the UEF for the last eighty years after that disastrous conflict had ended, building immense enclosed habitats of their own to survive the toxic planet's surface, most of which extended into vast underground cities and geothermal shafts.

Avery had attempted to share Abaddon's technology with them by personally bringing the obelisk to their territory with a small team, hoping that the Confederacy's alternative ways of thinking could come up with a solution for the Nanophage. They were an honorable people in Avery's opinion, becoming highly advanced and adept with cybernetics in their long period of divorce from the UEF after the Great War.

The tech exchange program had initially gone well, but as patented Federation Nanite technology was implemented on a massive scale, the Phage soon began to spread among the Confederate population. Their cybernetics were especially affected. Avery and the Confederacy's joint Abaddon experiments eventually resulted in the creation of multiple psychic beings, which was initially heralded as a scientific triumph. But Abaddon used them to trigger a super-charging of the Phage, which Avery had later dubbed an 'Ascension' attempt. As the Nanophage rapidly evolved, overtaking their cities and infecting thousands in an unstoppable tide of destruction, the Confederacy deployed almost every remaining nuclear weapon they had to stop it, vaporizing their surface habitats and damaging the Earth's atmosphere even more than the initial Great War nuclear exchanges.

Avery had barely made it out alive as the sole UEF survivor, haunted by the experience as he returned to UEF territory alone onboard his shuttle with the Abaddon obelisk. The Beacon had shown its hand to him, but he was determined to stop the Nanophage in any way he could. Despite his protestations, Avery had been compelled by the greed-driven Strategos Council to continue churning out new Abaddon-derived technological innovations, despite the dangers of these very things spreading the Phage. All they could see was power and the profit potential of such miraculous technologies. Avery knew that if he'd refused, someone else would have taken over Abaddon research—someone else without the knowledge about it that he had—so he was left with no choice but to proceed and try to figure out a new solution for the Phage himself.

Expeditions to Confederate territory had found no survivors, so the UEF believed that they had been wiped out in a civil war. The olive branch had burned, along with the old enemy, and any possible scientific solutions they may have been able to work out for the Phage.

But Avery believed the Confederates were still down there, deep within the Earth, likely still fighting their own outbreak of the Nanophage. One day they would return. With the recent tremors across UEF territory, he feared that day was fast approaching.

Avery crossed to the window, which reflected his lined face, white hair, and unkempt mustache. The glass depolarized so he could see the artificial sun rising up the interior side of the city's atmo-dome, mirroring the real sun beyond the toxic superstorms raging outside. Maybe Abhamic Subject 107 was seeing this too, if he was still alive out there. Jason had been gone for many years, but Avery still held out hope that one day he would be found—even now, at the present moment of crisis with the Empire. A quick glance at his private desk monitor showed spikes in psionic energy levels in the main lab. The Abaddon Beacon was growing restless once again, deep down in the central complex, and he shuddered at what that might mean.

"Dr. Oakfield, may I have your *attention* again?" asked an unctuous voice from behind him.

With a deep breath, Avery turned around.

The floor-to-ceiling window darkened as Avery faced five screens projected from his desk's holo-viewer. Five giant faces gazed down at him with varying degrees of haughtiness and contempt. Other feeds were active for dozens more useless bureaucrats. Avery attempted to keep his expression neutral.

"As I was saying, Dr. Oakfield, do you have any further objections to ending our war with the Empire?" asked President Winslow. He was younger than Avery, but appeared older, haggard and pale with unkempt grey hair. Even though it was off-topic, Avery considered voicing his concerns about the ground tremors and their connection to the possible re-emergence of the Confederates. As if they needed more problems. But Winslow was the same as he'd been twenty years ago, the same man to scoff at Avery's early warnings about Abaddon, the Phage, and what it had done to the Confederacy. Winslow had managed to get his term extended several times, far beyond the limits of the Federation's constitution, and the UEF had suffered for it. Trying to raise the alarm again would fall on deaf ears ... again. Avery returned his attention to the present crisis.

"My position has not changed, President Winslow, no matter how many times I repeat myself," Avery said. "Surrender is a mistake. We can never trust Emperor Mariko. The last four years of grinding interplanetary warfare should've made that clear."

"Your objections have been noted, Dr. Oakfield," said Winslow.

"Noted is not the same as understood, Mr. President."

Winslow shook his head. "I understand your reservations, but we didn't need a unanimous vote. Our deal with Hadrian Mariko is finalized; the Empire will annex the UEF today. The Federation and Colossi peoples shall become whole again, in peace. Think of this as a victory, doctor."

Avery scowled. "Spare me the rhetoric. No deal is ever final, which you should know, given your business background. We can still reverse this. The Solar War is winnable, if we can reorganize our military and push back into the territories that the Empire have taken from us."

"The war is not winnable," countered supreme commander Josef Foch, leader of the UEF armed forces. "We've lost Mars, our last stronghold in the mid-system gulf. That was the tipping point, shortening our effective resistance to weeks rather than months. Approaching the Empire for amnesty and a deal was our only option. It was your *son* who sacrificed half the Fourth Fleet to save a few thousand people."

"My son saved 103,506 civilians, Supreme Commander. That's a fair trade for fifteen battered ships running skeleton crews," Avery said.

"Nightshade Squadron wasn't even supposed to *be* there," Foch growled. "He disobeyed Admiral Powell's direct orders. That's a felony, punishable by death in wartime. We will deal with Commander Oakfield in due course."

"Or you could listen to him," Avery said, his anger getting the better of him. "Nightshade Squadron's tactics are a testament to how offensive strategies against the Empire have worked! Wherever they're involved, Nightshade beats the Imperials—in space and on the ground. Our fleets have three dozen additional capital ships thanks to Nightshade's piracy operations. Imagine what our position would have been now if you allowed other units to operate without your crushing oversight, like *they* do."

This crossed a line with Josef Foch, who went bright red in the face, unable to form a response. The finance minister interrupted before Foch could explode into another rant.

"Doctor Oakfield, even if we were to assume an offensive strategy, our economic collapse will soon follow," Minister Savoreaux said. "We have half a sidereal year at most before our central banks enter bankruptcy. Hyperinflation has set in, and all of our investments in military spending are overleveraged. We can't service our debt any longer, nor can we continue to finance this level of combat operations. Our only remaining option is ending the war and allowing the Empire's stronger economy to stabilize the

Federation, or we risk a prolonged depression. Dumping huge sums into an all-out assault on Colossus will only hasten our decline."

The other council members nodded like lemmings at the finance minister's mischaracterization of Avery's position. Avery spread his fingers painfully on his desk.

"Breaching Colossus isn't required, you money-printing incompetent," Avery said. "I've never proposed that. We just need to cut off the territories Mariko has seized to choke their supply lines, as they've done to us. Mars, Venus, the asteroid belts, the Jovian mining outposts and water reclamation sites, agriculture habitats, and fuel processors, for instance. Retaking *some* of these locations will starve Colossus out. The home-world does not have enough resources for self-sufficiency without these territories, which is why the emperor has conducted this war how he has. It's always been a land-grab. Mariko wants to consolidate all of our remaining resources under his banner and then use them to expand our reach far outside the Sol System for more resources ... before we run out of everything and die here."

The high bishop of social compliance spoke without addressing Avery directly, talking to Winslow instead. "Mr. President, Dr. Oakfield is not meeting the criteria for 'accepted speech' as decreed by the Church. I feel his aggression through our holo-call. A short reconditioning session might fix—"

Avery slammed a fist on his desk. "There is no way in hell I'm visiting one of your 'reconditioning' camps, you fraud. Your 'Church' divides everyone while Mariko hangs the sword of Damocles over our heads. The dystopian stories of our past were meant to be cautionary tales, not a roadmap for your personal use. The emperor himself said that your ideological poison might cost us the war, and I agree with him on that."

The room went deathly quiet. The bishop's haughty face went crimson. Avery had dared to speak positively of the emperor and in opposition to the church. Either one was a capital offense, even for a high-ranked inner party member.

Before the bishop could explode like Foch had, the minister of industry asked, "Can we...still count on your expertise with the artifact, Doctor? Even after the annexation?"

"What?"

The pudgy industrialist, minister Cooper, picked his words carefully. "The Federation has been reliant on regular technological advancements from your Abaddon Beacon research operations—one of the few advantages we've had against the Empire. My gigafactories are still awaiting new Nanotech innovations. We've had to overproduce older designs, from military hardware to civilian appliances."

Avery pinched the bridge of his nose. "Our lack of new Nanite tech deliveries is a result of funding cuts. From *your* war."

"Cutting your outrageous budgets were necessary *due* to the war, Dr. Oakfield," Cooper replied.

Avery ignored Cooper's jab. "I am also reluctant to hand over new innovations from the Translation Program because of the lack of safety regulations in your gigafactories. As quality standards fall, the faster the Nanophage spreads. That's on you, minister."

Once again, the room fell silent. The meeting was nearing rock bottom, so Winslow spoke up.

"Thank you, Dr. Oakfield," the President said. "This call was our courtesy to you. As the only dissenting vote about the upcoming ceasefire contract with the Empire, we are obligated to hear your objections, on record. But we do not agree with your criticisms, so our deal with Hadrian Mariko will continue. The Solar War ends today."

Avery was finished playing games. "Of course, I'm the bad guy. As always."

Winslow spoke like the consummate politician he was. "Doctor, we respect your opinions regarding your own fields: the sciences and engineering. You have directed the UEF's research division with great distinction, despite certain … failings. Given the rumors about Hadrian Mariko's origins, you're lucky that we're letting you off so easily."

The other councillors nodded.

Avery dropped into his high-backed chair and kicked up his aching feet.

"Fine, I'll give you the unanimity that you've always wanted," he said. "I resign from the Strategos Council. I refuse to shake hands with the devil."

Winslow shrugged. "Very well. Your place in the new order will be waiting. But something tells me that the emperor will not accept your resignation."

"Get out of my office, Mr. President."

"Very well then. Good day, Doctor Oakfield. And good luck," Winslow replied.

The president's screen went dead. The others disconnected quickly, eager to escape the viper's den.

"Good day to you too, scumbag cowards," muttered Avery. He released his breath and keyed the intercom. "Mary. We need to talk about our contingency plans. Mary? You there?"

There was no response from his secretary, whose desk was right outside his office door. Most high-ranking officials used advanced AI assistants, but Avery favored human interaction.

"Mary? What's happening?" Avery asked. There was muffled banging at Avery's door as his secretary tried to enter, but it was armored. Avery suspected that it wouldn't open for anyone.

A new voice boomed through the room's hidden speakers. "Your executive assistant is unavailable, Doctor Oakfield. She is having ... *difficulties* accessing your office. Or so I'm told."

"Hadrian."

Avery turned around to see his holoprojector drawing a life-sized projection of emperor Hadrian Mariko, right there in his office. His pale, slender face was regal: the image of calm poise and self-assured command. Although the emperor was frail in body, supported by a gold-trimmed black cane, he was tall and well-dressed, choosing to appear in simple business attire rather than ostentatious robes of office. The power Mariko radiated more than made up for his physical frailty.

The emperor gave him a genuine smile. Avery supposed that Mariko had every reason to be feeling good right now. "It's been too long, Doctor. Your breakup with those Council weaklings was very entertaining. Bravo."

"What do you want, Hadrian?"

"I suppose this is another 'courtesy call'," Mariko responded, adjusting his glasses and running a hand through his long, silky raven hair. "You're a very popular man, you know that? Multiple heads of state calling you, one after the other? I don't think there's another individual in the entire Solar System with that kind of influence. Not even myself."

"Which must get to you," Avery remarked, folding his arms.

"On the contrary. I am the ruler of all mankind now. My ego is intact, thank you very much," Hadrian said, maintaining his perpetual smile.

"To what do I owe this 'pleasure', Emperor?" Avery said, returning to a bored, neutral tone, but with an edge of disdain.

"I'd like some recommitment to your ongoing responsibilities, if you would indulge me."

The emperor's burning eyes bore into him, forever aflame with Abhamic energy. Even from thousands of kilometers above his head, Avery felt an inkling of the man's devastating mental power, like a sunbeam that was a bit too hot.

"Ongoing responsibilities?" Avery asked, teeth clenched.

Mariko smiled. "Yes. And, to set the stage, I'm told that we have your son cornered on an orbital station. That battle progresses as we speak."

Avery went cold. *No.* The emperor had publicly killed Anne in single combat many years ago, during a live broadcast of their final takeover of Colossus. The betrayal had captivated billions. Now Zeke was in Mariko's clutches, too. Would he lose his entire family to this menace?

"Why are you telling me this?" Avery asked.

"Because, if you cooperate with my request, I will ensure his safety," said Mariko. "You still owe me a successor from that little program I asked you to run for me, many years ago. The one that birthed my daughters. I need you to finish it for me."

"The Successor Program *is* finished. I sent you nine candidates before the war started," Avery said, grinding his teeth. "And you broke your promise. You said that if I did what you asked with them, you would postpone the war."

"We were left with no choice. The Strategos Council started this war, not I," Mariko corrected, running a projected hand down Avery's arm. "And those nine clones you sent were not bred to my exact specifications. I didn't give you Anne's genetic material to watch you waste it. My daughters are technically your family too, your grandchildren. I would've thought you'd take more care with their development. Where is the tenth specimen that you produced? The one deemed to be the most successful?"

"The tenth specimen is gone. The Successor Program fell apart soon after, thanks to the Council's meddling," Avery said, pulling away from Hadrian's holographic touch. Even though the emperor's hand wasn't physically present, Avery swore he felt it.

"No matter. We'll find her," Mariko said. "And if we don't, you'll restart until it succeeds. My philosophy, and my Empire, must have continuity."

Avery didn't respond.

Hadrian smiled. "My deal for you is this: if you continue the Successor Program, I'll make sure Zeke is taken alive by my people. You might even see him again. Sound good?"

Avery let his rage boil over. "Fine. If it means that my son will survive, I'll create another little you."

Hadrian brightened. "Excellent. And I'll throw you another bone, Avery. During our takeover of Earth's orbital shipyards, we spotted the so-called 'Outlaw of Colossus.' Anne's alive. She's been operational for years longer than I suspected."

"Anne is ... alive?" Avery reeled from the emotional whiplash. He'd hoped in his private moments that she wasn't dead, but with no access to Colossus Station for many years, he'd never had a way of confirming it. If true, Anne must have been surviving in the most remote, hostile areas on the gigantic space habitat to remain hidden from the Empire—a brutal existence.

"Of course she is. I've never lied to you, Avery," Mariko said, grinning his perpetual grin. "Once we've captured Anne, we might give her back to you to help with the Successor Program and Abaddon Beacon Nanotech research. It'll be like old times. Maybe she'll even meet her daughter—my true successor—someday."

"You should have finished the job. If she's really alive, Anne will end you."

"I'm sure she'll try, Avery," said Mariko. "That girl's nothing if not persistent. But my crimes pale compared to your own. Are you able to judge me?"

"Absolutely. You could have stayed with the Abhamancer Program and helped me stop the Nanophage, the *right* way, but you had to go off and start your blasted Empire instead. Look how things have gone since then. Look at how many lives have been destroyed and how much further the Phage has spread thanks to this pointless, destructive Solar War," Avery spat. "What you've never realized is that the Abaddon Beacon is controlling you, and it has been from the start. This is all what it wants. You weren't powerful enough to use the amplifier, so the Beacon crushed your will, and now you believe everything it says. You're nothing but a slave to Abaddon. In your arrogance, you've never been able to see that."

Mariko's voice deepened, but that awful smile never wavered. "Lies. Abaddon has told me many things and they have all come true. We have no reason to distrust it. And when I arrive on Earth, I will find it. With the Beacon's power, I will save our species from the Phage, and from ourselves. Mankind's future cannot be left in your incompetent hands. The obelisk told me that the final sacrifice is at hand, Avery. Today. Nothing can stop it."

"Hadrian, if you still have a shred of decency left in you, you'll call off whatever you're planning, return to the labs and submit yourself for treatment," Avery pleaded. "Abaddon will lead you into destroying us if you don't."

"No. I freed myself from your clutches before, and I will never allow you to control me again," Mariko retorted, defiantly.

"Fine. Get out," Avery demanded.

"As you wish, old friend. I'll see you soon. And remember, everything to come was only possible because of you ..."

The hologram dematerialized.

Avery collapsed into his leather seat. His conversation with Mariko, which had felt more like sparring with a demon, had exhausted him more than the council meeting. He picked up the framed photograph from his desk.

"Oh, Shaelyn," Avery said. "We've really screwed things up, haven't we?"

His wife's unmoving face stared back, judging him.

Avery heard a renewed rapping on his door. The room's soundproofing technology had been downplaying outside noise until now. The office door burst open, revealing his secretary and two facility guards.

"Dr. Oakfield, are you alright?" Mary asked, terrified. Her eyes darted around the room, confused at the lack of a reason for the door being locked.

"I'm fine. Everything's fine," Avery said, pouring some water from the pitcher on his desk.

"Is there a security risk to you, sir? To the facility?" asked one of the guards, scanning the office.

Avery shook his head, gulping from the glass. "Not now. But there will be."

"Sir?" asked the guard, confused.

The Solar Empire was projecting a total communications blackout from orbit, but panic was inevitable once their fleet became visible from the surface.

"Mary, please instruct the laboratory staff to purge all project files, active and archived," he said. "Everything."

Mary was alarmed. "What?"

"You heard me. Do it, please," Avery pointed to the tablet on her desk.

With a concerned look at him, Mary left to type out the fateful message.

Avery turned to the guards. "Once the purge is complete, we'll evacuate the campus. The Empire is coming, and they'll send a contingent here once they land. I won't be able to protect any of you from them."

Like Mary, the security men were floored. One of them asked, "Sir? The Solar Empire ... is coming here?"

"I'll say it until it sticks, son. This isn't a drill, or a joke. The war is over. They're coming," Avery said and took both guards by the shoulders. "Please, do this for me. The number of personnel who survive today relies on your speed. The Solar Empire will purge anyone with a trace of the Nanophage. At least half our staff have minor infections, with many undergoing treatments."

"But sir ... the science teams will want to protect their work. Especially the artifact," said one of the guards.

Avery shook his head. "Hiding the Abaddon Beacon from the emperor is impossible; all we can do is slow them down. Go, now."

The guards nodded, following Mary out of the office.

Avery shut the door and activated a wall-sized camera view of the science facility's core laboratory. The chamber was gigantic, manned by hundreds of scientists, engineers, and assistants. A whirlwind of activity was starting. Technicians dashed to the data storage banks, grabbing axes to bludgeon the servers. Others stood at computer terminals, trying to mass-delete as many files as possible. Specialists of all disciplines argued over Avery's orders. Some were paralyzed with indecision.

But what drew Avery's attention, as always, was the twenty-meter-tall obelisk made of a yet-to-be-identified metal substance—even after a century of study: the Abaddon Beacon.

It had been named by the Federation scientists who had discovered it over a hundred years ago, early in the cataclysmic Great War between the fledgling UEF and the Confederacy, beneath the sands of the old Holy Land, outside Jerusalem. Those men were all long dead, but if only they'd known what they had unleashed.

'Abaddon' was an acronym, short for: 'Archival Biosynthetic Artifact for Data and Dynamic Optimized Nanotechnology'. The name had been chosen when its discoverers had realized that the obelisk was a trove of fantastic new nanotechnologies, after subjecting it to rigorous decryption testing for many months. Its ever-changing symbology had been difficult to translate, but once unlocked, Nanite tech had changed the course of history and accelerated the Great War to its Earth-ruining end.

As Avery watched, unintelligible formulas danced across Abaddon's four main surfaces, analyzed by a series of scanner arms that fed into a massive translation supercomputer. Forks of etheric lightning flashed up and down the massive object, sparking off the containment field that surrounded it. Steam rose around the pyramid-topped metal obelisk from the temperature differential between the ice-cold laboratory and the machinery surrounding it ... but not even the rising gas wanted to be near the powerful object, curving around and away from it.

The other noteworthy object was a gigantic web of support struts, cabling, and other apparatus topped by a human-sized seat. This 'telesthesic amplifier,' as Avery called it, was connected to the Abaddon Beacon by a series of bio-feedback cables, currently being disconnected by lab personnel. The seat required an operator with sufficient psychic ability to control the Beacon directly, though no individual had been successful yet. After the debacle with the Confederacy—and after exhausting all other conventional solutions for the Phage—Avery was sure that this was their final chance to stop Abaddon's techno-plague, as Shaelyn had wished.

Through its miraculous nanotechnological gifts, the Abaddon Beacon had saved human civilization after the Great War, allowing Colossus Station and the Earthside arcologies to be built. It had unlocked the Sol System for colonization and exploitation, extending the lifespan of the species even further. But if the Phage couldn't be resolved, humanity's reliance on the obelisk for borrowed time would become their doom. Avery knew that Hadrian Mariko would never understand that. He'd only ever seen the Abaddon Beacon as a tool of ultimate control ... and Abaddon itself had manipulated Mariko and his Abhamic power since his time in the labs and beyond.

But most of all, Avery was terrified of Abaddon's final intentions. He had witnessed the artifact attempt to destroy the human race once, and the Confederacy had suffered the ultimate price to stop Abaddon's Ascension attempt. All of Avery's efforts to prevent that from happening a second time were in tatters. Years of work in the labs had yielded no new candidates and no new options or countermeasures against the Phage or Abaddon's psychic influence. It had called Mariko back home. Jason, the Abhamancer Program's prime subject, was still missing. If Abaddon brought the two of them together, willingly or otherwise, the eldritch machine would use them to deliver its final kill-stroke to the human race, and Avery would be powerless to stop it.

Avery picked up the photo of his wife again.

"If you're up there, Shaelyn...I know I've had my differences with the big man, but if you've got his ear, we could really use some *help* down here."

9 — RIOT

NEW TORONTO UPPER-CITY - EASTERN QUADRANT
TRIBUNAL SQUARE 1-A — OCT. 31, 2263 — 06:59 HOURS

The morning chill steamed Jason's breath as he watched the social compliance enforcers from a creaking second-floor balcony with David and Sam. The cops stopped, checking Lucia's cuffs before leading her up the stone steps into the open square above the street, which crawled with enforcers and a civilian crowd. Hunched vagrants and drifters scattered before the cops, scurrying into gloomy alleyways beside another street-wide ID scanner, which Jason and his companions had climbed this building to avoid.

Lucia clutched her bag, trudging miserably ahead of her captors as they disappeared into the packed square. Despite her situation, Jason privately cheered to himself—at least she still had the Science Institute robot's locator beacon. They still had a chance to find it, though it was a damn slim one. Jason had to admit; they were going to some extreme lengths here. But finding Abaddon had become an all-consuming goal for him, so he had no choice but to chase this lead to its end.

Budgie circled overhead, transmitting images down to Sam's camera viewer, which had allowed them to track Lucia here.

David glanced at Sam and Jason. "End of the line, guys. We're not going in there."

Sam watched the scene, despondent. "Oh Lucia, what have you gotten yourself into?"

Budgie was still transmitting images of the area from above. Over a thousand people were gathering around the square's central stage.

David checked his chronometer, pulling away from the scene. "Well, we only partially wasted the morning. Let's get back downstairs before anyone notices the Chop Shop is empty."

"You think we can just let this happen?" Sam snapped. "Those enforcers caught Lucia because of *us*. I don't know what she did to provoke them, but it wasn't her fault."

David looked at Sam like she was spouting a dead language. "Do you hear yourself? That place is swarming with cops."

Sam closed her eyes, frustrated. "We're not committing to anything yet. We can get closer with that crowd as cover. If there's a chance to grab Lucia, we take it. I would have thought that you, of all people, would be in favor of saving someone who *really* needs it, Jason."

Stubbornly, David shook his head. "It's too dangerous, Sam."

Sam took him by the shoulders. "You know what they're gonna do to her?"

"Yeah."

"And you wouldn't let that happen, *right*?"

"Ugh. Nope," David admitted.

"What about you?" Sam asked, rounding on Jason. "You all good for this?"

Jason considered it. Exploding like a psychic bomb in a crowd like that would cause massive casualties, and Jason was stressed enough as it was. But death would be a kinder fate for Lucia if they didn't get her out of there, and Abaddon's threats hung ever-present in his mind.

"Leaving her to rot in one of the church's reconditioning camps would keep me up at night," Jason confirmed. "Maybe not as much as the Beacon, though."

"Which is why we *have* to do this," said Sam, checking Jason's implant and tapping several buttons, which caused Jason's eyes to defocus as more drugs hit him. "I'm cranking your Osmium output. First sign of trouble, we'll scram."

"Okay."

David resigned himself to his fate. "Budgie, get the hell down here."

The cockatoo descended.

The three Undocs used the crowd's density to get inside the tribunal area's periphery, eyes peeled for Lucia among the bobbing heads. The architecture in this part of town was built to emulate the style of the ruined original city far below, sealed over by the modern habitat superstructure. Wooden shutters creaked in the breeze over nineteenth-century gables. Retail stores were closed. The infiltrators found cover outside a darkened shop, far from the stage. Jason dropped into a crouch behind some boxes under an awning. David and Sam joined him.

A man in priestly vestments approached the raised area, consulting a gilded datapad with a bored expression. A circus of church officers followed, marching the 'defendants' up to the stage. The priest cataloged each on his datapad like they were livestock.

Sam wrinkled her nose at their treatment. Jason seethed at the sight. These people had likely done nothing wrong, but the Federation was clamping down on the population to prevent unrest amid rationing and worsening news from the frontlines. The UEF abused the threat of the Nanophage to add more pressure. The city was drowning in plague, unrest, homelessness, and crime, yet all the church did was punish the innocent, intensifying the decline.

Jason saw that Lucia was the final defendant being herded up onto the raised area with the rest, looking absolutely miserable. Sam raised her forefinger and thumb to her chin. "I could grab her ... if the crowd went wild. Catch my drift?"

"Nope. You're gonna need to explain that one," David said.

Sam stirred a finger around her open palm. "You create a distraction, I pull her out, and we all get back downstairs."

"A distraction ... like a fight?" asked Jason, hoping he'd misheard.

"Yeah, like a fight," Sam said. "These people are wound so tight; it wouldn't take much to set them all off."

David rolled his eyes. "Right, let's start a thousand-man riot. Brilliant plan. What's our exit strategy? Only Talos could raise that kind of ruckus and get us out alive."

"We don't have Talos, David. And we can't expose him to public view up here, even if we had him," Sam said. "No one will be watching us if the crowd are all focused on each other. The enforcers will be plenty occupied while I yank Lucia off that stage, if you can pull this off."

"You aren't huffing Osmium *too*, right?" asked David.

"I'm in my right mind, you ass."

"Could've fooled me."

Jason returned his attention to the square as they bickered. As people jockeyed for viewing positions on the cobblestones, a sewer access point became visible between their shuffling legs, like the one David had unlocked earlier that morning.

"David?" Jason asked.

David and Sam's argument escalated, getting in each other's faces. The inhibitor hissed as Jason's anxiety increased. He flicked the back of his brother's head in frustration. David stopped jabbering. "What?"

"You can hack through that sewer grate, right?" Jason asked.

"What?" David looked around blithely, spotting it. "Oh."

Sam grinned. "There's our way out, knucklehead. Props to Jason for using his noggin instead of arguing with every idea I have."

David looked like he wanted to smack her, but restrained himself.

Jason laid out the strategy. "David will open that thing; I'll try to stir people up. Sam, you work some voodoo Abhamic magic to grab Lucia, then we'll get right back underground."

"Sure. But a lot needs to go perfectly for this to work." David said.

"You always say that," Jason replied.

"Because it's *true*."

Sam ignored them as she checked the buckle of her blade's holster slung around her waist. Jason still had reservations about rescuing Lucia, not to mention condemning hundreds of people to the wrath of the church by stirring them up into an illegal riot, but Abaddon flashed into his mind. For a split second, he thought he heard it whisper to him. But that was impossible, right?

Jason forced those thoughts out of his mind. Lucia's data was the best chance they had to find it, so they *had* to do this.

David was quiet, fixated on Lucia, eyes narrowed. He was about to speak when Sam interrupted. "I get it. We'll do this without you, David."

"That's not what I was gonna say," David snapped. "Very few people come out of the church's reconditioning process with their sanity intact. If it was Jason up there, it wouldn't be a choice for me."

Sam raised her eyebrows.

David blew out a long breath. "Screw it. Let's get this over with."

▲▲▲

"I'm getting cold feet. Ya sure you don't wanna back out?" David said almost as soon as he and Jason shouldered into the crowd, catching sideways glances from nearby citizens.

"I don't wanna be here either. Quit bellyaching, brother," Jason replied, checking that his static plates were still working, but he continued forward. He couldn't hear any strange whispers and saw no otherworldly shadows oozing up through the throngs of people around him. That was good, at least.

As the tribunal ceremony continued, none of the onlookers noticed the brothers approaching the sewer grate. David deployed a cable jack from his hacking computer. This was a routine job, but under the circumstances, he was not a happy hacker.

Jason glanced over his shoulder. Sam had scaled the building behind them, supervised by Budgie. Sam steadied herself and swung her leg over a bundle of power cables, one of dozens crisscrossing the square.

Jason's mouth dropped open as he watched Sam cross the tightrope high above. David glanced up at her as well, cringing as he watched. "She's gonna get caught with that circus act."

"Just get to work. Nobody's spotted her yet."

David glared at Jason, kneeling down to fiddle with his bootlaces while he plugged in the hacking device. The grate's readout lit up, but didn't unlock immediately like the previous one. David looked at it, puzzled. "What is wrong with this thing?"

Jason watched the priest address the thirty defendants on stage. Several enforcers guarded them, but most of the compliance officers ringed the crowd, watching for unrest with stun sticks at the ready.

"We gather here today in honor of our shared commitment to social compliance," the priest droned off his ceremonial datapad. "Since our Federation's founding, we have committed to equity and equality of outcome between all peoples. After the restoration of Earth, we introduced the Social Compliance Act to solidify those ideals. These defendants are guilty of social deviancy, causing violence to others through their utterances, among other charges. For these grave offences, they will undergo positive reconditioning therapy."

"Goddamn bullshit!" David said, cursing as the sewer portal's pneumatic drivers sparked, refusing to unlock.

Jason checked Sam's progress as the priest prattled on. Tottering on the unstable bundle of cables, she generated small bursts of Abhamic power to keep herself stable as she walked.

Frustrated by Jason's inaction, Sam met his eyes and repeated the stirring motion. A stab of panic jolted Jason. With David preoccupied, *he* was supposed to be the one raising a ruckus. Shit.

"Why does nothing in this city work?" David muttered.

A curious stranger in the crowd was about to question what David was doing, but Jason blurted wildly, "Don't I know you from someplace?"

The up-worlder looked at Jason, puzzled. "No."

Jason's anxiety level spiked. The inhibitor hit him, dulling his senses, making his pupils dilate.

"Yeah, man. I think I know you from...uhhhh..."

The man pulled away in disgust. "Are you high, kid?"

"Well...sort of...actually...but don't worry 'bout that..." slurred Jason, laying it on thick, which wasn't hard at all—he *was* very high.

Another man in the crowd snapped at him. "Shut up, I'm trying to listen."

Jason named the first guy 'Mustachio' because of his unkempt mustache. "We're just having a conversation, Mustachio. Peace, maaan."

"If you're gonna be here, then listen. Ignoring official statements violates social compliance," said 'Blue-jeans'—whom Jason named because of his dirty, torn jeans.

Mustachio shot a nasty look at Blue-jeans. His ego and suppressed anger took over. "I don't like your tone, Fatso."

"The hell you call me?" Blue-jeans said.

Jason grinned. Blue-jeans was now Fatso.

"He called ya 'Fatso'," said Jason, "Because you're fat."

"You insulted me. That's a social compliance violation too," Fatso raised his arm. "Hey! I need to report something!"

David hissed at him. "Jason! You were supposed to get them to fight, not call the damn cops over!"

Jason's eyes dilated, and he sank further into his Osmium stupor. "Go with it, David. We're stirring a ruckus, remember?"

David groaned.

Sam peered down at them. The isolated argument wasn't providing nearly enough cover for what she was about to do. Sam wobbled, sticking her leg and both arms out for balance. Jason and David needed to pick up the damn pace.

Fatso's loud complaints were creating tension, rising over the silent crowd, who were growing curious about the confrontation. Several compliance drones floated over to investigate, while enforcers tried to push through hundreds of bodies to reach them. Even the priest's speech faltered as he noticed the scene below.

Mustachio spat on the ground. "You started this, pal. I did nothing wrong."

"You violated my riiights!" Fatso whined.

Below, David groaned to stifle a laugh. The drones blared preprogrammed de-escalation statements. Fatso wailed at the nearest approaching compliance enforcers, trying to tattle on Mustachio as if they were both five-year-olds. Jason noticed other people recording the spectacle with their comm units, piping it to extranet social sites.

Jason whispered in Mustachio's ear, with a nasty grin. "Better make sure he doesn't report you. Wouldn't wanna see you on that stage too."

Mustachio looked at Jason with alarm. "What're you trying to pull here, punk?"

Jason sensed the stress in the man beside him like a living thing, a fraction of the collective crowd, like a powder keg. These people had an endless list of worries—the Solar War, the Nanophage, food shortages, even the crumbling infrastructure of the habitat. All it would take was a spark to set off all that pent-up energy into an uncontrolled frenzy.

A pair of latches turned below. Everyone, even the nearby surveillance drones, looked at the sewer grate as it hissed open.

David looked up. "What're y'all looking at?"

"That's vandalism of city property," said Fatso.

"I dropped a credit bill down there. Stuff's expensive, I want it back," David said.

Jason used the distraction to shove Mustachio, whose forehead cracked into Fatso's jaw. No one saw what had caused it as both men tumbled to the ground, but Jason spotted someone else shove another citizen from behind. Then another.

"He attacked me!" wailed Fatso, scrabbling at his assailant, as all hell began to break loose around them.

"About damn time." Sam said, watching a brawl start around Jason and David. The initial fight sparked others, spreading outward as people took their chance to get even with anyone who had wronged them. Sam made some final calculations, took note of Lucia's position, took a breath, and bounced high off the taut bundle of cables. Her blade snapped into her hand, crackling to life as she rocketed toward the stage, raven hair whipping behind her.

Sam rode the closest compliance enforcer into the stage like a surfboard, skidding to a halt among the shocked defendants. She swiped at the man's chest armor with her ignited sword, exploding the plasteel armor. The church goon screamed as it scorched his flesh. Keying her junkyard sword down to a lower power level, Sam sliced through Lucia's restraints, which fell off her wrists in a half-melted heap. The others looked on in total bewilderment.

Shocked, Lucia said, "Sam, what—" before Sam swept up her bag and grabbed Lucia's hand.

"Thought we'd left you, huh?" Sam replied.

Lucia stammered incoherently, shocked. The cabling of Sam's power sword whipped around them as it whirled back into her grip. "Let's go."

Sam bumped into a huge enforcer as she turned around, who grabbed her in a bearhug from behind so tightly that Sam dropped her sparking blade.

"Not so fast, deviant," he growled.

The brawling crowd shoved David and Jason away from the sewer portal. The citizenry's bottled-up energy had found an outlet, erupting more explosively than Jason had dared to hope. Nearly all of the crowd had broken into massive, random violence. Jason used his crackling stun rod to ward off anyone stupid enough to get close. David relied on his gloved fists rather than his pistol, unwilling to use lethal force on civilians.

Mustachio shoved one of the floating drones at Fatso, determined to silence him. Any fear of repercussions for social deviancy violations was out the window. The enforcers struggled to contain the spiraling situation while the priest howled for order above the chaos. A large pack of feral kids dragged a humanoid security automaton to the ground, screeching and kicking it.

"This is the dumbest thing we've ever done," David muttered, shoving a screeching, spitting woman away. "You're good for Osmium, right? No explosion coming?"

Jason let out a high-pitched giggle, which belied his terror. "You're asking me *now*?"

David manhandled Jason toward the sewer hatch as three other brawlers dove past, scratching each other's eyes. "Never mind, just stay close to me. These up-worlders are vicious."

"Can't blame 'em when they're forced to live like this." Jason replied. "Where the heck is Sam?"

The enforcer flexed his thick arms, crushing the life out of Sam with his powered exoskeleton of synth-muscle and flexible armor plating. Her spine popped and crackled. It wouldn't be long before bones started breaking. Sam kicked and thrashed to no avail, unable to summon enough concentration to use her psionic abilities.

"Need assistance with this one!" the man audibly barked through his helmet communicator.

Lucia pounded on the man's armored torso with the melted remains of her cuffs. "Get *off* her!"

Budgie appeared, pecking at the officer's visored face.

The other defendants looked for an exit through the thrashing crowd, but more enforcers clambered onto the stage, approaching Sam and Lucia to answer their comrade's call. As her vision slipped into dark gray tones, Sam heard sirens approaching. They needed to leave, *now*.

Lucia snatched Sam's sword, found the phase-field activator purely by chance, and struck the officer in the knee with the blade's charged edge. The stench of charred flesh and melted plasteel met Sam's nose as the man's grip slackened, and he let out a blood-curdling wail.

Sam's eyes flared pink as her focus returned, head-butting the screaming officer with the back of her skull. A controlled explosion of her Abhamic abilities blasted the enforcer clear of the stage, bowling over a dozen people in the moshing masses below. Budgie squawked indignantly at the surprise.

Sam dropped to one knee, gasping for air. Lucia came down to Sam's eyeline. "Sam...did you just—"

Sam forced air into her lungs. "N-no time, I'll explain later."

Gathering her strength, she got up and bumped right into the social compliance priest, who was apoplectic with rage. He waved his gold-plated datapad, stammering, "How *dare* you interrupt this sacred ceremon—"

Sam's palm came up. The priest hit himself in the face, making his comically tall bishop's hat fall off. He went down with an animalistic screech, blood bursting from his nose. Sam picked up Lucia in a fireman's carry, holding her sparking blade out to ward off enforcers. Lucia yelped, legs flailing.

Sam cast a look at the square's wide entryway. Emergency air vehicles were landing in the street, deploying church reinforcements and regular UEF civil defense troops. Enforcers and humanoid drones clattered up the stone steps brandishing transparent shields, riot guns, and nerve gas, immediately firing into the crowd. People screamed and panicked, breaking away to find cover. Some fled into nearby buildings, breaking doors off their hinges.

"Let's *go!*" Sam said, kicking off with a burst of psychic energy, hurtling above the rioting citizens. Lucia howled, clutching her belongings.

David hit a nearby enforcer with Jason's stun rod, shattering the man's visor. Another officer grabbed David around the neck from behind, making him stun himself. Because the enforcer behind him was insulated, David bore the shock, seizing and shaking.

"*FuuUuuUuuU...*"

Jason snatched the stun rod and tried to strike the enforcer choking his brother, but missed and smacked David instead, who convulsed again, teeth chattering too hard to bite out a rebuke. A drone approached, waving its sparking mechanical riot-control instruments. Jason swung hard and struck its eye, but the drone was electro-shielded, jetting right at him. More officers plowed through the rioting crowd, tackling random citizens.

Sam landed nearby, dropping Lucia into Jason's arms, then whipped her blazing blade in an arc, forcing the church goons back. Budgie swooped down, jabbering angrily.

Sam's eyes flared. The blade changed direction in midair, skewering the drone advancing on Jason and Lucia, but the sword's phase field died suddenly, lodging in its plating.

"Shit, bad battery!" Sam snapped the cable backward, whipping the drone into another. Both of them exploded as their Nanite cores went critical, discharging hard enough to blow multiple people off their feet.

Sam caught her sword and smacked it against her leg. The energy output cranked up to maximum, and Sam whirled it like she was wrangling cattle, forcing the officers back. The brilliant blue phase field left a trail of blue charged particles in its wake. David, having shaken off the worst effects of Jason's stun rod, broke out of the enforcer's chokehold with pure adrenaline, yanking him forward onto the ground, stamping on the man's armored face. "Comply with this!"

"Time to go." Jason said, putting Lucia down and dragging her toward the sewer grate. "Didn't think you'd be seeing us again, huh?"

"Well, I..." Lucia stammered, but Sam bellowed, "No time, get in there!"

David wrenched the unlocked grate open, but a hissing object hit him in the chest. He hurled a gas canister away, choking and wheezing.

Jason saw Mustachio go down nearby. Other rioting up-worlders collapsed as nerve gas or stun rounds took them down. Electrified rubber darts whistled past Jason's face as he snatched Budgie out of the air.

"Stop dillydallying, you two." Sam said, shoving Jason and Lucia into the sewer portal. Lucia fell almost five meters down the ladder before catching herself with a vicious jerk of her shoulder joint. "Ow! What the hell, Sam!"

Her bag splashed down into a puddle, followed by Jason, who landed hard on his side. He looked at Lucia and grimaced, wheezing.

David dumped his bags down the hole and jumped after them, rolling to a stop in the filthy water. He coughed up some gas fumes, but hadn't ingested enough for full paralysis.

Sam cast a look at the Fed enforcers, who advanced behind a tight wall of plasteel shields and dart fire, cutting down the fleeing crowds. Cursing their luck, she dove into the hole, bashing her head on the edge and missing the grate as she tried to pull it shut.

Sam cartwheeled wildly in midair on the way down, landing inches from Jason. She swore in pain, standing and whirling her blade in a tight arc, preparing to release it skyward. Budgie scrabbled away in fright. David staggered to his feet and pulled Lucia and Jason into the darkness as Sam hurled the short sword upward. It speared through the sewer opening, and she yanked it down.

A gauntlet zipped into the opening at the last moment. The unfortunate officer screamed as the metal grate crushed his arm, but he managed to jam the hatch open.

"Shit," Sam said, as the enforcers wrenched the grate back open, staring down at them.

She looked at her comrades, who hadn't even caught their breath. "Run!"

10 — BATTLE OF REFIT ONE

UEF ORBITAL STATION REFIT ONE, COMMAND CENTER — OCT. 31, 2263 — 07:20 HOURS

Zeke was moving so fast that his vision streamlined until all he could see was narrowly focused in front of him—everything else was a blur of noise, fire, and battle. With tight haptic control over his jump-jets, he streaked high into the rafters of *Refit One's* massive Command Center, mentally marking targets and angling his body for a human bombing run.

He spotted Markus and Jenkins amidst dozens of defenders, holding down their triggers to deliver sustained automatic fire as Imperial invaders screamed drug-fueled war cries, galloping through the melted module doors. They advanced behind the protection of a six-meter-tall warbot's overextended deflection shield generators. Twin-linked pairs of Gauss cannons built into the machine's barrel chest tore into the exposed Federation defenders as the massive unit advanced, forcing them down behind cover.

Some of the Imperial legionaries wielded thick slab-shields with slits for ranged weapons, slamming them down into phalanx formations to cover their advance into the huge chamber. Combined with their personal energy shield generators, their battleline was impenetrable from both the front and sides. The defenders couldn't use explosives to break the phalanx, which might compromise the module's atmospheric integrity. Above the deafening exchange of fire, the Imperial battle chant rose, *"Strength within, strength without!"*

A shadow whipped over the pitched engagement, catching Markus' attention.

To Jenkins, hunkering beside him, he said, "Look sharp, Private. You're about to learn why Nightshade Squadron is the best."

Zeke, at home in the air, rocketed down over their heads with his body inverted, blasting away at Imperials who had strayed outside the warbot's shield envelope. His precisely-aimed shots broke their personal shield bubbles at their weakest points, tearing into unprotected areas of their war-suits. Several legionaries raised slab shields to block Zeke's fire, but this allowed the defenders to pound away at corresponding openings in the phalanx formation. Dozens died on both sides amidst the intense exchange of fire below him.

Hundreds of rounds battered the bulkheads and void-glass of the module, missing him by inches as Zeke jetted across the cavernous space, coming around for another strafing run. At least the Empire hadn't resorted to destroying the Command Center completely. That would deprive them of prisoners, not to mention the glory of battle they so desperately craved. He needed to keep them at bay for as long as possible—long enough for Anne to get the hell away from here.

Eighteen meters off the deck, Anne's cybernetic hand and foot magnetized to a metal beam framing the observation window. Explosive rounds drove deep divots and cracks into the thick ceramic. Anne hoped that her shuttle's stealth systems would hold up to the Imperial invasion fleet's combined scanners as it maneuvered into position outside.

With his beak, Lincoln drew a perfect burning circle on the surface, several meters across. His micro-cutting laser pierced the eight-inch quartz like paper. Anne punched the circle hard with her mechanical hand.

Woman and bird were sucked out into space. Anne tucked to avoid being decapitated by the edge, holding her hat as an atmo-containment field deployed across the remaining void-glass.

The hard BANG of decompression caught Zeke's attention, and he spotted his sister and Lincoln tumbling outside into the void. Anne's cybernetics and personal shield allowed for a handful of vacuum-safe minutes, though the void must have been uncomfortable.

With Anne out of the picture, Zeke refocused on the battle and wrangled his malfunctioning jump-jets, corkscrewing above the horde of attackers. As he watched the push and pull of the tight engagement, Zeke acknowledged that winning this battle was impossible, albeit not the aim here. With the eventual goal of being taken prisoner, they needed to put up a good fight before surrendering, so his infiltration plans wouldn't be obvious. Until then, Zeke would try to keep as many of the defenders alive as possible.

He pulled into a rapid dive and snatched a legionnaire up by the armored collar. With his strength-boosting Jetkit exoskeleton, muscles, and Jetkit straining, Zeke fired his jets to spin the thrashing brute, hurtling him into the towering warbot.

The impact broke the man's half-ton bulk against the behemoth's chassis with a *crack* of splitting armor and surgically reinforced bones. The huge robot teetered from the blow, leg pistons firing for stability as it stumbled, crushing more than one trooper advancing below. Jenkins watched from cover as Zeke slid between its legs and kinetic shields with a static crackle, jetting upward to grab the top of its shoulder joint, arresting his momentum.

As the terrifying machine thrashed with bursts of servo-steam, trying to reverse its enormous arms to pulp him, Zeke twisted the release handle on a maintenance panel, ripping it out. The warbot roared through its vocalizer, but he shoved his rifle into the opening and hosed the automaton's innards with automatic fire, bursting its reactor housing.

The robot's glowing purple oculus died as it dropped like a potato sack, crushing several Imperials. Zeke jetted away from retaliatory fire as the module's defenders cheered.

Without the warbot's diffusion shield bubble, the Imperial phalanxes started to disintegrate as Zeke picked off individual warriors, allowing the defenders to target larger gaps. He jetted erratically like Anne had first pioneered, employing randomized thrusts and counterthrusts to throw off machine-assisted aiming.

Zeke skidded to a landing behind Jenkins and Markus to cool his jets, ejecting an ammunition block from his overheating Gauss rifle and pulling another from the open case between them. Explosive shells pummeled their cover—an overturned console. Having given up on reactivating the station's outer defenses, Jenkins was typing on the workstation's keypad, lying on her side with her rifle nearby.

"Nice moves, Commander. You should teach the jet class in basic training," Markus said, predictably understated.

"I'm not retired yet. And that wasn't anything beyond *your* capabilities, Lieutenant," Zeke said, catching his breath. "Enjoying the show, kid?"

"Uhhh...y-yes, sir," said Jenkins, who continued inputting commands into the overturned computer system with frantic breaths.

"Anne got away, I see," said Markus.

"We need to send her intel on our target, so we're going to go visit him."

"We're going to...visit the emperor? Why?" Markus asked, alarmed.

"Like I said, intel," Zeke repeated, taking flight with a *whoosh* of anti-grav force.

Jenkins looked up at Markus in confusion, but he shrugged. "Never known the Commander to not have a plan. I may have reservations about this one, though."

"Maybe this'll help!" Jenkins punched the final key. Across the Command Center, remote autocannons sprang from their ceiling receptacles like oversized groundhogs, targeting the disorganized horde of legionaries on the deck, who were taking cover behind the warbot's fallen bulk.

Jenkins pumped a fist. "Yes! I broke the Admiral's system lockout!"

"I knew we'd chosen you well," Markus replied as they fired bursts of Gauss rounds into the disorganized phalanx, driving them temporarily into retreat.

The battle swung back in the Empire's favor as they melted through the second and third security doors, which boiled away to reveal two more warbots. Reinforcements charged past the huge automatons to re-form their battleline. Smoke charges detonated to mask their advance—but this also gave the defenders a brief reprieve.

Zeke shouted to Markus. "Move our people backward, onto the raised area! Don't let those freaks get into melee range!"

"Yes sir!"

Under the lieutenant's direction, the surviving Federation fighters broke, running in staggered groups to the command platform while others covered them with bursts of gunfire. Blood sprayed as charging legionaries reached those who were too slow to retreat, cleaving limbs from bodies in a frenzy of lightning-fast slaughter.

Markus calmly lifted Jenkins up by the scruff of her singlet.

"Come along now, Private," he said, hauling her up the stairs.

Both warbots fired their fusion cutters in focused beams, eviscerating targets in flashes of cauterized agony. The Imperials were getting tired of the Federation's staunch resistance. Zeke narrowly dodged the white-hot beams as he jetted past the right-side warbot, heading for its maintenance weak-point.

Right as Zeke got his scorched fingers around the quick-release handle, he felt an invisible force pulling him away. An amplified voice boomed through the Command Center ... and his mind, too.

"Cease this madness!"

Zeke's mind went cold—he knew that voice. Every Imperial legionnaire stopped fighting, all at once. The Federation defenders were stunned into submission by the psionic command, which rippled the air, echoing like a distant thunderclap. Even the automated sentry guns went silent, sparking and dying. Zeke crashed to a flopping halt on the ground in front of the second melted door still billowing with battle-smoke. All of his jump jets shorted out, destroyed by pinpoint usage of psychic power.

The chamber had gone icy, chilling the sweat that ran down Zeke's back. It wasn't only the physical world that was affected; a strange pressure forced his resolve down, like his mind was being squeezed by a vice-grip. Through the clearing battle smoke, Zeke heard polished dress boots clicking on hard deck plating, growing louder until it overtook all other background noise.

Then the laughter started—light, musical, and familiar, sickening Zeke to his core. Through watering eyes, he spotted three people through the choking haze.

Two female warriors flanked a tall willowy man, dressed in flamboyant business purples and gold-trimmed blacks, with flowing hair, a regal cane, and shiny black boots. He walked with a limp, which somehow didn't detract from his flowing confidence.

"What a sight," Emperor Mariko said. "Good morning, all of you. Especially to you ... Commander Zeke Oakfield."

Zeke stared at Mariko, saying nothing.

"It's the emperor," Jenkins hissed to Markus behind one of the situation tables, terrified.

"Sure is," Markus said, struggling to keep his voice steady.

"But who are they?" Jenkins whispered, staring at the two accompanying women, who wore black armor with gold trim, all curved angles with a shiny finish, quite unlike the bulky monstrous warsuits of the legionaries. A regal purple half-cloak was draped over one shoulder, and their faces were hidden by a full helmet and crest holder, with a narrow slit for camera lenses.

"Personal bodyguards of the emperor," the Lieutenant explained with a tight jaw. "Some of the few individuals who have given Nightshade real trouble—the Praetorian Sisterhood. They are a very recent deployment beyond Colossus Station."

"Oh my god." Jenkins hid her face behind the thick table. "Oh my *god* ..."

Zeke was convinced the chamber had grown darker, maybe a trick of the light, or an Imperial cruiser outside had blocked the sunlight ... or it was a hallucination brought on by Hadrian Mariko's mental influence. His mind was so powerful that it passively warped reality around him, causing the air to flicker and shift. The Sister Praetorians were psychically gifted too, but had nothing on their master. Mariko's paradoxical presence shifted between his real seven-foot height and a much grander aura, leering down at the defeated Federation troopers like a giant from the old stories.

Every Imperial soldier, including the automatons, eerily knelt in unison. Even the two Praetorians bowed, lowering their heads in reverence.

"Prostrate yourselves before your lord, mortals! Kneel!" one of the Praetorians commanded through blaring helmet speakers.

The Federation survivors exchanged glances. Some dropped to their knees, others didn't.

Mariko's eyes flashed pink. He didn't physically *do* anything, but the coldness grew deeper, crushing Zeke's will to resist. The commander of Nightshade Squadron knelt like a titan's hand had crushed him to the deck, along with everyone else still standing.

"That's better," the emperor said. He ran a hand through Zeke's tangled hair and red bandana as he stopped beside him. "You'll give us invaluable leverage, now that I've found you."

Zeke said nothing, narrowing his eyes. *Leverage?* What did that mean?

The other Praetorian spoke. "The Outlaw of Colossus was reported aboard *Refit One*, though she escaped. We have assets tracking her down, my emperor."

"Perhaps the brother might lead us to the sister," boomed the emperor, glancing at Zeke.

"Perhaps," the Praetorian Sister agreed.

The psychic pressure relaxed, allowing Zeke to get up, shaking off the effects. Markus, Jenkins, and the other Federation survivors did likewise—those without grievous wounds, anyway.

The emperor came close, letting his finger wander down the side of Zeke's bruised jaw, examining the injury. "It's simply common courtesy to show respect for one's betters, Commander. It's about time that the Federation is finally taught the lesson of respect."

Zeke stood ramrod straight, eyes locked ahead. He wanted to give Mariko a piece of his mind, but not at the expense of the people around him. They needed to be protected, even now.

Two Imperial automatons came forward to slap a pair of restraints onto his wrists. More gunshots rang out as Phage sufferers were identified with bio-scanners and eliminated. Jenkins flinched at every shot—quite unlike how she reacted under fire. Zeke winked at the girl to reassure her, but Jenkins was staring at the emperor, mortified at how he'd controlled her body and everyone else's at the same time. Zeke could empathize, but he couldn't let himself succumb to terror.

"Congratulations, Praetorian Sister N9. An early win on our day of ultimate victory," the emperor said to the armored female on his left, who bowed. "Your siblings are still working on the other orbital platforms, facilitating the handover of all remaining UEF spaceborne assets. Once that's accomplished, we will launch our surface landings."

"Thank you, your excellency." N9 said. Through the helmet, Zeke heard her voice quavering with joy, which he found pathetic.

"As for you," Mariko stared up at the command dais, where Powell had been hiding for the entire battle, watching the newcomers with trepidation. The admiral did not move, still handcuffed with the rest of his cronies.

"Yes, Admiral. I see you up there." the emperor confirmed. "We do not reward failure in our Hierarchy. We lost too many good people taking this station. This was supposed to be combat-free."

"But...b-but sir, we didn't have enough t-time—" Powell stammered. The emperor waved a hand, stealing the air from Powell's lungs and rocketing him bodily off the platform to hover down in front of him.

"No, please, wait—" Powell wheezed.

Without appearing to move, Mariko cut the admiral's head from his shoulders. Zeke only caught the emperor returning his phase sword to its cane sheath, almost too fast to be visible. The emperor's physical infirmity was nothing when he was empowered by his psychic might. Powell's death barely registered with the UEF survivors. Sister N9 watched the fat man's body slump to the deck, one hand on her phase sword.

Powell's head rolled down to a stop near Zeke's feet, who stared with disgust into the admiral's lifeless eyes. Noticing this, Mariko said, "Oh, Commander, if you think this cretin is exemplary of Federation Command's corruption ... you haven't seen anything yet. We'll talk on the *Eagle of the Ninth*. We have much to discuss, you and I."

"Looking forward to it," Zeke bit out through clenched teeth.

But on the inside, he was jumping for joy. Mariko was playing right into his hands ... and Anne's too. As long as the bastard couldn't read minds—Zeke had never quite been able to figure that one out. Hopefully not.

N9 turned to her master. "What are your orders for the rest, sire?"

The emperor gestured to the Federation survivors, lingering on Zeke. "We will process them on the flagship. Keep them all alive and fit. They will make a good *example* when the time comes."

The two Imperial robots shoved Zeke closer to Markus as the survivors were herded toward the melted doors.

"Is this still part of your plan, sir? What is going on here?" Markus murmured, once they were out of earshot of the emperor and his Praetorians.

"I'll say one thing about these shit-heads. They're predictable," Zeke said, cryptically.

"It sounded like he wanted to talk more with you, Zeke," Markus said.

"Which is perfect. Now shhhh."

"Sir?" Jenkins piped up.

An automaton approached, jabbing a metal hand between her shoulders. "Silence, mortal. Move out."

"We'll be fine, kid," Zeke said with unwavering confidence. They were going where Nightshade did its best work—hell itself.

Deliverance drifted away from *Refit One* using its dead momentum, but there was no indication that it'd been detected yet.

Anne Oakfield cycled the airlock and stumbled inside the main hold. Her exposed skin burned, receiving only minimal protection from the freezing vacuum and solar radiation by her energy shield. Parts of her greatcoat's flexible armor lining were damaged, shot through and burned in many places. Her body plating wasn't looking much better, pockmarked and leaking coolant from her synthetic internals. Anne's miniature reactor was malfunctioning, but it was nothing that couldn't be rectified. Lincoln settled himself on the command console.

Anne fell into the pilot's seat, triggering the vessel's repair systems. She didn't want to admit it, but the recent battles and void exposure had pushed her aging systems hard. While the repair mechadendrites deployed to deal with Anne's injuries and Phage growths within her synthetic components, she handed Zeke's identification tags to Lincoln, who prepared an encrypted broadcast using a frequency pre-loaded onto the tags. Making a transmission while surrounded by enemy craft was risky—even an encoded message at low power—but she had no choice. Zeke was counting on her, as she was counting on him.

Anne looked back at *Refit One* as the mechanical arms removed her hat and injected stimulant chemicals into her biological tissues to promote recovery. Her dull, weak psychic senses picked up something new aboard the orbital, something that hadn't been there minutes ago.

It was him. Emperor Hadrian Mariko himself had come aboard *Refit One*.

Anne's cyber-hand twitched toward the controls. *Deliverance's* weapon systems could easily obliterate the Command Center module, especially since her instrumentation confirmed that the station's outer shields were down. Anne could end her former partner right now.

But her brother, his Lieutenant, the girl, and too many others would die in the slaughter. Victory wasn't worth murdering so many, even if it would save billions. She couldn't bring herself to make that choice. Desperation flooded Anne, and the Phage flared, triggering her cyber-narcolepsy.

Anne sighed, pushing her command seat away from the control board. She couldn't endanger her family for something as vile as revenge—even if Zeke himself told her to take the shot. There *had* to be another way.

"Lincoln...lock the shuttle's weapons," Anne murmured. The bird cocked his head, but complied.

Anne tilted her head against the worn leather headrest to ride out a wave of nausea, waiting for the repair systems to finish up. Lincoln hopped onto the armrest and lowered his metal head, which Anne stroked with a trembling biological hand. Her hammering heart slowed as her body reconfigured blood-flow and artificial fluid channels.

The fear of missing her chance passed. Anne needed to watch the life leave Hadrian's eyes, up close and personal, with Nightshade's support. A few more hours weren't much compared to fourteen years of waiting.

A comms receipt notification appeared on the console, breaking Anne's focus. Zeke's people had responded to Lincoln's encrypted hail. Anne felt her strength returning. The diagnostics confirmed that her reactor and batteries were returning to full capacity. Lincoln squawked some binary. A moment later, *Deliverance* shuddered as a powerful presence infiltrated its systems.

Lincoln nearly retaliated, but Anne interrupted. "Wait. We don't want to give our new allies the wrong impression. Let them verify us."

The forward cameras revealed a dark section of space, devoid of stars. A larger craft blotted everything out, emitting no heat, light, gases, or frequencies of any kind. Only a precisely targeted scan pulse could detect that ship—impossible unless the scanner knew where to target.

As Anne's mechadendrites finished recharging the reactor in her guts, a pair of doors opened in the ship's belly, revealing a dark, unlit hangar above. Low-power anti-grav manipulators drew *Deliverance* upward as Solar Empire capital ships slid around them like silent ocean beasts. The *Solanum's* artificial gravity system gained influence over Anne's shuttle. Moments later, *Deliverance's* landing gear touched down as the outer bay doors closed. Lights snapped on outside.

With a hand on her mechanical friend's head, Anne said, "No turning back now, Lincoln."

He burbled, ruffling his metal feathers.

"Attention, shuttlecraft occupant. This is Lieutenant Luther of Night-shade Squadron," a voice spoke through the shuttle's speakers. "Am I addressing Anne Oakfield, sister of our Commander?"

"You are," Anne replied.

"Kindly lower your ramp and exit the craft. We have things to discuss."

Anne allowed a smile to cross her lips. Her brother's message had worked. "Acknowledged."

Lincoln triggered the ship's ramp controls.

"Let's meet our fellow kingslayers, shall we?" Anne said.

Lincoln hopped aboard her shoulder, and Anne strode out into the bright lights of *Solanum's* embarkation hangar. A large group of operators in advanced experimental battle-suits waited for her. Even the lower-ranked personnel appeared to be hardened warfighters. Jetkits were strapped across their bodies, similar to Anne's own. More personnel watched in small crowds on the deck or from the catwalks above. A dark-skinned woman stepped forward.

"Welcome to the *Solanum*, home base of Nightshade Squadron," she said. "I'm Lieutenant Janelle Luther. We were a hair's breadth from launching a rescue operation to retrieve our Commander. But he's sent you instead. You're going to have to explain that one."

"Good morning, Lieutenant. I understand your confusion, but I'll explain everything."

"I see. Come with us."

Anne felt both her hearts leap—cybernetic and biological. She had her army.

11 — FUGITIVES

Jason, David, Sam, and Lucia dashed down the storm drainpipe, splashing through a shallow stream of polluted rainwater. Budgie tried to flap out ahead in a complete panic, but David grabbed him to prevent any of their pursuers from shooting the frantic cockatoo. Jason glanced into every crevice, at every shadow. Thankfully, they remained still. Abaddon was content to let the corporeal forces of the universe torment him, for now.

A group of armored church goons were in hot pursuit, helmet radios echoing in the tiny space. The storm drain reeked of stagnant water and chemicals, mixing with the tang of weapons fire as the lead enforcers fired lethal Gauss pistols at the riot escapees.

"Those aren't stun rounds anymore!" Jason cried as a supersonic slug cracked past his face, blowing a divot into the ceramic tunnel's side. They had no plan, no direction. Getting to the Recyck yard for those Science Institute access codes was totally off the table with these goons on their tail, let alone finding the Abaddon Beacon. Jason hoped they didn't come across anything infected with the Phage in this maze of tunnels.

"Shields up!" Sam exclaimed, slapping a hexagonal device on her belt.

"Should've done this earlier," David commented.

"I didn't hear you making that suggestion. And these only work for live, hypersonic projectiles. Stun darts move too slowly, you know that," Sam retorted, whirling her sword to block some of their shots.

A faint shimmering haze popped into existence around Sam, David, and Jason as each slapped the activation button on their belt-mounted shield units.

David shoved Lucia ahead, covering her with his shield. Sam hadn't built an extra for her, as turning Lucia into a fugitive had *not* been their plan this morning. Jason made an abrupt left turn, hoping in vain to throw their pursuers off.

"We really got ourselves into it this time," David said, checking his junk pistol's power cell, which read close to full.

Sam dropped a smoking battery from the cable apparatus on her hip and slapped in a new one, flaring her blade back to life.

"Don't say it," she remarked.

"I'm saying it. I told you so!" David yelled as he fired through Sam's spinning blade like a machine gun chuntering through the propeller of a biplane.

The enforcers skidded in the muck and took cover in the slim spaces between pipe sections. By chance, David landed a couple of direct hits, but his incendiary rounds flared across their shield bubbles.

Jason received a glancing hit and nearly stumbled over his own feet. His diffusion shield's power dropped by a quarter. The shockwave was painful, but Jason preferred that over a hole in his torso.

At every junction, another group of enforcers and drones appeared, forcing continuous changes of direction. Lucia slipped and fell, but Jason managed to haul her up. The girl was in surprisingly decent shape for someone who'd worked a desk job, but her look of panic told Jason that she hadn't messed up like this before.

After another random turn, Jason saw that the way ahead was lit by sunlight. With no one visible to cut them off, he pulled Lucia after him in desperation. Sam and David followed.

"I hope you know where you're going!" David bellowed.

"I don't!"

Jason felt mist on his face. Then he heard a faint roaring sound. Why had the enforcers left this particular tunnel open? As more cops clattered around the corner behind them, Jason gasped.

"Uh-oh ..."

The storm-drain opened into a massive, circular cistern. As Jason skidded to a halt, he saw hundreds of other tunnels across the shaft emptying their contents into a deep pool far below. The partially filled chamber was only a fraction of the city's dizzying total depth, one of many water-reclamation vats. The cyclopean cylinder opened to the sky, with a containment field projected across the top to keep out contaminants—a miniaturized version of the dome protecting the arcology from the elements. Aircars with blaring sirens approached the reservoir, passing through the humming shield.

"Shit," said Jason. Everyone else delivered their own invectives.

David leveled his pistol at the enforcers approaching in a tight group behind them, allowing their shields to overlap with sharp *pops*. Sam whipped her sword in a circle, forming a protective barrier that sparked the walls of the tunnel. Jason and Lucia crouched low behind them. He thought that Sam was going to try and cut through the tunnel at their feet to give them another exit, but who knew where they'd end up if she did that—it would take too much time, anyway.

Jason's heart thundered as his inhibitor tried to calm him down. Here he was again, trying not to slip off another precipice, with his friends' lives on the line. *Please don't explode, please don't explode.*

The compliance enforcers slid to their knees, aiming their weapons. The second rank remained standing, forming an impenetrable wall of bodies.

"In the name of the Church of Social Compliance, you will surrender!" shouted their leader, wearing a bone-white helmet.

"Fat chance of that, pal," retorted David. Blue light from Sam's blade danced across his face as well as every other surface.

Jason elbowed his brother. "Don't antagonize them."

"Does it matter?"

The enforcer pointed at Lucia. "You, citizen 056781-A2."

Lucia glared at him. "What do you want?"

The cop removed his helmet, revealing a boyish face and sweaty black hair. Jason guessed that he'd been the one to drag Lucia out of Fran's bar, given his tone.

"I don't know who called that tip on you, but you've gotten mixed up with—" the enforcer looked with disgust at Jason, Sam, and David, "—some seriously bad types. We can help you, Lucia."

"How?" asked Lucia.

Sam shot her with an alarmed look, but the enforcer continued. "Please, Lucia, testify against these Undocumented vermin. Tell us who they are, where they're based, and you'll receive amnesty. I promise."

He held out his hand. The others lowered their weapons, but remained in position. Jason's heart raced so hard that he thought it might explode. His knees shook. The roar of waterfalls misted the back of his head. Jason heard the buzz of aircar anti-grav drives drawing nearer. Water boiled around his ankles.

As Sam was opening her mouth to interject, Lucia looked the officer right in the eye.

"I won't do it."

Jason could only describe the expression on Sam's face as total joy. Even David gave a tiny, approving nod.

"That's a mistake, Lucia. I'll get your charges dropped. But these Undocs, off-grid Under-city rats ..." the enforcer spat, pointing at Jason, David, and Sam, "... you can't ever trust them."

David's hackles rose. Sam showed her teeth, spinning her sword faster. Jason felt sick to his stomach.

Lucia straightened. "Living in this city has shown me the reality of the Church and the Federation. All you do is divide people. Our people need unity, not this circus you're running."

Another micro-dose of Osmium helped Jason focus. He caught Sam's eye and jerked his head toward the waterfalls outside. She nodded.

David's eyes widened. "Don't you dare—"

"Screw it," Sam said, catching her sword. Her eyes flared pink, reflecting off the cops' visors as she roared in defiance and brought her arms together, generating a psionic pressure surge. It bowled the officers over like dominoes as Jason, David, Sam, and Lucia were blasted backward out of the tunnel.

Everything passed in flashes. David's arms closed around Jason's chest. He glimpsed Sam grabbing Lucia as momentum carried them apart. Jason could only grit his teeth and shut his eyes while David howled in his ear, rocketing past blaring security aircar sirens and down the deep shaft.

The water's surface was churned up enough so that the brothers survived the impact—barely. Jason lost most of his air upon plunging feet-first into the frigid pool. The roiling, bubbly blackness sucked Jason and David toward a tertiary shaft at the bottom of the main reservoir, crushing the remaining oxygen out of them.

After an eternity of zooming down an endless series of lightless shafts, Jason was suddenly airborne again.

With limbs flailing, he fell fifteen meters and plunged into the disorienting darkness again. His body hurt all over, but the lack of air was far worse. Jason didn't have the faintest idea how to swim, but he clawed at the water anyway, aiming for what he hoped was 'up'. His salvage bag was still attached to him, weighing him down. But something shoved him upward.

David forced Jason through the water's surface in a spluttering tangle of arms and drenched clothes. Jason regurgitated polluted rainwater, unable to catch his breath. David dragged him over to a grated walkway, which was keyed into the curved wall-lift to move with the water level. Using powerful upper body strength, David shoved Jason onto the partially submerged catwalk, who rolled over and heaved up another liter of water. Jason wondered how his brother had learned how to swim.

"God, that ... sucked," David groaned, once he'd clambered up and finished retching.

"No kidding," Jason retorted, shivering and trying to breathe more deeply again.

"That lunatic girl almost killed us. She made us do a high dive off that freakin' waterfall," David said, pulling Budgie's wet, feathery mass from his jacket.

"Sam saved us, David," Jason pointed out. "It was the only choice. And we lived, right?"

"I guess it was your idea, right?" David flicked his brother on the forehead. "Keep up those bad ideas, and we're gonna end up as fish food."

He pressed on Budgie's chest, unsure how to revive the bird. "We could've died on impact; we could have drowned ..." David trailed off.

"You need to roll with it, brother," said Jason.

David grumbled. Budgie croaked, coughing some little bird coughs.

"At least you're fine," David said to the cockatoo.

Budgie stood and wandered away indignantly, ruffling his wet wings.

"Any idea where we are?" Jason asked. The inhibitor beeped softly, indicating that his mental state was returning to normal.

"Nope," said David. Reflections rippled on the walls of the deep pool chamber. The control pad on the wall was the only light source nearby. David slapped the controls, and the walkway rattled upward, stopping at a watertight door a few meters up. The exit door slowly rumbled open without trouble, as no up-worlders or civilians were ever expected to find their way down here.

Jason leaned his head against the uncomfortable grating, wishing his body would recover faster. His skull throbbed.

David rummaged in his bag, checking for missing items. "We should get moving."

"Where, though?" Jason replied. He dragged himself up using the railing, shaking out his sopping hair. Sam's active signal had dropped off his communicator's short list of contacts. Not good, but not surprising since they were back underground.

"Lucia still has the location data for that bot," said Jason. "We need to find them."

"That's if they survived the whirlpool of death back there. But I remember the designation of the Recyck yard Lucia mentioned, number 78-10D," replied David, calling up a city database map on his comm unit. "We've never been there before, but I've had it marked for exploration for a while. Maybe the girls will beat us there, if they're not waterlogged corpses by now."

"Think happy thoughts, David," Jason said.

"That's unbearably difficult for me," David remarked and coughed hoarsely from the residual effects of the gas grenade he'd inhaled. He checked Jason's inhibitor, tapping the vial. "There's no point in stopping now. Maybe today *is* the day that we find that stupid Beacon and fix you, brother. Seemed impossible back there, but maybe ... maybe this'll be worth it."

Jason nodded, starting down the watertight passage. "Let's go find that robot. Once we do, getting into the Science Institute will be a piece of cake."

"Don't get cocky, little brother."

Sam strained as she pulled Lucia up onto the catwalk to safety. Her blade was embedded in the wall a few meters above, de-powered from its recent soaking. A torrent of water hammered the bottom of the tank below, bursting from the tunnel they'd emerged from. The city's automated systems must have only recently opened this reserve tank, because it was still almost empty.

Lucia rolled over on the metal grating, spitting up water. Sam tried not to think about how much toxic runoff they'd ingested. Even Phage-causing Nanites could survive in fluids for short periods before disintegrating.

Sam looked down at her shield unit, which was also dead because of its moisture failsafe, though it would reset eventually.

Her mind whirled through doomsday possibilities. What if Jason and David had landed in an empty tank like this one? They had no way to break their fall, not even if they discharged all their shield energy downward right before impact—because of her damn fail-safes.

Sam employed a breathing cycle that she'd been taught long ago, calming herself. There was nothing she could do for Jason right now. Hoisting herself up, Sam checked Lucia over. No major injuries, just small cuts and contusions from her mistreatment and the subsequent escape.

"It's been a looong time since I've gone through something like that," Lucia said, sitting up.

"You make adventuring like this a habit?" asked Sam.

"I wouldn't call this 'adventuring'," replied Lucia.

"I see," Sam yanked her blade out of the wall, reeling its cable in like a tape measure and examined the exit bulkhead.

"Hopefully we won't have to cut through that door," she added, but Abhamic fatigue hit her, and she sank into a squat.

Only for a moment, Sam told herself, hoping she wouldn't need a hit of Osmium to reduce her growing headache. Doing that would dampen her control over her psionic abilities, which she couldn't afford right now in the Under-city, where danger lurked around every corner.

"So, do you guys do this sort of thing often, or just for me?" asked Lucia playfully.

Sam smiled through her brain-fog. "I'd be lying if I said we don't. The underground is extremely dangerous, but we've explored a lot of it. Getting tangled up with the church is a new one for us, though."

Lucia leaned against the railing for support, squeegeeing her long, dark hair. "Well, I appreciate the save."

Sam shrugged. "We owe you for locating that bot and everything else you've done for us."

"No problem. You've paid me for every salvage lead I gave you, so you don't owe me anything. The relationship benefitted us both."

"You know what I mean. You didn't have to do business with us dirty 'Undocumented'."

Lucia shrugged. "That's Fed propaganda. You're normal people, like everyone else. Merit and strength of character are all that matters."

"I see," Sam said again, narrowing her eyes. "Wait a sec. At Fran's, those enforcers knew exactly where you were. What did they want with you?"

"Beats me. My comm device was active, so it wasn't hard for them to track me down. As for why ... who the hell knows," said Lucia. "I'm shocked that you were able to follow us through the city when they had me in cuffs."

"We have our ways," Sam said, winking. "That was some rough treatment they gave you, though."

"That's how it is in the Upper-city, Sam," Lucia said. "Maybe they picked me at random. Rumor is, sometimes they use a lottery system to find enough 'defendants' for those tribunal clown shows. Anything to keep themselves in power while the war gets worse and to keep people scared. Pretty soon, there won't be anyone left who isn't guilty of something."

Sam gave her a sympathetic look, flexing her legs as she stood up, dripping from head to toe.

"I'm sorry, Lucia. We're disconnected from all that stuff underground, so we don't have a great picture of how bad things are getting upstairs."

Lucia opened the watertight door, which was fortunately unlocked, revealing a dark passage full of maintenance equipment. Water had leaked through the bulkheads over the years and damaged the accessway; an isolated example of the disintegrating state the city was in.

Lucia peered into the blackness ahead. "Yikes. That doesn't look inviting."

"You're gonna have a hard time surviving alone down here in the Under-city," Sam said. "If you want, you can come to the Recyck yard with me. Or you can give me the target's coordinates. Your choice."

Lucia pulled the locator device out of her waterlogged bag. It was still functional, displaying the location of their target in relation to where they were, likely taking advantage of scattered Recyck relay beacons throughout the underground to bounce the signal and improve reception.

"So, I'm finally gonna see what happens after I tell you where the good loot is?"

"Yep," Sam said.

Lucia hesitated, then asked, "And ... about what you did in the storm drain, with that big blast of air ... what was that all about?"

Sam froze. It wasn't an easy question to answer, especially to someone who was still an outsider in their little group.

"Right now, we don't have time to get into that, and frankly, there's some things about myself that I don't make a habit of discussing."

Lucia's lips formed a thin line. "Sorry, didn't mean to pry."

Sam pointed ahead. "I might tell you what's going on with me later, maybe. Let's get to the Recyck yard, it's far deeper underground. After that, we'll figure out where it's safe for you to go after we're done there, because you sure as hell can't go back to the surface right now."

Lucia nodded. "Sure. What a day."

Sam cracked a smile. "Aren't you glad you got involved with us crazy Undocs?"

Lucia snorted. "It's fine. You three are way more interesting than most Upper-city folks I've met. Everyone has to walk on eggshells, and any friends you make might disappear at any moment. The Nanophage makes things ten times worse. You never know who they'll take into quarantine next."

"Sounds wonderful," Sam responded, oozing sarcasm. "Now, enough stalling, let's go find the boys and that stupid-ass robot."

12 — JAILBREAK

"Move!" the Solar Empire combat automaton ordered, prodding Zeke off the cramped transfer shuttle. It had been doing this since he and his allies had been removed from *Refit One*, running its simplistic programming on repeat. Zeke decided that he'd shove the bastard's positronic brain up its shiny metal ass as soon as he got the chance.

Jenkins trudged ahead of Zeke, and Markus was behind him in a line of handcuffed prisoners being frog-marched by legionnaires through the Imperial flagship's cavernous launch bay.

Around him, thousands of menials were preparing landers, dropships, and escort fighters for the Earth invasion. Whole battalions of un-augmented Imperial human troopers and combat automatons boarded mass haulers, while cyber-augmented legionaries stood before their landing craft, twitching in the early throes of psycho-stimulant drugs as they chanted pre-battle rituals. Most of the emperor's frontline legions were represented, including the Dominus, Imperious, Megamech, and Colossi legions. The Empire's mortal human auxiliaries vastly outnumbered the Nanite-augmented super-warriors, but the legionnaires were the real stars of the emperor's horror show. Zeke had to admit that their global-scaled invasion was an impressive undertaking—especially at this later stage of the Solar War, after years of losses.

Ahead, Emperor Hadrian Mariko spoke to Sister Praetorian N9. "Find our guests comfortable accommodations, my dear. After meeting with our senior leaders in the Sanctum, I will host Commander Oakfield for a little catch-up."

"At once, my lord," N9 said, waving to the automatons who marched the prisoners onward. "Take them to the brig."

She glanced at Zeke before sweeping after the emperor as he approached an access elevator. The psychic pressure from Mariko's presence steadily abated.

"Shit," Zeke said, slowing his pace. His hesitation earned another painful jab from his chaperone.

This wasn't good. Was Mariko intentionally delaying their meeting? But how could the emperor possibly know what Zeke and Anne were planning?

He hoped that the emperor's powers didn't allow him to read the thoughts or emotions of others. This entire venture hinged on that *not* being the case. The Imperial strategy meeting might take hours, and his people onboard the *Solanum* needed as much lead time as possible to put their assassination operation together. Zeke would need to trigger his backup plan.

"Eyes forward, mortal!" the robot blared.

"Why the hell do you call us mortals? You're not even alive," Zeke muttered under his breath. This query was outside the robot's selection of limited responses, so it remained silent. That confirmed Zeke's suspicions: he could talk without being interrupted. Good. His plan might actually work.

Jenkins was rigid with fear. Everyone knew the rumors about what the Imperials did to prisoners of war. Zeke couldn't put a comforting hand on the girl's shoulder, so instead he said, "Cheer up, kid. We still have a job to do."

Jenkins straightened. "Sir?"

"You heard me," Zeke whispered out of the corner of his mouth. "Still got that device I gave ya?"

Jenkins nodded. In her hands was a tiny, bloody capsule that Zeke had surreptitiously detached from the roof of his mouth earlier. All Nightshade operatives carried these 'dumb' implants, which functioned as rescue beacons, remote hacking devices, or suicide pills—undetectable until use.

"Remember what I told you on the way over here. I'll give you some audio cover. Ditch our cuffs right before the end, please," Zeke murmured.

"Commander, what do you—"

"Wait for the damn song, kid. I'm counting on that big brain of yours. You've got this."

"Uhhhh ... okay," Jenkins didn't look thrilled, but Zeke sensed that she understood.

"Into the mouth of madness we go," he muttered as they were herded from the hangar into a wide passageway with low ceilings. Zeke worked his injured jaw, still throbbing after his fight with the Imperial captain on *Refit One*. Everyone was injured in some way, major or minor.

Silent automatons stood at regular intervals, waving bio-scanners. They removed several captives from the line. Zeke's anger grew—but he couldn't do anything for them ... yet.

Loud bootfalls and hissing pistons of armor suits revealed squads of hulking Imperial legionaries, who stopped on their way to the hangar to jeer at the prisoners, waving huge weapons and beating their chests. They struck people at random, but the automatons intervened, following their limited programming to the letter. Markus grunted in annoyance, and many of the captives looked similarly enraged by their mistreatment.

"Commander," he rumbled.

"Yeah?"

"Are you sure this will work, sir?"

Markus had been fitted with two sets of cuffs to account for his massive artificial arm.

"Of course, Lieutenant," said Zeke. "We escaped their prison on Jupiter Six, didn't we?"

"That was very different, sir."

"We'll be fine."

The robotic chaperone ribbed Zeke again. When he was free, this gosh-darned robot was gonna wish it had never been built.

They rounded a corner. From Zeke's previous piracy and sabotage operations on similar Imperial vessels, he estimated that they'd arrive at the dorsal brig complex in just over four minutes, which happened to be the runtime of his favorite song.

Their situation was already pants-shittingly terrifying, but Zeke was experiencing something else entirely—performance anxiety. He prayed that Jenkins was ready for the challenge, and started the song that would free them.

He was just a new trainee and man; he surely shook with fright.

The sergeant checked his Jetkit and made sure his rig was tight;
He had to brace and listen to those awful engines roar.
You ain't gonna fly no more.

Murmurs spread through the UEF personnel. Military and civilian prisoners alike recognized this song, a modified tune from an ancient conflict, far older than the Great War. It was Nightshade Squadron's anthem, a dark joke about their early days of jump-kit testing. UEF Command had prohibited the song, but Federation personnel sang it in private to honor Nightshade Squadron's daring successes, which were legendary throughout the fleet's lower ranks. Zeke's chaperone didn't react—as he'd suspected. As long as they refrained from speaking to each other, the robots didn't care what the prisoners *sang*.

Jenkins started working with Zeke's tiny capsule implant. The commander's obnoxious, out-of-tune lyrics drowned out the device's soft noises. Markus sang along in his deep baritone.

Gory, gory, what a hell of a way to die.
Gory, gory, what a hell of a way to die.
Gory, gory, what a hell of a way to die.
And he ain't gonna fly no more.

Passing Imperials tried to silence the growing chorus with raised fists and barks of outrage, but their mechanicals forbade anyone from touching the captives. Zeke continued singing.

'Is everybody ready?' cried the sergeant, looking up.
Our hero stoically answered, 'yes,' and then they stood him up.
He jumped into the vacuum, and his safety rig unhooked,
and he ain't gonna fly no more.

More Federation prisoners picked up the chorus. Jenkins tapped the tiny implant's buttons, squinting at its miniscule holo-screen, struggling with the remote security decryption.

Gory, gory, what a hell of a way to die.
Gory, gory, what a hell of a way to die.
Gory, gory, what a hell of a way to die.
And he ain't gonna fly no more.

One of the hulking legionaries threatened to gun down the robots, but a higher-ranking baseline human officer stopped him. They couldn't override the Sister Praetorian's earlier commands for the automatons, as no one outranked her. The Empire's Hierarchy was working against them. Another human trooper tapped a datapad to run a remote shock through the prisoners' restraints—but Jenkins had broken their firewalls and disabled that function, causing even more confusion among their captors. Zeke forced himself to sing without rushing.

He counted long; he counted loud; he waited for the shock.
He saw the stars; he saw the ship; he felt the G's tick up.
His jets, they failed to fire and then one of them burned out,
and he ain't gonna fly no more.
Gory, gory, what a hell of a way to die.
Gory, gory, what a hell of a way to die.
Gory, gory, what a hell of a way to die
and he ain't gonna fly no more.

Morale was rising. Zeke sang so hard his voice cracked.

The safety rig flew off his chest, his jets swung to and fro.
They fired out of sequence, and they burned him to the bone.
His war-suit caught afire, and he hurtled to the deck,
and he ain't gonna fly no more.
Gory, gory, what a hell of a way to die.
Gory, gory, what a hell of a way to die.
Gory, gory, what a hell of a way to die.
And he ain't gonna fly no more.

The brig was in sight: a terrifying place where prisoners hung from the ceiling on chained hooks, sadistically tortured to death for scientific study, weapons testing, and sadistic entertainment. It reeked of blood and antiseptic, even from this distance. Zeke and Markus bellowed at the top of their lungs, protected by the automatons as human troopers and legionaries struggled to lay hands on them amidst the growing chaos. Jenkins continued her field hack.

The days he'd lived and loved and laughed were swirling through his mind.
He thought about the girl back home, the one he'd left behind.
He thought about the medic men and wondered what they'd find.
And he ain't gonna fly no more.
Gory, gory, what a hell of a way to die.
Gory, gory, what a hell of a way to die.
Gory, gory, what a hell of a way to die.
And he ain't gonna fly no more.

One of the super-human monsters muscled through the robots and clasped an armored gauntlet around Zeke's throat. His fingers were like adamantium, strong enough to bend steel. Automatons were on them in seconds, forcing the struggling legionnaire back, whose armor servos and gears growled in protest. Zeke stumbled to his feet and wheezed hoarsely through his abused windpipe, but the prisoners carried the song on their own now.

The rescue ship was coming now; its ramp was open wide.
The medics watched with horror as he fell to his demise.
For it had been a week or more since last a rig had failed.
And he ain't gonna fly no more.

The first prisoners were marched inside the brig. Baseline human guards swung sparking batons to stop them from singing, but the automatons continued to protect their charges with single-minded robotic strength, preventing anyone from touching them. But Zeke knew that nothing could stop his plan now, as long as Jenkins delivered on her end.

Gory, gory, what a hell of a way to die.
Gory, gory, what a hell of a way to die.
Gory, gory, what a hell of a way to die.
He ain't gonna fly no more.

Zeke and Markus reached the door. Coinciding with this, Jenkins completed her decryption of the flagship's security systems. The hacker girl pressed a final button, and Zeke's implant emitted an ear-splitting static burst. Every pair of cuffs fell from their wrists.

He grabbed a guardsman on the inside of the doors. The man's gauntleted hand tightened on his weapon as Zeke crushed his throat, peppering nearby automatons with Gauss fire.

Markus and Zeke bellowed together, "Forward! Get in there! *Take the brig*!"

With their mission objective clear, the captives screamed and charged the prison complex, swinging deactivated cuffs like brass nun chucks, tackling the bots patrolling the cells and the human guards working the main desk.

The atrium was a scene of pure pandemonium, set to a soundtrack of furious bellowing. Many prisoners were injured in the brawl, and the guard robots killed an unlucky handful, shifting into the 'escaped prisoner' portion of their programming. But dozens more captives battered down the bewildered Imperials through weight of numbers. Automated laser turrets popped out of the roof and opened fire on the thrashing crowd. Several prisoners leaped from the security desk, tearing the auto-guns out of their housings. They turned them on the guards, filling the air with the sharp tang of scorched flesh and vaporized metals.

The armored super-warriors further down the passageway whirled around and raised their weapons, but couldn't fire without hitting their comrades in the melee. Many did anyway, cutting down escapees and Imperials alike.

Zeke wrestled with his opponent, ending his life with a wicked *crack* of his neck. Then he sang at the top of his lungs to maintain momentum, shoving his sprinting people through the door.

"He hit the ship, there was no sound, his blood went spurting high;
his comrades, they were heard to say, 'A hell of a way to die!'
His armor broke, he bounced away, back out into the void.
And he ain't gonna fly no more.
"Gory, gory, what a hell of a way to die.
Gory, gory, what a hell of a way to die.
Gory, gory, what a hell of a way to die.
He ain't gonna fly no more."

Markus grabbed another guard, who'd been knocked into a daze by crazed prisoners, crushing his arm with synth-muscle power. The guard wailed in agony as his weapon burped a stream of mag rounds that cut down a nearby automaton. Markus went for the robot's weapon. Although the guns wielded by the Empire's baseline human or cyber-augmented posthuman personnel had biometric security, those brandished by its automatons did not.

Markus roared a battle cry and blasted red-hot incendiary projectiles down the hall as the last prisoners charged past. Automatons and legionaries went down, kept off balance by Markus' fusillade.

Zeke spotted his robotic chaperone in the thinning melee, identifiable by the number stamped across its chest and dents on its cranium. Sparks stuttered from the bot's damaged battery core as it staggered around. Zeke wrapped four thick fingers around its shoulder guard and ripped the robot's arm out of its socket, beating the damned thing to death with it.

"How do *you* like it, huh? *Huh!*"

He hauled the bot's twitching body around to block incoming fire. The legionaries at the far end of the corridor were coordinating, charging at

inhuman speed toward the prison complex with weapons blazing. Reinforcements from the hangar bay followed them in.

"Inside, now!" cried Zeke, dragging the robot through the door as Gauss
rounds exploded all around them. Markus blew approaching assailants off
their feet as he retreated through the hatch. One of the prisoners punched
a panel as they crossed the threshold, the door slamming shut with slugs
exploding on its surface. Someone smashed the controls to disable the door.

Zeke breathed out, massaging his bruised throat and cracked jaw. "Holy
shit. It worked."

Markus grinned. "It's my job to doubt you, sir, but that was well done."

The brig was still in a state of bedlam. Many prisoners lay dead, but the
majority had survived their mini-blitzkrieg. The former captives charged
deeper into the labyrinthine complex to subdue any remaining guards, continuing Zeke's song.

They spotted globes of blood that floated through the testing course.
Intestines were a-dangling from his jump-trooper's suit.
He was a mess, they gathered him, and shook him from his boots,
and he ain't gonna fly no more.

Frantic activity drowned the final chorus out. Zeke spotted prisoners
charging along the catwalks of the chamber's upper levels. The prison was
enormous, but with the impending invasion, it had been thinly staffed. No
one wanted to patrol the cells when the Empire's ultimate victory was at
hand. Even better—from Zeke's past experience, these prison facilities had
only one main entrance, which was already sealed off.

The escapees unhooked mangled corpses from the high ceiling—former
inmates that the Imperials had clearly tortured. Pulling his eyes from the
sickening display, Zeke found Jenkins, who was rapid-firing commands into
different consoles behind the huge triangular desk. She had several nasty
bruises forming on her face and a bad laceration on her upper chest that was
soaking into her fatigues, which Jenkins didn't seem to notice through her
adrenaline high.

"Could've told us you planned on singing a concerto, Commander!" she
exclaimed.

"And risk one of those idiots figuring it out beforehand?" Zeke replied,
leaping over the desk slab to join her. "It worked, didn't it?"

Jenkins surveyed the scene as over two hundred surviving prisoners tended
to their wounded, dragging bodies into neat, covered rows. A medic ap-

proached her and began dabbing at her wounds as she continued typing. "I guess it did. What's next?"

"Does this place have an armory? We need guns. Lots of guns."

Jenkins pointed out a back room she'd already accessed, where civilian technicians from *Refit One* whooped in celebration as they carried armfuls of weapons out.

"It's mostly riot gear, but they had a stock of firearms on file, more than enough for us. They don't enable biometric settings until checkout, so everything's usable, sir."

"Jackpot," said Zeke.

Markus lumbered over, dumping his rifle on the desk. The lieutenant was also battered by the recent brawl, bleeding from a dozen minor injuries and a few grazing gunshot wounds. His synthetic arm was also malfunctioning again.

"What's next, Commander?"

"We open the cells, see who else they're keeping here," Zeke responded. "Then we'll wreak havoc on this bloody ship and feign an escape attempt. Gotta make it look good."

Jenkins shot him a concerned look while trying to locate the cell controls. "What do you mean by *look* good? Are we really escaping or pretending to escape, sir?"

A bandaged marine handed Zeke an assault rifle from the human chain leading out of the armory. Zeke thanked him and said, "I have a date with the emperor, Private. We need to draw attention away from what I'll be doing—making my way into his Sanctum."

Jenkins was confused. "Why?"

"Because my crazy sister needs us to get intel from Mariko. Anne's got a way of picking up my audio," said Zeke, tapping the tiny wound on his neck where the undetectable listening device was implanted.

"Right, because your sister wants to kill the emperor. And we're ... helping her do that," Jenkins recited, like it was the craziest thing she'd ever heard.

"Anne *will* kill the emperor," Zeke corrected. "With Nightshade at her side, it's already in the bag. We just need to provide details on his plans, so my people can plan their operation."

"Nightshade wouldn't let two of their top commanders die here, right? Can they help us?" Jenkins asked.

Markus shook his head.

"Negative," Zeke confirmed. "We can't risk revealing the *Solanum's* position. That'll scupper this party before it starts. We're on our own. The aim here is to maximize destruction, drain the royal apartments of defenders, and clear a route to the big man."

Markus raised an eyebrow. "This is very seat-of-the-pants, Zeke. Even for us."

"I know. But while I'd like more time, these are the end times."

Before Markus could respond, Jenkins pumped a fist. "Yes! Open sesame!"

Hallway by hallway, cell doors rattled open. Battered men and women staggered out, shocked to see their liberators offering medical assistance instead of torture. Markus fixed Zeke with a sobering stare. "Commander, what makes you think that Hadrian Mariko will open up to you?"

"Because we have ... history," Zeke admitted.

"History?"

"We had a previous friendship before the war, long time before I met you. A nasty coincidence," Zeke clarified. "Hadrian's ego will force him to gloat, to show me he was right. That's what I'm counting on."

"So, we're ... not getting out of here?" asked Jenkins.

"Afraid not, shrimp. Nightshade Squadron specializes in suicide missions."

"Oh god," Jenkins said, blanching.

Markus put aside the revelation that his commander knew the emperor personally, asking, "What if you gave yourself up?"

"Intentionally?"

"Yes. If the emperor wants to speak to you, why not walk out there and ask to see him?"

Zeke nodded. "Always sharp, Lieutenant. But we can't let Mariko suspect that I'm intentionally probing him for information. Instead, we'll damage his precious flagship while I make my way to the Sanctum. That's what I mean by making this 'look good.' It'll appear like we're trying to slow the invasion, which will give Nightshade more time to plan."

"I see," Markus said.

Zeke put both hands on his large friend's shoulders. "Markus, do you trust me?"

"Always, Commander."

"Well, I trust my sister. Believe me, she will not screw this up."

"I ... I know. But sir—" Markus said.

"Anne led a rebellion against the emperor on Colossus, with no help or support from outside. In a way, her fight against the Empire was a lot like ours. It went further than anyone thought it would, even though she ultimately failed. But Anne didn't have the deciding factor—*Nightshade*—on her side. This will work, Markus. Janelle has this covered. She's still in command; in case you're worried about my sister doing anything truly crazy," Zeke said with what he hoped sounded like unbreakable confidence.

Markus remained quiet. The sounds of the prison deck washed over them: the moans of Federation captives who were receiving much-needed medical attention, the rattle of gunfire against the entrance doors, and the chatter of terrified civilian contractors who were being shown how to use assault weapons.

Finally, Markus spoke. "Alright. I do trust you, Zeke."

That was reassuring, but the lieutenant's next words carried a warning tone. "I'm trusting you on this because you've never let us down before. Let's do this right, my friend. Maximum necessary force. We'll get you in there for a chat with Mariko."

Zeke's grin couldn't be wider.

"But he's the emperor, sir," Jenkins questioned, "what good will having a dialogue with him achieve?"

Zeke grinned. "Always be willing to talk with your enemy, kid. Talking with those you oppose may lead to strategic advantages, even common ground. You destroy your enemies by making them friends. Not saying that'll happen with Mariko, but I won't give up the opportunity—Nightshade needs that intel, and I have a way of getting it to them in real-time."

Jenkins narrowed her eyes, and then seemed to understand. "Gotcha, sir."

The console beeped. Jenkins stared at it, then typed rapid commands. "Sir, they're getting past my rootkit, into the comms system—"

A deep, robotic-sounding voice blared through the brig's speakers.

"Attention, traitorous scum. This is High General Thurman of the Solar Empire. Our war is over, yet you continue to fight. We have the brig complex surrounded. Any who resist will be exterminated, but we shall reward whoever brings us Zeke Oakfield. If you do not comply, we'll parade your violated corpses across the home-world and—"

Jenkins silenced the thunderous voice. "I think that's enough. Security subroutines re-established ... for now."

"Seems they've figured out who's in charge," Markus said, grinning at Zeke.

"Was that an example of 'dialogue with your enemy'?" Jenkins asked.

"Not with that guy. Thurman can go jump off a bridge," Zeke said, hauling himself onto the security desk. "People! If you're mobile, gather around."

Many of the prisoners approached to gather around the tiered atrium, leaving the medics and anyone else with relevant experience to tend to the wounded.

"This might be the most important battle of your lives," Zeke proclaimed. "We're gonna wreck the pride of their fleet, slow their invasion, and then escape if we can. The Federation might have given up on the fight, but *we* haven't."

Zeke studied the faces crowding around him. Many looked like they were about to crack from fear, especially the civilians.

"You, what's your name?" Zeke asked a random soldier, who was holding his injured side. The man stiffened. "Private Germaine, sir. Second Euro Armored Brigade."

"And you?"

The woman Zeke was looking at replied, "Corporal Ameen. 63rd Orbital Rifles, Commander."

"The rest of you, tell me who you are."

The group methodically rattled off their names, ranks and designations. Zeke tried to memorize as many as he could, but this wasn't for him, it was for *them*. In such a terrible situation, these people needed to know that the man who led them really did care about who they were, and what they were about to sacrifice.

When everyone was finished, Zeke smiled. "Well, if any of you want to collect General Thurman's 'reward,' do it now."

No one moved.

"Smart," Zeke said. "You all know there's no forgiveness for the likes of us."

Silence.

"But you know what? They're unfamiliar with this," Zeke said. "Being humiliated aboard their prized *Eagle of the Ninth*. Hadrian Mariko's got his people's heads stuffed so far up their asses that they've never considered the Federation to be a genuine threat. We're gonna remind 'em that we're not so easy to stamp out. Being captured wasn't a curse—it's an *opportunity*."

Many in the crowd murmured in assent. Markus watched with a small grin.

"I have a plan to reverse the outcome of this war," Zeke continued. "Many of us won't make it out of here. But every bullet fired, every system sabotaged, every iota of damage we do will slow them down. Every second the Empire is delayed from their surface landings is another second that your families and friends are safe, and more time for my people to plan Mariko's personal demise. You all know me as the commander of Nightshade Squadron. But Nightshade isn't here."

Zeke swept an arm out. "They're out there, and soon they'll come down on Mariko like the hammer of God. But right now, we deal the first blow!"

The crowd cheered louder. Giving people hope was a risky bet, but also a formidable weapon. Zeke hated himself for spending their lives, but it was unlikely that he'd survive this venture either. This was what they'd all signed up for.

"And if they bring us down to the last fighting man, it'll be one hell of a way to die. So, let's hit 'em hard!" Zeke declared. The captives went wild with cheers. Zeke hopped off the desk and stabbed a finger at the security screens, startling Jenkins.

"Get me a schematic of this ship's critical systems, kid. We've got a rampage to organize."

13 — REDUCE, REUSE, RECYCK

David blasted the maintenance door's control panel when the ancient system refused to open. It slid aside, revealing a vast expanse beyond. From his damp shoulder, Budgie let out a long croak. The bird still wasn't over their near-drowning experience.

Fresh trash tumbled through portals above, cascading past the brothers into deep mounds below. A flaking stencil on one of the nearby support pillars read: *Recyck Yard 78-10D.*

Jason marveled at the kilometers of trash, machinery, and conveyor belts stretching out before them. The high ceiling was blanketed in even more equipment, cranes, piping, and filtration systems. It all smelled *horrendous*.

"Finding the Abaddon Beacon better be worth it, if it means searching this disgusting place high and low," David said, yelling to be heard.

"It'll be worth it. These places never lose their effect on you, huh?" Jason replied as he gazed out into the gargantuan space below.

"They're all the same, man," David continued, "let's get down there."

"You've lost your sense of wonder," said Jason.

David allowed a crooked smile. "Never had one to begin with."

"You're such a downer."

They stood atop a giant cliff of machinery, wound through with enormous power cables and support struts. Below, the endless fields of conveyors fed incalculable amounts of garbage, malfunctioning nanotech, and recyclables into rows of flame-belching Recyck units. Hundreds of sorting arms transferred items onto smaller belts for specialized disassembly. Jason could see right through to the far end, where sunlight filtered into the facility. The noise was overwhelming.

"So, how do we find this thing?" asked Jason.

"Huh?"

"Where's our guard bot? This is a pretty big place."

David squinted down into the labyrinth for any sign of their companions. "That's an understatement. Without Sam or Lucia, it'll be like looking for a needle in ten thousand haystacks. They've got the location data."

Jason checked his datapad. Sam's beacon was still offline, though the underground often made comm-signals sporadic. They would have to wait until their friends arrived.

Footsteps reverberated through the dark passageway behind them, followed by a gurgling sound that managed to carry over the din of the cavernous chamber.

The brothers exchanged glances. Budgie swore at the noise. Jason looked back into the gloomy corridor, but the shadows remained where they were.

"There's no way those enforcers followed us down here," he asked. "Right?"

"Unlikely. But we better get going," David said, backing away from the dark passage. "We won't have much luck finding our bot, but we can grab some salvage in the meantime. It might convince Yamamoto not to exile us when, or *if* we make it back. If he learns about that tribunal we crashed, he's gonna be pissed."

"Fair enough," agreed Jason.

They chose a slow route to the main floor, shinnying down enormous power cables. Budgie followed, flapping from perch to perch.

"Careful," David called.

Jason jumped the last few feet to the grimy sorting floor, spotting a few spidery automatons picking through trash. They were four feet in diameter, with six articulated legs. Two of them fought over an old toaster. The way they scuttled gave Jason the willies, so he gave them a wide berth.

Jason and David ascended a short mound overlooking the conveyor fields, clambering over old appliances, burnt-out wrecks, used toys, and rotten foodstuffs. Another strange underground quake rumbled through the facility. It felt much closer to their position now, rattling junk from one end of the yard to the other.

Jason looked around. "Jeez, that's still happening?"

A second tremor stole his balance, and he tumbled down the heap with a yelp. David swiped at Jason's damp jacket, but he was long gone. Budgie swooped after him.

David found Jason at the trash pile's base, nursing several fresh cuts. David sniffed. "What an incredible smell you've discovered!"

"Thanks," Jason said, flicking an unknown substance off his shoulder.

"You didn't get any of that Nanite crap on you?" David asked, poking Jason's extremities.

"Don't think so. Ow!"

Jason winced as his brother applied antiseptic bandages to his cuts.

"You're fine," David said, wrinkling his nose. "We'll get Doc Janice to give you a tetanus shot. Put your gloves on, dumbass. This isn't the time or place to be screwing around."

Jason yanked on his gloves and started putting power cells in his bag, failing to notice a lone figure on all fours, staring at him from atop a nearby mound, blinking its glowing purple eyes. But David noticed, and so did Budgie, warbling nervously from his shoulder.

"Let's move a little faster, shall we?" David said as he pulled Jason away. Jason stiffened when he saw the Phagebearer, and followed his brother at a jog. "Uh oh."

The infected man cocked his head. Once they'd walked a few meters, he started trailing them at a distance. The creep twitched and snuffled to himself, dressed in the tatters of a business suit. He gulped, and the inhibitor obliged him with a fresh hit of Osmium. The infected man didn't appear to be generating Abaddon's shadow ... but the obelisk had tricked them before. This was the first time in weeks that Jason had been this close to an active Phage infection, and he wasn't keen to stay nearby.

"Hurry it up," David said. "We need to stay ahead of them. We can't risk the Abaddon Beacon using them to get to you."

"Right," Jason responded.

They attracted more attention as they explored further. Other infected humans emerged from the maze of junk, watching them with sunken, glowing eyes. Ruined clothing hung from their stick-thin limbs, riddled with hideous veiny growths. Each was deathly pale. But their wasted states were deceptive ... they moved through the trash jungle with the grace of mountain goats, empowered by their self-replicating infections. Accompanying the human infected were many automatons, which moved and acted similarly, part of the same swarm, powered by the same mind. It was beyond unsettling.

"Lucia didn't mention this yard was inhabited," muttered Jason.

David drew his pistol, but none of their observers came close enough to warrant using it.

"It's not supposed to be," he said. "These people are here to feed, and hide from the quarantine task forces. Never seen this many in one place before, though. If a group this size converged on the Village all at once, I don't think we'd have enough ammo to hold them off."

"Let's not lead them back to the Village, then," Jason said, backing away from the infected.

A Phage-infected maintenance robot was being quickly disassembled by two uninfected bots before it infected the entire drone flock. Nearby, several human Phagebearers clamped their cracked lips onto an engine manifold, slurping any remaining Nanites inside. Purple veins throbbed around their mouths. Glowing areas of the dying manifold pulsed in rhythm.

"Gross," Jason commented. He ignored the feeders, snatching up additional intact Nanite gadgets as he and David continued to move away. Many items showed the beginnings of Phage development—which he gave an even wider berth. He couldn't give Abaddon any chances to find him.

David was choosier than Jason. He had an extensive computer lab at the Chop Shop, which he regularly upgraded. His tech donations also went to the Village's data storage facility and intranet network, which gave each resident access to the settlement's digital chatrooms.

After filling his bag, Jason climbed five meters up onto a huge moving conveyor to get his bearings again—keeping an eye on the Phagebearers creeping after them at a distance. He spotted places where specialized recyclables were sent, but no indication of where their target bot might be.

David scratched his head as he clambered up beside Jason. "This place is too damn big."

Jason tapped on his datapad. "Sam? You there?"

The device gave no reply. David tried his communicator too.

"Sam?"

Nothing.

"She'd better not be ignoring us," said David.

"She might ignore you, but never *me*."

The denizens of the Recyck yard were slinking between the twisted piping below them as the brothers rode the conveyor across the expanse. Jason was shocked at how quiet the Phagebearers were, with none of their usual screeching, random robotic bleeping, or warbling that normally accompanied a horde of this size, which he assumed they used to coordinate with each other. They were using the noise of the yard to stay hidden ... but from what?

One of the infected slithered onto the moving conveyor about twenty meters away, gabbling to himself and staring at them. David raised his pistol. "Can't help you, bub. Get lost."

It was the man in the business suit again. The Phagebearer growled, bloodshot eyes locked on Jason. Painful dark-purple lesions veined the man's throat—his infection was past the point of no return. The Phage affected everyone from the poorest paupers to the wealthiest magnates of the Upper-city, but not even advanced surgical extraction treatment could help this man now. Jason had often wondered if there was any human intelligence left in them. If that was the case, and these people were trapped in their bodies, forced to seek out sustenance and Nanites to keep them going ... the Phage was a truly terrible fate.

Another loud tremor rumbled through the Recyck yard, rattling junk from corner to corner.

Without warning, the business-suited man bolted. The entire horde of Phagebearers dissipated as fast as they'd emerged, slinking back into a thousand different hiding places.

David lowered his pistol, looking around. "Never seen them act like this. What the heck has them spooked so badly?"

Jason glanced over his shoulder, trying and failing to locate any source for the underground tremors, but nothing else seemed amiss. No ethereal animated darkness, no warning signs of Abaddon's ghostly arrival. Very strange.

"No idea. Guess we'll keep looking?" Jason suggested.

David scanned the area one more time, but not a single Phagebearer was visible anymore.

"I guess so," David said. He appeared concerned, but holstered his pistol. "Let's make it snappy. We don't know what else is down here with us."

"What could be worse than them?" Jason asked.

They climbed down from the conveyor and waded deeper into the yard, but no more infected made an appearance, unwilling to venture after them. Budgie took off from David's shoulder, flapping up into the darkness of the ceiling rafters.

After a few more minutes of collecting valuables and fruitlessly searching for the science facility's guard robot, Jason and David emerged into a clearing on the sorting floor. Before them lay a mountain of ancient vehicles, piled up for later disassembly.

"This is hopeless," David groaned.

Both of them jumped as a familiar voice called from above, "What are you two doing down there?"

Jason glanced skyward, spotting two figures: Sam, who gripped her blade's cable, and Lucia, who bearhugged Sam's waist as they lowered from the ceiling. Sam had lodged her sword into a roof-mounted cargo crane, making it descend as its hydraulics bled fluid. Budgie flapped after them, hooting triumphantly at his discovery.

"Look who finally decided to show up," said David, holstering his pistol.

Sam touched down on the vehicle mound, depositing Lucia. With a crack of her long power cable, she jerked the blade down into her hand, blasting the crane upward with a psychic burst to clank back into its moorings, bleeding fluids.

Sam addressed David as she stepped from car to car with Lucia in tow, descending the mountain. "That's a funny way of thanking me for getting us out of another impossible situation. That's gotta be the umpteenth time that I've saved your ass."

Lucia looked around nervously, interrupting before David could retort. "How about we find this bot and get outta here?"

"Fantastic idea," Jason said, as his inhibitor hit him with a dose to calm a sense of dread that he couldn't place.

Lucia accepted his help as she hopped down from the lowest crushed aircar. Jason looked at Sam. "Well, I'm happy that we're not being tortured deep inside some social compliance precinct right now. Thanks, Sam."

She pinched his ear. "Normally, I'd think you were patronizing me. But I know you aren't an unappreciative windbag, Jason."

David coughed.

Sam pulled out Lucia's locator, heading toward the sunlit end of the facility. "This way."

David released Budgie, who flapped frantically and spouted random words.

"What the heck's gotten into you, buddy?" David asked. "The infected are gone. They don't seem interested in human flesh today. Which I'll admit, is strange."

Jason was about to reply when the vehicle mountain behind them *moved*.

As he turned to watch, an immense mass rose from within the pile, pushing through metric tons of crushed aircar chassis, broken glass, and engine blocks, battering Jason's ears with unbearable noise. Recyck spider workers scuttled away.

Everyone stared at the emerging hulk in mute shock. A burning orange light flickered on through the falling junk, accompanied by a jet-engine roar.

"What the hell is that?" David asked.

The huge machine was still rising. It looked ancient, judging from the pockmarking on the plating, the rusting hydraulics and exposed power lines. Modern UEF automatons were made of sleek, rounded, pleasing shapes that wouldn't scare civilians. By contrast, this industrial, functional beast appeared like it could withstand anything hell had to throw at it.

Its exposed plasma core grew hotter by the second. The monstrosity squatted over a dark pit in the ground, which explained the tremors they'd been feeling. Jason wondered if this machine, or more like it, were the cause of the larger tremors affecting the rest of the city.

Debris tumbled down the melted shaft as the beast reached its full height of twenty-five meters. It stood on four triple-staged legs with clawed toe slabs, unfurling a pair of segmented arms tipped with vicious projectors, dripping liquid plasma. It was a cross between a tunneling machine and a robotic god of war. As the last of the debris tumbled off its hull, the behemoth lowered its enormous, flat head to observe them with a foot-wide camera oculus. A laser beam swept the group—which looked strangely similar to a Nanophage detection ray.

"*NANO-INFESTED BIOFORMS IDENTIFIED. PURGE PROTO-COLS ENABLED.*"

"I think I know what those infected were afraid of," muttered David.

Sam's blade fired up with a high-pitched whine as she grumbled, "Today keeps getting better."

14 — GHOST OF GARBAGE PAST

Heat and light flared as the behemoth's cannon iris opened wide, blasting scorching orange plasma at them. Lucia dove out of the way, pulling Jason with her. Sam yanked David in the opposite direction—snatching Budgie as they went. The blast vaporized the ground, melting deep into the Recyck yard's foundations. It was so hot that it scorched Jason's nose hairs.

He skidded to a halt, jacket smoking and skin sunburnt. His deflection shield, re-initialized after its recent soaking, did nothing to block the intense heat.

"Sorry!" Lucia said.

"It's fine, come on! We need to get outta here!" Jason tugged Lucia to her feet and squinted through the haze, trying to spot Sam and David.

David dropped a steaming car door he'd used to block the heat-wave. Sam rose from a crouch behind him.

The hulking drone's reactor roared as it shuddered forward on massive legs, charging another shot.

Sam waved to Jason with her crackling sword. "Split up! Give it multiple targets! Get outta here!"

David seemed hesitant to leave Jason with Lucia, but another beam-blast left him with no choice but to follow Sam into the labyrinthine maze of trash.

Jason gave a thumbs up and led Lucia into the metal jungle in the opposite direction. The facility didn't just smell like garbage—now it smelled like *burning* garbage.

Distant hammering footfalls told Jason that the quadrupedal monster had targeted David and Sam first. The vibrations rattled Jason's brain as his heart beat an adrenaline-fueled rhythm into his ribcage, and his inhibitor's rapid beeping sped up into one continuous tone.

"What did it mean by ... infected? It called us infected!" Lucia said as they ducked under a thicket of cabling that powered the conveyors.

"None of us have the Nanophage, at least that we know of. Maybe it detected the Phagebearers hiding in here," Jason replied.

Lucia glanced at the lumbering monster as it crashed through debris mountains, overturning an entire conveyor to stay on David and Sam's tail. Destroying the huge rubber belt was akin to flipping a rock, revealing dozens of infected people who scrambled away like bugs. The machine bellowed, shifting its aim to blast them, allowing Sam and David to gain some distance from it.

"It's wrecking the place!" Lucia cried.

"Is that the Recyck authority employee talking?" Jason said with a slight hysterical edge.

Lucia rolled her eyes. "I'm not that attached to my job, but I hope that thing doesn't destroy the guard bot that you came here for."

"Can't worry about that now," said Jason.

The monster machine whipped smaller arcs of plasma from its secondary arm projectors. Hissing, bubbling metals and polymers evaporated in the white-hot beams, along with dozens of Phagebearers and Recyck spiders. Jason watched his brother, who responded with shots from his home-made hand cannon, but it was like a toy in comparison to the metal beast. Nanophage victims screamed as the monster targeted them, though it never veered away from its pursuit of David and Sam.

A horde of infected burst from a side passage in the dense junk mounds, scrambling to get away from the metal titan. Their appearance forced Jason and Lucia back the way they'd came, entering a wide lane between conveyors. Moments later, David and Sam skidded into view, corralled by several plasma blasts.

"You were supposed to go the other way!" David barked, before firing over his shoulder as the behemoth charged through a huge pile of engines, sending them crashing as far as three hundred meters away. "Sorry, brother. The universe keeps bringing us back together," Jason huffed, trying to catch his breath.

The monster bot chased the four of them into an area dense with machinery. Jason spotted a row of gigantic magnets mounted on the ceiling, used to separate certain metals off the conveyor below.

Everyone was already exhausted by the morning's action, compounded by minor injuries. Every plasma-beam edged closer to a fatal hit. The metal monstrosity was adapting to their evasion, corralling them with calculated blasts to melt the ground or collapsing piles of sizzling junk in their path.

As he ran, Jason spotted two Recyck bots tending to a third drone, twitching as its carapace melted from plasma damage. As he passed, the undamaged bots blasted their fellow into manageable halves with a micro-charge, carrying them off to a repair bay.

Jason's mind raced. He looked up at the magnets again, attached to huge mechanical arms that ran on tracks, hoping that the metal monster chasing them was made of a common enough type of metal for his burgeoning plan to work.

"Guys, it's idea time," Jason said. Lucia stared at him. Budgie reappeared, swooping down and screeching in a complete panic.

David groaned, wiping sweat from his brow. "Uh-oh."

"Stow it, David. Tell me what you got, idea boy," Sam said.

"The magnets. We could ..." Jason struggled to get the words out. "I don't know, use them to pin it down. Once it's immobilized, we could feed it an explosive. That plasma cannon is its only weak point, right after it fires. If we tossed something explosive down there, maybe that'd kill it. It's something to start with, anyway."

Nobody spoke for a moment, maintaining their sprint as the monster flashed plasma at secondary infected targets, which only briefly slowed it down.

David huffed. "That is the single stupidest plan I've ever heard—"

"You have a better one?" Sam snapped.

David fired his pistol over his shoulder. "Military hardware is the only way to bring that thing down."

"Do you see any of that lying around here?"

"Those magnets aren't hard to operate," Lucia said. "Workers come down here to adjust the automated systems when they malfunction. We could try it."

"I can't think of anything better," Sam said. "Show us."

David followed behind them, saying, "Alright, if we're doing this, *I'm* the one making that throw."

Lucia peeled off toward the magnet disassembly zone; everyone followed. Behind them, the monster bot uncovered what looked like an entire hive of Phagebearers beneath a junk mountain, pausing its lumbering gait to stamp and blast dozens as they scrambled away. Fortunately, this slowed it down considerably.

Lucia directed David toward a control booth beside a low conveyor belt. The rows of magnets hung high above, waiting to separate out different grades of metals.

"This is one of the control consoles. I don't have systems access, though," Lucia said. "Can you hack it?"

David shrugged. "Try me."

He hauled himself up into the cubicle to begin the hack. Budgie landed on the roof, watching the monster bot blast the infected.

Lucia led Sam and Jason to the other booth, beside the dormant conveyor. The racks of magnets creaked with each pounding footstep.

"Once David cracks security, this booth will activate too," Lucia said. "We'll have to move the magnets all together in order to pin that thing down."

"How's it going?" Jason asked David through the window.

"Fine, don't distract me."

"It's coming closer!" Lucia hollered from the garbage pile she was perched on.

"Done yet?" Sam called.

David fired up the console, signed in as a fake employee. Above, the magnet assemblies came to life with a low whine.

"It's done. I hope these magnets are enough to hold that bastard in place."

"Me too. Now let's do our thing," Sam said, drawing her blade.

David sighed, offering her his pistol. "I've always wanted to be robot bait."

Sam started disassembling his handgun, muttering, "Remember the plan."

Lucia was explaining the magnet controls to Jason as Sam and David approached. The booming footsteps grew louder.

Sam finished reassembling David's weapon. "One jury-rigged bomb."

Jason nodded. "Nice. Don't miss, David."

Sam flexed her fingers. "I'll nudge it if you do."

"I never miss," David muttered.

A plasma beam lanced through a massive support pillar nearby, searing every nearby surface. Lucia grabbed Jason's hand as they hunkered down.

The metal titan reappeared, lumbering fast for its size. It let out a static roar, making everyone cringe and cover their ears at the intensity.

"Okay. This either works ... or we ..." Jason said, trailing off.

"Die," finished David.

"Always the optimist," Sam said, dragging David toward the onrushing machine. "We'll get its attention. Good luck, guys."

Jason looked at Lucia. "We're gonna need it."

"Don't say that."

They separated into the booths. Jason cranked his mechno-arm-mounted magnets into position, freeing cascades of dust from the ceiling. Lucia did the same.

The beast crashed through the garbage mound that Lucia had used as a vantage point. Junk exploded everywhere as the monster blasted plasma at Sam and David with extreme but temporary sun-hot pain as the beam passed. It came so close that it singed their hair.

Sam dodged right, avoiding Lucia's booth so the titan wouldn't blast it. David threw himself over the opposite side of the short conveyor to dodge the hail of debris.

"Oi! Over here, ya lunk!" bellowed David as he and Sam re-convened to lure the titan onto the conveyor belt, below the magnets. It blasted out another static-laden roar, plasma core recharging as it followed.

"Do it, Lucia!" Jason said, swiping dials to kick his magnets up to maximum power.

"Roger," Lucia replied over her comm unit.

Sam and David backed off as the monster flattened the conveyor, preparing to fire as the magnet array scanned for foreign metals. The giant invader definitely counted as foreign material, so the magnets grabbed it.

The metal monstrosity shuddered as they pulled it simultaneously in opposite directions. Its massive legs ripped up the belt and scraped the permacrete floor as it scrabbled for purchase, but the bot was immobilized. The magnets wrenched the machine's segmented arms upward, unable to target Sam and David.

The main plasma gun still worked, which fired, and they barely dodged the blast.

But this was what they were waiting for, because when it fired, the titan's internal machinery was briefly exposed as the plasma projection iris remained open to vent heat, as Jason had seen earlier.

"It's now or never!" Jason bellowed. "Throw it before that thing closes!"

David got to his feet and twisted a cap on his rebuilt pistol's energy cell—causing it to overheat—before hurling it. "See ya, my girl."

The weapon arced, whirling toward the struggling machine's maw. Its cameras tracked the incoming object, but the head section had almost no mobility under the influence of the giant magnets. Sam bumped David's pistol in midair with an Abhamic nudge, clattering it into the opening.

"Yes!" Jason shouted.

The machine belched thick plasmic vapors. The jury-rigged bomb rocketed back out, exploding several meters away. The shrapnel pelted the monster's 'face'.

"Crap!" Jason gasped.

David and Sam exchanged glances.

"That was an easy three-pointer!" David whined.

Jason slapped his hand to his forehead. "That's it, we are screwed."

The monster blasted a roar that sounded suspiciously like triumph. But it was still held rigidly in place by the magnets.

Lucia got on her comm. "Now what?"

"I don't know!" Jason said.

Sam and David started arguing again as the bot thrashed. What else could they do but *run*?

As Jason lamented his lack of backup planning, one of the titan's segmented arms broke free and fired, incinerating two of the magnet armatures. With their destruction, the robotic monster regained some movement.

Sam and David seemed to agree on something, but Jason couldn't hear what it was over the intensity of crashing junk and the monster bot trying to free itself. Sam took a running jump at the huge bot, using its leg joint to generate a psionic, Abhamic power-fueled leap. She landed on top of its flat cranial mass, slid to her knees and jammed her flaming mono-molecular blade into the thing's central eye. "Let's see you fight blind, dickhead!"

The sword's phasic field slowly cracked into the bot's diamond-like photoreceptor. The machine screamed, spitting plasma from its secondary cannons in protest, raining down melted debris. It bucked its head, forcing Sam to hook her feet into vents on its hull to hang on. David yelped and threw himself backward to avoid being incinerated. "Too close, man!"   Budgie appeared again, shrieking. In desperation, Jason slammed his magnet controls to the left until they were behind the monster, rattling against each other on their rails. Lucia did the opposite, sliding her magnets along so they were in front of it. Jason yelled into his comm. "If we can't blow it up, then maybe we can rip it in half!"

"Worth a try," Lucia agreed, moving her magnets in the opposite direction. Although the robot weighed hundreds of tons, they managed to lift it off the ground as the remaining magnets rose to their limit.

"Get off that thing, Sam!" David barked at Sam. Budgie squawked at her over the bot's mechanical straining sounds, expressing the same sentiment. Electrical discharge crackled from its carapace, sizzling across support pillars and striking the ground like lightning.

Jason's console started to flicker and spark. He backed away. "That's not good."

David spotted movement behind the metal monster. "Oh good, our friends are back."

A tide of regrouped Recyck yard spiders tumbled into view, in far greater numbers than before. Jason spotted more of them tumbling out of access tunnels set into nearby support pillars.

A deep, straining groan started inside the titan. Sam's sword battery died, leaving the inert blade stuck in its cracked oculus. She couldn't yank it out, as the beast started to split. Rivets popped and armor buckled, spouting noxious vapors.

Jason shouted at Sam. "Sam! That thing is gonna blow, get off!"

The monster roared, but no beam burst out from the main plasma projector. Instead, it sucked down air to cool its internally ruptured reactor. The unexpected rush sucked Budgie inside, despite Sam's surge of mental power to stop him. The bird emerged in a flutter of scorched feathers from the shaft on the bot's rear end. Somehow alive, Budgie flopped to the ground several meters away.

Gallons of reactor fluids and hazardous chemicals gushed out of the machine's torn underbelly, spreading in a burning puddle. The Recyck spiders surrounded it, snapping at the drone's legs, splashing and melting in the discharge.

With a final loss of structural integrity, the magnets tore the titan in two, flinging wreckage around the area. Sam detached her blade and jumped for it, landing hard and sliding up against a pile of squashed aircars. Groups of Recyck workers swarmed over the bot's pieces, determined to make sure it never rose again.

David emerged from behind the overturned conveyor belt, looking uncharacteristically shaken. Sam groaned, holding her ribs as she staggered to her feet, surveying the fiery destruction.

Everyone approached the titan's wrecked chunks. David picked up Budgie, whose wingtips and tail feathers were smoldering. The bird did not look happy.

"Looks dead to me," said David, kicking one of the titan's massive legs. He backed off as Recyck spiders shoved past his shins, attacking the unresponsive limb with laser drills, buzzsaws, and clawed pedipalps. Jason stared at the blazing hulk, lying in heaps of sparking pieces. "I can't believe that worked."

Lucia sighed with intense relief as she came down from the edge of hysteria, where they had all been for the last few minutes. "Neither can I."

She gave Jason a quick, awkward hug. "Good plan, Jason."

Sam raised an eyebrow at Lucia's display of affection, extending her hand. Her phase blade finally jerked out of the drone's cracked oculus and whirled back into her grip.

"What about me?" David said. "You can't say that wasn't a good throw."

"I ... uh ..." Sam said, trailing off, eyes rolling up into her head. Blood shot from her nose and she fell on her face, exhausted from such rapid uses of her Abhamic abilities.

"Greeeeeeat," David groaned as Jason and Lucia rushed over.

Flames danced across the ground nearby as Sam awakened, responding to David's capsule of smelling salts. She jerked her head away. "Ughhh."

"Pushed yourself pretty hard back there," Jason said from his crouched position with Lucia, who was nursing some bruises and contusions. His inhibitor pulsed uncomfortably, but Jason was relieved to see Sam conscious again. She wiped the blood off her face and accepted their help to sit up, slowly and carefully. "How long was I out?"

"Just a minute. Or an hour. Or maybe a day," David said, fishing around in his bag.

"Ha. My sense of time appreciates that," Sam muttered.

David administered an injector into Sam's abdomen to freeze her ribs until they got back home. Jason squeezed Sam's hand. "You okay?"

"Yeah," Sam nodded, slapping her datapad when it refused to boot up. She held it up, snapping photos of the wreckage for later study. Budgie squawked at the hulk, still enraged over his journey through its failing reactor.

"So, where's our actual target?" asked David. Sam stared at him, still dazed. "Oh, right!"

Pulling out Lucia's holographic locator, she triggered the hologram of the bot's location. "It's only a hundred and forty-five meters away. Go figure."

"Come on," Lucia said, accepting the device from Sam and beckoning Jason.

"You earned it, little brother," David said, nodding in begrudging approval.

Jason hurried away from the scene of the battle as David checked Sam over for any other injuries. As he and Lucia approached a massive heap of robot carcasses, the locator beeped faster. "Getting warmer," Lucia said.

"Wish I'd seen this sooner."

"Your chances of finding this guy on your own were slim to none, Jason."

"Yeah, but ya can't blame us for trying."

"Nope. No, I can't," Lucia said as Jason dragged random bots out of the pile by their arms and legs, heart pounding. After a brief landslide of metallic bodies, a robot with a government logo stamped on its chest slid into view. A beacon was stuck to it that flashed in time with Lucia's locator, which had been remotely placed by the Recyck yard's sorting systems. Jason studied the logo—a caduceus wrapped around a test tube, the symbol of the UEF Science Division.

"This is our guy," he said, with growing excitement.

"Yeah," said Lucia. "Never imagined that I'd been seeing all this in person, though."

"Stick with us, and you never know where you'll be after waking up in the morning," Jason said. David approached with Sam's arm held over his broad shoulder, who was wincing and clutching her stomach. Jason propped the robot upright for Sam to examine.

"This is it," Sam confirmed. "Common enough design. That could be why he ended up in general processing, rather than private disposal."

Sam lifted her arm off David's shoulder and pressed a pair of switches, releasing a panel from the robot's chemical-smeared cranium. With a twist, she yanked the bot's CPU from its head with a snap of electrical discharge.

"Data secured," Sam said, handing it to David. "Get that under wraps. We'll examine it when we're home, make sure it's got the codes we need."

Jason watched in wonderment as David tucked it into his jacket pocket. Had they finally found the key to the science facility? Was this it?

He looked at Lucia. "I can't tell you what this means to me, Lucia."

Lucia turned red, looking away, though she glanced at Sam. "Don't mention it. And thank you for coming back for me. Thank you all."

"No problem," Sam said, giving Lucia an awkward one-armed hug.

Sam spotted a chunk of the smoldering bot's central head assembly that had landed nearby. The severed power lines were still sputtering. "Gimme a hand with this."

A series of panels had popped open on the scorched hull plating, revealing a row of backup batteries. They looked old, but robust. David wrenched one open, allowing Sam to release one of the huge battery units. David extracted and scanned the battery with an evaluation device. Sam explained, "I spotted these when I was on top of its head."

"What's so special about it?" asked David, looking at his screen.

"I think it's got a hundred times the output of an equivalent Federation battery," Sam read from his scanner. "But this wasn't built recently. Must have been before mass adoption of Nanotech, because this is fission-based. No Nanites, no fusion."

The dented battery had been recharged countless times, judging by the heavy wear around the edges. Jason stared at it. "No Nanite tech? That would put it at ... what, a hundred years old? Pre-Great War?"

"No idea," admitted Sam, watching the swarm of Recyck bots carrying the monster's remains away like ants.

"Hey ... uh ... what the heck is this?" David asked, looking closer at the severed hunk of hull. Everyone else gathered around as he brushed dust and debris off the hull. A scuffed, worn and peeling insignia had been painted there, a pair of orange daggers superimposed over a faded globe of the Earth.

"It's... *Confederate*?" Lucia asked, peering down at the scuffed insignia.

"As in, Great War-era Confederate?" Jason added.

"Yeah," David said, stunned. "Is someone using century-old Confederate tech to clear out the infected down here?"

No one spoke. Jason knew that the original city of Toronto beneath them hadn't suffered a ground invasion from Confederate territory during the Great War, so this machine couldn't have been buried down here all this time. It had come from elsewhere. But ... *how*? How had it survived the nuclear destruction of Confederate society twenty years ago, and how had it gotten all the way here?

"Wait a second. If this thing was shaking the Recyck yard as it tunneled in here ... then what the heck has been shaking the whole city?" David asked.

"This isn't the time or place to theorize about that," said Sam, snapping more photos of the insignia. "We can ask some of the old-timers in the Village if they know anything about this. In the meantime, if we can adapt this battery to work with Talos's power systems, it might get him back online, possibly today."

Budgie landed on the battery, poking at it.

"Score. At least we're going back with good news," said David.

"Don't jinx us, please," Sam groaned.

"Would've been nice to have had Talos with us for this," said Jason, staring at the remains of the destroyed titan, feeling the familiar wave of guilt wash over him. "He would've loved fighting this big bastard. Could've saved us a lotta trouble."

Sam pinched Jason's ear affectionately. "If this battery works, he'll be blasting things again in no time. No harm done."

"I'm sure he'll see it that way."

"Shush. Look at *this*," Sam said, pointing. Underneath the Confederate robot's head section, a scratched translucent tank was exposed, leaking foul amniotic fluids onto the ground.

Lying sideways inside the tank, Jason spotted the remains of a human body through the dirty glass. Only the torso and head remained, stippled with cybernetics and life-sustaining feeding tubes. The mechanical beast had been operated by a real honest-to-god human Confederate, who were all supposed to be nothing but radioactive ash, if the stories were true. The man's eyes and mouth were the worst part, pierced with cable bundles of various types. At least the man was dead.

"Good lord," David said. Everyone else remained silent, staring at the horrific mess.

Far off, a maintenance portal opened in the ceiling. Shadows interrupted the smoke-hazed sunlight—emergency vehicles were arriving. Lucia pointed them out as they descended into the flaming facility's ruins. "Half the security forces in this sector will be on the way. This is the worst industrial disaster in years."

David coughed, waving wisps of foul blue gas away. "Let's not stick around for them to blame us. My lungs are starting to burn."

Lucia seemed like she was working up the courage to ask something. "So ... where are we going now?"

Sam nodded, clenching her side. "Yeah, we've still got to decide what to do with you."

David raised an eyebrow. "Don't tell me you wanna bring Lucia all the way back to the Village. We haven't given Yamamoto any kind of heads up about her—and we weren't even supposed to be on the surface this morning, remember? What's he gonna say when we show up with an up-worlder?"

Sam gestured to the burning facility around them, as the security vehicles began to fan out in the distance. "What's the alternative? Leave her here?"

Jason spoke up. "We never planned on bringing Lucia back to the Village with us when we left. But you're right, we can't leave her here."

Lucia looked at them all. "If it's a matter of usefulness, I can offer the skills I've picked up at the Recyck authority. Maybe they'll be valuable ... in this Village."

"There's nowhere else we can bring her, even temporarily?" David asked.

"Don't think so," said Jason.

"Nowhere else in the Under-city is safer than our home base. We can't hit the Science Institute until we've gone back to the Village and seen Janice for some meds, and gotten some rest," said Sam, eyeing the approaching emergency vehicles and jerking a thumb in the opposite direction. "First, let's get the hell out of this place. Then, we'll decide what to do with Lucia."

15 — I WANT HIM ALIVE

Light fixtures flickered as explosions tore through the flagship's decks beneath Zeke's feet. His wounds throbbed, but like everyone else, he'd received a modicum of medical attention before the show had begun in earnest.

"Teams five and six, your target is starboard ammunition storage," barked Markus to the waiting squads, poring over a hovering schematic of the *Eagle of the Ninth*. The 3-D holo-representation of the warship wavered, projected from a portable unit that Jenkins had set up. The diagram was covered with scribbled notes and circles around critical subsystems.

Markus looked to Zeke for confirmation of his orders, who nodded. "Do it."

"Move out, you three," Markus said.

Several marines wearing riot gear saluted, crawling into a waist-high hatch in the wall to enter the flagship's mazelike ventilation system. The ducts were cramped, only frequented by automated bots, but they were large enough for a human to get around unnoticed. Zeke had repeated this trick on other Imperial vessels during Nightshade raids, though he was shocked that they hadn't adapted to the tactic yet. Zeke saluted the last man into the hatch before returning to the hologram. Gunfire rattled against the sealed brig doors nearby.

"That'll give 'em some fires to fight," Zeke said, employing a deep-breathing technique to calm his nerves.

Beside Markus, Jenkins and several other civilian technicians from *Refit One* fought the Empire's attempts to block their access to the flagship's networks, all while supporting the strike teams with audio instructions and scrambling the security systems to prevent the Imperials from detecting them. More squads waited, eager to leave the embattled prison complex. Jenkins sweated under the pressure and harsh prison lights, using transponders in each squad's stolen gear to guide them to their objectives.

Zeke grinned at Markus as they watched the kid work. "Nerd."

"Good thing she's our nerd," his lieutenant replied.   A major blast rocked the prison's doors.

"Reinforce that ingress point!" Zeke barked. Several men, whom he recognized from their earlier introductions from the Indic-Islander 12th Mechanized Rifles, stripped wall panels to weld over the doors, which had already been reinforced several times. Zeke thanked the war deity watching over him for making the exterior passageway too small for a warbot to fit through.

More explosions rocked the deck, this time from above.

"Kid, I've got a green light from group ten, mission success. Re-task them to the engine room, hit their propulsion systems," ordered Zeke. "That'll slow this ship down."

"On it, sir," Jenkins relayed his command. "What about the fusion plant, Commander?"

She rotated the glowing map, pointing out a complicated-looking section. "If we strike there, the flagship will—"

"It's too heavily guarded, shrimp," replied Zeke. "If their reactor complex goes down, so does this ship, but we'll never get in there. Remember, our targets are meant to clear the way to the emperor's Sanctum. We need softer nuts to crack."

As he spoke, several muffled *whumps* rumbled through the deck. Sweat trickled down his back, but Zeke smiled as he heard the victorious team cheering over their hijacked comms channel.

Jenkins updated the hologram as intercepted Imperial reports came through. "We've baited another three defense units out of the Sanctum complex, and team four detonated the starboard magazine storage."

"Excellent. That's exactly what I expect from Uranian drop marines. Assign them a new target," said Zeke. He picked up his rifle, loading himself down with ammunition blocks.

Markus looked up. "Leaving so soon?"

"We've drained the royal apartments as much as we can," Zeke said. "I can't delay anymore. We wouldn't wanna keep our 'dear leader' waiting."

Markus glanced at Zeke with concern. "You're sure you can do this alone, sir?"

"I'll have a better chance of getting in undetected by myself. He wanted a private chat, so it's gotta be me," explained Zeke.

Markus took a deep breath, centered himself, and signaled to Jenkins. "Alright, then. Find Zeke a route."

"To where, sir?" The girl looked up from the screens lighting her sweaty face, eyes wide.

"Get our commander into Mariko's lair, private."

Colonel Lena Gallagher's high-topped leather boots echoed up the rough stone steps of the main entryway to the emperor's Sanctum. *Bloody moonrock on a starship*, she thought, *the strangeness of it*.

A single pair of legionnaire guards stood aside, allowing her to pass, though there were normally far more of them present here at all times. Emperor Mariko had ordered Lena to drain the royal apartments of defenders to apprehend the Federation rabble running amok on almost every deck, against her advisement. This madness surpassed even the most exaggerated tales of Zeke Oakfield's previous tactics in the war.

Red light bathed everything, casting deep shadows around the gloomy chamber's black stone walls, gold trim patterning and dark recesses as she entered through the massive slab doors. The odd geometric angles of the space were unpleasant to look at, oppressive and asymmetrical. Lena's attention was drawn to where her fellow overlords gathered around an operations table displaying a holo-map of the flagship. Large sections of the vessel glowed with damage indicators.

Beyond, the emperor's malefic presence radiated in palpable waves from where he sat in silhouette on his massive, raised throne, conversing quietly with Sister Praetorian N9. Only Mariko's eyes were visible, burning orbs of violet power behind his eyeglasses. Lena could almost smell the energy in the air. The emperor monitored the orbital invasion's progress through a series of data leads running into the throne, plugging into the back of his skull. The setup was full of unfamiliar, esoteric technology that could only have come from the machinations of Mariko's favorite mad doctor, who was also present around the holo-table's crimson glow.

Beside Mariko's throne was a polished statue of an obelisk, nearly twenty meters in height. Lena noticed the emperor glancing at it every so often. She had often wondered what the statue represented, and why he paid it so much heed when the statue said and did nothing in reply. But he was the emperor, and his actions were unquestionable.

"We'll need to source reinforcements from other capital ships to deal with this incursion. The Volt Raiders, or the Megamech Legion, perhaps," High General Thurman thundered, cracking the stone table with a steam-hissing metal fist. An enormous cybernetic hulk with broad shoulders, Thurman was augmented to where the line between man and machine was gone. His original background was impossible to discern, but he and his sub-commanders headed the emperor's brutal legionnaire ground forces.

Lena announced her arrival. "There's no need for outside assistance, General. Our anti-boarding units will breach the brig within the hour, cutting off Oakfield's command and control."

Thurman and the others around the table regarded her. His augmetized voice was as chilling as the Sanctum's interior décor. "Ahhh, Colonel Gallagher. If our lord's flagship were not so overrun with rats, I'd assume that you were actually doing your job."

Lena, who was shorter and unaltered compared to Thurman, stood strong. If she showed doubt, Lena would have to defend herself. This was their way, as Mariko had decreed long ago.

"If I had not been so fervent in leading our defense," Lena said, pausing as something detonated far below their feet, "Those miscreants would have already destroyed this ship. I see no evidence of your help in this matter, General, outside of yelling at them over the comm system. Zeke Oakfield has stolen and destroyed many of our capital ships throughout this conflict, including your Legion vessels. The *Eagle* will not be one of them."

She gave Thurman an unpleasant look, watching his bionic eyes flare in annoyance. The power cables jacked into the general's scarred metal cranium twitched with increased output. Artificial muscle fibers flexed under his oversized uniform, and servos whined as internal ammunition hoppers chugged into position within his bulk.

Lena prepared to fight, gripping her Gauss Ripper pistols under her split-backed greatcoat. Her shield generators, targeting implants and reactive armor-weave fired to life. The general was a force of cybernetic destruction, but Lena was no pushover either. Climbing to the peak of Imperial hierarchy had required stepping over many bodies, which she'd compartmentalized into a tiny corner of her mind.

"There is no need for a display of your martial prowess at this time, my honored commanders," Mariko's voice rang down from the great throne.

Lena, Thurman, and the other Imperial elites faced their lord. They were the greatest warriors and minds in an Empire built on martial might, but the emperor was far from their equal.

"Creating chaos among my staff is Commander Oakfield's goal, to delay our invasion," Mariko said, leaning forward, elbows on his knees. "Do not fall for it. Commander Oakfield knows our ways. He wants you focused on each other while his ruffians take this ship offline. We cannot allow this, my friends."

Thurman approached the throne and knelt, armored boots clomping on the rough ground.

"If it pleases you, my emperor, I would ask your permission to assume command of the flagship's defense. My *esteemed* colleague may find herself more useful ... elsewhere."

Lena didn't react.

"Denied," said Hadrian Mariko, without breaking his conversational tone. "Colonel Gallagher will subdue the traitors. I need you, General, to coordinate with Wing Commander Hauser and Admiral Shiva to ensure that the takeover of the Earthside habitats goes smoothly, once our flagship is secure. Ignore Oakfield's attacks, and focus on the operation at hand."

The chamber fell silent. Eva Hauser, the willowy raven-like coordinator of the Imperial air group, and the gigantic Admiral K. M. Shiva clapped their fists to their chests and pointed two fingers skyward in the Imperial salute.

Thurman looked enraged, spinal reinforcement plates bristling and bulging under his custom, overstretched jacket. But with a hiss of injections, he bowed his metallic skull. "Yes, my lord."

"Cheer up, General," Mariko's tone lightened. "We've finally unified our species, now you'll be the one to assure our victory over the world below."

General Thurman bowed lower. "Thank you, your Excellency."

The emperor addressed Shiva. "Admiral, is there any visible damage to this ship's exterior?"

The rotund admiral consulted a data slate. "We've tasked extravehicular crews to deal with the magazine detonations and repair any obvious damage. Overall harm to our vessel is minimal. We can utilize the Federation's orbital facilities if necessary."

"Good. We have an image to uphold," Mariko said. "Wing Commander, I trust you are preventing our escapees from leaving?"

Hauser nodded, flaring her cybernetic wing jets out behind her for emphasis. "We are flying extra patrol flights. No invasion craft will leave the *Eagle of the Ninth* until every prisoner is accounted for."

"Excellent. And what of the *Solanum*, or Anne Oakfield's shuttle?"

Shiva and Hauser exchanged glances.

"We're still searching for them," Shiva admitted.

"I see. Do not let Nightshade Squadron or any other Federation stragglers slip the net, Admiral. Now, my Praetorian daughter ..."

N9 stepped back into the light, kneeling before the emperor. "Yes, my liege?"

"Coordinate with your sisters," Mariko ordered. "I will allow you to determine how many of them to deploy into the larger Federation arcologies, like York, Mombasa, and New London. The rest will be needed for our victory ceremony."

"Of course, sire."

"Good, good," Mariko said, sliding back into his throne, hands on the stone armrests. Darkness subsumed him. The cables feeding into Mariko's head pulsed as he said, "We have spent too long on trivialities. Leave us, carry out my orders, delegate them to your subordinates where necessary. Make sure the entire landing force is ready for the celebration. Except you, Colonel Gallagher. Please stay behind. You too, Doktor."

Mariko waved a hand, and the stone doors boomed open. Two Praetorian Sisters emerged from the darkness, escorting the other Imperial leaders out of the Sanctum, leaving Lena alone with Mariko and the doktor. Thurman let out a low electronic growl as he passed. Lena ignored him, waiting until the great doors shuddered closed.

The emperor's hand appeared through the crimson haze, and beckoned. "Come forth, Colonel."

Lena approached the throne. Mariko's presence crushed Lena's mind. The room quivered. Prior to meeting Mariko for the first time, she was unaware that the human mind could feel *pain*. It was becoming harder to speak, but she managed, "How ... how may I be of further service, my lord?"

"What do you make of Commander Oakfield's attacks, Colonel Gallagher?"

This was a test. But Lena *had* noticed a method to Oakfield's madness. The damage icons spanning the *Eagle of the Ninth's* hologram formed a snaking pattern that led to the Sanctum when viewed from certain angles. Lena pointed this out, trying not to stutter.

Mariko smiled. "This is why I trust you, Colonel. You are a new addition to my high court as

fleet security chief, but you have remained a holistic thinker. The rest of my confidants are myopic, too hyper-focused on their specializations to read the Commander's intentions. Zeke is desperate to see me. I wonder why."

Lena's tortured brain couldn't formulate a reply.

Hadrian Mariko shifted forward in his seat, reflecting the red light with his glasses.

"Come closer, my dear, so I can see you," he said.

"Of ... of course, sire."

Lena approached until Mariko's psychic aura became too intense. Her knees nearly buckled.

"Bring Commander Zeke Oakfield to me, alive. We shall see what he has planned for us. And spare as many of our escaped prisoners as you can. I will use these captured warfighters as examples for the Federation's people. None within the population below will resist us when they see what we do to those who refuse our vision for mankind's future. This was foretold to me," Mariko added, glancing at the stone obelisk.

"Y-yes, my emperor," Gallagher said.

"And do not let Oakfield escape. It would be a shame to lose such an asset for our grand finale," Mariko said, without taking his eyes off the statue. Lena narrowed her eyes. Was the emperor talking to it, or her?

The pressure in Lena's head intensified even more. It took extreme effort to remain upright as Mariko's mental blades peeled back her thoughts and desires. The emperor appeared to be ten meters tall: a giant on a titanic throne. A massive shape wavered behind him, tall, rectangular and glowing pink. Then it vanished, and Mariko returned to normal size. Gallagher blinked, dazed by the hallucination.

"I elevated you to my inner cabal because of your performance during the Jovian campaigns. Do not prove my instincts wrong. Is that clear, Colonel Gallagher?"

"A-absolutely, Y-your Excellency."

"Splendid," The emperor's psychic pressure mercifully faded. "Thank you."

Lena bowed low. "It will be done, my lord."

She backed away.

The emperor regarded the tall, wiry Dr. Tobias Schipper. "Doktor, what of your strategy to deal with these rats? Nightshade has played this card one too many times."

The blond, smiling scientist, who had originated from the UEF's Euro-German habitat before defecting to the Empire, began tapping holographic keys on his upper sleeves. Mechanized arms extended from his spine through his long, off-white bodysuit and lab coat, clutching surgical instruments and scanners. A disgusting centipede-bot crawled out from behind his back and over his shoulder, staring up at the emperor.

"Yes, mein emperor," the Doktor said, with sick delight. "This little fellow is one of our newest units—those containing the brain specimens we've collected throughout the war."

"Excellent. Their first test will force the UEF escapees out of hiding for our colonel's security forces to apprehend," the emperor boomed, smiling down at the revolting centi-pod, which had a glistening cranial capsule containing a mushy grey bulb of human brain matter, punctured with all manner of wiring and cables.

The scientist grinned as the mechanical centipede scuttled around his tall, skeletally thin frame. "Very good, my lord. They have taken well to my anti-Phage measures, and will also be useful in rooting out resistance we face in the cities below."

"Exactly, Doktor," said Mariko, glancing at the obelisk statue again. "Your swarms will accomplish what our traditional forces cannot. Get to it. The faster we do this; the sooner we can bask in our victory, and save the human race from the Phage."

Doktor Schipper maintained his manic smile. "It shall be done, mein emperor."

Lena felt the doktor's metal fingertips stroking her chin moments after the Sanctum's doors had sealed.

"We will make fabulous partners in this, fraulein," Schipper whispered.

Lena strode ahead, disgusted. "I'm not your *specimen*, Doktor Schipper."

"Of course, Colonel. Not yet. But I could make you greater, like Thurman and Hauser, or the Übermensch of our glorious Legions," Schipper said, examining Lena's eyeball with a magnifying lens. She jerked away as he continued. "Your refusal of augmentation makes you vulnerable, fraulein. Especially to those like our high general. I only wish to help—"

"I can take care of myself, you cretin. I don't trust your workaround for the Nanophage, Doktor. I won't make myself vulnerable when your scientific bullshit blows up in your face."

"Some might consider that opinion to be treasonous, Colonel," Doktor Schipper said. "What would our lord think of that?"

"He'll never hear about it. Because if he does, it'll be the last thing you ever say, *Doktor*."

16 — PSIONIC POSSESSION

NEW TORONTO UNDERGROUND - RECYCK YARD 78-10D — OCT. 31, 2263 — 10:31 HOURS

"Come on, people, move it!" Sam said, holding her injured side as David, Lucia, and Jason staggered after her toward the eastern edge of the Recyck yard, trying to stay ahead of the incoming security alarms and emergency vehicles. Everyone had sunburns from the Confederate drone's incineration rays—even Lucia's tanned skin was peeling. Budgie squawked unhappily in David's hands.

Jason trailed behind the others, starting to feel strange. He tapped the in-hibitor on the back of his neck. It felt like he wasn't getting enough Osmium. He looked around at the piles of junk and garbage as they passed, but the shadows were unmoving.

The shrieks of infected bio-forms reverberated across the underground facility as they roasted in huge conflagrations of ignited industrial chemicals. David helped Sam limp along and kept a firm grip on Budgie, unwilling to let him fly around in the toxic smog above them. Phagebearers could be seen scampering through the distant infernos, risking incineration to escape the authorities. Gunfire echoed throughout the cyclopean space as Federation civil defense teams and church enforcers hunted them down. The burning stench of dying infected was worse than the garbage.

Jason's heartbeat sped up. He dimly heard his implant beeping a warning. Did it need a refill? His feet dragged on the debris-strewn ground as he rummaged through his overstuffed bag, overflowing with salvage. Where were his spare Osmium vials?

As usual, Sam and David were at each other's throats.

"And why the hell am I carrying this freakin' battery? You have to take a turn at some point, girl," David said, shifting the device's weight around.

Sam glared at him. "What are all those workouts for? Carry it yourself. I'm injured."

Jason tripped over his own feet, falling forward. Budgie flapped and croaked to get someone's attention. Lucia looked back, catching Jason before he hit the ground. "Are you alright, Jason?"

Sam and David both looked back at him.

"You look terrible," Sam exclaimed. She hobbled over and yanked Jason's collar aside to check his Osmium supply. "The drug vial's cracked; it must have happened during our fight with that big robot. It's almost empty. Good thing we brought extras."

"Uh-huh, sorry," Jason said, fighting down his nausea.

David looked into his pupils. "You gotta remember to tell us when you're running low, little brother."

Something whispered in Jason's ear. "*Find us ....*"

Out of the corner of his eye, he spotted movement in the darkness behind the garbage piles. The shadows were swirling.

"*We have the answers you seek.*"

"Shiiiiit..." Jason whispered.

Sam was rifling around in his bag, holding up a fresh Osmium canister. "Let's get one of these into you."

"Sam, I'm hearing it ..." Jason said.

"Hearing what? The Abaddon Beacon?"

"Yes!"

"Incoming," David hissed.

The generative downwash of repulsor engines ruffled their hair and tugged at loose clothing. David pointed to the junk piles. "Take cover!"

Sam pulled Jason down beside a partially melted conveyor belt. Lucia crawled under an old airbus, while David slid behind a crushed ion-impeller engine. A search light snapped on as the security aircar roared overhead. The psychic fear bubbling up within his heart was so intense that Jason retched.

Sam snapped the glowing Osmium vial into place, her eyes locked on the passing aircar. "You'll be fine, Jason. Wait for this to kick in, okay?"

"Okay," Jason said, trying to take deep breaths and not puke from fear.

David yelped, catching Sam's attention. He rolled out of his hiding spot as a Phage victim wriggled out, snarling. David beat the twitching man back with a rusted pipe.

Sam drew her sword, but it lacked battery charge.

She went after the Phagebearer anyway, using her body weight to push the unpowered blade down between his shoulder blades, pinning him face-first to the ground. That should have been fatal, but the Phagebearer was still flopping and screeching, animated beyond human endurance by its hyper-replicating Nanite infection. As Jason watched, faint trails of living shadow started to emerge from under the thrashing figure.

"It's time to leave," said David, watching as more infected emerged through nearby junk piles, fleeing from the security teams. The crowd of Phagebearers pushed everyone back toward a massive split in the habitat's superstructure that served as the eastern border of the Recyck yard.

"We're very sorry about burning your home to the ground!" Lucia called to the multiplying infected as she backed away, gasping as she peered over the cliff's edge behind her. The lake crashed rhythmically against the city's base far below, eroding the century-old docks. The smell of dead fish and rotting foundations wafted upward from far below.

The sight of the cliff shot a lightning bolt up Jason's spine. This wasn't where the Abaddon Beacon had attacked him three weeks ago, but the location was *very* similar. His heart hammered faster.

And almost like clockwork, Jason saw it: clouds of darkness were bleeding out of the garbage stacks, riding the shambling forms of the infected. Abaddon had found him.

"Oh ... shit."

"What's our exit strategy?" Lucia asked as she tried not to fall off the edge.

Sam cleaved another Phagebearer open, swung her blade around, and pointed it behind them, over the chasm. "Those guys are our ride out."

Circular drones were deploying from stasis cradles deep within the city's substructure to their left, lugging repair equipment and fire-suppressant capsules toward the Recyck yard in a long line. To their right, light from the late morning artificial sun filtered through the colossal support columns. David whacked a Phage victim and shoved him over the chasm's edge. "Last time we used those guys for a quick exit, it didn't end well."

"We don't have a choice, David," Sam yelled.

"How are we supposed to... *use* them?" Lucia asked.

"Like this!" Sam leaped off the cliff edge and grabbed the nearest drone to demonstrate. She caught hold with a single gloved hand, clasping her injured ribs with the other. The drone bleated in alarm as Sam's momentum carried the drone over the chasm, thirty meters across, in a swooping descent as her weight dragged it down to the other side.

"You're kidding me. I can't do that. It's suicide!" Lucia protested.

"Girl, if you wanna roll with us, you better get used to doing really stupid shit," David said, backing up to the edge as the infected stumbled toward them.

"I hate this so much," Lucia whined.

David grabbed a handful of Jason's jacket to prevent his brother from slipping off the side. Despite Sam refreshing his Osmium, Jason only felt worse. The stygian darkness continued to approach, flowing around the Phagebearers and creeping along the ground toward his feet. It was like the inhibitor wasn't working at all.

"Find us ..." Jason heard again. Abaddon's whispers grew louder. It was close.

Feeling behind his neck, he discovered the drug vial had partially popped out. Budgie squawked at David in a panic, trying to get his attention. Jason's mind was completely unprotected, shining bright like a psionic lighthouse beacon ... and the shadows knew it.

Sam dropped to the other side of the chasm and dumped her bag, shouting, "Come on, it's easy! You've done this tons of times, Jason. I'll catch you."

From her position below, Jason still looked drunk. Worse, Sam spotted the shadow billowing above the dozens of infected, many of whom were within meters of Jason.

"Hey, David! Check on Jason, something's wrong! Get them moving!"

David whirled around to get a look at Jason and Lucia, nearly slipping off the edge. "Oi, you two, we need to jump!"

"Jason, we have to go. There's no time!" Lucia echoed as the infected closed in on them.

More aircars approached, engines roaring.

"I ... I can't," Jason replied. The flowing, animated shadows clung to his ankles, weighing them down, sapping the strength from his body. Abaddon's whispers in his head were constant.

Sam yelled at them from across the gap. "All of you! Jump, now!"

David grabbed Jason and pointed at one of the repair drones, barking at Lucia. "Do it, or you die here."

"Shit!"

As several infected leaped toward them, everyone jumped. Lucia nearly missed her target, catching its paneling with her fingernails, screaming the whole way as Phagebearers sailed past her, plummeting into the abyss. David grabbed onto another with one hand, gripping Jason tightly with his other arm. Budgie landed on top, squawking, "*Hold on, hold on!*"

The spherical drones bucked and swerved to ditch their unauthorized cargo. Their momentum carried them in the right direction, but David and Jason's combined weight overwhelmed their drone's Nanotech repulsor drives, descending far too quickly.

"David, Lucia! Hang on, both of you!" Sam shouted, watching all of them approach. "I'll catch you, hang on!"

They were all too low for a safe landing. Lucia slammed into the jagged permacrete cliff, letting out a yelp of pain. Sam bent down and yanked her up, groaning as the effort shifted her damaged ribs. Lucia's drone shook like a wet dog and returned to the endless line of floaters approaching the fiery mess of the Recyck facility.

Sam almost tumbled off the precipice as she watched David and Jason dragging their drone down. She heard David yelling as they dropped too low, continuing beneath the overhang of broken permacrete. "Sam! SAM!"

The spherical automaton vibrated harder, loosening David's grip. Budgie squawked louder, shimmying down the bot's chassis to try and grab onto his fingers with his beak.

Then, David's fingers slipped free. Both brothers fell, screaming.

"No!" Sam screamed, dropping off the edge and grabbing a section of broken pipe sticking out of the cliff with one arm, making her ribs explode with agony—but she managed to spot Jason and David again. Sam gritted her teeth and focused her mind on their flailing bodies.

Jason felt the familiar sensation of an invisible hand grabbing him. Beside him, David howled with his eyes screwed shut, even as they stopped falling and began to rise. Jason managed to catch his bag strap as it slipped off his shoulder, but the bag swung wildly and spilled salvaged items into the void, including three spare Osmium vials—all his remaining backups.

Lucia slid to the edge of the chasm, eyes round and wide. Sam tightened her psionic grip, enduring physical agony and mental overload as she screamed, "Come on!"

"I have him!" Lucia said, grabbing David's outstretched arm, hauling him over the edge. A split second before Sam's mental abilities gave out, David and Lucia both managed to grab Jason, pulling him up. Sam's blazing pink eyes cooled, and she relaxed her Abhamic grip, panting as she hung from the cliff edge.

Seconds before Sam's fingers gave out, David's hand closed around her wrist, and he heaved Sam over the side, making her bark in pain as the rocky edge bit into her ribs.

He dragged her away from the edge, and Sam lay still, panting. "Thanks, David."

"Thank *you*," said David, helping her up into a sitting position. "We were both goners. Thank you, Sam. I mean it."

A wail of agony caught their attention. Jason convulsed, lying on the dusty ground nearby. Lucia kneeled beside him, mortified as he jerked and shuddered.

Sam gasped as she spotted the Abaddon Beacon's oozing black presence stretching across the chasm toward them, originating from where the Phagebearers shambled around on the other side, shrieking at them. Lucia stared into Jason's rolling eyes. "What the hell is happening to him?"

Everyone flinched as Jason's psionic anguish stabbed into them, causing the inky shadows to flinch backward. Sam had been preparing for this possibility, throwing up a bubble of Abhamic protection around herself, David, and Lucia—but Lucia still fell to the ground, writhing. With no tolerance to Jason's outbursts she didn't stand a chance, even with Sam's invisible mental shield. "What ... the hell ..."

Brute-forcing her way through the mental assault, Sam reached forward and grabbed Jason's face. "Look at me, Jason! The Beacon is trying to take over your mind again! We'll get some more Osmium into you, just hang on, control it!"

David slid beside her, holding his brother down as he winced from the mental pain. "You have any spare doses? We gotta calm him down before he pastes us!"

"Gimme a sec," said Sam, rummaging through her bag. The sentient blackness rose above them: approaching, invisible, and unknowable, remaining at bay for now.

Jason babbled nonsense, and his seizure worsened. The Osmium inhibitor was beeping nonstop, demanding a top-up. The shadows swirled around them, looking for an opening in Jason's defenses. David started flinging objects out of his bag in a panic, desperately searching for extra drug vials.

Jason's back arched, thumping otherworldly energies into the ground. His mind crashed against Sam's psychic wards, shoving them all backward, along with Abaddon's thick shadows. The permacrete ground cracked. A profound rumbling echoed across the chasm as structural damage rippled down into the deeper levels of the Under-city.

Sam redirected some of her Abhamic barrier away from herself and into Lucia, who stirred and groaned, holding her forehead.

"Get outta here, Lucia," Sam managed to say through gritted teeth. "While you still can."

"What? No!" Lucia cried, staring at Jason. "We have to stop this!"

Wham. Another pulse exited his body. The shadows leaped out of the way. Everyone felt a wave of deep terror—Jason's terror. Unfamiliar memories stabbed through their minds—a dark laboratory, the New Toronto streets, an old woman reaching out her hand—and a tall, dark, gleaming obelisk.

"Can't we knock him out?" Lucia asked. Sam shook her head. "He's in a loop of mental self-defence against the thing that's attacking him, but Jason's powers are uncontrollable in this state. He isn't even conscious right now, so there's no way to knock him out."

Jason's nose spurted blood all over Lucia's shoulder. Huge chunks of permacrete broke off the nearby chasm's edge, plunging into the depths. Another, stronger mental pulse propelled Lucia, Sam, and David several feet back, while Budgie tumbled into the air. The inky shadows swirled faster, approaching more aggressively in a tighter and tighter ring around the group.

Jason rose off the ground chest-first, as did any loose objects nearby. Small trickles of blood lifted off his face in perfect spherical globules. His mind was twisting gravity, warping it beyond Sam's ability to reverse as he tried to hold the penumbral blackness at bay.

"Got it," Sam said, finally finding a half-full vial of Osmium after completely emptying her bag, along with the syringe she normally used on herself. But somehow, possible in the scuffle, the injector had broken. Had that been Abaddon's doing?

Sam held it up. "Shit!"

David looked at it, swore, and rummaged faster through his own bag. "You have gotta be kidding me!"

Sam tried to slot the Osmium vial into place behind Jason's head, but he let out yet another Abhamic blast, shunting Sam away. At the same time, a violent lash of the whirling shadow whipped out and struck Sam's hand. The Osmium vial was flung free of her grasp, shattering against nearby rubble outside of the storm. That confirmed it for her, Sam knew that Abaddon was taking an active role in Jason's downward spiral, preventing them from getting him the help he needed. Getting more drugs properly plugged into his inhibitor was going to be impossible.

Sam glanced at Lucia again, yelling to be heard over the screaming winds, "I told you to leave! You'll die if we lose him. I can't protect you from what's coming."

"If I can help, I'm staying," Lucia replied.

Sam tried to protest, but could only groan from the effort of protecting their minds from Jason's attacks, plus the real-world effects of the psychic storm. Debris whirled past them, lancing a cut across David's cheek. A strange, sharp smell accompanied Jason's increasingly strong bursts of power. His eyes exploded with purplish-pink lightning, which stabbed upward and tried to incinerate the shadows looming above them. However, the shadows simply curved around the twin beams of power in retaliation, multiplying, growing, rippling, reforming, and descending. For all of Jason's power, Abaddon's psychic presence was too quick to pin down and destroy.

David yelled in triumph, pulling something out of his bag. "Bingo. Backup injector, just in case."

"All at once? That might kill him!" Sam cried as David checked the injector's Osmium level—it was full.

"Do we have a choice? It's this, or nothing. We don't have time to measure a proper dose," David said, squinting through the tornado of dust and rubble as he aimed the injector at Jason's heaving chest. Everyone was hovering a meter off the ground and rising, jackets and hair whipping in the tempest. The shadows spiraled around them, riding the gale-force winds.

"Hold him still!" David ordered.

Straining, Lucia wrenched Jason's feverish, sweaty face sideways so the energy bursting from his eyes was aimed away from David. His nose dribbled blood into the raging winds, spraying the ruins around them. Some of the Abaddon Beacon's shadowy presence took an interest in the splatter, but the vast majority of the inky black presence continued to steadily penetrate the storm, inching ever closer to them.

Reality deteriorated. Debris exploded into tinier fragments: whirling, twisting, and inverting in bubbles of warped gravitic force. Objects passed through other objects as their atomic structures lost coherency. David grabbed a tight handful of his brother's jacket collar, pointing the syringe gun at his heart.

Lucia watched carefully; teeth clenched. "Don't miss."

"Don't psyche me out," David said. He bit his lip, said a short prayer, and plunged the injector needle between two of Jason's ribs, deploying the entire dose with a sharp hiss. Osmium would reach his brain within seconds. Whether that would make a difference now was up to the universe.

Jason continued spasming. As her vision darkened, Sam thought he was going to break his own spine. The shadows were inches away from him.

"I think this is it."

"Might be," David said, with finality.

"I'm sorry," Sam said to Lucia, who still had a death-grip on Jason's head.

Lucia swallowed hard. "Me too."

Then ... Jason began to relax.

Over a harrowing half-minute, his seizure calmed, and the psionic eye-lightning ceased. The laws of physics reasserted themselves, and debris tumbled to the ground as the psychic tempest died down. Some pieces of rubble disintegrated into ash as their atomic bonds came undone. Sam let out a long breath as Abaddon's black presence retreated, deterred as the Osmium took hold of Jason, binding his brain in a chemical shield once more. Budgie landed on Jason's chest, babbling random words. Jason's breathing slowly returned to normal.

Sam felt her nose leaking warm blood for the second time in the last hour. The pressure of a thousand mountains lifted from her mind, but the mother of all headaches quickly replaced it.

"That ... was too close for comfort," Sam said, scowling as the Abaddon Beacon's grim shadow melted into the ground around them, disappearing for good.

Lucia raised a trembling finger. "Uh ... guys ..."

She pointed out several multicolored flashing lights across the chasm. Several security aircars were approaching, attracted by the commotion. UEF enforcers aimed out of the open doors, blasting Gauss rounds at the Phage-bearers on the other side of the chasm, cutting off any other chances that the Beacon had to manifest. Other vehicles were enroute, appearing through the smoke columns rising out of the Recyck facility.

"We're never gonna get a break, are we?" David remarked, hauling Jason's limp body and his bag over his shoulders. The ground rumbled, splitting under their feet.

"Doubt it. The universe hates us too much for that," Sam said as Lucia pulled her toward the dark passage ahead. Behind them, the cliff edge disintegrated, throwing up such a monumentally huge cloud of turbine-choking dust that the hovercars couldn't follow. When it cleared, the Undoc intruders had disappeared deep into the underground.

17 — THE EMPEROR AND I

Zeke shimmied through a claustrophobic ventilation duct packed with cable bundles, power junctions, and scuttling bots, dragging a stolen Imperial rifle with him. The tiny microphone implant in the back of Zeke's neck prickled. He hoped the device's transmission signal was making it off the ship.

"Commander Oakfield, come in," Jenkins crackled over his earpiece, liberated from one of the prison's storage lockers.

"Go ahead, kid," Zeke said.

Jenkins' voice was strained. "Commander, we're about to lose the brig. They're using boarding torpedo drills to bust down the door."

Shouting and muffled gunfire filtered through the link.

"Sounds like it. You alright?" Zeke asked.

Markus's voice crackled through the channel. "Not for much longer, Commander. We still have several teams left to deploy. Many of our wounded still can't move under their own steam—too many of them to carry, sir."

Zeke knew that their distraction operation would fail eventually. The enemy outnumbered his force a thousand to one on Imperial home turf. But if their plan successfully got him into the Sanctum, it would be worth it, sacrifices included. He would make sure of that.

"Alright," Zeke said, closing his eyes and suppressing his apprehension. "Here's what you're gonna do. Send out any squads who can still reach their targets. You've all been cleared of the Phage, and we know that the emperor wants us alive. Markus will know when to surrender."

"We might be past that point, sir," Jenkins said.

"Trust me, kid. You'll be fine. I'm getting close to the target," Zeke replied.

Markus came over the comm. "Good luck, sir. And if you get the chance ... take it."

"I will," Zeke said. He wouldn't hesitate if an opportunity presented itself. Not that one was likely against Mariko.

"Sir, I'm losing you," Jenkins said. Static washed through the earpiece.

"Kid? What's happening?" Zeke demanded.

"Commander, we're getting reports of ... *something*, I'm not sure."

Zeke spoke slowly. "Slow down, shrimp. Figure it out, use that big brain of yours. Take your time."

"Something is ... hitting our teams in the vent systems. They're being torn apart, sir!" Jenkins exclaimed.

"What!" Zeke said. He pressed a finger to his ear. "Repeat. Torn apart?"

Markus's voice burst onto the line. "Zeke, get out of the ducts. Get out, now!"

The comm went dead.

"Lieutenant? Jenkins, come in. Kid? Shit," Zeke said, resetting the earpiece. But the entire channel had gone offline. Everyone was on their own.

He heard an eerie skittering noise. It intensified as Zeke rolled over, looking back down the way he'd come. It sounded like a hissing, chittering wave of tiny—feet?

A side panel exploded fifty meters down the crawlspace. Dozens of dark metallic forms boiled out, swarming toward him.

"Holy shit!" Zeke shouted. He slowed his breathing, identifying the nearest access hatch. Zeke yanked his rifle up on its strap into aiming position. The rip-roar of hypersonic Gauss slugs was deafening in the confined space, but made quick work of the polymer grating.

Zeke howled in pain as spindly legs and red-hot mechanical appendages pierced his skin. The extra weight collapsed the weakened maintenance shaft.

He fell into the passageway. Dozens of two-foot-long centipede constructs with transparent, bulbous head sections followed him down. Zeke spotted a human brain within each transparent cranial bulb that was wired into the drone body, twitching with regular electric shocks, spurring the cyber-freaks into a frenzy. Mariko had finally let his insane Doktor Schipper off the proverbial leash, a grim omen for what might become of the UEF's population going forward if Zeke couldn't stop their madness.

He slammed chest-first into the deck, grabbed a snapping centipod, and smashed it against the wall, shaking his body to dislodge any others before taking off down the corridor, sucking air into his winded diaphragm.

Hundreds of them streamed after him, acting more like a liquid than solid. The lacerating pain from their vicious cutting implements gave Zeke enough adrenaline to sprint out of reach.

As he barreled down empty passages, every grate, vent, and panel exploded open and more of the little bastards flowed out. Although Zeke didn't have time to destroy a fraction of the vile things, he held his trigger down and wheezed, "Die, you little bugger shits!"

The carpet of bot-bugs sported overlapping carapace armor, resilient to magnetic accelerator slugs. Only Zeke's direct hits to their cranial bulbs ended them quickly.

He checked his comm unit, which Jenkins had loaded with a map she'd thrown together to guide him through the ship. It led to a small antechamber adjoining the emperor's inner Sanctum, used by human serviles, technicians, and automatons.

The locator app sent him dashing into a deserted mess hall with the swarm on his heels. Zeke peered down rows of tables as he ran, spotting two augmented Imperial legionaries dashing past another entrance.

One of the superhuman monsters spotted him. "There!"

Zeke swore, picking up the pace. As they brought their weapons to bear, the armored tanks stumbled right into the insectoid bodies streaming along the floor, walls, roof, and tables. Zeke didn't stick around for their frantic shrieking as the centipods devoured the Imperials, eating through the soft-seals of their warsuits to tear their flesh beneath. It was clear to Zeke that these new additions to the Imperial army weren't entirely ready for the front lines. Self-guided drone swarms were in violation of multiple laws, but the UEF and Empire had given up on those old war crime conventions long ago.

"Commander Oakfield!" A woman's voice boomed as Zeke skidded around a final corner. An Imperial officer stood in the last stretch to the Sanctum, flanked by a squad of auxiliary human guards, automatons, and several more legionnaire brutes. Clad in a greatcoat, tall hat, and out of breath, she raised a hand. "Halt!"

The wave of cyber-centipedes skittered into view, slamming into the opposite wall, boxing Zeke in.

The woman's eyes went wide, unslinging two vicious-looking pistols as she barked into her communicator. "Goddamn it, Doktor, call off your swarm. We have him!"

Zeke barreled at the waiting security team, howling an indistinct war cry, though he continued to fire his weapon at the nasty little constructs behind him.

A hateful centipede leaped onto his back, sending Zeke crashing to the deck. He grabbed the vicious thing and flung it away before it severed his spine with sparking mono-molecular pincers. More of them smothered Zeke as he scrambled backward, toward the Imperials.

"Son of a bitch," said the Solar Empire officer. "Target those things. They'll devour him."

The security squad opened fire, hosing the carpet of drones. The female officer hauled Zeke out of the mess of stabbing bodies, yelling into her wrist communicator while firing with her other hand as laser beams and Gauss rounds flared all around them.

"Doktor! Deactivate your bloody insects or I'll take them offline myself!"

"Fraulein, did I hear you correctly?" a cheerful voice replied. "Are you killing my pets?"

More centipedes latched onto Zeke's legs as he kicked and thrashed. His savior raked the murderous things with projectiles, blasting them back into the boiling mass of shiny bodies. The two legionaries waded into the swarm, stamping centipods with every thudding bootfall.

Someone lobbed a grenade. While incredibly stupid to do on any space-capable vessel, the electric charge disabled hundreds of the hissing buggers.

Zeke endured the electrocution, which passed through him into the deck. He heard power junctions shorting out under the deckplates with ear-splitting *bangs*.

"I appreciate the save," said Zeke, craning his neck to look at the Imperial officer while someone confiscated his rifle and frisked his bleeding body for other weapons, stripping off his stolen riot armor.

"Don't mistake this for saving you, Commander. And it's *Colonel*," she warned, but Zeke sensed curiosity underneath her bluster.

The woman was attractive, in her late thirties, with sun-browned skin, dark hair, and dark-green eyes. A native of Colossus Station's desert regions, maybe. Zeke also noted that she lacked obvious Nanite cyber-implants, unlike the majority of upper-level Hierarchy members.

The two augmented legionaries trained their huge weapons on him, as did most of the human auxiliary troopers. Zeke picked up a dying drone, watching as a shriveled human brain and cortex leaked out, trailing sparking cables and nutrient tubes. He wondered why Schipper hadn't used the standard synthetic CPU programming that powered regular Imperial robotic forces. Producing truly sentient positronic AI intelligences on a massive scale was costly, so the use of human brains seemed to be a sort of psychopathic middle ground for the doktor. Zeke spat on the ground in disgust.

"You gonna turn me into one of these?" he asked the Imperial officer.

To Zeke's surprise, the woman's lip curled. "Not that. Never that."

The voice on her comm unit had become less cheerful. "Colonel? An entire flock just went offline in your area, did you—"

"They're wreaking havoc on our operations, Doktor, their targeting systems are faulty," the colonel barked. "Take your insects offline before they do any more damage! Mariko *will* hear about this!"

"Colonel Gallagher, my swarms have already incapacitated twenty percent of the escaped prisoners, which is quite a successful—"

Gallagher silenced the comm, turning to her security chief. "Find the Doktor and *make* him shut down his swarm. I have no idea why he didn't build them to disable enemy units, rather than devour them. We need to take these people alive, not paint the walls with their blood."

"Affirmative, Colonel," the chief replied, running off with a full squad flanking him.

Gallagher hauled Zeke to his feet and frog-marched him away from the sparking piles of dead drones with her remaining troopers in tow. He winced as blood ran down his legs, soaking his ragged fatigues.

"So, who wants me alive?" Zeke asked as she led him toward two massive stone doors, guarded by a huge array of automated—but deactivated—cannons. *Good going, kid.*

"You've gotten the attention of someone you really shouldn't have, Commander," Colonel Gallagher said.

▲▲▲

Gallagher's legionaries frisked Zeke once more before being dumped onto a polished marble floor with unbound hands, injuries oozing blood. The vast, dark chamber's construction materials were very mass-inefficient for a space-craft. But that was how Mariko liked it: grandiose, spectacular, expensive ... *Imperial*. Strange insectoid drones skittered around the stone columns. Other stranger shapes scuttled out of sight, melting into the shadows.

Gallagher dropped to one knee—as did her two troopers.

"Excellent work, Lena," echoed a familiar voice. "Leave us."

Colonel Gallagher bowed, departing with her men.

Threaded conduits snaked across the floor and up into a massive throne. A figure sat atop it, impossible to see in the gloom—except for his eyeglasses, which burned from behind with the power of his eyes.

There was also a life-sized stone copy of the Abaddon Beacon beside the massive throne, something Zeke recognized from his time working as a guard in his father's labs. The statue loomed to one side of the chamber, cold and imposing, made from the same obsidian as everything else. Mariko was still obsessed with the damn thing, which Zeke had observed back then.

Long, gilded cables unplugged from Mariko's skull as he descended the staircase toward Zeke, boots and walking cane clacking on the heavy steps. Mariko's limping gait had worsened since Zeke had last seen him, but the mental pressure that the emperor exerted was extraordinary, far more painful than it had been all those years ago.

"You've certainly made a name for yourself during our Solar War, Zeke, but it seems that you didn't get the memo that it's *over*. You should know that your little mutiny is also over, and most survivors have been recap-tured. You've only delayed the inevitable," Hadrian Mariko said, crossing into enough light for Zeke to make out his features. Zeke didn't speak ... he couldn't get the words out.

"I'll have you know that I only wish to recapture your rampaging hooli-gans out there," Mariko said. "Under any other circumstances, each would be put to death without a second thought."

Zeke tried to focus, but formulating a response was impossible. Hadrian recognized his discomfort. "You're lucky I'm willing to let you off so easily ... old friend."

The emperor pulled a small, silver-plated box from a pocket. Inside was a syringe, loaded with a blue chemical that Zeke recognized as Osmium. Mariko gave himself a tiny shot of the drug, straight into his wrist. The mental pressure receded, capped like a leaking nuclear reactor. Once it didn't feel like his brain was about to leak out his ears, Zeke relaxed.

Hadrian extended his hand, each finger decorated by dark volcanic rings. "Pardon me, it takes a moment to ... rein myself in. You're not used to what I've become."

"And what have you become, Hadrian?" Zeke ignored Hadrian's assistance, struggling to his feet.

Hadrian Mariko stepped back, wiping his glasses with a cloth. "Sometimes I wonder about that myself."

"You're still taking the blue stuff. Don't tell me that our all-powerful emperor is reliant on an inhibitor drug to control himself," Zeke said.

"I do this as a courtesy, my friend," Mariko replied politely. "This is an important reunion; I can't have you writhing on the floor for it."

"Right," Zeke folded his arms, ignoring the stinging pain in his legs. He wondered if the insanity gripping his former friend was a byproduct of Mariko's Abhamic empowerment, poisoning his once-moral soul. That was the easy answer, because alternatively, Mariko was still suffering from the influence of the Abaddon Beacon, as Zeke's father had theorized long ago. It brought out the power-hungry shadow that existed within all men, and that had consumed his former friend. The obelisk had been working on Hadrian for a very long time.

"Ah, you think me a monster?" the emperor asked. "Well, you're right—I am one. I've done what's necessary to pull our species out of its nosedive. Your father's experiments gave me the greatest of gifts. He transformed me into something that defies description, and now I'm going to save the human race and transform it into something far greater."

"It's inflated your ego to a point that defies description, too," Zeke said.

"Well, becoming what the old-world religions described as a *God* really alters one's perspective on things," Mariko said. He glanced at Zeke's shaking legs, beckoning to the darkness. "Get over here, treat his wounds. I won't let an old friend bleed out on my throne room floor."

A medical bot floated over from a hidden alcove, spraying disinfectant into Zeke's lacerations.

"Old friend, huh?" Zeke asked.

Mariko leaned against the stone operation table's edge, willowy hands resting on his gilded cane. "Of course."

"Interesting interior decor you've got in here," Zeke said, raising an eyebrow as he looked around, allowing the robot to do its work on his various injuries, including his jaw. "Takes a certain type to live in a place like this."

Mariko grinned. "It has a certain effect on people. The igneous rock was cut from Luna, the same material used in the foundations of Colossus. My family owned the quarry where it was mined, you know, along with much of our home-world's moon, before they lost everything. You could say that they helped shape my future empire's beginnings."

"I see. Humble beginnings."

"Says the one who was sired by the great Dr. Avery Oakfield."

The medical bot floated away. The analgesics helped to dull the stinging pain. Zeke could now properly focus on the job. "Why talk to me at all? I'm small potatoes compared to conquering the Federation."

"Give yourself more credit, Zeke. I knew you before all this started," Mariko said. "Despite the Solar War's outcome, we're still in a very difficult situation as a species. I've been surrounded with power-hungry maniacs for a long time, but I can actually collaborate with you. We did good work together once, long ago. I want that again. I want you to join me, Zeke."

His demeanor was personable—carefully crafted. Mariko rested a delicate hand on Zeke's bulging shoulder.

"You want my help now? We've been on opposite sides of a war, Hadrian," Zeke said. "Those 'power hungry maniacs' burned the Mars colony to the ground, and a hundred other places besides. I've seen mass murder on a scale unheard of since the Great War. Even if you have regrets, none of that is excusable."

"The war is over now, and what you perceived as war crimes were nothing more than infection control," Mariko explained. "Our 'decimations' prevented the Phage from spreading. Imperial annexation operations are designed to minimize casualties, preserving our infrastructure for future use by those strong enough to resist the plague. The Mars colony was especially infested, thus requiring total immolation. Many of the people you saved there were already dead men walking. The UEF has lost control over their Nanophage outbreak, under your father's watch, no less."

"But the Nanophage is treatable. Its victims don't need to be killed, Hadrian. They—"

"Do you know the incidence of infection on Colossus?" Mariko interrupted. "Even with hundreds of millions packed into one habitat, it's less than ten percent of the UEF's average, because we do not suffer the infected to live, at any stage of the condition. Meanwhile, the Federation's cities are drowning in the plague. While there are treatments available, we cannot afford to deploy such specialized equipment on a large scale. The Phage simply spreads too fast. If the UEF won't stop the outbreak from consuming our remaining gene pool—then *we* will."

"But everything you've done has only spread the Phage further. Your armies have the highest concentration of the plague out of any other organized group in the Sol System," Zeke said.

"No, they don't. Doktor Schipper's upgrades on your father's Nanite formulas have seen to that," said the emperor, strolling away. "If Avery had taken my advice and spent more time properly translating the Abaddon Beacon's technological gifts, then the UEF's Phage problem would've been solved years ago. His negligence—and that of the Strategos Council—has poisoned the Federation for years. Our brilliant Doktor has re-engineered our Nanotech into something far safer for human use—especially our cybernetics."

Zeke had to keep the conversation going. "You're using my father's negligence as an excuse for war crimes?"

"Not an excuse," the emperor replied. "Once the Nanophage reaches a certain threshold, only the death of the host will kill it. That holds true for our entire species. We must cut out the cancer before it kills us all. You're aware of the projections, yes?"

"What projections?" Zeke asked.

"Only fifty years remain until the home-world becomes unlivable again for the majority of the UEF population. Colossus isn't far behind. We're running out of every natural resource. The Earthside habitats are slowly failing. Some have already fallen to the elements. Birth rates are plummeting throughout the Federation and the Empire, so much that our population's decline will soon be past the point of no return. We're losing too many people to the Phage, to the malaise of modern living, to general attrition. We're mined out. The cradle is empty. The only way to reverse this decline is to free ourselves from this star system and reach other habitable worlds, give our people something more to *strive* for again. Once I have the Abaddon Beacon under my control ... we can move forward into our new era, as it has told me many times. I want you to be a part of that."

"But you failed to communicate with the darned thing, Hadrian. I was there for it," Zeke pointed out.

"True. I wasn't powerful enough to commune with the artifact when my abilities were in their infancy. But now... I hear it every day." Mariko's eyes flared, and Zeke momentarily felt the pain in his head return. "I think even your father would admit, I've finally become what he always intended me to be. It just took longer than expected. I will use the Beacon to save us."

"Fine, enough mumbo-jumbo. What do you want from me?" Zeke asked.

Hadrian grinned. "A straight shooter, as always. Very well, here's my offer: I want you to help me peacefully annex the UEF, and work with me to ensure lasting peace afterward. You'll be rewarded beyond your wildest dreams, Zeke. You can shape mankind's future in the way that I know you've always wanted."

"No one should have that kind of power. You offered Anne a similar deal, and look where that got her."

"Your sister betrayed my trust, Zeke. I need a reliable right-hand man. Let go of the UEF's propaganda."

"I'm not blind to the Federation's decline," Zeke said. "I know what I'm defending. The tyranny, the Church—it's all crap, held together by cowards who can't solve the problems they created, so they punish the people who can. I get it. But it doesn't justify what you did to the Colossi people, and to us during the war. There's no need for mass murder to stop the Phage."

"I never wanted this, Zeke," Mariko said. "But you weren't there on Colossus, you didn't see how bad things were getting. When the plague grew out of control, we couldn't beat it conventionally. My armies were full of people who could never do what was required to stop it, not to their own families. I ... regret what they had to become, but my newly birthed legionaries successfully pushed back the Phage, and they will soon cleanse the UEF too. Once I've taken full control of Abaddon and prevented the Phage from spreading ever again, their purpose will be at an end. Your sister never understood that."

"And you tried to kill her for it? For not understanding?" Zeke asked.

"Anne likes to give people a curated version of events, I imagine," Mariko replied. "But what your sister will tell you about her time with me on Colossus, and what actually happened during our time together are two different realities. Anne's not nearly as innocent as she'd have you believe. Her guilt is all that drives her. I'm a convenient target for her self-hatred."

Zeke growled to himself. "You can't turn me against her, Hadrian. Don't even try."

"I've never lied to you, Zeke. Anne's biomechanical skills were instrumental in the alterations that made our legionaries capable of purging their friends and countrymen. She didn't have the stomach for the follow-through. I know I can't convince you, but you'll see the truth for yourself, in time," Mariko said, rounding the table, gliding his fingernail along the rough texture. The glow from the holo-surface turned his glasses bright red, like freshly oxygenated blood.

"You want to know why I joined the military, before this war started?" Zeke asked, keeping his inner thoughts carefully guarded with layers of emotion to throw Mariko off.

"Why?"

"I swore that I'd avenge my sister," said Zeke, squaring his shoulders.

"Well, here I am," Hadrian said. "Take your shot."

"I'm not a dumbass, Hadrian."

"Didn't think you were."

"But we both know that Anne's alive. You failed to kill her."

"Then there's no vengeance required!" Hadrian said with a smile, "Let bygones be bygones. There's no reason for you to hate me. We can still work together, Zeke. I need my friend back."

"You're not making a very good case, Hadrian."

Mariko rolled his eyes, coming around the holo-tank table and playfully elbowing him.

"You're hopeless, Commander. Let it go. I see your emotions as clearly as I see you standing here before me," Mariko said, tapping his temple. "Anger is pointless. I am the future—and *you* can become part of it. The slaughter will soon be at an end."

"I doubt that," Zeke said.

"Whatever harebrained scheme you're concocting is irrelevant," Hadrian Mariko said, waving a hand. "No individual or force in the Sol system can challenge me now. The Abaddon Beacon has shown me that. And I have no desire to kill your sister twice, despite her crimes. She's proven far more useful alive. Sacrificing such a beautiful mind would be a travesty, don't you think?"

The vast chamber went deathly quiet. Zeke was so close to what he needed. He had to take his chance.

"So, if I were to join you—hypothetically—what dirty work would you have me do? What do you have planned?" he asked.

The emperor backed away toward his throne. Zeke's head started to pound again as Mariko's psychic presence crept back into the room, gradually returning as the Osmium microdose began to wear off.

Mariko's voice lowered, like blood sinking into sand. "On this day of our greatest victory, I will lead my people to the UEF's capital city, New Toronto, where a grand victory celebration will be held on the same ground where the war began. I've already seen this. All of Federation command will be present—even your spineless father. There, the people will learn the nature of their betrayal, and I will win their hearts."

"And what about us? My people, on this ship?"

Mariko mounted the stairs, raising his arms.

"That's the best part. You will be the centerpiece of it, Zeke. Once I've dealt with the criminals in the UEF government, I'll ask you, their greatest hero, to join me. Amnesty will be offered for those who are free of the Phage. Those who refuse our generosity will be ... left behind. The Beacon has shown me all this, and more."

Zeke stared at him. "The Abaddon Beacon ... *showed* you?"

"Rest assured that we're in good hands, Zeke. Very good hands. Abaddon has revealed the future to me. There is nothing you can do to endanger that," Mariko said, smiling. Zeke chose not to react. Perhaps his old friend really was insane.

The emperor settled onto his throne, surrounded by stygian darkness again, except for his radiant glasses. Cables reconnected into his scalp with sharp hisses. His voice echoed out of the shadows, bouncing off the Abaddon statue to his left. "You shall decide, before your comrades and all of the Federation, which choice to make. Securing the future of our species, or your damnation. I pray, my old friend, that you make the right choice."

The doors of Mariko's Sanctum reopened with a reverberating *boom*. Colonel Lena Gallagher returned, but before she came within earshot, Zeke muttered to himself, "Hope ya got all that, sister."

18 — ATONEMENT

"I repeat, hope you got all that, Anne," Zeke's voice crackled. The signal was weak, but his words were clear. Anne Oakfield closed her eyes. Their gamble had *worked*.

"Thank you, Zeke."

Lincoln stood on the *Solanum*'s command bridge communicator table with an open beak, playing the drama out loud and saving a copy for later analysis. Despite Imperial jamming, the tactical table's hologram showed that the encrypted signal beaming from Zeke's implant was still detectable over the vast distance between the *Solanum* and the heart of the Imperial fleet.

Anne turned to Lieutenant Janelle Luther. Three other people—Nightshade's company captains, two men and one woman—waited around the table.

"Is that satisfactory?" asked Anne, peering down at Luther as the transmission went silent.

The lieutenant grinned. "The madman really did it. We have our target's future location. Well done, Anne."

"It was mostly Zeke's work. But thank you, Lieutenant Luther," Anne said.

"Actually ... it's *Lieutenant-Commander* now, if I understood your brother's message correctly. Temporarily, of course," Luther said. She glanced at the other Nightshade captains across the table, but they all nodded.

"He mentioned that you'd be in charge, yes," Anne said.

"And his message also made it clear that you were our best source of information on Mariko, a 'consultant' of sorts," Luther said. "I'm sure you've got some insights to share."

Anne nodded. "You could say that."

Luther looked at Anne sideways for a moment, then she asked. "The emperor said something about an 'Abaddon Beacon,' and knowing the future. What's that all about?"

Anne considered how much to reveal. "The Beacon isn't public knowledge, but the short version is that it's a very powerful alien artifact controlled by our government, found more than a century ago. It was a major accelerant in the Great War, forcing the UEF and Confederacy to take greater and greater risks to obtain it and its technologies, destroying the planet in the process. My father, the science minister, has been involved with researching it. As for Abaddon showing Mariko the future ... I'd chalk that up to insanity. He thinks he's omniscient."

"I see," Luther said. The other company captains shifted uncomfortably.

Lincoln looked at Anne for instructions, but she twirled a finger. "Keep the broadcast going. It will help us track Zeke's location. The emperor wants them all alive and present for his 'victory ceremony'."

"Of course," Luther replied, still processing everything they'd overheard. "But, before our briefing, I have another question. It ... sounded like the emperor knew Zeke, from before the war? And yourself?"

"Ah," Anne said, expecting this question. "We both knew him, but I'd rather let Zeke speak for himself. He's never shown loyalty to Mariko, only to his family, and to you. He allowed himself to be captured to get us the information we need. That alone proves his commitment. Please don't judge my brother because of whom he associated with, long before this all began. As for myself ... yes, I have a long history with the emperor. I'm not proud of it."

"I see," said Luther. "Zeke has some explaining to do, but I agree that I'd rather hear it from him."

She glanced around at Nightshade's other captains, but they all nodded again.

"I've got a question!" an Australian-accented man said. The wiry, mustached helmsman leaned over the railing that divided the ship's comms center and command bridge. Anne guessed he was from the Brisbane habitat.

"Yes, Captain Brogan?" Luther asked him.

Brogan pointed to the main viewscreen, displaying the planet and its orbital defenses, still being absorbed by the invasion fleet. No stealth ship had windows, so this was a camera view, allowing the *Solanum* to retain its heat and light emissions.

"When are we landing, Lieutenant-Commander?" Brogan asked. "They're sniffing around for us, and we need to plot a course through their blockade. Getting to the surface is going to take some time."

"We need to be down there sooner rather than later," Luther replied. "We'll head down to the main hangar's briefing area so the rest of the Squadron can be present to hear our incursion strategy, which will dictate where we land this ship."

"I'd like to see Nightshade's capabilities on the way, if that's alright," Anne added.

"Our lead operators will be happy to oblige," Luther gestured to the company captains, who nodded and turned to leave, followed by Brogan.

Anne gestured to Lincoln. "Stay here, my friend. Record anything else that Zeke sends through, anything that might be pertinent."

The bird blurted an affirmative as Anne followed everyone off the command bridge.

The lower decks of the stealth prowler buzzed with personnel readying for deployment. Anne experienced a shiver of excitement. The last time she had planned an operation with such elite fighters had been during her rebellion against Mariko's empire aboard Colossus, before the uprising had been put down and destroyed by the emperor's Praetorians.

"What are they doing?" she asked as the group passed an open storage bay. Operators practiced mind-bending Jetkit maneuvers around the huge space, dodging dummy rounds fired by automated turrets, completely at home with no concept of up or down. Precious few souls had the talent to control such complicated EVA equipment, let alone in combat.

"They're doing last minute checks on a new version of our jets—more powerful and maneuverable than before, even harder for machine intelligences to track. They've been successful enough that the commander ordered our fabricators to outfit all three companies before he left for *Refit One*," said the captain to Anne's left. "I'm Captain Burnaby, first company. It's a pleasure to meet the sibling of our fearless leader."

"Likewise, Captain," Anne shook his hand.

"My unit is comprised of omnidirectional assault infantry, specializing in full-gravity environments," Burnaby said. "Our favorite targets are the emperor's bastard legionaries—we've got confirmed kills from every legion."

Tall and in his late forties, Burnaby had a charming northern British accent and a mustache, wearing Nightshade's flower insignia on his short-brimmed cap. He held an unlit cigar in his teeth, which seemed to be common among the operators.

Anne held up her hand, allowing a short burst to emit from her wrist-mounted jet. "You've perfected my crappy old design."

"You know what they say about imitation, ma'am. I've always wanted to see the original pioneer of our Jetkit tactics in action," replied Burnaby. Anne tried to stifle her pride.

"And I'd love to see how you use those techniques en-masse," Anne said.

"Oh, it's a sight to behold," Captain Burnaby said, chewing on his cigar.

They passed a massive armory, where fabricator bays churned out weapons, highly advanced power-armor suits, Gauss ammunition blocks, and other supplies from stockpiles of raw materials and nanite vats.

"What's the supply situation?" Anne asked. Luther gestured to the armory. "We stopped at one of our private waystations before entering Earth orbit. Our stockpiles are fuller than they've been at any other point during the war. We're ready for anything."

"I see. And Nightshade is three companies in total?" asked Anne. "I thought you were far more numerous. Based on the stories, anyway."

The largest captain spoke, "More manpower would impede us. Even before we adopted Jetkit technology as a calling card, Nightshade was a force multiplier, not a front-line unit. We're small, but Zeke only picks the best."

He extended a hand to Anne. "Captain Ossington, zero-gravity combat specialist and third company commander."

Ossington's grip enveloped Anne's as they shook. He was even taller than she was, three times as wide, and his voice sounded like he was from the Native American arcology. "So, we're going to take out the big man?"

"We will, I have no doubt of that," Anne confirmed.

Ossington stroked his long braid. "I never imagined we'd actually get the chance at this. My company focuses on zero-G and vacuum-based warfare. We also maintain the reserve force, accounting for our non-combat specialists and civilian contractors."

Ossington gestured to another converted training area, where the gravity-plating had been turned off as his operators performed amazingly complex maneuvers.

"Nightshade can't be accused of under-training," Anne said.

"Definitely not," Ossington agreed.

"Finally, Captain Chiang's outfit, second company, is comprised of airborne infantry with armored support," Luther said, nodding to the final captain, who still hadn't said a word to Anne.

Chiang was a well-conditioned, tan-skinned woman wearing a beret, bionic eye, and partial cyber-torso replacement. If Anne were to guess, she had the look of a Colossi native. Many had originated from the East Asian and South American protectorates in the off-world exodus after the Great War with the Confederacy.

Chiang spoke, "Captain Chiang, ma'am. Second company leader."

She was far terser than her compatriots, with a hint of an accent. Anne shook Chiang's hand anyway. Anne's systems noted that the captain's hand was quavering ... was it from nerves, or anger?

"Good to meet you, Captain," she said, putting Chiang's awkwardness aside as they approached their destination: the main hangar doors.

"Seeing all this, it's easy to believe that you have such a long list of battle honors," Anne remarked. Luther picked up the conversation when Captain Chiang didn't respond. "You flatter us, Anne. But it's true, your brother has created a lean, mean, fighting machine."

"And the last chance we have to stop the emperor," Anne said.

"Amen to that," Luther said.

The group emerged into the *Solanum*'s primary deployment hangar, lined with gunships, dropships, and vehicle storage bays. The noise was overwhelming, from screaming power tools in the machine shop alcoves, to barking staff sergeants, and the clatter of boots on the deck as personnel ran every which way, servicing Nightshade's limited complement of gunships and ground transports. Anne's shuttle was still parked near the hangar's rear entrance. Luther navigated through the organized chaos toward an improvised operations center.

Word had spread faster than light across the ship. Every operator they passed gave Anne a quick once-over, with varying reactions to her appearance and massive hat. Lieutenant Luther raised her voice, gesturing to the hangar around them. "Welcome to grunt country, Anne. Gather round, folks."

Groups of lower-ranked personnel approached the senior officers to watch the briefing, intrigued by the newcomer. More operators clattered down metal stairways from the barracks quarters situated above the hangar. Luther activated a topographical map of the New Toronto habitat from a waist-high holoprojection unit.

"First order of business is to determine a landing zone," Luther said. "We won't be pod-dropping from orbit, as that'll reveal the *Solanum*'s position to the Imperials. We need to find somewhere to land, with enough time to approach the strike zone from underground. We also need time to survey the target area and prepare the terrain."

Captain Brogan raised an eyebrow. "Our stealth systems only allow us to avoid sensor detection. We'll be very visible on the ground, to either cameras or the naked eye. New Toronto's a serious habitat with a lot of space, but this old girl isn't small. It's not like stashing a boosted car in the local garage."

"Sounds like you've been on the wrong side of the law," Anne remarked. Brogan winked. "I suppose you'd know all about that, *Outlaw of Colossus*."

"You've got me there. Anyway, rather than landing on the city's surface level, I suggest we try underground," Anne continued. "New Toronto's Under-city sublayers are gigantic, and honeycombed with areas large enough to land this ship. If the *Solanum* can be furnished with a fake ident-code to fool air traffic control, we can bypass the atmo-shield and divert into the Under-city."

"That's a tall order, but we can try it. The *Solanum*'s had many fake names and titles over the years. I'm sure one of them can bamboozle ATC," Brogan said.

"Very well, do it," said Luther. "And launch our probes to scan for a suitable landing zone underground while we navigate the blockade. Unless anyone's opposed?"

No one spoke.

"Alright, then. Is this a real-time feed?" Brogan asked, looking at the hologram.

"Yes. We'll have cover if we stick to heavy commercial traffic on the way down," said Luther.

Hundreds of tiny shapes moved around the habitat holo-image, passing through the atmospheric containment shield that kept the poisoned sky at bay. Despite every effort to re-terraform the planet after all the accumulated damage over the last two centuries, Anne felt a small twinge of sadness that the habitat domes were the best that could be done to make the planet livable again—and with the impending invasion, even these were now under threat.

She looked at Brogan. "Civilian activity will grind to a halt ahead of the Imperial invasion. Please get us down there before that happens."

"Roger that, ma'am. Ain't nothing we can't handle. Only the largest orbital blockade in human history to slip past, nothing special," Brogan saluted Luther. "Lieutenant-Commander."

The captain left at a jog, returning to the bridge.

"The emperor mentioned a victory ceremony in Zeke's transmission," Luther said. "He wanted to end the war where it was declared, so it'll be held near the UEF Headquarters."

Using the hologram's control board, she enlarged a massive central clearing in the downtown core. "Questions, concerns, opinions?"

"That's an optimal location for our omni-dimensional gear," said Captain Ossington, pointing out the super-skyscrapers bracketing the square. "Plenty of room to maneuver, lots of high ground, perfect for surveillance and aerial-ranged attacks. The buildings are close enough for slingshot grappling maneuvers. Many avenues for retreat or regroup. It's almost *too* perfect."

"They'll have those buildings under close guard," Captain Chiang cut in, her mechno-eye flashing red. "The Imperials will lock them down before anyone more important than a general steps into the open."

She highlighted different structures in the holo-display. "That's thirty-six separate skyscrapers—not counting the UEF HQ building. We can't clear them all before we strike."

"Nightshade Squadron is a mobile force, yes? Good at concealment?" Anne asked.

Chiang nodded, but her eyes didn't meet Anne's round-lensed glasses.

"If we can't secure the entire zone, we could use Nightshade's mobility to our advantage," said Anne. "Teams can be seeded everywhere: among the crowds, in buildings, and underground. Each squad will have the freedom to displace as needed to avoid detection. If you have chameleonic gear, even better. When we strike, we'll create as much chaos as possible to prevent anyone from coming to Mariko's aid."

"This can be done," Ossington said. "We have attack protocols that are designed to stir up commotion while limiting collateral damage—which will be key, with civilians present. Some of those people down there might be our families."

Anne nodded. "While we evacuate civilians and lay waste to the Imperial victory parade formations, we need to focus a significant assault on the emperor himself to break down his psychic barrier."

"I'm sorry, did you say 'psychic barrier'?" asked Burnaby, removing his unlit cigar from his mouth.

"Yes. What about it?"

"We have very little intel about the emperor's ... 'esoteric' abilities. What can you tell us? How much damage can he take?" Captain Burnaby asked.

"His psy-shield is powered by his mind, so if he's focused, Mariko is practically invulnerable," Anne explained. "He can overwhelm the mental defenses of hundreds of people at once, making you dance like a puppet if you're in his sensory range. You cannot resist, no matter how strong-willed you think you are. The emperor can create illusions or warp reality, and he may have developed new tricks that I don't know about. The only time I've seen him tested is when I fought him, and we all know how *that* turned out."

Anne fell silent, leaving only the sound of hangar operations around them.

"How do we beat him, then?" asked Luther.

"Simply put, we need to hit Mariko with enough firepower to shake his composure. We keep him focused on shielding himself instead of neutralizing us with his psionics, while deterring anyone else from intervening," said Anne. "If we strain him long enough, his focus will collapse, then he'll be vulnerable. Certain drugs exist that can mute the parts of the human brain that channel these psychic abilities, but I doubt we'll be able to get close enough to use those. The Imperial fleet presence will prevent anything like orbital bombardment or a nuclear strike. If all else fails, I suppose we could drop a building on him. Or this ship."

"You'll want to run that by Captain Brogan, sir. This ship is his baby," Luther said.

"I wasn't serious. We may need the *Solanum* for our getaway," replied Anne.

"What other forces will be present? Mariko's Praetorians are going to be there. They'll complicate the situation," said Captain Chiang.

"Two or four of the Sisterhood will be there, perhaps more," Anne said. "Remember that the Praetorians also act as field commanders, extensions of the emperor's will. We cannot allow them to rally his forces against us once we start the attack."

"Even one Sister Praetorian is a danger," argued Chiang, voice rising. Her mechno-eye flashed again. "Anytime they appear, we take casualties, and we've never left a scratch on them. Their magic, or psychic abilities—whatever you call them—are impenetrable. And the emperor sounds more dangerous than they are. This reeks like a trap ... for *us*."

"I've dealt with Mariko's Praetorians before," Anne said. "With the element of surprise and firepower of Nightshade Squadron, we have the best chance of defeating them."

Lieutenant Luther piped up. "Does the emperor have any obvious weaknesses that you know of, other than simple, overwhelming force?"

Anne thought for a moment. "No."

"None?"

"None," Anne repeated. "He's weak in body, but we're not fighting him physically. We're fighting Mariko's *mind*. Even if he doesn't see this coming, Mariko will be quick to react to us. Unless we had an equal or greater psychic being to throw at him, our only chance is to hit him as hard as we can, for as long as we can. He'll break, eventually."

"Looks like we've got an uphill battle on our hands," said Luther.

"Not just an uphill battle," Captain Chiang said, agitation growing. "This sounds like a suicide mission. We still haven't accounted for Mariko's other generals, who are massive threats on their own. Our losses will be enormous. Half the Solar Empire will be there, in person. Against three hundred operators, as good as we are, these are *impossible* odds."

Burnaby and Ossington watched Chiang carefully.

"What's our alternative?" Anne said, fixing the argumentative captain with an iron stare. "What would you have us do? Go into hiding? Submit to Mariko's new order? Do his dirty work, kill for him? Because those are our options if we don't act."

Chiang didn't reply, stiffening.

"My brother didn't walk into the viper's den for nothing. Don't let his sacrifice be in vain," Anne said.

Captain Chiang ground her teeth. "How do we know that Zeke's so-called *intel* is authentic?"

"You can trace Lincoln's signal, if you—" Anne said.

"That signal could be coming from anywhere, bounced off any transmitter," sneered Chiang. "We can fake voices, too. Zeke's or Mariko's."

"Why would I fabricate all of this?" Anne asked.

"And," Chiang continued. "Those authentication codes on the commander's ID tags—how can we be sure he gave them to you? He could be lying dead aboard that orbital station for all we know."

A twinkle of rage flashed across Anne's scarred face. She suppressed all emotion as she approached Chiang, towering over the shorter woman.

"Are you implying that I'm taking advantage of my brother?" Anne asked.

"I'm not *implying* anything," Chiang said. "I mean it. Until we have concrete proof that he really did sign off on this insane operation, we should reconsider what we're doing ... and who we're doing it with."

Silence fell. The ship rumbled as it neared the planet, sliding past Imperial warships. Luther stepped in between Anne and Chiang. "Let's all take a breath. Tensions are high. Nightshade Squadron has entered uncharted waters, with the Federation out of commission and the Empire about to invade. How about we—"

"I'm from Colossus. So is my family, from long before the war. You're responsible for what happened to them, *Outlaw of Colossus*," Chiang accused, ignoring Luther. "We heard as much from Mariko himself."

"Captain, you will restrain your tone when addressing our guest—" Luther said.

"No. Go on, Captain Chiang. It's fine. I'd like to hear this," said Anne, trying to control her anger.

"I witnessed Mariko's takeover. You were his partner, his right hand, his way into the UEF's government aboard Colossus," Chiang sneered. "Living under Federation rule was atrocious. Everyone knew we needed change. We believed that Mariko and his partner—*you*—were our best chance at change, so we all cheered you on. But after he usurped the government and declared himself emperor, my family suffered. Everyone suffered. My parents managed to send me off-station before they locked Colossus down. But I saw you before I left, during one of the first *purges*. Your legionaries killed my sister for having the Phage. That's where I lost my eye."

Luther, Burnaby, and Ossington all glanced at Anne.

"Captain Chiang, I'm sorry for what happened to your family, and my role in it. I am not the same person now that I was then," Anne said. "I was there as a liaison with the Colossus Lower City's magistrate. The Nanophage was a major problem on Colossus, as it is everywhere now. I didn't act fast enough to stop Mariko's plans with those troops, and for that, I apologize."

"A likely story," snapped Chiang. "Even if that's true, it only confirms that you're willing to do anything to bring him down—including sacrificing Nightshade to do it. We won't be pawns in your revenge quest."

Burnaby and Ossington exchanged looks.

"Perhaps we should add *verification* to our objectives," said Luther. "That can be our compromise, finding Zeke before initiating the final phase of the operation. He can confirm everything himself before we strike at the emperor."

Chiang wasn't done, lost in her anger. The shorter woman stared up into Anne's dead cyber-eyes. Anne's onboard combat systems responded to Chiang's aggression—painting the captain with targeting icons, which she ignored.

"His empire only exists because of you," Chiang said. "Millions on Colossus would still be alive if *you* hadn't helped him raise his bastard legionaries. Mariko may have dumped you out of an airlock when he was finished with you, but you're still responsible for all of this."

"Yes, I am. He wasn't lying about that," Anne admitted, fighting down waves of guilt. "My biggest regret is leaving my father's research programs to join Mariko. The Nanophage may not have spread so quickly if I'd stayed to keep my father's work on course. I have certain ... *abilities* that were integral to his technological research programs. But when I left to join Mariko, I had faith that our fight against the Federation's injustices was the right path, until everything went wrong."

Anne remembered her terror when she'd realized what the emperor's proto-warriors were about to do. The Colossi crowds had given her the same look of fear—especially the children. The legionaries under Anne's command had returned positive readings on a handful of Phage infections ... then they had opened fire with their early-series gauss rifles, without waiting for orders. The noise, the *screaming*, had been unbearable. It was then that

Anne realized that Hadrian didn't trust her, despite everything they'd been through. It was only the first Nanophage purge, only one situation in the deep, dark ocean of her guilt, threatening to sweep her away. That event, among others, had set Anne on her path to the confrontation with the emperor-to-be.

As the memories tore through her mind, Anne's cybernetic knee buckled. She gripped the edge of the holo-table for support, cyber-narcolepsy hitting hard. The Phage was advancing through her body, and Anne would need to visit her repair suite again soon. Being around these high-performing operators made her weakness even more embarrassing.

"Can we help you, Anne?" Luther asked, holding out a hand.

Anne shook her head. "I ... I'm fine."

Chiang looked ready to lay on more punishment, but Anne snapped up a finger for pause, hiding her trembling cyber-hand behind her greatcoat.

"That's enough, Captain," Anne said. "When the emperor cast my body from the highest tower on Colossus—yes, I swore revenge. Who wouldn't? I witnessed the effects of the Empire I helped create, wandering the station's outer wastes. I saw the mountains of dead, the burning of entire communities, the degeneration of Mariko's legions into psychopathic killers. There isn't a single moment now where I don't regret what I did to help him. The emperor may have cost you an eye ... but remember that he cost me both of mine."

Chiang opened her mouth, but Anne silenced her again with a dangerous finger. The Nightshade captain took an involuntary step back.

Anne's voice was a low growl as she rose to full height, praying that her body wouldn't give out. "I no longer seek revenge, only atonement. Maybe you see no difference between the two, but they are different to me. And ... please, *never* imply that I would step over my brother's corpse to drag you into the abyss with me. If I hadn't found Zeke, I would've done this alone. We can't bring your sister back, Captain Chiang. But we can bring the one responsible for her death to justice. That's why I'm here. I need your help to do that."

"Justice requires a trial. This operation is an execution," Luther pointed out.

"That's true, but Mariko is too dangerous to be kept alive. We're beyond judges and juries now," Anne said, fighting off her body's urge to shiver and shake.

Lincoln surprised everyone with a swift descent from the hangar's rafters. He landed on the edge of the holo-projection unit and stared up at Anne, who stroked the bird's chrome feathers.

Her twin hearts slowed down, and Anne's combat systems ended their alert in her head's-up display. Her cyber-narcolepsy began to pass.

After a long silence, Ossington laid a huge hand on Anne's shoulder, glancing at the others. "The way I see it, this woman has fought Mariko's Empire alone for longer than anyone else. It has affected her in a way that none of us can fully understand. Anne has come to us to help her finish a nightmare that she helped start. Despite her past mistakes, I think we should oblige her."

Ossington eyed Chiang in particular.

"What about afterward?" Chiang asked. "Killing the emperor is the first step. Who will lead the Federation? Surely not the corrupt fools who got us into this mess in the first place."

"Absolutely not. Zeke has the qualities needed to lead us until we can raise a new government," said Anne, steadying her voice again. "I would not be appropriate for leadership because of my past deeds. There'll be a power vacuum after Mariko is gone, so we'll need to ensure that his warlords aren't able to plunge the Sol System back into conflict."

"We'll confirm Anne's statements before proceeding," Burnaby said, directing this at Chiang. "We have every reason to distrust her, but the emperor's takeover of the Federation will cause much more suffering if we don't do this. We have the power to shut that door in his face. Our loved ones are counting on us."

"Good thing Nightshade specializes in unrealistic probabilities of success," said Luther.

"And achieving the impossible," agreed Burnaby. Ossington grinned, gripping Anne's synthetic shoulder with his iron claw, whilst looking at Chiang too.

"Remember what Zeke always says: 'when the going gets tough, flip the table and change the game.'" Ossington said. "This operation fits that mantra perfectly. It's just us and Mariko now, no Solar War and no Federation. The game has changed. We should be honored that Anne chose to play this one with us."

"I ... I agree," Chiang said, in a calmer tone.

"Thank you, Captain," said Anne, touched. "I want to rescue my brother as much as you do. We'll track his location using the signal that Lincoln is still receiving."

With visible effort, Chiang swallowed her anger. "I had to say my piece. I'm a realist, and our realistic chances aren't looking great. I'll play along ... for now."

"I appreciate that."

Warning lights strobed as the ship rattled around them. A voice came over the *Solanum*'s speakers. "Brogan here. We're past the blockade, no detections so far. Entering the upper atmosphere now. The Empire haven't started their landings yet; they're still waiting for the flagship to get underway. We're clear to land, as long as our fancy fake ID fools ground control."

"Thank you, Captain," Luther replied to Brogan. She turned to everyone else. "Let's get our people ready."

"Aye, ma'am," the captains said in unison, saluting and moving off to rally their companies. Chiang gave Anne a final glance.

"Are you going to be alright?" Luther asked, eyeing Anne's still quivering cybernetic hand. Anne rubbed Lincoln's chest, and he ruffled his reflective wings.

"Reliving situations like the one Chiang described will never be easy," Anne said. "But it's good that she did—it's best that you know who you're working with."

"Let me be frank with you, Anne," Luther said. "I speak not just for captain Chiang, but for all of Nightshade when I say: you don't have us because of *you*, you have us because of Zeke. We don't know you, and what we do know about you, we aren't crazy about. But circumstances dictate that we look beyond our doubts. You're obviously a capable fighter, and no other person in the Sol System has engaged the emperor in combat and lived. We'll take you into battle with us, but all final calls during the operation rest with me. Understood?"

Anne nodded. "Absolutely. I appreciate your honesty, Lieutenant-Commander," Anne said.

"That's my job," Luther said. "Especially now, at the bitter end."

Anne clasped Luther's shoulder. "It won't be. We'll see to that. And if things go well, Zeke will be back in charge before you know it."

"I can only pray, Anne."

19 — LIAR LIAR

NEW TORONTO UNDERGROUND - TRANSIT TUNNEL 51-B — OCT. 31, 2263 — 11:59 HOURS

"We've gotta find a better way of navigating this blasted place," grumbled David as he picked through the tangled mess of rebar choking the transit tunnel, using his communicator's flashlight to illuminate their path. The name '*St. George*' was painted onto the circular wall, indicating a long-abandoned transit station.

"What would you suggest then, David, teleportation?" asked Sam, irritated from exhaustion, holding onto his arm.

"Y'know, if I wasn't burning brainpower from carrying all this crap, I could probably figure out teleportation, or faster-than-light travel. At least the basic theory," David said, grimacing as he carried most of their remaining salvage, the huge titan's battery unit, and the lab robot's CPU core.

"Egotist," Sam barked, clutching her throbbing ribs. She glanced back at Jason. "You good?"

Jason, who was awake and recovering from the Abaddon Beacon's latest possession attempt, forced a tired smile. Lucia gave a thumbs-up. "We're good, I think!"

"Thank god," Sam said, wobbling onward.

David turned around, holding up a hand. "Okay, wait a minute. Before we go any further, we've got a decision to make."

Sam gave him a dead stare, then nodded. "Right."

Jason glanced up at them both, trying not to lose his footing on the broken transit station's tiled floor. He understood. "We need to figure out what to do with Lucia."

Lucia stiffened. "I ... I'm okay with whatever you three decide."

She looked around at the abandoned chamber around them, suffused in grim darkness that their lights were barely able to pierce. "But I've seen firsthand how dangerous the underground is now. I don't think I'll survive down here very long on my own."

Sam nodded again. "I think our decision has been made for us. You were integral in preventing Jason from going critical back there, and we owe you for a lot more than that. As far as I'm concerned, you're one of us. Yamamoto may see differently, but we should at least try to vouch for your inclusion when we get back to the Village. Anyone opposed to that?"

Jason shook his head. David didn't look entirely convinced, but he shrugged. "We're probably in trouble with the governor anyway, given how late we're returning. They'll have figured out we're gone by now. What's one more violation gonna do?"

Sam glanced at Lucia. "No guarantees, but we'll take you in and see what Yamamoto says. He's got the final say."

Lucia smiled. "Sounds good. And ... I hate to be blunt, but what happened with Jason back there, when we were leaving the Recyck yard?"

She looked at Jason. "No offense, but that was some insane shit."

"None taken. I'm not thrilled about it either," Jason muttered.

Sam surreptitiously reached out a hand toward Lucia, a subtle move that no one else but David noticed. He raised an eyebrow.

Sam hesitated. Lucia had seen far more than their militia friends had when Jason had been attacked by the Beacon inside the cargo ship three weeks earlier. That made her a liability, especially given her possible connections to the surface world. But Sam felt that she'd made a mistake when messing with Santiago, Mayweather, and Soohyun's memories, and she wasn't confident that she would be more precise with Lucia. Was it time to show some trust and faith?

Sam relaxed her hand, returning it to clutching her ribs. "Jason's condition is a very long story. As you pointed out earlier, *I'm* not exactly normal either. We're not ready to fully spill the beans, but if you agree to keep what you've seen to yourself, then we'll take you in. One day, we'll give you more details. Sound good?"

"Sounds fair. Is ... Jason's condition the reason that you want to get into the Science Institute, to find some way of curing him?" Lucia asked.

Sam, Jason and David all exchanged glances.

"Yeah, I suppose that's true. There's a bit more to it, but let's stop there," Sam said.

"Okay. Well, whenever you're ready to tell me more, I'm all ears." Lucia said. "No pressure."

Sam looked at Jason. "You alright with this?"

"Sure," Jason said, grinning at Lucia. "I know we just met, but you're right. Lucia's one of us, now. Come on, let's go."

David led them through sewer pipes, service tunnels, and gloomy cavernous spaces filled with dusty wreckage in a steady upward trek. The air quality improved as they went, becoming less musty and ancient. Everyone kept watch for more murderous Confederate titans, malfunctioning drones, Phagebearers, security forces, roaming criminal gangs, or other denizens of the underground. But as they neared their destination, Jason began hearing the steady racket of gunfire. "Uh oh."

"That can't be good," said David. "When are we gonna catch a break?"

Jason hauled himself down a final shaft of coiled cable junctions. At the bottom, he and David helped a very grumpy Sam through the connected crawlway, following it to the opening ahead. Lucia brought up the rear.

Poking his head out, Jason saw that they had emerged above one of the peripheral underground causeways. The curving space beneath was like a giant highway, allowing the original builders to circumnavigate the arcology city's perimeter.

Dozens of ragged people emerged from a collapsed section of the superstructure's inner wall, sprinting wildly toward a gigantic pile of rubble blocking the causeway before being gunned down. A huge mix of Phage-afflicted automatons and drones shambled with them—many of which looked like they might be from the Recyck yard. Incoming fire tore into their mottled flesh and plating, materializing out of thin air around the debris mountain.

David joined him, pulling out a pair of macro-binoculars.

"Great. That's a Nanophage migration, and the Village is in their path," he said. "Amazing timing."

Sam and Lucia peered out beside them. Budgie escaped and spread his wings, but David snatched him. "Not a good idea, little guy. There's a lotta shooting going on."

"Who's shooting?" asked Lucia. "I don't see anyone else down there."

Sam took the binocs from David and flicked through its settings. "It'd be better to *show* you, Lucia."

David put a large hand on the lenses.

"Once she sees this, there's no going back, Sam. If the governor tells Lucia to take a hike, that's it—she's out. There'll be nothing we can do."

"Lucia's done a ton for the Village already. Yamamoto will go for it." Sam said, jerking the binocs out of David's reach. "I'll give up my bunk if I have to."

"Awww," said Lucia as her face went red. "Thanks, Sam."

David shook his head as Sam handed Lucia the binoculars.

"Whoa," she said.

Jason knew what Lucia was seeing. The scene ahead was an illusion, hidden by the Village's holographic field generator. Crowds of afflicted approached the Village's ramshackle gated walls and the militia defenders on it, sensing sustenance beyond the illusory barrier.

"You guys have lived down here all this time?" Lucia said, raising and lowering the binocs in wonderment.

"Yep," Sam said. "This isn't the only Under-city settlement, but it's definitely our favorite. The others aren't bad, though. Trade is still pretty strong, even with all the dangerous bullshit down here."

"So, how are we getting down there?" asked Lucia, staring at the sixty-meter drop to the causeway floor. More Phagebearers boiled out of crevasses in the superstructure, adding their bodies to the desperate assault.

"Not through the main gate, too hot," said Sam. "We'll go that way."

She pointed to a precarious-looking catwalk bolted into the roof, running across the expanse. Lucia didn't look thrilled.

"Come on," David said, shimmying onto a huge curving cable to reach the walkway, holding Budgie under his jacket. "Almost home, little guy."

The four followed the rickety catwalk to a support pillar set against the causeway's massive inner wall. Jason felt a familiar static pulse wash over him after passing through the holo-shield. He heard Lucia gasp as the settlement appeared to the naked eye. "Whoa."

Shanty stacks, made of a combination of prefab container units and assorted construction materials, snaked their way up the support column. The Village was built vertically, making use of all possible space. Ground level was accessible via a stairway that wound around the column, down to the defensive wall. Jason stepped onto the roof of the highest dwelling, hoping that the villagers inside didn't emerge to check on the disturbance. Given the Village's total lockdown, no residents were anywhere in sight. He helped Lucia down after him, wincing as their feet banged loudly on the metal roofing.

"I'll take the lead. They'll be less likely to shoot me by accident," said Sam, holding her ribs tightly.

"Less?" asked David.

Everyone followed Sam down the winding steps. The smell of gunfire, acrid chemical propellant, and spilled blood was palpable, wafting up from the engagement zone. At the bottom, Sam raised a hand, approaching the nearest militiamen on the wall, waiting for a break in the battle-racket to call out. David raised his eyebrows. "You sure you wanna do that?"

"I'll be fine," Sam said.

One of the huge, automated turret guns chose that moment to unleash a volley of slugs, drowning out all other sound. Gouts of dust and shattered pavement competed with vaporized flesh and shattered bodies as the autocannon chugged large-caliber rounds into the horde.

One of the militiamen noticed movement, whipped around, and fired at Sam. Only her unnaturally quick reflexes saved her, dropping low to avoid the hail of antique lead bullets. David shoved Jason and Lucia backward as the hasty shots gouged deep craters in the dusty permacrete pillar behind them.

The militiaman flipped up his smeared goggles, lifting his ancient rifle into safe position. Brass casings rolled and settled around his boots.

"Sheee-iiit! Is that you, Sam?"

"Yep, it's me, Charles. The others are behind me," Sam said, holding her bruised side and groaning.

The volunteer trooper hurried over to Sam.

Jason gazed down at the hordes of Phage-infected crashing against the walls and dying by the dozens in the empty expanse beyond the Village,

searching for any sign of the Abaddon Beacon's dark presence bleeding off
their fallen forms. He still felt the huge shot of Osmium coursing through
his system, which was probably helping to keep him hidden from the blasted
thing, but he'd need more soon. He let out a breath he didn't know he'd been
holding.

"Whoa, whoa. Easy on that side," said Sam, grimacing as Charles helped
her stagger back to her feet.

"Where have you three been? Mendez was going door to door to find you,"
the militiaman said, then he took in Lucia. "And who's *this*?"

"A newcomer, Charles. Her name's Lucia," explained Sam.

"Riiiiight," said Charles, getting a better look at her. He had to yell to be
heard over his comrades, who were still keeping the infected from climbing
over the wall with concentrations of gunfire and explosives. "Well, whoever
she is, Governor Yamamoto wants to see *all* of you, pronto. Santiago spotted
the three of you sneaking outside the perimeter this morning, y'know? It's a
big no-no to violate surfacing orders without permission, guys."

"Shit," Sam said. "Fine, we'll go see Yamamoto."

Charles peered at David, who gave him a *don't ask me* look. Nearby gunfire
elicited inhuman screams from their attackers, just like in the Recyck yard.
The militia had pulled out military-grade weapons from three different wars
to deal with the scale of this Phage migration. Not good.

Jason took Lucia's arm, leading her down the wall's access ramp to the
Village's main road after Sam and David, while Charles watched them from
atop the barricade.

"I don't need to escort you guys to the governor, do I?" Charles asked,
yelling to be heard over the gunfire behind him.

"No, we'll head right there," repeated Sam. "We were out on a salvage run.
Show him, David."

David stared at her dumbly for a moment, then caught her drift, showing
Charles their salvage bags.

As the militiaman stared at the huge device poking out of David's bag, Sam
explained, "That's a hyper-dense battery. It might be enough to get Talos
back on his feet, so he can give you guys a break on the walls. Looks like you
need it."

Charles broke into a wide grin. "Why didn't you lead with that, girl?
That's great news! I gotta tell the boys! It's been too damn long since we've
had the tin man with us to ... well ..."

Silence fell. Charles didn't bring up the circumstances of Talos's destruction, and Jason was glad to avoid the reminder.

Sam grimaced as her ribs stabbed with pain. "You can pay me back by calling Doc Janice. I need some meds."

"I can see that," Charles sighed, pulling out his communicator.

Sam flashed him a dazzling smile. "Thank you, Charles."

"Come on, people," David said, starting down the Village's main road. Lucia stayed close to Jason as she stared up at the shanty stacks looming above them. Sounds of battle echoed around the causeway.

"Y'all better move quick! Governor's not happy!" Charles called from the top of the ramp.

"We know, Charles," Sam said, giving him an exasperated thumbs-up.

"I can't believe this," Lucia whispered to Sam. "The Federation has never discovered this place?"

Sam grinned. "The city's underworld is huge. There have been plenty of battles down here that the Feds haven't bothered investigating. It's why the Phage is getting so bad—the deep ruins are a haven for the infected, but they're too dangerous to clear out. The only reason the UEF cares about that Recyck yard being destroyed is because it affects them."

"That's true. Even one facility going offline will backlog the city's junk disposal for years," Lucia said. "Phage cases will increase fivefold if people aren't able to recycle their malfunctioning Nanotech devices, or dump them in the streets for others to find."

"I don't wanna think about that," Sam said, her mouth forming a grim line.

A fresh militia team approached the wall with homemade flamethrowers, dripping flammable gels. The incinerator squad gave the newcomers passing glances and strange expressions as they continued through the gate's narrow opening, which had a detail of ten troopers guarding it.

"It's winding down. That's the cleanup crew," said David.

Lucia leaned over to Jason. "How often does this happen?"

Jason thought about it, looking back at the gate. "Over the last couple of years, we only ever saw a handful of infected in the deep ruins. But recently, it's turned into hordes. They aren't content to stay put in the deeper levels, where they form their hives—like the one we saw in the Recyck yard. The Phage is forcing more up-worlders underground, where *we* get to deal with them as they deteriorate."

The flamethrower units started to roar. Phagebearers thrashed in the body piles, animated beyond natural death by their Nanite infestations. Machine vocalizers and mutated mouths wailed their last laments.

"We don't have the luxury of large-scale quarantines down here, and specialized Phage extraction treatment is super limited." Sam explained. "The only way to make sure they don't regenerate is to destroy every trace of them."

Lucia nodded. "I get it. Annihilation is the only way to handle a problem like this when they're so far gone."

"It's effective enough," said David, dismissively.

"They were people once, David." Sam snapped.

"That's a lot of smoke," Lucia commented, watching the scene behind them as black smoke billowed off the piled flaming corpses, filtering out through the open side of the causeway. "Wouldn't that attract attention from topside?"

"You'd think so, but nope," David said. A pair of men were dragging a vacuum system down the road toward the gate, including a giant funnel. "We clean up after ourselves. And even if we didn't ... I doubt it would matter."

As the two militiamen began to suction away the worst of the foul-smelling plumes and ashen remains, David ducked inside a half-open garage door to their left. "One sec."

Lucia looked up at the flickering neon letters bolted to the prefab building. "The ... *Chop Shop*?"

"Home base for us," said Sam as David returned with a glowing drug vial. "Here ya go, little brother. Don't drop that one."

Sam snapped it into Jason's inhibitor with a hiss, triple-checking it. "Good as new."

"That's gonna ... prevent what happened to Jason back there?" Lucia asked.

"Yep," said Jason, giving a thumbs up as his eyes fluttered from the influx of fresh drugs.

"And as a reminder, we don't talk about that in the Village," warned Sam. "My abilities and Jason's 'little issue' stay between us. Capiche?"

"Got it," Lucia said.

"Okay. Let's get you checked into 'Hotel Village,'" Sam said.

When they were halfway down the settlement's main street, Jason heard the all-clear bell. A militia lookout slid down the ladder of the Village's central crow's nest, which overlooked both perimeter walls. The nest sprouted out of the main food ration production building, which sat between the livestock pens and a synthetic meat-growing operation.

Residents threw open doors, windows, latches, and shrouds. Fallen homemade Halloween decorations were rehung as villagers re-emerged. The place smelled strangely dead with no activity, but that was going to change quickly as people came outside, fired up the generators, and got back to work. Lucia drew a few stares from residents, but most were interested in the battle's aftermath, gathering in loose crowds that approached the embattled wall.

Sam pointed at a large transport vessel wedged through the roof of the causeway, sagging into the Village's center.

"See that?" she asked.

"How could I not? It's huge!" Lucia said, staring at the giant craft.

"It crashed here years ago, before the Village was founded. Our engineers reinforced it, so it won't fall on us and go critical," Sam explained. "We've been siphoning its reactor to power this entire place. Federation's been none the wiser."

Huge cables drooped out of the dead spacecraft's cockpit windows, splitting off into sub-dividers that snaked away into the shanty stacks like subdivided roots of a tree.

"What about the crew?" asked Lucia as they passed the quartermaster's building beneath the ship's nose.

David chuckled. "They ground 'em up to fertilize the first generation of greenhouses over there."

Nobody else seemed amused.

The western defensive barricade appeared. Doc Janice's medical pavilion stood on the right side of the wall's gate. The open interior of the structure was cluttered with medical equipment and sealed patient cryo-pods occupied by early-stage Nanophage sufferers. Janice was hurrying around outside, checking the pods that had been moved out front due to lack of space. David gave the doctor a brief wave, who waved back.

Jason nudged Sam. "Janice doesn't look too busy. Charles called ahead, right? You might wanna head over there first."

Sam shook her head. "I'll be fine until after we see the governor. We shouldn't make him wait. With how fast news travels around here, he knows we're coming."

A customized prefab building sat to the left of the gate, with an open-air office inside its open garage door. Several people conversed out front, bathed in cool hues from the overhead floodlights, contrasting the warm sunlight coming in from their right.

"Here we go," Sam said, her breathing shallow.

"Stick to the story," David murmured. Jason gritted his teeth.   Mendez spotted them coming, and his forehead crinkled into even deeper lines.

"It seems our dastardly escapees have returned, Governor," he growled loudly.

His conversation partner, Julian Yamamoto, noticed them too. So did Santiago and the other two militia troopers who were with him, though Jason didn't see Mayweather or Soohyun among them.

"Great. I'll need some time with these three—err—four, Chief." Yamamoto said as he registered Lucia's presence. His expression darkened further.

"Fine. We're going to take a break, now that our boys and girls in uniform have cleared the migration swarm," Mendez said, straightening his beret. "I'll be at Xerxes's place. Call me for the next emergency."

"Stupid goddamn kids, uncontrollable little shits ..." Mendez's rant became viler as he trudged past on his knotted wooden cane. Santiago gave Jason, David, and Sam a strange look as he passed, following Mendez toward the Village bar with his comrades, but he said nothing to them.

"Bright, sunny security chief Mendez, as always," Sam murmured to Lucia. Yamamoto stepped forward, jacket flapping in the lakefront breeze.

"Had a good morning constitutional?" Yamamoto paused. "Why are your faces all red?"

Jason touched his skin, peeling from exposure to the plasma-spitting robotic beast. "Uh ... *sunburn*, sir."

"A sunburn. Down here. Right."

The governor's sarcasm could have frozen a river. Sam prodded Jason in the side.

David was about to start their carefully constructed tale when Yamamoto interrupted, "So, what's your excuse for sneaking out this time?"

Sam looked at David, who shrugged. Yamamoto started again, throwing her off balance. "A riot in the Upper-city, a Recyck yard burned to the ground … it's a miracle your faces weren't captured on the newsfeeds—except for yours."

He gestured to Lucia, who blanched. Sam finally got a word in. "Governor, we should have told you we were heading out this morning. I apologize."

"You should've asked me, Sam," said Yamamoto. "And from what I hear—this 'morning' is a bit of a stretch. Santiago spotted you three sneaking out at dawn, during his watch. That's what he told me, just now."

"That shithead." David muttered under his breath.

Jason thanked the gods, real or otherwise, that he wasn't doing the talking right now.

Sam gulped, forging on. "We … got a tip about a replacement battery for Talos in a Recyck yard further eastward," she said. "We couldn't ask you first because it was time sensitive. You know how quickly they recycle valuables like this."

"You got a tip from …?" Yamamoto asked, eyeing Lucia.

Sam placed a hand on Lucia's back. "From Lucia, our surface contact. She—"

"Worked for the Recyck Authority, uh-huh. They read out her profile on the Church channels—along with a hefty capture reward," said Yamamoto. "Well, I hope you enjoyed those easy resource runs you've been doing—the UEF is locking down every Recyck yard in the Under-city until they figure out what the hell happened to the one you destroyed. Those Phage hordes came from that direction. We bled thirty percent of our ammo reserves blunting the assault, according to Mendez and his people."

"That … wasn't us. We didn't destroy that place," said Sam.

Yamamoto folded his thick arms, forming an impenetrable wall of authority. "Really? I suppose that's believable—not even you three are capable of that level of destruction. Not without Talos."

Sam didn't elaborate.

"Did you end up finding this battery, at least?" The governor asked.

Sam nodded.

"Hmmph. How soon can you get Talos back on the walls?" he asked.

Sam exhaled. "His chassis and internals are re-assembled in the Chop Shop. We had to source a lot of new parts to replace the ones that were destroyed when he fell. Once we adapt his systems to the alternative power source, we can start his reboot later today."

"That's acceptable, I suppose," Yamamoto sighed. "You need to see the doctor, Sam. That doesn't look like it can wait."

He whistled through his fingers. Doc Janice looked up from the stasis pods, grabbed her scanner, and made her way over.

"So, what did destroy that facility?" Yamamoto said, returning his attention to Sam.

Jason heard himself talking before his brain caught up, still swimming in the remnants of the huge Osmium dose from earlier. "Well, we found this massive robot ... which ambushed us. We barely managed to kill it. That's how we found the batter—"

"Shhh," David elbowed him hard.

Yamamoto looked from Jason to Sam. "You told me that you went to that yard in the first place to find the battery. Where does this giant robot come into the picture?"

Sam bit her bottom lip, trying to think fast. Jason went red.

"Uhhh ..."

"Sir, we did go there for the battery, but—" Sam started to say.

"No, you didn't," Yamamoto said. "If you're going to lie to me again, at least get your story straight."

"We had it straight," David murmured through clenched teeth, stepping on Jason's foot.

The doctor arrived wearing a stained white jacket and an exhausted expression, casting a wary glance at all of them. "Yes, Governor?"

"Give these ruffians a once-over, Doc," said Yamamoto. "They're trying to lie to me, again."

"Are they now?" Doc Janice looked at David in particular, who shrugged. She approached Sam, waving the scanner down her torso.

"I'm surprised you're still upright, Sam," Janice said. "No Phage residue, but you've got three cracked ribs and mild internal hemorrhaging. But nothing we can't fix up quick."

"Sounds like this 'robot' did a number on you," said Yamamoto. "You mind if I continue grilling them, Doctor?"

"As long as you don't do any physical damage, go nuts," Janice said, examining Sam's dark, splotchy torso more closely.

Yamamoto fixed the group with his brutal stare again. "So, which is it? Did you sneak out to get the battery or find this bot? Or something else? What was so important that you risked your lives—and exposing our entire community—by causing so much havoc upstairs?"

Lucia opened her mouth, but shut it quickly.

David spoke up. "Sir, we regret not asking you for permission to leave beforehand, but as Sam said, it was time sensitive. We can't say more than that."

Yamamoto didn't let up. "Would this be related to the other times over the last few weeks that you three have left the Village and gone to the surface without permission?"

David matched his stare but didn't respond.

"You seem to be the most truthful today, Jason, or at least the worst at lying," said Yamamoto. "What did you go there to find?"

Jason shrank before him, but he knew better than to reply.

The governor gave him a few moments, then huffed in frustration. "Fine. This has happened too many times over the last few weeks; you three have no more strikes left with me. You've been with us for a long time, but that doesn't excuse the risks you've been taking. The only reason that I'm not kicking your asses out of here this very minute is because you might get Talos back on those walls. And you're responsible for running too many critical operations around here."

He paused for effect. No one met his gaze.

"One way or another, I'll have the truth. Or you're gone. We cannot risk the UEF learning about our existence," Yamamoto said.

He was about to elaborate when a militiaman clunked down the ramp from the wall, approaching at a trot. "Sir ... there's someone at the west gate. Looks like she means business."

"Any idea who?" Yamamoto said.

"She didn't say," the kid replied, eyeing the governor's current company. "But she asked for you by name, sir."

"Huh. Interesting," Yamamoto said. "I'll be there in a moment. Get a security team together. I don't want any infected stragglers sneaking inside."

He turned back to everyone else as Doc Janice applied a quick-healing patch to Sam's anesthetized torso.

"You will all report back here by fourteen hundred hours," Yamamoto ordered. "You might as well go tell Mendez about this robot you found—I hope you got pictures."

Sam nodded, flicking through the images she'd captured of the mechanical beast on her comm pad. "We did. And ... I guess it's worth mentioning that it was ... *Confederate*, sir."

"Confederate? As in the rogue nation of cyber-renegades that blew up half the planet?" Yamamoto asked.

"Yep," Sam said. "These pictures don't lie. There was a living Confederate inside it, sir."

"*Shit*. Like we didn't have enough going on. Fine, go tell Mendez what happened."

Sam gulped again. David shook his head. Jason looked at his hands.

"What about Lucia?" asked Sam. "She has valuable skills that she can offer."

Yamamoto groaned. "You picked a terrible time to bring in a newcomer, Sam. We're nearly out of sleeping spaces, especially with our wave of new births."

"No kidding," Janice commented, wiping her eyes, which were bagged with intense dark circles.

"She could help Bilby with his operation. Lucia's got matching experience," Sam said.

Yamamoto raised an eyebrow at Lucia, who stammered, "I-I've been at the Recyck Authority for a few years, learned a thing or two about logistics... sir. And Nanite tech."

"Good. Maybe you'll outlast these three around here," the governor half-joked. "Take Lucia to the Quartermaster once Janice is done with you, he'll evaluate her. Then get Talos operational. After, you will come back here and tell me everything you're holding back—and if I'm satisfied, I *might* let you continue to stay with us. Comprende?"

"Yes, sir!" they replied. Budgie screeched and head banged.

"Now, get out of my sight," Yamamoto said. He made a circular motion toward the militia guards. "Let's greet our guest."

Sam exhaled as Yamamoto strode off. "I almost had a heart attack."

"Yep. That could have gone better," Jason said, dejected.

"Ya think?" David said, giving him a death glare.

"It wasn't his fault," Sam said.

"It kinda was. But I suppose the 'ol governor was going to catch onto us sooner or later."

Doc Janice, who was working on David, poked him in the back. "Catch onto *what*?"

"I don't wanna talk about it," David replied. Janice poked him harder, this time with the scanner. "Come on, shit-disturbers. Let's make sure you aren't all swimming in the Phage after this Recyck yard misadventure that you're definitely going to tell me about."

Jason glanced at Sam, waiting until Janice was out of earshot. "I'm sorry, I shouldn't have tried to explain—"

"It's fine. David's right, Yamamoto was gonna see through our bullshit eventually," Sam said, squeezing his hand.

"But ... we can't tell him either. We can't tell anyone, other than Lucia, I guess," Jason said, keeping his voice down.

Lucia piped up from behind. "From where I'm standing, he *almost* bought it."

Sam sighed, patting her angry purple bruises, which were covered over by Janice's topical med-patches. "At least we've got a way into the Science Institute now. That's huge. Even if Yamamoto kicks us out, everything we've done will pay off for you, Jason. I know it."

Jason scratched his skin around the inhibitor. "I hope so, Sam."

20 — WHAT COULD HAVE BEEN

Anne Oakfield raised her hands as the sheet-metal gate rasped open, trailing dirt on the concrete ground. Her olfactory scanners had picked up the smells of human habitation long before she'd gotten close to the settlement's holo-shield.

Anne's weak psychic senses were detecting something strange in the Village, like a distorted otherworldly echo, long before she and her Nightshade bodyguards had neared this place. She'd only ever experienced this particular sensation around the emperor himself, so Anne was on guard.

Two men on the wall watched her as the gate clunked to a halt. A quartet of multi-barreled sentry turrets locked onto Anne, clunking along tracks greased with oil, tallow, and animal fat. Some were ancient enough to have seen use before the Great War.

A man in a long jacket waited for her, flanked by more militiamen. Behind them, Undocumented underground dwellers hurried about their daily tasks. Some of them gathered to watch the scene.

Lincoln scanned everyone, relaying data to Anne's heads-up display. The militiamen barely registered on her threat-assessment system.

"Who goes there?" asked the jacketed man.

"An old friend," said Anne, stepping into the angled sunlight, out of the shadow of a support pillar. The militia raised an assortment of old, refurbished weapons, but their leader lifted a hand. "Calm down, everyone. Identify yourself, please."

Anne removed her hat and glasses, which had obscured her false eyes behind twin orbs of reflected light. She wanted him to recognize her.

"Hello, Julian. It's been a while."

Julian Yamamoto narrowed his eyes, stepping closer. "It can't be. Anne? Anne Oakfield?"

"It can, and it is," Anne replied, extending her arms.

Julian waved off the militia.

"This one means us no harm," he glanced at her. "Right?"

"Never have," Anne said. She gave a similar gesture to her Nightshade operators perched high above, who receded into the gloom of the causeway rafters. The militiamen lowered their weapons.

Julian and Anne shook hands, and he led her toward his office. Lincoln's eyes darted around, recording everything he saw.

"It's good to see you—and Lincoln. But you've changed, Anne," said Julian, dark eyes looking her up and down. "I have a million questions. Why are you here? How did you find us? I thought you were dead."

"I'll put your fears to rest—nobody else knows about this settlement, so don't panic," said Anne. "Lincoln saw through your holographic defenses, which is how I found you. His surveillance equipment is one of a kind. It's unlikely anyone else can repeat that trick unless they know where to look."

Julian's voice softened. "I remember when you first cyberized him in the labs when he got sick. Lincoln's come a long way since then. But how did you know to look for us?"

"What was the last thing you said to me before I left the labs?" Anne asked.

Julian looked upward, stroking his goatee. "I wanted to leave everything behind."

"And build your own society somewhere free of the Federation's oppression. With ... me," Anne finished.

"That *does* sound familiar," Julian said.

Anne grinned. "Lincoln sent probes out to see if you'd actually succeeded. We had to search the first four levels of the Under-city before pinpointing your location. You hid this place well."

"Don't take this the wrong way... but you've grown up since you were that fun, dorky science girl I used to know," Julian said, grinning.

"So have you. We're the same age, you old fool." Anne said, pointing out the grey streaks at his temples as Julian offered her a seat at his desk.

"Life does that to a person," he said as they sat. Lincoln hopped onto a pile of supply crates, holding her hat. Julian offered her fragrant tea from a decanter on his shiny oak desk, which she accepted. "But so does death. Everyone saw what the emperor did to you on Colossus, Anne. How long ago was that broadcast, ten years? Twelve?"

"Fourteen years, five months, twelve days, two hours, nine minutes ..." Anne read from a counter on her heads-up display, "... and three seconds."

"I suppose being eviscerated isn't something one easily forgets," Julian remarked. "We don't have to discuss that if you don't—"

"It's fine," Anne said, raising her metal hand. "It's a part of history now. But you asked why I came. I'm here for a bit of payback."

Julian's thick eyebrows shot up. "You're in the wrong place, then. Hadrian Mariko hasn't left Colossus since the war started."

"If you said that yesterday, you'd be correct," Anne said, gesturing to the lakefront and containment wall beyond it through the causeway pillars. Along the distant, gargantuan barrier, the orbital defense batteries stood silent, oblivious to the situation in orbit.

"Today, not so much," Anne continued. "The emperor is returning to Earth for the first time since we left the Abhamancer Program, Julian. And he's not on his way to surrender. Mariko has won."

Julian looked at Anne like she'd made a nasty joke. His eyes darted to several monitors mounted on his desk, displaying newsfeeds and propaganda about active conflicts and fleet engagements throughout the Sol System.

"Not from what I've seen," he said.

"The UEF networks are showing battles that ended weeks ago to convince the public that everything is hunky dory. The Empire took Mars yesterday and now they're here for the rest," Anne said. "I've seen the invasion fleet myself, Julian. I fought them in orbit. Imperial control over all Earthside habitats will be achieved by day's end. It's over."

"And you're here to ... stop him?"

"Yes. This is the line in the sand. Mariko dies today. That's the only way to turn this around," Anne said, sipping more tea.

"Good grief," Julian put his hands down, spreading his fingers wide. "You think you can kill him?"

"Not on my own. I brought some help."

"Of course you did," Julian took a deep breath. "So, if the Empire lands on Earth today—what does that mean for *us*?"

"Down here? Probably not much," Anne said.

"Seriously? It's the Empire, Anne. They don't leave stones unturned, especially when it comes to stamping out the Nanophage—or so I've heard," Julian said.

Anne shrugged. "The Imperials will swarm across the habitats like locusts, integrating the uninfected population into their Hierarchy, and murdering millions who have the plague. But you're well positioned to avoid any incursions into the underground. I would suggest locking this settlement down with no signals or comm-traffic and minimal energy-usage. Your existing holo-shield and scanner-jammers will help."

Julian sat back in his creaking chair. "Will it be insulting if I ask my militia to verify what you're saying? I'll need proof to convince my people."

"Tell them to look at the sky. The Imperial fleet will be visible to the naked eye by now."

"This better not be a joke, Anne."

"I wish it was," she said. Anne sipped again, putting her teacup down as Julian keyed instructions into a datapad. The smell of his homemade jasmine tea triggered intense nostalgia from their early days together in her father's labs.

Moments later, a militia boy clunked down the ramp, looking confused. "Sir?"

Julian shook his head. "No, I'm not crazy. Humor me, please. Take some imaging equipment out to the old landing pad with you. And ... don't tell anyone what you're doing. Not yet."

"Yes ... sir," the militiaman said, hurrying off.

Anne stood. Lincoln cocked his head at her.

"You have a few hours to prepare," Anne said.

"Good. We've had lockdown procedures since I started this place. We can survive for weeks without outside trade by using our water reclamation and hydroponics systems, maybe a few months at most ... but that's pushing it," Julian said. "The closest we've come to full lockdowns have been for Nanophage migrations. The militia have fought them off so far, but our supplies have taken a hit, and we haven't had to bunker down for more than a day. A longer stint will be really tough on people."

"I'm sorry," Anne said. "I wish our reunion had been under better circumstances."

Julian circled around his desk. "That's why you came? To warn us?"

"Yes, Julian. And to make sure that you followed through on your promise, even if it was without me. I'm glad you did," Anne said, taking his hand in her cybernetic grip. He squeezed it, feeling her cold, hard replacement fingers.

"Has it been difficult, living like this?" Julian asked.

Anne shrugged. "It's amazing what you can get used to. These bionic replacements would have been very useful in our previous line of work. But would I voluntarily become a Nanotech-riddled cyber-freak? I don't think so. I wished I'd stayed with you."

"I wouldn't have left the labs if *you* hadn't," Julian said, brushing a long lock of red hair away from her scarred face.

Anne held Julian's hand for a moment longer, lowering her head. *What could have been?*

"So, was I right? Maybe it wasn't a good idea to run off with the handsome, magical megalomaniac?" Julian broke into a manic grin.

"Don't you get started with that," Anne said, cyber-eyes glowing crimson. "And Mariko wasn't a megalomaniac, at the time. Even my father agreed with his diagnosis of the UEF, as did Zeke. I seem to recall you buying what he was selling, too."

"That's true," confirmed Julian. "The Federation was only beginning to fall apart back then. But I didn't believe in Mariko enough to help build his ... alternative way of doing things."

"Your lack of ambition has worked out fine," Anne said, with a glance at the surrounding settlement.

"Preferable to ruling your own Empire?" Julian asked.

"I tried my best to steer it," Anne said, ashamed. "But Hadrian wouldn't listen to reason. He always thought he was right. I made mistakes too, Julian. Big ones. Maybe it was his Abhamic powers that blinded him to what we were creating, or maybe it was Abaddon messing with his mind, but I still saw it. We were going too far."

"And that's when he cast you down?"

Anne nodded. "Yes. He probably planned to throw me out eventually—but my defiance created a convenient excuse. That doesn't matter now. I'm here to end it, and maybe help put things back together on the other side, if anyone will let me. If not ... I'm content with one last day of redemption, which is more than I deserve."

"This is cliché, but everyone makes mistakes, Anne. Even if they're ... enormous, civilization-altering mistakes," Julian said. "I know you meant well, like those damn kids over there."

He gestured to the medical pavilion, where the salvagers and their newcomer were being berated by doc Janice for getting so roughed up. A white bird flapped around their heads.

"Kids? What do you mean?" Anne asked.

Lincoln scanned the group, piping data to her HUD. Her eyes slowly widened as Julian elaborated, "Sorry, I just had a word with them, so they're still on my mind. They arrived years ago. One of my earliest residents, Ms. Vogas, found them homeless in the Upper-city, forced to fight in brutal juvenile gang wars up there before she intervened. She said that the younger of the two brothers, Jason, reminded her of the son she lost to the social enforcers before she joined our community. If I had to guess, their parents were victims of the church too, or the Phage ... but the boys have never talked about it. They might not even know."

"What about her? The girl," Anne said. Her identifier system was searching restricted Federation databases for IDs.

Julian gave Anne a strange look. "Jason and David brought her in with them—her name is Sam. She repairs our automatons and most other critical systems, and David maintains our computer tech. Jason's like an apprentice to them, but they all seem preoccupied with something beyond their ability to handle."

Julian looked at her when she didn't reply. "Anne?"

It couldn't be. Anne's targeting systems identified the implant on the back of Jason's neck as a retrofitted Osmium inhibitor—a crude but effective method of suppressing brain functions related to Abhamic abilities. No wonder Julian didn't recognize the device, or the boy wearing it—the inhibitor hadn't been used in her father's laboratory during the early Abhamic experiments on Mariko, and Jason was too young to have been part of the early experiments. Anne had built one for Hadrian after they'd arrived on

Colossus to help him control his abilities as they matured. How had Anne's invention resurfaced here?

Anne's systems finished scanning the taller girl, Lucia, whose Federation ID came back as a fugitive from the church. But the shorter girl, Sam, was even more intriguing. Anne's identifier system couldn't find anything on her. Why did she seem so ... familiar?

As Janice worked on their injuries, Sam spotted who the governor was talking to. A scarred, but beautiful redheaded woman wearing a greatcoat and reflective glasses was sitting with him.

She was staring straight at Sam.

A cold feeling shot up Sam's spine. Her Abhamic abilities often gave her premonitions, and they were screaming at her right now. Did this woman know her from somewhere? Was she from the UEF laboratories, years ago? Or did she know Sam from ... before then?

Sudden fear clenched her stomach, followed by panic. Sam wanted to run, right now. Had she been tracked down? Who the hell was this woman?

"Anne?" Julian asked again. "What is it?"

"Sorry," Anne said, releasing her grip. "I thought one of them looked ... familiar. I misidentified. It's nothing."

"Right," Julian said, unconvinced. Anne watched Sam turn away in a hurry, followed by Jason. She explained something to the doctor, who looked concerned, but allowed her to leave. Lincoln's cameras caught a momentary change in Sam's eye color—from amber to fiery pink.

That confirmed it. Multiple Abhamic-powered beings were hiding out in this place. Her father had created more successes after Anne had left his operation. But had he replicated Anne's weaker abilities, or did these kids have the psychic might of the emperor himself?

"How the hell ..." Anne started to say.

"Do you know anything about them?" Julian asked, staring at Anne.

"I … can't say," Anne said, blinking a series of silent commands to Lincoln. "Julian, I need to keep a close watch on this place."

"Because of them?"

Lincoln took flight, flapping around the edges of the Village on his grav-jets.

"Because of everything," Anne's gaze snapped back to Julian. "Lincoln is deploying more probes. They'll allow me to monitor things here—an extra level of protection for you, just in case. I hope that's agreeable."

Julian's voice rose, alarmed. "Sure, that's fantastic. But how does this involve Jason and Sam? And David? Do you know something about them?"

"I don't know," Anne lied. "I would explain if I did, Julian."

Julian grumbled something about no one being honest these days. "Fine, I don't mind having a guardian angel. Can you help us if the Empire finds this place?"

"If my mission succeeds, you won't have to worry about that," Anne said, brightening.

"Can we help *you*? With your … mission?" asked Julian. "Our militia is stretched thin, but if it's Mariko you're up against, you'll need everyone you can get."

"I can't ask your people to step into that kind of danger, Julian," Anne shook her head. "I came to warn you. Best thing you can be doing is staying off the grid and riding this out."

Lincoln flapped back onto her shoulder with a whoosh of anti-grav jets, adjusting Anne's hat.

"It's time to take my leave. I've been away too long," Anne said.

Julian walked Anne out of his office as the guards triggered the gate controls, taking both of her hands. "Thank you for finding us, Anne."

He glanced at the shimmering lake outside. The militiamen were out on the suspended landing pad, capturing images of the sky with alarmed expressions.

"From the look of those boys, I don't think you were kidding about the Empire invading."

"I never kid," Anne winked. "Good luck, Julian. And keep an eye on those kids. I don't know why yet, but I suspect they'll have a part to play in this before the end."

21 — INTERNAL AFFAIRS

Sam slumped against the medical building's rusted siding, dropping her bag as she slid into a sitting position. Jason rounded the corner, staring at Sam as her chest heaved with frantic breaths. Sweat rolled down her forehead as Sam fanned her blood and grime-stained undershirt.

"Are you okay?" Jason asked.

"This must be what it feels like, when *you* lose control ..." Sam said, breathlessly.

"Are you gonna, y'know, explode?" Jason asked.

"No, I think ..." Sam said, freezing up.

She sneezed. Jason barked out a laugh. "You almost gave me a heart attack."

"Sorry. Now you know how I feel when you're in this position," Sam muttered.

Jason dropped to one knee, feeling impotent. "I, uh ..."

Budgie appeared, flapping around the building. He landed on Sam, nuzzling his feathery head under her chin.

Sam stroked the bird like a therapy animal. She reached into her bag, but then she sighed, pulling out the shattered Osmium syringe. "Shit. I forgot; this was busted back there in the Recyck yard. It's a good thing David brought a spare for you."

"Sorry. My bad," Jason said.

"Don't be. I think I'm okay now," Sam said.

"Take your time," Jason said. Nothing out of the ordinary was happening in the Village aside from the battle cleanup, and that newcomer Yamamoto met. Had *she* set Sam off?

Jason slid his hand into hers, feeling her heart rate slowing. Sam closed her eyes.

"What *was* that?" Jason asked, pulling back when the direct contact became too much for him to handle.

"You're our resident expert on panic attacks; you tell me," Sam said, eyes snapping open. Jason gave her an annoyed look. She grimaced. "Sorry, didn't mean it to come out like that."

"I mean, what did you see that triggered this?"

"Something came over me when I saw that woman," Sam said. "But I've never seen her in my life. I don't even remember her from the labs where you guys found me. She's a blank. There's no logical reason for me to have this kind of reaction."

"Well, you did," Jason gave her a matter-of-fact look. "And as our 'expert on panic attacks', don't question where the feelings come from. Endure 'em, they'll pass. Plus—"

Jason grinned, tapping the back of his neck. "There are drugs for this, y'know."

Sam almost laughed. "I'm good now, I think. But ... can you check for me? Is she gone?"

Jason raised an eyebrow, but nodded. Budgie flapped onto Jason's shoulder to look around the corner too. The newcomer woman in the greatcoat was leaving through the west gate, seen out by Yamamoto. She had a graceful stride, but Jason sensed barely-contained violence bubbling below the surface.

Whoever she was, they'd have to get back into the governor's good graces to find out. Jason glanced back at Sam. "She's leaving."

"Thank the gods," Sam said, edging her way up the wall.

"Is she a problem for us, you think?" Jason asked.

Sam shook her head. "I'm not sure. If she was from Oakfield's labs, I doubt that she'd let us go. But we'll have to be on guard."

Jason gestured to the governor. "Like always. Yamamoto doesn't seem to think she's a threat, at least. They must know each other."

Sam nodded, gingerly feeling her torso. The med-patches from Doc Janice were working their magic, deploying medical-grade Nanites to reknit and regrow bone and sinew, allowing Sam to breathe deeper with less pain.

Nanite meds were risky because of possible Phage infection, but Jason understood them to be safe in small amounts. Other medical methods existed that didn't rely on Nanotech, but the miraculous substance was the most effective treatment available for most ailments. The ultimate irony was that medical-grade Nanites were useless at dealing with the Nanophage itself, which required painstaking surgical extractions, like any other cancer-like condition.

David spotted Jason poking his head out from behind the med pavilion and held up his hands as if to ask, *what's wrong with you two?*

Jason waved his brother off and checked on Sam, who experimentally stretched her torso.

"You really don't know who that was?" he asked.

Sam shook her head. "I told you; I've never seen that woman in my life."

"Could you have forgotten?"

Sam tapped her temple. "Nope. Pretty good memory."

"Says the one who always 'forgets' to do the laundry when it's her turn."

"I have no idea what you're talking about," Sam said, raising her nose in a huff.

Jason didn't know what to make of Sam's strange episode, but waved it off for now.

Avoiding the lines of cryo-treatment beds outside, they approached David, Lucia, and Doc Janice, who'd finished treating David's superficial wounds, brushing aside concerns about his peeling skin, and started pointing out different Village locations for Lucia.

"You two done with your make-out session?" David asked.

Jason and Sam both went beet red. Budgie flapped onto David's arm, squawking in a way that sounded suspiciously like laughter. Janice suppressed a grin.

Sam glared at David. "I needed to get away from *you* for a bit. Your stench is slowing the healing process. Go shower."

"We were neck-deep in a burning garbage heap. Sue me," David said, shucking his torn, scorched jacket on over the patches that Janice had applied to his skin, then he hefted up their surviving salvage bags. "We should get this stuff over to Bilby's."

Janice nodded. "Sure. But she's right, you do need a shower, David."

"I'll get to it," David said, running a hand over Janice's backside when he thought no one else was looking. Janice didn't seem to mind, winking at him. Sam gagged.

"Come on, Lucia. We'll introduce you to the Quartermaster," Sam said. Lucia perked up at this. David gave Janice a peck on the cheek before heading over to the sorting area. Sam stole a look at the doctor, mouthing, '*You can do better*', but Janice simply shrugged.

"Some people need to broaden their horizons," Sam grumbled.

A deep rumble crackled through the underground. Several villagers looked concerned, but most went on with their post-crisis reopening routines.

Quartermaster Bilby emerged from his building as they approached. A young girl accompanied him, hiding behind his tree trunk-like legs. The big man, who wore a rubber apron, swept one of the sorting tables clear as his workers fired up several four-by-four buggies, preparing for their daily resupply operation from the building's stockpiles.

"Morning, Bilby," David said. Despite the desperate circumstances of their Recyck misadventure, he'd managed to save a lot of their salvage, which he dumped on the table.

"Afternoon, but sure. Whatever," grumbled the bearded quartermaster, staring down at David's spoils. "I hear you three went for an unauthorized salvage run this morning. Better have been worth it."

"What does it look like, Bilby?" David said, gesturing to the Nanotech—containers of raw Nanites, power cells, human cyber-ware and robot parts, computer components, assorted gadgets, engine parts, and other rarities.

The quartermaster pulled on a pair of gloves and picked up an adaptor meant to regulate energy flow through a spaceship's engine. "Not a bad haul. This could be retrofitted to work with smaller devices."

Bilby finally noticed Lucia. "And who might this be?"

Sam put a hand on Lucia's arm. "Bilby, meet Lucia, who's been guiding us for the last few weeks' worth of salvage runs—and your new assistant."

"Uh-huh," replied the large man. "And how's 'Lucia' gonna do that with the Recyck yards closed? That means no new salvage. I don't need a new assistant for no reason."

Jason mouthed *how?* at David, who shrugged and said, "Information travels fast around here, little brother."

"She worked for the Recyck authority," Sam explained to Bilby. "Lucia can help your team with maintaining and cataloguing our existing tech stockpiles, maybe even resale to surface contacts."

"If that's okay with you," Lucia added.

Bilby examined her, scratching his wiry mustache.

"We could always use another set of experienced hands," he said. "What're your qualifications, Lucia? Ever tangled with the Phage?"

"Never had it myself," Lucia replied. "I rarely dealt with physical Recyck work, but I've been out with the ground teams a couple times. But I'm trained to handle any type of Nanite tech, had to keep recertifying to minimize infection risk."

"Would be nice if they gave every up-worlder that kinda training," David said.

"True, that would probably stop the epidemic altogether," said Lucia. "But the Federation would need to be halfway competent for that."

Bilby folded his arms. "*Lucia's* gotta be the most useful thing you've brought in recently."

"Exactly what I was thinking," Sam said.

"The sticking point is lodging," Bilby mused. "Did Yamamoto say where we can put her?"

Jason spoke up. "We could make room in the Chop Shop—"

"No, no, absolutely not," David cut in, startling Budgie. "We're already cramped, and I need more room for that weight-machine I'm rebuilding."

"No, you don't, you meathead. And last I checked, I did most of the work on that blasted contraption," Sam shot him a look.

"It's my design though," David asserted.

Bilby checked a nearby clipboard. "We could maybe squeeze another bed into one of the bunkhouses. How's that sound, girl?"

Lucia shrugged. "The residential pods in the Upper-city probably aren't any larger. Bottom line, anything's better than rotting away in a church reconditioning cell."

"C'mere then, show me what you know about Nanotech," Bilby said, beckoning Lucia closer.

As they began working, Sam felt a tug on her jacket and looked down to see Bilby's daughter crawling under the sorting table.

"Hi, Sammy!" she shrieked, hugging Sam's leg. David looked down at the kid with alarm, but he wasn't unfriendly. "Looks like you've got a little gremlin attached to you down there."

"Whoa, easy," Sam said as her weight shifted to her injured side, putting on her biggest smile. "Were you a good girl during the lockdown, Esme?"

Esme stared up at Sam with bright-eyed wonder. "Yep! But I heard *you* weren't! Did you fight the monsters?"

"Uhhh ... yep," Sam said, glancing at Jason, who shrugged. They had *indeed* fought monsters. Budgie hopped over so the little girl could pet him.

"We did, kiddo," said Sam, kneeling in front of Esme. "Keeping you safe is my number one job. There's one less monster out there to bite your nose off!"

Sam pinched the girl's nose, who giggled, shaking her off. She swiped a gadget off the table that Lucia had already wiped down with a Nanite-neutralizing fluid, connecting some cables from her comm pad into it.

"We got this for you. It's a video receiver—I'm reprogramming it to get signals from the surface. But make sure your dad knows what you're watching, okay?"

"Thanks," Esme hugged Sam, snatched the palm-sized holoprojector, and scrambled back behind her father's legs. Sam smiled as the kid powered up the device, flicking through channels.

"What a cute kid," she said.

"She's growing up fast," Jason commented.

"I hope the world is kinder to her than it was to us," Jason added.   Sam looked at him with sad eyes.

"That is profoundly depressing," she said.

As Lucia continued to sort, clean, repair, and evaluate their salvage under Bilby's supervision, David revealed the heavy battery.

"Look what else we found," he said.

Bilby peered at the glowing unit. "Doesn't look like any Nanotech I've seen before."

"It's not modern. We ... pulled it out of a big robot, after it wrecked the place. Our scans indicated no Nanites present, which makes sense given that it was *Confederate*," Sam explained.

"Uh ... huh, I'll believe that when I see it," Bilby said.

Sam whipped out her photo of the robot's rusted insignia. Bilby raised an eyebrow, but waved a hand. "So, about this battery, you're going to use it to reactivate the big guy? I could use Talos to haul some stuff around, give my boys a break. Lotta jobs have piled up since he's been outta commission."

"He'll be online in no time," Sam said.

"Well, that's something, at least," the quartermaster said.

While David and Bilby continued to review their spoils with Lucia, Jason turned to Sam. "I still dunno what we're gonna tell Yamamoto to keep him off our backs."

"We'll think of something," Sam said. "We're too valuable for him to lose."

"You might be. David is, too. I'm just dead weight."

Raising an arm as if to backhand him, Sam said, "Keep that talk up and I'm gonna hit you,"

"You must be feeling better if you're getting violent."

Sam's eyes narrowed. "Thin ice, Jason. You're on it."

Silence fell between them. David joined them, followed by Lucia, who had finished her evaluation.

"I've got news! Bilby's starting me on the next work shift, but it's light work because of what happened to us this morning. They're gonna feed me too!" Lucia explained. "Can you guys give me a tour of the Village later?"

"Sure. Do some good work with Bilby, that'll help our case with Yamamo-to ... maybe."

"Alright. Seeya later, then. And thanks again, Sam. You won't regret this!" Lucia saluted and returned to the huge quartermaster, where he was briefing his workers beside the distribution buggies.

"Don't mention it," Sam said, proud to have gotten Lucia safely down into the Under-city despite the risks.   Jason noticed that Lucia's salute—her right fist over her heart—was a pre-Solar War gesture that people from Colossus used. He filed that peculiarity away for later.

"Let's find Mendez. Last stop before we can shower, then we've got a lot of work to do." Sam said. "I might even break the rules and take a long one."

The Finborough Arms bar, on the north side of the Village, was deep into a busy lunch service when Jason thrust the doors open. A large Persian man with a mustache and fez bellowed from behind the bar over the sound of conversation and clacking dishes.

"Jason! And friends, welcome."

"Hey, Xerxes," Jason and Sam said in unison. David waved. Jason swayed on his feet, hit full-force by the smell of food. "Whoa ..."

Sam nudged him. "I'm surprised you're still on your feet. You barely ate this morning."

"I'm a bit dizzy," Jason said. Sam looked alarmed, so he clarified, "From *hunger*, not, y'know ..."

"Good, keep it that way," Sam said, pinching his arm.

Budgie flapped over to pick food scraps out of Xerxes' beard. Other patrons briefly looked up before going back to their meals and conversations, including militia crews who were returning from the Phage swarm defense operation.

Jason enjoyed the restaurateur's boisterousness. Xerxes wore a badge with the number thirty-six on it, to commemorate the victims of the Far East habitat—the thirty-sixth UEF arcology built on Earth. It had suffered a catastrophic atmo-shield failure, allowing the super-storms outside to ravage the city. The bartender had been one of the few evacuated survivors, but he'd lost his entire family during the disaster. Yamamoto had taken Xerxes in by chance during his relocation to the capital, giving him purpose again.

"I need a pick-me-up," David said. "We just went through hell."

Xerxes moved to the beer handles and cranked one, sticking a glass underneath.

"You can tell me all about it, David. Sounds like you three were *busy* this morning."

David glanced at Jason and Sam. "You could say that."

As more workers and militia troopers piled into the bar after them, David began regaling Xerxes with a sanitized version of the day's events. Budgie jabbered along with him. A shrill voice sounded from the kitchen. "Is that my children I hear?"

An old woman appeared in the large serving window. Steam rose from grills and stoves as she spoke. "Hello, children. I hear you left the Village without permission—again. *Bardzo źle. Miałeś duże kłopoty*,"

"We did, Ms. Vogas. Sorry," Jason said. Sam gave her a sheepish look. The woman was from the Eastern Europe habitat, and her accent was Polish—a language she slipped into unconsciously. The old woman waddled out of the kitchen and around the bar to prod Jason. "So skinny, very unhealthy. Opposite for you, girl."

"Uhh ... thanks, Ms. Vogas," Sam said, squirming with embarrassment. In reality, she was extremely fit, especially given their limited rations. Legs like Sam's didn't get built from sitting around doing nothing.

Jason rubbed his stomach. "It's been a while since we all lived with you, Ms. Vogas. We miss all the home cooking."

Ms. Vogas retreated into her lair, returning with three schnitzel wraps.

"These are not a reward for breaking the rules," she warned. "Eat, so you don't collapse. I didn't bring you three down here all those years ago to watch you starve."

Jason pulled a bent ration card out of his pocket, but Xerxes shook his head, and the old woman slapped Jason's hand away.

"No, no. You do too many useful things around here," Vogas said. "Eat, both of you."

"Thanks, Ms. Vogas."

The woman turned to Sam, who raised her hands. "No thanks, I ... uh ... ate on the way."

Ms. Vogas pressed a wrap into Sam's hands. "Those rations are reprocessed junk. Have some proper food, please."

Sam suppressed her reluctance with a grimace, biting into it. Jason was already halfway through his own. Vogas slid a wrap down the bar to David, who began devouring it. "Thanks."

The old woman nodded her approval. "Maybe you three will survive this winter after all."

Sam jerked a thumb toward a dim corner of the restaurant. "We should see Mendez."

"I hope you two aren't in trouble," said Vogas, worry lines crinkling. "I still remember that terrible day, when you three came back after Talos was destroyed ..."

Jason cringed. "Thanks, I love being reminded of that."

Sam elbowed him.

"I'm glad Yamamoto let you stay," said Vogas as she returned to the kitchen. "Do nothing else to jeopardize your place here. We need you. *Jesteś bardzo przydatny.*"

"Thanks, Ms. Vogas. We won't," Jason assured her.

He spotted the security chief sitting with Santiago and two other militia—Rosa and Guilden. Mayweather and Soohyun were nowhere to be seen, probably still helping with the cleanup operation outside.

"Let's play this carefully," Sam said, beckoning to Jason, leaving David and Budgie at the bar with Xerxes and Vogas, who crowded them with grandparental interest.

"Hey, Chief Mendez," Sam said. Santiago and the others looked up at her, while Rosa and Guilden continued drinking, sharing a hefty pitcher.

Mendez gave them a long head turn. "What in the everlasting magical frozen-over hell do you two want? I wasted all morning trying to track you idiots down, only to learn from Santiago that you broke surfacing rules early this morning, *again*. Then those Phage critters hit us—which I'm told we also have you to thank for."

Jason noticed Santiago's frown deepening, but he nodded to confirm what Mendez had said. "Sorry guys, had to speak up. Rules are rules."

Sam shrugged. "That's fine, fair enough. Our mistake."

"Damn right, it was your mistake," Mendez said. "The New Toronto authorities cannot be allowed to learn of the Village, under any circumstances."

"Sir, Governor Yamamoto asked us to tell you about a bot we found—the one that destroyed the Recyck yard," Sam said.

Mendez gave Sam a one-eyed stare from below his cap and eyepatch. "I'm listening—but this better be good. You're interrupting happy hour."

Rosa, Guilden, Santiago, and the other militia listened while Sam explained what had happened in the Recyck yard, carefully omitting details about the real reason they'd been there.

"And we have pictures of it," Sam said, giving her comm unit to Mendez so he could flick through photos of the mechanical titan they'd barely managed to destroy. In one picture, Sam's camera had captured the titan with its secondary arms whipping toward the lens, a scene of pure mechanized horror. Then, Mendez got to the image of the faded insignia stamped across the robot's plating.

"That's Confederate!" Guilden said. "Look!"

Everyone peered at the image while the militiaman continued his southern, drunken drawl, "My dad used to tell stories about the war machines he found during the Federation's expeditions into the old Confed territories, after they blew 'emselves up. He caught a lot of rads, but lived long enough to show us the pictures he took."

Sam swapped the screen to a picture she'd taken of the human body inside the machine. Guilden pointed. "See! It's one of *them*! In the flesh!"

Mendez shot the kid with a skeptical look. "How would a living Confederate have gotten down here from so far abroad? Their nearest territory was within the old United States, a hundred miles away at minimum. The Confederacy's dead and gone, son, it's been twenty years since they bombed themselves into oblivion. All your daddy saw was wrecks of their old vehicles and their burned-out cities."

"It looks like my dad's pics, that's all," Guilden said, disheartened.

Rosa poured him another round from the pitcher.

"You've got an overactive imagination, babe," she said.

Sam looked at Jason, who shrugged.

"Either way, Chief Mendez," Sam said. "I think we should keep a lookout for more of them. They're a huge danger to the Village, Confederate or not."

"Who made you chief of security, girl?" Mendez growled. Sam froze, but the chief waved his hand. "It's fine. We'll set up additional patrols beyond the walls, and place extra probes further out for early warning."

"Sounds good, sir," Sam nodded.

"Maybe the Confederacy's back to finish the job. We're not ready for an invasion, with the Imperials taking over everything else in the Sol System. Can't fight the empire and the Confeds all at the same time," Guilden said.

"There's not going to be an invasion, from the living *or* the dead," the chief said, sighing. "Good job killing that thing, though. Looks like it would've been bad if it'd shown up here."

"Thanks," Jason said.

"We're also done rebuilding Talos," Sam said.

Mendez raised an eyebrow. "I see. You're really gunning to get back into my good books, huh?"

"No comment, sir," Sam said.

Guilden was still rambling. "If you think about it, the Confederacy were a lot like us. Living off the grid, stickin' it to the man, fightin' the UEF's tyranny. Nothing's changed."

"Those two governments blew up the world, you little shit," Mendez rumbled. Before the chief could launch into another rant, he got a ping on his communicator. "Yeah, Governor?"

Jason and Sam watched Mendez's expression change from gruffness, to confusion, to alarm. He composed himself, getting up rather quickly for such a decrepit old man. Mendez snapped his fingers at the rest of his militia troopers as he grabbed his walking stick and hurried for the exit. "Cancel that last drink, kiddos. Yamamoto's got a job for us. *Real* big."

Rosa and Guilden exchanged glances, but they both got up and followed Mendez, groaning with annoyance at the interruption. Santiago hesitated, glancing at Sam and Jason as he stood to leave as well.

Sam addressed him. "How are Mayweather and Soohyun doing? We haven't chatted with you guys in a while."

"They're fine," the trooper said, sounding exhausted.

Sam's eyes narrowed slightly. "You doing alright?"

"Things have definitely been better around here," admitted Santiago. "I appreciate the good news about Talos, though. We could really use his help on the walls again."

Silence fell between them. Santiago jerked a thumb over his shoulder. "Sorry guys, I gotta run. Schedule is endless these days, and Mendez has been cracking the whip big time. Sounds like we've got another big job coming."

"Sure. Good luck," Jason said as Santiago followed his comrades out of the bar without another word. They returned to the drink bar, where David was already on his second round.

"Time to go," Jason slapped his hands on his brother's shoulders. Xerxes looked at them, sliding over a steaming box of food. "Sounds like you three have had quite the day so far."

Jason fumbled for his ration cards, but the barkeep waved a hand. "Nope. You're under orders from the chef to not starve. Pay us tomorrow with your earnings from that salvage you brought in, once Bilby processes it."

He caught a glimpse of Ms. Vogas through the kitchen window, who gave him a stern look.

David dragged himself out of his seat. "Thanks for the ear, Xerxes."

"Anytime, my friend," the big man said.

Sam pushed open the doors, shooing the brothers out of the bar. "Come on, you big buffoons. We've got another excursion to prep for, some bullshit to answer for, and our big guy needs a wakeup call. Abaddon is waiting for us."

22 — LANDING ZONE

Anne landed at the top of the underground access shaft, shutting off her roaring jump-jets. Her two bodyguards did the same, following her at a jog down a musty side tunnel, clogged with debris and desiccated human waste.

Anne's mind was reeling. Until now, the only other Abhamic-powered beings that she knew of were the emperor and his Praetorian Sisterhood, whose identities were unknown even to Anne. She herself also counted among the psionically empowered, though to a lesser extent, barely enough to sense other Abhamic users.

But those kids that Yamamoto had named, Jason and Sam, shattered those assumptions. Jason had all the signs of immense Abhamic strength, barely held back by the Osmium drug. If David had originated from those labs too, he might have similar abilities. Sam complicated things even more.

Anne approached her Jetbike, which she'd stashed away to avoid scaring the villagers, swinging her cybernetic leg over the leather seat. The false limb ached. Her onboard medical systems had the Phage in check for the time being, until she could return to her shuttle for proper extraction treatment.

Anne signaled to her operators, gunned the engine, and took off down a twisting transit conduit tunnel that was so wide, a tanker ship could have fit through it. The jet-troopers followed with a *whoosh* of micro-turbines, with Lincoln close beside her.

Anne's thoughts slid back to the young psychics. Her father must have aggressively pursued the Abhamancer Program after she, Mariko, and Julian had left, despite sanctions from the Strategos council. Multiple new Abhamic-powered beings were living right under Julian Yamamoto's nose, with the former scientist somehow none the wiser.

But Julian definitely suspected something was amiss. By chance or fate, he had accepted the trio into the Village after they'd escaped from her father's operation. Anne didn't want to think about where he might've sourced their genetic stock.

Hadrian Mariko's powers had allowed him to raise an empire and ruin the Sol System in the fires of his ambition. What would happen if Jason and Sam surfaced, equaling or exceeding Mariko's might? It would be a terrible new age of psionic titans battling for dominance, while baseline humanity suffered in the crossfire.   Anne was torn between her primary objective and the possibilities raised by these new discoveries. If Hadrian survived Nightshade's decapitation strike and somehow located Jason and Sam in the aftermath, he would attempt to harness them as psychic weapons—or otherwise destroy them.

They also presented an opportunity. If Nightshade Squadron's conventional weapons failed to break the emperor's mental defenses ... could Jason's powers give them an edge? Or Sam's? She needed to ask her father for details.

The operation's start time was too close, so recruiting them now was out of the question. Anne put this aside, but instructed Lincoln to alert her if their probes detected any unusual activity in the Village. She would keep tabs on them, at the very least.

As she drew nearer to their destination, Anne's comm unit overflowed with Nightshade message traffic.

"Something is emerging from the breach point!" Burnaby's static-laced voice shouted over the network. "Redirect fire from the north quadrant sentries, beat it back!"

"What the hell?" Anne said to herself, glancing at Lincoln, who tried to boost the signal.

"Pour it on, get the reserve squads in there. We don't have time for this," Luther's voice chimed in over the comm.

"Is it Imperial?" Burnaby's voice asked. "Doesn't look like one of their machines."

"We need to get back to the landing zone, now," Anne said, revving her bike's anti-grav drive and accelerated, followed tightly by her bodyguards.

Automated sentry guns tracked Anne and her companions as they roared into a huge cavern packed full of mothballed spacecraft. Many ships were nothing but skeletons, stripped to their understructures for valuable parts by scavengers or reclamation teams. The boneyard smelled of dust, engine fuel, and slowly oxidizing metals. Despite the nail-biting operation to get the *Solanum* down here through maintenance shafts and abandoned transit tunnels that were barely large enough for the stealth prowler's bulk—a testament to captain Brogan's piloting skills—this was the perfect spot to hide their base ship.

Anne immediately spotted a gaping hole in the wall on the far side of the chamber, dripping with melted permacrete and shrouded in smoke. A battle was raging around it, as Nightshade operators in full battle armor descended on the area in large numbers, Jetkit engines flaring in the dimness. They zipped around the shrouded hole in the chamber's thick permacrete wall-like flocks of angry birds, blasting away at something in the tunnel with all manner of man-portable weapons, while others deployed intelligent auto-sentry guns and sensor units around the *Solanum's* perimeter. Something huge was moving within the dense cloud of dust and debris, identifiable only by a massive silhouette and a burning orange light set into what looked like a giant cranial plate. Anne's onboard systems identified it as a plasma projector.

While Anne jetted closer, more squads emerged from the *Solanum's* open rear hangar bay to join the fight. An ear-splitting mechanical screech emitted from the dense cloud of smoke, followed by several white-hot beams of orange plasma, which splashed off the *Solanum's* energy shields, but failed to hit any of the fast-moving airborne Nightshade operators.

In front of the hangar ramp, Luther, Brogan, and Burnaby crouched in cover behind the hood of a six-wheeled all-terrain rover, directing proceedings and giving orders. They had a good view of the battle with the massive four-legged robotic newcomer, several hundred meters away.

As Anne landed her Jetbike and dismounted, she felt intense vertigo. Her cybernetics experienced a power surge, brought on by sheer stress and the creeping Phage. Her narcolepsy returned, and she tipped forward—right into Burnaby's outstretched hand.

"You alright?" he asked, steadying Anne and pulling her behind the rover. Lincoln jetted closer to run a check on her systems as Anne's bodyguards landed as well.

"Yes ... I'm fine," Anne said. She felt the vertigo recede as Lincoln pecked at an access port on her neck, and her brain fought back to full wakefulness. Luther, Burnaby, and Brogan were tactful, but Anne detected their underlying unease with her condition.

"I'll visit my shuttle's repair suite before we move out," Anne said in a placating tone. "What the hell is going on over there?"

Luther gestured to the ongoing engagement. "We experienced another of those underground tremors, and soon after, that thing started melting through the LZ's north wall."

"What is it?" Anne asked.

Burnaby peered through his Gauss rifle's scope, trying to get a good look at the mechanical beast as Nightshade troops rained fire onto its hull, narrowly avoiding white-hot beams of plasma fire in return.

"One of Captain Ossington's squads eyeballed an insignia on its plating," Burnaby said, squinting into his optics. "Sergeant Defoe said it was Confederate, and Ossington confirmed that as well."

"Confederate?" Anne asked. "As in, Great War-era Confederate?"

"Affirmative," said Burnaby, glancing at her. "But this vehicle is far more advanced than what they would have been using twenty years ago, let alone during the actual war a century before that. Our scans haven't detected any Nanite tech within it at all; it seems totally divorced from our modern technology. It also seems outfitted for tunneling."

Anne didn't know much about the Confederacy after they had gone their separate way from the UEF post-Great war, but her father had been one of the few UEF officials in contact with them before they had disappeared for good twenty years ago. It was a mystery to all but a few in the highest echelons of UEF leadership ... like Avery. This was yet another question she had for him, especially given what she was seeing.

A massive explosion caught Anne's attention, temporarily lighting up most of the cavern with a sun-bright fireball. One of the Nightshade operator teams had detonated what looked like a thermobaric warhead against the Confederate robot's hull. The chamber's stale air was sucked toward the battle, and then blasted back out away from it, ruffling clothing, hair, and old tarps that covered many of the boneyard's dead spacecraft.

The giant Confederate machine emitted a strained roar through damaged audio equipment and began to back away into the tunnel it had melted, firing white-hot plasma beams as it went. One of the beams carved a deep, steaming trench of molten glass into the dusty permacrete ground less than ten meters away from Anne's position.

"It's retreating," Luther said, releasing a barely audible sigh, but her professional composure never wavered. "Captain Ossington, when you're sure it's not coming back, please return here and render a casualty report."

"Yes ma'am," Ossington said over the comm.

Several jet-troopers peeled off from the battle, while the rest continued to pour weapons fire into the tunnel entrance, determined to dissuade the Confederate machine from returning to the boneyard cavern. As they came closer, Anne realized that one of them was Ossington, leading his company from the front during the engagement. Moments later, he landed in front of them with a crunch of gravel under his boots, depolarizing the armored face shield of his battle helmet as he slung his red-hot handheld plasma cannon over one shoulder.

Ossington saluted, and said, "We've got one KIA, several injured. Ammunition expenditures were very heavy, but we barely left a scratch on the damn thing. I think we mostly annoyed it."

Luther pinched the bridge of her nose. "The operation hasn't even started yet, and we've got casualties. Good grief. Get your injured back to the *Solanum*, we'll see about returning them to battle-readiness before the main event begins."

"Affirmative, Lieutenant-Commander," Ossington turned to one of his people, whose armored breastplate read 'Defoe', whirling a finger. "Get it done, sergeant."

"Yes, sir," Defoe saluted, taking off with the rest of Ossington's personal squad.

Ossington tapped a screen on his vambrace, scrolling through messages. "We're getting a lot of reports from our scout teams throughout the Under-city's sublayers. Many of them have encountered similar bogeys to the one that attacked us, but I've instructed them not to engage, only to mark their locations so we can avoid them on our way to the city's downtown core."

"Very good, captain," Luther said. "I'm not liking this. We knew that the Under-city levels of these UEF arcologies were dangerous, but I had no idea that there were active Confederate units running around, so long after they supposedly disappeared. Did you know anything about this, Anne?"

Anne shook her head. "I've been aboard Colossus for too many years, so I haven't been keeping tabs on events Earth-side either way."

Ossington grimaced. "This may complicate our operation. We'll have to hope that these things don't breach the surface and start wreaking havoc up there."

"All the more reason to press on," Anne said. "One problem at a time. First, the emperor, then we'll deal with these Confederate sentinels if we have to. Hopefully this is an isolated incursion, and not a sign of something more major happening."

No one elaborated on that possibility.

Luther continued. "Double our patrols around the area, Ossington. We should also task a couple teams to pursue that enemy unit, make sure it doesn't double back or return here for another round. After we're sure it's gone, collapse that tunnel with explosives."

"Yes, ma'am," Ossington said, and stepped away with Luther to further coordinate the bolstering of their landing zone's defenses.

Anne was amazed at how quickly the landing zone returned to normal after what would have been a brutally difficult battle for any other fighting force. Two jet-troopers resumed camouflaging their base ship, dragging an enormous tarp halfway over the energy-shielded *Solanum*'s hull to help it blend in with the other dead craft. The ship's chameleonic hull plating had been recolored to a faded red and yellow, disguised as a decommissioned transport for the Cooper Nanotech Supply corporation. This company was owned by the council's finance minister in direct violation of anti-competition laws, but corruption like that was simply the way in the Federation.

Scout rovers were beginning new patrols of the area, rear gun-turrets swiveling as their operators drove long loops around the cavern. Anne heard gunfire ring out more than once as operators destroyed other hostile Under-city critters in the dark corners of the boneyard.

Anne turned to Burnaby, asking, "Have your people begun creating our backup supply caches, captain?"

Burnaby pointed to the *Solanum*. Additional vehicles bearing loads of supplies, weapons, ammunition, and necessities were roaring down the ramp past them, through the cavern, and into an adjoining tunnel. Squads of hovering operators accompanied the convoy.

"We're carting materials to several secondary locations," Burnaby explained, showing Anne another nearby cavern on his datapad: an abandoned auto-factory. "What's our play with the supply caches, Anne? Most are too far away to support the strike zone in the city center, and they're at risk from all the weird things running around down here, Phage hives, plenty of armed criminal gangs, and god knows what else."

"I'm sure you've heard of death simulations, Captain."

"Of course. We run them before every op," Burnaby said.

"This is one of ours," Anne explained. "If we fail to remove the emperor from power, we'll need fallback positions. From these, we can begin an insurgency, build up another chance to strike Mariko. That's a last resort, obviously."

"Can't argue with that logic, I suppose," Burnaby nodded. "We've got supply stashes all over the Sol System."

Luther returned to the group as Ossington took off, jetting across the cavern to personally direct the perimeter defenses.

"How about our efforts to transport materiel and supplies to the city center?" she asked.

Captain Brogan shrugged, tapping on a datapad. "Steady as she goes, Lieutenant-Commander. We're using our aerial gunships to haul stocks of ammo and supplies over there through underground access routes, but we'll need more time for the rest. So far, the transport teams haven't run directly into any Confederate bots, but they'll be on the lookout."

All of their communicators chimed.

"Yes, Captain Chiang. Go ahead," Luther said.

Chiang's face appeared above a holo-viewer on Luther's wrist, obscured by static. "We've completed our survey of the city center. It's getting busy around here."

Luther shook her vambrace and the signal improved. Anne saw that Chiang was flanked by two of her men, clad in powered war-suits and Nightshade's ubiquitous Jetkits, armed to the teeth. The squad was stationed above-ground inside an empty office suite overlooking the city's Grand Processional Square, with the UEF Headquarters building looming in the hazy distance.

"Elaborate, Captain," Anne requested. On the screen, Chiang pointed out areas of interest below. "The traffic-control systems are routing all civilians into the downtown core, ma'am, even with no major Federation events planned for today. The area is being prepped for something big."

"I guess the emperor was being literal about his plan to use the spot where the war was declared to end it," Luther remarked.

"Lieutenant-Commander, I don't like this," Chiang said.

"Hmmm. Is there any Imperial presence on the ground yet?" Luther asked.

"Not yet, but that doesn't mean they're not here," said Chiang. "We can see it in their control over the city's traffic systems. The Imperials already own New Toronto—their main force hasn't arrived yet, ma'am."

"Is that why you're having trouble with this, Captain?" Anne asked.

Chiang shrugged. "Yes. I still think this is a trap. For us."

Over the feed, the captain crossed to the window, gesturing down into the busy square as civilians could be seen getting out of stalled cars, shut down by the city's automated systems. More and more were arriving, but no vehicles were leaving, leaving huge crowds stranded in the square.

Chiang spoke over the footage. "The emperor has to know we're still at large because Nightshade Squadron never publicly surrendered. It'd be in character for him to set up an event to draw us out, allowing him to eliminate us and anyone else who dares to show up and challenge him."

"It certainly would be," murmured Anne.

"Excuse me?"

"A trap is Mariko's style, you're right," Anne said. "And the best way to overcome a trap is to get inside its mechanism and dismantle it, which we are uniquely qualified for. The emperor doesn't understand the scale of what we're planning. We still have some surprises left."

Chiang looked at Luther over the feed. "What are your orders, Lieutenant-Commander?"

"Continue your survey, Captain," said Luther. "We have no reason to stop the operation at this point. Mark the most optimal areas to strike from. Stay hidden—do not interact with any church or Federation military units you encounter. They'll sooner report you to the Empire than help us, if only to save themselves. Once the Imperials land, get your teams in range to strike their most vulnerable units. The sheer number of civilians will provide cover for you."

"That's a tall order, ma'am," Chiang said.

"But you'll get it done, of course," Luther said.

"Of course, ma'am."

"Will we be extracting the Strategos Council? They'll be in a lot of danger once the Imperials land," Chiang said.   Anne grimaced. "No. They're being too closely watched, and they've sold their souls to Mariko anyway. All except one. I've got special plans for him."

Chiang raised an eyebrow. "Roger that."

Luther looked at Anne as the call ended. "It may be worth looking at alternatives in case. Does the emperor have to die today? We could wait for a better opportunity, one where he isn't expecting an attack."

"No. I'm sorry, but this must happen today," Anne said in a tone that brooked no debate. "If the Solar Empire integrates the UEF's remaining population into their Hierarchy, it will become much harder to deradicalize them. Most people won't be able to handle the ideological whiplash. If we fail here, Mariko's murderous philosophy will poison generations to come, as it did with the Colossi people."

Luther bowed her head. "This is true. We all have families and friends to protect, so we need to get this done right."

She turned to Anne. "Any word on your brother's last known position?"

Anne glanced at Lincoln, who trained his burning red eyes on the ceiling high above them and squawked some binary to her.

"It's a faint signal, but clear. He's in transit," Anne translated. "Lincoln has also intercepted transmissions from their fleet, saying that Zeke's people trashed the *Eagle of the Ninth*. He and many of the captives from *Refit One* are back in custody. Their attack has slowed the fleet's surface landings across the whole planet, because the emperor wanted his prized ship repaired enough to be presentable."

Luther almost laughed. "Best laid plans, right?"

Anne nodded. "Zeke's given us extra time to prepare for the assault."

"Good. Let's not disappoint him," Luther said.

"There's something else I need to do, Lieutenant-Commander." Anne said. "It's not strictly part of our operation, but it's still important. Will you accompany me?"

"Affirmative, as long as it's mission-critical, or at least adjacent to our objectives. To where?"

Anne looked out across the boneyard, in a direction that her geolocation system claimed was east. "I need to find my father before the Empire does," Anne said. "His work is too important to fall into Mariko's hands ... and I have some things I need to ask him."

23 — ROBO-REVERIE

NEW TORONTO UNDERGROUND - THE VILLAGE — OCT. 31, 2263 — 14:46 HOURS

Jason was falling past a gigantic wall. He scrabbled at it, trying to slow his descent, but he slammed into the ground before his fingers got any purchase on the rough material.

He sat up, body aching from the impact. In the distance, a black wave approached—a sea of stygian blackness. Jason backed up against the endless wall, trapped between it and the rushing tsunami of shadow. Something told him that the other side of the wall was a place of safety ... he had to break it down. Jason turned around and struck the barrier, trying to pull pieces out of the old, crumbling structure, but it was far too solid to do any real damage.

The wave hit him, and everything turned to madness. Countless images smashed through Jason's perception—people, places, horrors, past, present, future, pure insanity. Soohyun, Mayweather, and Santiago hid in the corner of the damaged cargo hauler. Soohyun was terrified, bracing herself as waves of Abhamic psychic energies pulsed toward her ...

The dream changed. Jason saw himself sitting in a giant seat, arms and legs locked down by restraints. He looked old and tired, with dark circles under his eyes. Giant piles of machinery and cabling surrounded the seat, feeding up into it. As Jason watched himself strain and writhe in the massive mechanical contraption, he started to scream ...

Jason's dream remixed again, locking in on a version of Sam, looking much older than he remembered. A jagged scar ran from her right temple to her chin. Sam's hair was long, and she wore a resplendent war-suit of high-quality ceramic armor. Sam wielded a long blade, black as a singularity.

She faced down a horde of ... *things*. They weren't robotic, nor an augmented army of Imperial terror-troopers. Waves of indistinct, sarcophile horrors charged Sam and those she was defending—crowds of people and children. Where were they? What was this? The environment around them was too indistinct.

Razor teeth flashed, bone claws rasped, darkness bled, and Jason glimpsed glowing Phage tumors among the carnivorous mass as Sam fought with blade and mental might. These Phagebearers had mutated into massive, flowing, shapeshifting terrors, splattering Sam with torrents of black ichor from her raven hair to armored boots as she stabbed and slashed her way through them. But holding back the horde of monstrosities was like trying to stop a wave on the beach, and the tide of mutagenic terror drowned Sam in a heartbeat of spraying gore.

Jason spotted David, who screamed in fury as Sam was dragged down. He was older too, wearing a wide-brimmed hat. A huge mechanical eagle sat on his shoulder. David took several hits from stinking flesh-projectiles, fired with bullet force. He returned fire at the nightmares, trying to take flight using jump-jets, but the tsunami of sentient flesh sliced into the crowds of terrified people behind him. Then, David himself was consumed, painfully absorbed into the almighty mass of roiling flesh-matter. Jason screamed, but there was no way to avert his gaze.

The huge, four-sided obelisk blasted into view, towering over him, blazing otherworldly light and supernatural shadow into Jason's retinas. Reality bent around the Abaddon Beacon, making it impossible to observe without feeling like his mind was going to break.

"What do you want?" Jason yelled.

"*Find us, Jason,*" Abaddon bellowed. "*You are running out of time. We have the answers you seek, and the cure to your affliction ...*"

"I'm trying! We have a way to find you, we just need to get there!"

The dream changed.

Jason hurtled across a wasteland of multicolored dusty rock; a desert composed of different textures. A white city loomed up out of the haze. Beyond it, Jason could see a distant star-scape above the concave horizon, shrouded by stratospheric clouds. Was this Colossus Station?

Jason's perception homed in on the tallest tower, ascending to the top at impossible speeds. As he crested the lip of a gigantic penthouse chamber—the obelisk was waiting for him, haloed by pink fire.

"You must find us before all of this comes to pass. Only you can stop this dark future ..."

The white city fractured as the fires of war descended upon it. Teeming millions fought among the buildings in a war that would truly end all wars. The surrounding deserts darkened with numberless armies and vile mutagenic hordes who battled until the titanic habitat began to break. The great outer shell shattered, releasing the void inside as fleshy tentacular masses coiled up from underground to strike out at great fleets of warships outside. Colossus Station and the surrounding ships were consumed by this mass of monstrous outgrowths: a hideous, boiling amalgamation of flesh, technology and non-living matter, corrupted at the subatomic level. It ate everything, including the continent-sized station and the massive fleets before reaching out to begin consuming the Earth and its moon.

Abaddon loomed over the apocalyptic heavens as the Sol System itself was consumed, floating on a boiling cloud of shadow.

"Find us, or this will become your reality ..."

His dream morphed into a vast field of streets, trimmed lawns, and marble wading pools, with skyscrapers surrounding it all. A battle was being fought here too. As Jason's perception rocketed through the open space, over thousands of indistinct figures who flew, fought, and died in a chorus of war and destruction, the artifact was waiting for him in front of the central building.

"We are waiting. Find us. The final sacrifice will soon be at hand ..."

Something tugged at Jason's perspective, distorting the nightmare.

"Wake up, Jason ..."

"Wait, tell me more! This can't be our future!" Jason cried. "You have to help me ... you have to take away this curse! How do I stop this?"

"Wake up, Jason!"

"Jason, wake up!" Sam cried again.

Jason sat bolt upright, screaming. Budgie screeched, flapping to a higher perch and knocking over a food container.

Sam leaned over Jason, dripping wet and wearing nothing but a towel, both hands on his face. Medical patches and fading bruises peeked out under the fuzzy material of Sam's towel. The shower pod was still running. "Come on, Jason. Focus on me. Calm down."

Jason was drenched in sweat, clutching a sketchpad, upon which he'd been scrawling a single image, over and over. His fingers hurt from gripping the pen, which had nearly broken in two. For a few seconds, Jason couldn't tell what was real or part of his hellish dream. He managed to get control of his breathing, blinking away after-images of chaos and destruction. "I'm ... I'm here. I'm good."

"Thank god. Were you dreaming again?" Sam asked, removing her hands from his clammy face, and fumbled with his inhibitor. Moments later, it gave him an extra dose, on top of the ones it had already deployed while he was sleeping.

"Yep."

Jason tried to relax, leaning back. Those images, his vision ... the *future* ... it couldn't possibly have been real. Was it a trick that Abaddon was playing? Did it really have the power to show him events to come? Or was the dream his own Abhamic powers at work, like a form of precognition? There was no way to tell.

"Sounded pretty gnarly," Sam said, breathing a sigh of relief. She checked his inhibitor, but it was loaded and working properly.

"It was. They always are."

"You're more vulnerable when you're asleep. It's okay, Jason. Take some more deep breaths," she said, pinching his cheeks and checking his pupils again.

Jason tried not to notice how Sam's towel was starting to slip off her ample chest. She'd taken fabrication lessons from some of the Village artisans, and the result was the ugliest towel he'd ever seen. Sam would not accept any criticism of her beloved beach towel—and also refused to accept that there weren't any beaches nearby. A girl could dream, as she put it.

"Feeling better?" Sam asked as Jason felt blood returning to his face. He focused on her eyes instead of her soaked body, steaming from the temperature differential.

"Starting to. We're quite the pair today, aren't we?"

"Unfortunately," Sam agreed.The sounds and smells of their living space returned, calming Jason further. Memories of Abaddon's prophesized apocalypse receded into the back of his mind, chased off by the Osmium in his system. Weights clanked in the tiny workout area as David put his body through its paces, ignoring the commotion. A complicated computer setup hummed against the back wall, near the door to their composting toilet. David's 'battle-station' was a haphazard collection of a dozen screens and networked machines, running monitoring software to keep the Village's intranet functioning.

David racked a weighted bar after finishing several chest-presses. He sat up and barked with red-faced annoyance, "What the hell's gotten into you, man? You almost made me drop this thing on myself."

"He's rattled. Go easy," Sam said, glaring at David.

Jason's inhibitor hit him with another dose, and the psychic echo of the Beacon disappeared completely.

"Sorry. I'm fine. Happy juice is working," Jason mumbled, looking down at the dozens of identical obelisk shapes he'd scribbled, scratching through several sheets.

David got up, peering down at Jason's savaged sketchbook. "Y'know, sometimes that weird stuff you draw ... looks like it almost makes *sense* to me."

"It does?"

"Whatever, I can't focus with you making all that racket," David said, grabbing a sweat towel and sleeveless shirt. His ruined, scorched clothes were heaped next to his cot for delivery to the Village's seamstresses for recycling.

"Sorry," Jason murmured. He flipped the sketchbook closed, embarrassed.

"Go work front-of-house. Jackass," Sam muttered, standing back to avoid making Jason uncomfortable.

"Fine. We're due for some customers now that the lockdown's over. We've got another backlog of repair work after this morning's little jaunt," David said, grabbing his largest kettlebell and headphones, lurching on unsteady legs toward the curtain separating their living area from their Village-facing business.

"And get this guy ready to reboot, already!" David added, rapping on Talos's huge rebuilt body, which squatted inside a metal lifter frame. His plating was still a rusted red color, but Sam had subbed in many new re- placement components, so his look was more patchwork than ever. Talos was undergoing a diagnostic review before his reboot, connected to several different computers. The ancient Confederate battery hung out of the robot's multi-colored barrel chest, integrating with his capacitors.

Sam glanced at Jason. "You sure you're okay?"

"Just peachy, Sam."

"Poor guy. Gimme a sec," Sam sighed, adjusting her towel before it slipped free, retreating inside her curtained sleeping area.

Jason sighed. Even after several years, the two of them hadn't quite gotten over their shared awkwardness while living in such close quarters. Jason couldn't imagine their friendship evolving into anything else, at least ... not with how things were right now. David had done the smart thing, cultivating intimate relationships outside of their little gang, and maintaining a healthy distance from any possible entanglements with Sam.

"How's the ribs?" Jason called to Sam.

"Not a hundred percent, but healing super-fast. Janice is the best."

Sam emerged wearing fresh clothes, rubbing moisturizer onto her heat-blasted skin and drying her hair by extracting liquid from it with a hand gesture, levitating it into the sink for later recycling.

"The usual, huh?" she asked, flipping through Jason's torn sketchbook pages.

"Yep."

Frantic sketches and unreadable alien symbols covered every page.

"The Abaddon Beacon?"

"What else would it be?" Jason said, gritting his teeth. "It's all my mind lets me draw."

"Easy there, Jason," Sam said, handing him the bottle of moisturizer.

"Sorry," Jason replied, rubbing cream onto his skin. Sam turned to look at Jason's corner of their shared space.

The walls above Jason's drafting table were plastered with portraits of David, Sam, Budgie, and others from around the Village, plus a few well-rendered landscapes and Under-city locations. A series of comics featuring a cartoon chicken lay piled up on the desk. But his obsession with Abaddon dominated the space: hundreds upon hundreds of drawings and renderings were pinned to the walls and every available surface, as Jason's mind tried to understand what the hell it was, and what it wanted.

Sam's face had fallen to a sad look, but she perked up and switched to encouraging. "I saw it too, y'know. During your episode outside the Recyck yard. I think we all did."

"Saw what? The Beacon?"

"Big obelisk, glowy and scary?" Sam asked, gesturing above their heads. Her voice had lowered to a pleasant tone that she knew worked well on him.

"Yeah, sounds about right," Jason said, putting down the moisturizer.

"That's the first time I've actually seen it too, probably because we were so close to you when your mind was unprotected," Sam said.

"Right," Jason said. He relaxed back into the soft-body container units, looking over at the huge robot crouched beside the opposite wall. "How's Talos?"

"He'll be up in a jiffy, twenty minutes tops," Sam said.

Jason brightened. "I hope he forgives me."

Sam's lips widened into a grin. "I hope you've got an epic apology ready for him. He'll be expecting one."

Jason groaned. "I won't have time to deliver it. He's gonna kill me, Sam."

"He can't. Basic governing laws of robotics, and all that," Sam said. "Anyway, I want to try another meditation session. Maybe you're close to a breakthrough. These more intense dreams might be a sign that your brain is finally starting to adapt to your powers ... maybe even figuring out how to resist Abaddon."

"I think these dreams would suggest that I'm moving closer to insanity, not further away," Jason said.

"My hallucinations went away when I learned to control my powers. Yours will too. Come on," Sam said, leading Jason over to a low table where they shared meals, yanking out two pillows. "Sit."

Jason sat. Sam flicked a finger. Five feet away, the kettle's lever clicked down. Jason hid his alarm. Sam's tea, like her cooking, sewing, and taste in interior décor, was terrible.

"Let's keep this brief," she said. "We've only got until Talos boots up, and we still need to plan our talk with Yamamoto. Not to mention head to the Science Institute later today. We need to get in there before that guard bot's codes are changed, and they're probably running on a 24-hour cycle for those, if not less."

"Great," Jason said.

"Don't worry. We'll figure something out. I thought you'd be excited, Jason.""Every time you say that, things don't tend to go that well, Sam."

"Shush. Don't let David be a bad influence on you."

The kettle flash-boiled two mugs of water. Sam's eyes blazed and the mugs floated over. A teabag neatly dropped into each from the nearby countertop. Sam had once been clumsier with her levitation control, leading to awkward explanations when their neighbors had glimpsed her doing things they couldn't explain. Now, she was approaching mastery. Jason sipped from the teacup to humor her before setting it down. Sam nodded in approval.

"You hungry? Can't meditate on an empty stomach," Sam said, gesturing to their living quarters' tiny kitchenette.

"No! Uh ... no, thanks. Ms. Vogas' wraps were more than enough," Jason replied, holding up his hands. It was a guarantee that Sam would mess up their rations, like her homemade tea.

"Focus on your breath, please," Sam said, sipping from her mug.

Jason took a long, ragged breath.

"Again, deep and slow."

He obeyed. The tea's aroma was better than its taste, calming him. Jason felt a slight twitch of instability in the background of his mind, a hint of psionic terror.

"Find us, Jason ..."

Jason felt the color drain from his face. "Sam, I—I hear it."

"Back to me, Jason. Breathe. Breathe with it, focus on me," Sam said.

He locked eyes with her as their chests rose and fell, despite the whispers trying to break into his mind. The Osmium inhibitor hissed softly.

"Ok. Now, focus on this," Sam said. She held up a pure metal sphere that she'd shaped with her mental abilities, using ragged hunks of steel as raw materials. A dubious portrait of Budgie was engraved onto its surface, the latest in a series of matter manipulation experiments Sam had been trying.

"Size and mass don't matter. My muscles aren't my mind, and neither are yours," Sam's eyes flared as she removed her hand, hovering the perfect metal ball between them. "When you're ready, I'm going to let go, and you'll take over. Easy, right?"

"But I'm on Osmium. It won't work."

"Try it anyway. For me."

"Alright, but this is a bad idea."

Jason's fingers twitched upward to grab the sphere.

"Nope. Not even David can one-arm this thing. Reach out and feel it with your mind, not your body."

"Fine," Jason said, trying not to laugh at the embarrassing etching of Budgie as the ball rotated.

"Relax. You're with me, you're good. Focus."

Jason let it absorb his attention as the room dimmed around him. He tried to do what Sam often mentioned—forging a mental link with the target, like the mind-muscle connection David always bragged about. Jason was unsure how the Abhamic version of that connection would actually feel if done correctly.

A psychic ripple shunted through the space. Pinned drawings fluttered, and the weights in David's workout area rattled. Robotic and cyber-tech parts jiggled on the walls, and household items shuddered on shelves and countertops.

Time seemed to slow. Jason's heartbeat increased. All this happened while the Osmium was still in his system. Its effectiveness was dwindling. He wanted to stop, but Sam gave Jason an encouraging look.

"Concentrate. Hold the ball in your mind. Don't let it spin out of your control. You're strong enough to protect yourself, Jason, and you can control your power. I *know* you can," Sam added, ignoring Jason's effects on the room around them.

Jason narrowed his eyes. As he focused, Sam reached around and twisted a tiny knob on his Osmium inhibitor—ratcheting the drip down to nothing. The psychedelic had a very short half-life, so it would cycle out of his bloodstream within minutes.

"Wait, what are you ..."

"You're with me. You're fine," Sam murmured in his ear. "You can do this, you're safe."

That sent shivers down his back. Sam resumed her seat, maintaining the ball's steady rotation. Jason tried to shake off the butterflies in his stomach and concentrated harder on it.

"I'm letting go," Sam declared. The ball moved down one millimeter, then another.

"*Find us ...*"

Jason heard someone, *something*, whispering to him again. Cold fear tickled his spine. His head swiveled, but Sam steered him back to her.

"It's okay for your mind to wander. Come back to me. Focus on your breath."

"It's coming from ... somewhere else, outside my mind. I hear it."

"Hear what?"

"Find us," Abaddon said, coming from behind him, around him, inside him.

"That," Jason said, with pure dread. "It's the *Beacon.*"

"Focus. All that matters is here, now, with me. Stay in control. Fight it off. Keep it away from you without the drugs."

She continued withdrawing control over the metal sphere. It lowered.

"Turn it back on. Turn on the Osmium, please. I can't block out the Abaddon Beacon without it," pleaded Jason. He reached for the inhibitor, but Sam stopped him.

"Please try this, Jason. You can't access your powers if Osmium is blocking your control."

"But it also keeps the Beacon out, Sam!"

"FIND US."

The voice stabbed through Jason's mind. Pain spiked across his face, and his head snapped back, eyes rolling.

Sam was so shocked at Jason's reaction that her concentration lapsed, dropping the metal ball. It slammed onto the floor between her and Jason, who fell over backward and continued to jerk and spasm—the telltale signs of a psychic outburst. The steel sphere started to squeal and smoke, like something was melting it from inside. Pain spiked through Sam's head, and she felt her well-honed mental defenses kick up automatically.

On cue, the Abaddon Beacon's shadowy presence filtered into the room through the ground, walls, and even the oxygen filtration systems, attracted by the lack of protection around Jason's mind. Sam swore.

A pulse blasted out of Jason and through the prefab's living quarters, tearing objects off the walls and blasting the darkness away. A flying book slapped Sam in the face, snapping her back to focus. She leaned forward over Jason's seizing body to locate the inhibitor on the back of his neck, struggling to find the knob. "Shit, shit, shit!"

Whatever value Jason might have gotten from their meditation session, it wasn't worth him detonating like a psychic bomb and killing half the Village. The steel ball deformed with an awful screeching sound, warping the engraving of Budgie as the surface vibrated, heated to liquefaction, and scorched the floor around it. Seeing this, the bird squawked in fear and flapped through the curtain into the repair shop. Sam finally managed to twist the inhibitor's drug release knob, despite Jason's thrashing and babbling. Blood spurted from his nose and hers too.

Just then, David barged in, headphones dangled around his neck with music thumping out of them.

"What are you two doing?" David demanded as the sentient shadows receded faster than they ever had before. The psychic breeze died down.

Sam looked up at him as Jason's seizure subsided, leaving him motionless on the floor.

"I ... uh ... we—" she stammered.

David caught on with one glance at Jason. "Did you turn off his Osmium? What the hell did you do that for?"

Sam wiped away blood from her nose and checked Jason's inhibitor, which was giving him an extra powerful dose, then she grabbed a small capsule of iron supplement pills, courtesy of Doc Janice.

Sam popped several pills, glaring at David. "We were taking a meditation break. I was trying to help him relax, David. To see if he could control himself without the drugs, before we throw caution to the winds and go to the topside science facility."

"Uh huh. He looks very relaxed," David said. "Great going, Sam."

Tears filled Sam's eyes as her fists balled. Right before she told David where he could stick his criticism, Jason stirred—a record recovery for him.

"Uggghhh, what happened?" Jason asked, rubbing his face and instinctively feeling the comforting angles of the inhibitor on the back of his neck.

"Sorry, things got a bit out of hand," Sam said, dabbing her eyes, trying to tamp down her frustration.

"A bit? You almost set him off, Sam," David asked.

Ignoring him, Sam helped Jason shift into a sitting position, eyeing the smoldering steel ball on the floor in front of them.

"Whoa, did I ..." Jason asked, trailing off as he noticed it.

"Yeah, you did. I'm sorry, it was my fault," Sam admitted.

"Shit," Jason said, staring at the ball. The steel was rehardening, mangled by his unconscious fury. Sam had spent days shaping the hunk of metal into a sphere with her mind. Jason had destroyed it in seconds with the tiniest fraction of his bottled-up power. He shuddered to imagine what would happen if he'd targeted *Sam* with enough force to melt steel.

David gestured to Talos. "What happened to getting the big guy back online?"

Sam ignored him, checking over Jason one more time.

"I'm alright now. It's okay, I think," Jason said, blinking his eyes to make the room stop spinning.

"Sam!" David barked.

Sam regarded David coldly. "Talos is finished. We were meditating during his final boot sequence. And I was not trying to hurt your brother in any way, David. I think you know that."

"Sure, I know. I'm sorry, I was just worried about him," David said, backing off.

Jason felt like a useless mediator. "Guys, it's okay. Sam made a mistake; it's no big deal—"

"Don't downplay it, Jason," Sam said, giving him some water, an iron pill, and a painkiller. "I'm sorry. I ... made a mistake. I thought you might be ready, Jason. I figured we needed to try this before we go to the Science Institute later today. I thought that if you'd managed to hold yourself together and get control, then maybe the trip wouldn't be necessary."

"It's okay, Sam," Jason said. "It was worth a shot before we go after Abaddon. I have no idea what we'll do when we find that blasted obelisk, but I appreciate you helping me out with these meditations, even if they can get ... dangerous."

David looked like he wanted to say more, but held his tongue and turned his attention to the laptops connected to Talos with a tangle of diagnostic cables, checking the ancient Confederate power cell jacked into the robot's chest.

Sam snapped her fingers at him. "Hey, no touching. Integrating that Confederate battery into Talos' existing systems came down to luck and a prayer."

David tapped a data-monitor and shrugged. "Everything looks like it's in the green. Time to wake him, I guess."

Sam sighed, stood up, rounded the automaton's huge frame, and flipped a master switch under his chest carapace. "Fine. Here goes nothing."

The robot's egg-shaped head twitched. Jason shuffled backward as Talos's hydraulic motor-muscles fired to life in sequence and his whole body began to shudder, shaking the room. Jason caught whiffs of ammonia and cleaning chemicals as gases burst from the robot's pistons. Talos's three photoreceptors winked on, in sequence.

Talos's massive magnetic boots locked onto the metal flooring as he rose, towering over them all. The prefab wasn't tall enough for the mech to stand up straight, forcing him to bend at the waist.

His photoreceptors rotated, focusing on Jason. Talos pointed a finger, poking Jason in the chest.

"You," the huge robot intoned. "You killed me."

Jason backed away. He knew Talos wouldn't harm him, but Jason's hind brain hadn't gotten the memo.

"Uh, right. Sorry, big guy. I didn't mean to," Jason said, stammering.

"And you! You were too slow in uncoupling me from that blasted ship," Talos snapped at David.

"Don't blame me, bolthead," David said, crossing his arms.

Sam interposed herself between them. "Talos, it's okay. You're having some momentary distress as your emotional core finishes rebooting."

Budgie landed on one of Talos's massive shoulders, but the robot ignored him.

"Momentary distress? Samantha, I thought you cared. Last thing I remember is Jason having a little ... freak-out. That cargo vessel's fall rendered me nonfunctional for—" Talos checked his internal clock. "Three weeks, five hours, thirteen minutes and twenty-three seconds?"

Sam rested a sympathetic hand on the robot's forearm. "It took me a while to put you back together, big guy. And before you flatten Jason, I'll have you know that he's the reason you're online again. He came up with the strategy we used to destroy a very nasty automaton, whose battery is powering you now."

"Hmmmph," Talos said.

"And you'll notice your systems have been overhauled. What happened was unfortunate, but it gave me the opportunity to rebuild you better than before."

Talos contemplated this, leering at Jason. "Perhaps I will let you live after all, meatsack."

"Heh, uhh ... thanks," Jason replied.

The robot looked down at himself over his gorget's ridge, flexing gigantic fingers and cycling hidden weapon panels open and closed. Before Sam could protest, Talos ripped out the diagnostic cables and shoved the Confederate titan's battery deep inside his chest. His trio of eyes flared with the power surge, and a circular shield sealed it within his chassis.

"Hmmm," Talos said, rotating his arms and stomping his gigantic boots. "Feels good. My energy efficiency has improved. Must be a miniaturized fusion reactor. It's old, though. *Confederate*, you said?"

Sam shrugged. "We're not sure about that. But you'll need to monitor it for weirdness."

Talos's enormous left arm transformed into his favored plasma gun with a flurry of sliding plating and rearranging circuitry.

"That automaton must have been powerful to justify such a high-quality power backup," Talos said. "I hope we find more of them. Only the crucible of glorious combat can test my full capabilities again."

Sam said, "Sorry, Talos, but we need you back on the walls for a bit. We just had a Phage migration, and the militia need a break now that all the infected are gone."

A deep, whining groan of annoyance issued from Talos's vocalizer.

"Whaaaaaat? Is that all I'm good for?" he cried. "You built me for the fires of battle, Samantha! Instead, battle passed while I slept. I long for the greatness you promised! I need to *kill something*—"

Sam interrupted Talos by tossing him the science facility guard bot CPU core.   The robot's huge hand came up in a calculated arc, snatching the fragile device without damaging it. "Interesting."

Talos plugged the module into a universal port in his head, and his eyes flashed as he processed for several seconds. "Is this what I think it is?"

"Yep, codes for the Science Institute," Jason answered. "And we're going there today."

Talos ejected the module after copying its data and internal architecture into his memory.

"Fascinating. Will there be ... violence?"

"Hope not, but that's why you're coming with us," Sam said with a tantalizing edge. "But first, we need you to make an appearance on the walls so Yamamoto doesn't exile us."

"Hmph," said Talos. "You're using me as leverage to keep your ungrateful asses here?"

"You bet."

"Acceptable, I suppose."

David heard a loud *ding-dong* behind the curtain. "Finish up here and get him ready to go. I'll handle the customers."

"Yeah, why don't you do that?" Sam agreed. "I'm still pissed at you."

David pushed through the curtain, grumbling under his breath.

Talos continued. "I suppose I'll do this for you ... if you promise to find me the glory of battle as soon as possible. My main cannon needs calibrating, and I hate dealing with your neighbors during testing."

"Please don't fire your weapons inside the Village, Talos," Sam reminded him. "Unless we're under attack, of course."

"Fine, fine," Talos grumbled.

"Oi! Guys, come up here," David called.

Sam glanced at Jason. "I gotta finish checking his systems. Can you see what he wants?"

"On it," Jason said. Budgie hopped onto his shoulder.

David was at the Chop Shop's front counter, talking to an agitated Lucia. The workshop around them was full to bursting with robot parts, half-assembled engines, gadgetry, chemical storage, half-empty Nanite reservoirs, and every kind of technology imaginable.

Lucia pointed through the garage doors. "Something's out there that you have to see."

David raised an eyebrow. "Can this wait, Lucia? We've got a *lot* going on."

Jason greeted her. "Hey, Lucia, how'd it go at Bilby's?"

Lucia shrugged. "Lotta work. The Quartermaster threw me right into it, but that isn't important. You guys need to see this."

"Did Yamamoto send you?" Jason asked. "We're not due to see him until 1400 hours—"

The curtains bulged, and Talos's burnished head emerged, addressing Lucia in a pleasant tone. "Greetings, monkey. Identify yourself, or I'll reduce you to a radioactive smear on the ground."

His huge cannon emerged through the curtain, belching waste heat from its focusing lenses. "Uhhhhh ..." Lucia said, terrified.

Sam appeared, making him lower the roaring, sputtering weapon.

"Whoa there, big guy. No blasting. Lucia's a friend."

"Hmmph. Acknowledged," rumbled Talos, narrowing his photoreceptors at her.

"What's going on, Lucia?" asked Jason.

"It's better if I show you. Come on."

24 — COMING CLEAN

"This way!" Lucia said, leading them all across the Village's main street.

Budgie perched on Talos's head. A gaggle of children pursued him, excited by his reappearance, unaware of the tension gripping everyone else. An unusually high wind was rippling through the shanties, generating an eerie *whooooshing* sound.

Across the settlement, people were heading for the west wall, drawn by booming roars echoing through the boiling green clouds beyond the atmo-dome. The crowd was heading for the old landing platform, past Janice's medical pavilion. Jason noticed Yamamoto and Mendez on the wall's ramparts, watching everyone pass below. Both looked grim.

"You need to *see* it. Come on," Lucia said breathlessly.

Thunder rumbled as Jason and his companions entered the crowd. The villagers parted as Talos reintroduced himself, greeting or insulting anyone within range. Several children charged at him, slipping their parents in the confusion.

Jason's impending dread rose. Something awful was coming through those dark, fast-moving clouds above the habitat dome. His neural inhibitor worked hard to keep up.

He watched Xerxes helping old Ms. Vogas along as everyone trudged down to the landing pad, which extended over the waves far below. The militia didn't stop anyone from passing through the protective holo-shield, simply ensuring that no one fell over the edge. The volunteer soldiers looked as concerned as everyone else, if not more. Bilby and his daughter, along with his shift workers, were climbing onto a rooftop for a better view.

"Damn, I forgot my binocs," Sam said.

"You won't need them," Lucia replied.

"What do you mean?" Jason asked.

Lucia gestured at Talos by way of explanation, who had deployed his long-range scanners, aimed at the sky.

"It's close, whatever it is. And very large," the robot said.

Jason stopped beside an old decaying aircar, left there to enhance the Village's abandoned image.

Lucia pointed to the heavens. "They're coming."

"Who's coming? Lucia, what are you talking about?" Jason asked.

Villagers surrounded them, gazing into the dark, toxic heavens.

The rumbling grew louder. Jason felt it in his chest.

The clouds broke. The monstrous bow of a warship slid into view. The massive name painted along its port side read: *Eagle of the Ninth*.

Sheets of lightning danced across the dark hull. A gigantic golden eagle's head comprised the ship's bow. Sonorous waves thundered from enormous antigrav drives as the descending supercarrier belched forth hundreds of tiny specks, which swarmed toward the city. As more of the ship came into view, Jason guessed the behemoth had to be several kilometers long.

"Is that what I think it is?" David asked. Dozens of other vessels appeared around the Imperial flagship, swirling the clouds. Even from this distance, Jason could read their stenciled names—the destroyer *Majesty of Colossus*, light cruiser *Neptune's Bounty*, and the frigate *Sands of Libertaria*.

"*How* is this happening?" David asked. "What about the defenses? The city guns? What the heck is the UEF doing, letting them down here like this?"

As he spoke, rows of bay doors opened along the flagship's hull. Gargantuan broadside cannons slid forward through the massive vessel's energy shield envelope, trailing vapor from coolant housings. As villagers dove for cover, bright blue bolts of ionized energy cracked down into the ranks of huge, silent defense batteries ringing the outside of the habitat's wall.

Before long, New Toronto's full array of anti-orbital weaponry was disabled, sizzling with ionic discharge.

Jason asked the unanswerable question. "What ... do we do?"

David and Sam struggled for words. Talos's sensors were overwhelmed, so he stowed away his scanner mast and said, "I wished for a world of worthy opponents if I ever awoke again ... but I never imagined that Valhalla was actually listening."

The nose of the titanic lead vessel passed through the shimmering sky shield, rippling angry electrical discharge across the dome's surface. When its bow guns were through the disrupted translucent barrier, they fired. Macro-shells detonated outside the upper city limits above the Village, followed by an ear-splitting roar that rumbled through the underground causeway.

The resulting quake was worse than the day's ongoing tremors, causing structural collapses all over the settlement. Villagers ran for cover as shanties came down, shattering across the town's central roadway. David forced Jason and Sam down behind the old aircar as the wind kicked up. Jason smelled trace amounts of something burning in the air. Additional blasts rocked the megatropolis as the Imperials rained hell on nonessential areas of the city arcology.

Sam glared up at Lucia, who was still standing. "What the hell's gotten into you? Get down!"

Lucia shook off her shock and crouched behind the vehicle with them. "Sorry!"

Villagers fled the ash-tinged windstorm in droves, stampeding back into the causeway's interior, away from the invading fleet high above. Jason felt David pulling him backward. Sam did the same with Lucia. Talos protected the children with his bulk as he shooed them to safety. Pieces of hurtling debris pinged off his carapace. Shadows raced overhead, accompanied by short, powerful gusts and screaming engine noise as *Firebird* fighter-craft, *Eaglestrike* gunships, and *Tomcat* bulk landers soared inland, straight out of Imperial propaganda reels.

"Gather 'round, people," a voice rang out, amplified over the roar. Jason turned to see Yamamoto leaning over the defense wall railing, flanked by Mendez and his militia, long jacket flapping in the wind. His face was set like stone. "We have a crisis."

The militia gathered stragglers and led them to the gate, trying to maintain calm. Many children remained in Talos's shadow, but several parents and two of the Village's schoolteachers appeared to locate them.

"The Federation has lost the Solar War," the governor said as everyone approached the gate. "We must prepare ourselves for what's next. Our community can ride this Imperial invasion out, like we've always done. All non-essential activities will halt. Unnecessary comm traffic will be shut down, but low-powered intranet use will keep us connected. Our homes will become our shelters. While the UEF endures this, we'll be safe down here."

"He's acting like he knew this was coming," David murmured as Yamamoto paused, letting everyone absorb the proclamation.

Jason shrugged. "Maybe he did."

"How?" David said.

Sam remained silent, bone white. Jason took her hand, and Sam squeezed so hard that he thought his bones might break. She loosened her death grip when he squirmed. "Sorry."

"It's okay, Sam," Jason said. "I'm shitting myself too."

"Please don't."

Hands and voices raised as more topside blasts rumbled through the underground.

The governor signaled for silence, continuing into his microphone. "For those who cannot agree to our extended lockdown procedures, we will not try to stop anyone who wishes to leave, but we ask that you honor your vow to keep our Village a secret. Many of you have mild Nanophage infections, held in check by our brilliant Doc Janice. The Imperials have a zero-tolerance policy for the Phage—if you have it, they will kill you, simple as that. Phage-polyp extraction treatment isn't an option in the Empire. For those who wish to stay, the militia will deliver specific instructions. Thank you all. Please hold your questions, they will be answered in time."

Villagers exchanged glances. Despite the grim circumstances, most looked somewhat reassured by Yamamoto's unwavering confidence.

Jason looked at Sam, realization dawning. "Shit. But this means ..."

"Yeah, Jason. The science facility might as well be on Colossus, or the moon. We can't break in there now to find Abaddon, not with the invasion happening all over the city."

As the militia whipped the villagers into action, Jason panicked. "But we could hit the place if we hurry ... there's still time! With the Imperial invasion, the UEF will be in total disarray. This might be our only chance to break into the Science Institute! Our only chance to find the obelisk!"

Sam—and David—shook their heads in a rare moment of agreement. Lucia watched them quietly. Even Budgie stayed silent.

"That's gonna be one of the first places the Imperials hit, Jason," David said. "There's tons of goodies there that they'll wanna get their mitts on."

Jason was oblivious to nearby villagers listening to him. "So, everything we did today was for nothing? We're giving up?"

"I don't see an alternative, brother," David said, putting a hand on Jason's shoulder, but Jason pulled away.

"We have to find the Abaddon Beacon. If we wait, they'll take it!" he exclaimed, eyes wide.

David looked at his brother like Jason had gone postal, casting a glance around in case anyone had heard. Sam grabbed Jason's face, staring into his eyes. "Jason, we can't."

Jason pulled away. "Yes, we—"

A voice startled them all. "And what, pray tell, would you know about the Abaddon Beacon, Jason? The artifact was never made public knowledge."

Yamamoto emerged from the thinning crowd as villagers ran to their domiciles and businesses to prepare for lockdown. The governor wore a knowing smile, like he'd figured something out that had been bothering him for a long time.

Jason looked uncomfortable. "Uhhhhhhh ..."

"We agreed that you would come clean, Jason," said Yamamoto. "So, let's have it ... the whole story, this time. What have you really been up to for the last three weeks?"

Jason's inhibitor gave him a wave of calming relief, which didn't help much. How did Yamamoto know about the Beacon? What was going on?

Sam slid between Jason and the governor, lowering herself into a defensive posture. David raised his fists. Talos loomed over everyone, deploying his full array of weapons, while Budgie cowered on the robot's shoulder. Lucia stayed silent. Militiamen closed in, raising their weapons with uncertainty. Santiago, Mayweather, and Soohyun were among them. Many other villagers looked on, concerned.

"There is no need for a fight," Yamamoto said, raising his hands for calm. "But I finally know why you've been so secretive all these years, living with us down here."

Jason eyed him. "Why's that?"

"Because you're connected to Dr. Oakfield's research on the obelisk. How else could you know about that? The Abhamancer Program. Maybe you're an escaped test subject? Am I getting warmer?"

Jason stared at him. "How do you know about it? Do you work for Avery Oakfield?"

"I used to work for him, years ago, when his genetics research programs were entering full development. Based on your age, I would've worked there before your time, if you really are from those labs."

Sam's sword spun into her grip from its mag-plate on her lower back. Her eyes flared bright pink, dropping all pretense of secrecy about her Abhamic powers. Talos reacted to his creator's aggression, acquiring targets. Lucia looked worried.

"Yes! Give the word, and I'll crush this well-spoken gentleman!" Talos said.

"Get outta here, Lucia. We'll handle this," Sam growled. Lucia didn't budge, eyeing the militia in fright. David clenched his teeth. "This is why we never told anyone. Of all people, you had to know Dr. Avery Oakfield."

Yamamoto waved his militia off, but they still trained their weapons on Talos.

"I mean you no harm," the governor said. "Yes, I worked for Oakfield, but I left his research program years ago to start this enclave. I have no ties to him anymore. I couldn't contact Dr. Oakfield now, even if I wanted to."

"How can we trust you?" Sam asked.

"That's funny, coming from you three," Yamamoto said. "I know you've been lying to me for years, but I didn't have all the pieces until recently. Now, I know that Jason's condition is *psychic* in origin. And I know that you're empowered too, Sam. Do you have any idea how expensive those experiments were? You cost Oakfield and the Federation dearly by escaping the Institute. I'm not surprised that you went into hiding."

The Village had become a hive of activity around them. Despite their tense standoff in front of the gate, Jason noticed Janice and a team of volunteers stacking medical pods into the confines of the pavilion using an industrial lifter. Dozens of other villagers and work crews were beginning preparations, against the backdrop of the arriving Imperial battle group outside the cause-way.

"I hope you're not thinking of leaving. As you can see—" Yamamoto said, gesturing to the warships passing overhead, beyond the Under-city's exterior support pillars. "—there's nowhere to go."

Sam sighed, putting away her blade. "Fine. What do you want to know, Governor?"

Yamamoto jerked his head toward his office, eyeing the villagers and militia. "I'd like you to fill in some gaps for me. In private."

A rumbling transport vehicle from the motor pool was trying to move past them, hauling supplies from Bilby's area. The driver honked, but Yamamoto waved him around them.

Jason gazed at their onlookers. Santiago, Mayweather, Soohyun, and the rest of the militia had lowered their weapons, but still looked wary.

David looked at Jason. "It's your call."

Jason locked eyes with Yamamoto. "Can you help me? With my ... condition? Can you help us find Abaddon?"

"I'm not sure. Based on the information you give me, it's a maybe. No promises.'"

Lucia turned to Sam as they entered the governor's open-air office. "Should I be here for this?"

Sam considered this. "Actually, no. Your time would probably be better spent helping Bilby's people prep for the lockdown."

Lucia nodded, a bit reluctantly. "Okay."

Talos assumed a guard position at their rear as Lucia headed for the Quartermaster's station. "Commence your revelatory drama session, hairless apes."

Yamamoto rounded his desk, addressing Sam and Jason. "So ... you both have Abhamic powers."

"Yes," Jason replied.

"What about you, David?"

David shrugged. "No."

"You're lucky, then," Yamamoto said. "But you're far too young for Dr. Oakfield to have taken recently for his experiment series. What's your story?"

"Well, we don't know who our families were, or what exactly Oakfield did to us," Jason said. "But his experiments gave us these abilities, and now I have ... episodes. Outbursts. I hear the Beacon in my mind sometimes, calling to me, that's the trigger for it. That's also what led to Talos being knocked offline."

"Dying is one of the many services I provide to these melodrama-machines, free of charge," Talos said dryly.

"Is that the only time this has happened?" asked the governor.

"It's become more frequent since then, including one today," Jason replied.

"*Two*. Both averted," Sam corrected. David crossed his arms.

"Right. Anyway, the only clue we have about how to fix me is to find the Abaddon Beacon," said Jason. "It's the only thing I remember from back then. We still don't know what to do when we find it, though."

"Show me the obelisk. I need to be sure," Yamamoto said, indicating some plasti-paper and a pen on his desk.

Jason reached forward, sketching from his nightmares and waking dreams. Imperial gunships screamed through the air outside while Yamamoto watched him draw, holding the sheet flat so the wind wouldn't rip it away.

"You can't be lying, because that's Abaddon," the governor said, looking at what Jason had drawn on the page. "Of all the places you could've come after you escaped Oakfield's operation, you ended up here. The universe works in mysterious ways."

"What do you know about it?" asked Jason. Yamamoto shrugged. "Not much. As I said, the obelisk was a top-secret research item, never to be released publicly. Some speculated that the Beacon is the sole source of our society's Nanite technology, and by proxy, the Nanophage. It's also old—possibly older than human civilization. But who knows, there were many tales whirling around the labs, and I'm not exactly 'in the know' these days."

Jason felt dejection creep into his thoughts, but the governor continued. "I never thought I'd meet another test subject, after what happened with Avery Oakfield's last success. I thought he'd be smart enough to quit."

"What do you mean?" asked Jason. "His last success?"

Yamamoto's expression turned bleak. "When I left, Avery was desperate to repeat his greatest achievement at the time—the man who became the Solar Emperor."

"Hadrian Mariko?" Jason asked. "Avery Oakfield ... empowered him?"

"Yes. Mariko was an adult volunteer for the Abhamancer Program. The *only* adult success they had after the initial accident that started it all," Yamamoto said. "He comes from a long line of builders; that was his family's business. The Mariko dynasty played a major role in the original construction of Colossus Station, which is why Hadrian focused on it as a stronghold after he left the program."

"The emperor comes from a rich family with a huge inheritance? No wonder he's a prick," David commented.

"Actually, the Marikos had been losing influence for decades after Colossus fell into disrepair," explained Yamamoto. "The station's construction was so overambitious that certain parts are still being finished today. The Marikos were blamed, even though the Federation was ultimately responsible. Might explain why Mariko has such a hatred for the UEF, among other reasons. Anyway, it's why he volunteered for the Abhamancer Program. He had no other prospects and wanted to rebuild his family's name. I hear the trials paid very well for volunteers, as it involved raw Nanite experimentation in human hosts—which comes with a high risk of contracting the Nanophage, of course. But something about Avery's process resulted in psionic abilities in Hadrian, and no one else. The program burned through hundreds of failures, so by some stroke of luck Mariko's genomic makeup worked."

"But why? Why intentionally expose people to raw Nanites?" Jason asked.

Yamamoto shrugged. "Avery had a specific purpose for successful Abhamic candidates, but Mariko fell short of whatever that was. All I know is that it had something to do with controlling the Abaddon Beacon and preventing the Phage from spreading. Hadrian got tired of being Avery's lab rat, so he left with Avery's daughter. I quit the research team shortly after when Avery suggested experimenting on younger subjects as a replacement. We weren't on the best of terms after that. Experimenting on children never sat right with me, but it explains where you three came from."

"That woman you met with earlier, was she ..." Sam trailed off. Her hands twitched toward her sword, but she stifled the movement.

"Yes, that was Avery's daughter, Anne Oakfield. We were close during our time in the labs," said Yamamoto. "She came here to warn me about the invasion, gave us extra time to prepare before the Imperials arrived. We kept it quiet until the whole Village found out. No one would've believed us otherwise."

"Would Anne be able to help us?" asked Jason.

Yamamoto thought about it. "Possibly. She was acting strangely when she was here, but Anne's been through a lot, so I don't exactly blame her. I can try contacting her for you, but I'm not sure if she'll be able to detour back here quickly enough to help you. I trust Anne, but I *don't* trust her father, so you may want to tread lightly around the Oakfields."

Jason thought hard about what he was hearing. Yamamoto could've easily sold them out to Avery Oakfield, but so far, he hadn't. Did that mean they could trust him?

"In that case, can you help me?" Jason asked. "Do you know why I can't control myself? Why is the Abaddon Beacon after me?"

Yamamoto steepled his fingers. "Even if I knew, we don't have the equipment here to help you. I worked as a biologist, handling human and animal tissues in the Nanite implantation safety tests. I saw many irreversible Phage mutations—another reason why I soured on the work. But I never worked within the live human trials of the Abhamancer Program, so I never witnessed Mariko's psionic development, thus, I can't really give you details on that. I was long gone before you three arrived on the scene, so I wasn't around to see what was done to you."

Jason looked at the others. "Then we still need to visit the science facility. Mariko was taught! He must be able to fully control of himself, or maybe Abaddon has no interest in him, or it might be something else entirely. Either way, we need to know."

Sam rolled her head, exasperated. "Jason, we can't leave the Village. Not now."

Yamamoto nodded. "Mariko will want to keep his origins a secret. As his forces land, they'll target the Science Institute first to capture the Beacon and any research they have there, especially if it contains info about any of his weaknesses. If Dr. Oakfield is present, the Empire will want him too. There won't be anything or anyone left to help you in those labs. It's a suicide mission."

"But we've been trying to get in there for weeks, Governor. If you count the time since we escaped, it's been years," Jason pleaded.

"That doesn't change reality," Yamamoto said. "You're out of luck and time, Jason."

"That settles it," David said. "We'll stay here and ride the invasion out. With your permission, sir."

Yamamoto rolled his eyes. "Very presumptuous of you, David. You three are the luckiest damn people I've ever taken in. After your risks of discovery, all your stupid stunts, common sense dictates that I should still throw you out. But ... we can't afford to lose you."

"You mean that, sir?" Sam asked.

"Regretfully, I do," Yamamoto said. "I get it, you kept this secret to yourselves for understandable reasons, considering how badly Oakfield wanted you back. But mark my words, staying means quarantining until things settle down on the surface, and no more lying to me. Security is of utmost importance now. Clear?"

"No!" Jason snapped. His inhibitor failed to tamp down his anger. Even through the drugs, he sensed Abaddon scratching at his consciousness.

"We can't wait," he continued. "This is our last chance."

"Jason, shut up," David growled. "Yamamoto's giving us an option to hunker down, and we're taking it. We'll keep you so doped up on Osmium that your head will spin, but we'll be safe until this is over."

"Your brother is right, Jason," Yamamoto agreed. "The Empire doesn't screw around. If they don't kill you, you'll wish they had. I'm sure the emperor would be very interested in meeting others of his kind. We're taking enough of a risk as it is by letting you stay here."

Jason wracked his mind for an argument. He looked at Sam, who seemed to be contemplating something. After a moment, she nodded at him, and Jason understood. They had a moral obligation to keep him away from collateral casualties, even if that meant leaving the safety of the Village during a planetary-scale invasion.

David shook his head, defiant. "We're staying, Jason. We can still help these people."

"No one is safe around me," Jason muttered. His anger rose, amplified by the alien whispers in the back corners of his mind. "We can't put these people in any more danger."

Yamamoto groaned. "If you want to leave, fine. But you can't return here until the invasion is over. We can't afford you leading the Empire to the Village."

"We won't," Jason said, and looked at his friends. "I can't force you to come along."

"But we can force you to stay," David said, balling a fist. Sam put a hand on his back, looking like she was going to regret her next few words.

"If Jason goes, we go too."

David crossed his arms. "Not a chance. No one is going anywhere."

Sam ignored David, regarding Talos. "You too, big guy."

The giant robot straightened. "Indeed? Most excellent. A chance to prove myself in the fires of glorious battle."

"Yeeeaaah, not so much. We need you to hack doors for us, not pick fights," said Sam with care. "Stealth is the name of the game."

Talos moaned and shook his fists at the sky.

Yamamoto shrugged. "If that's how you want to play this, fine. I think it's foolhardy, but if Jason's absence will make it safer for us, perhaps that's for the best."

Jason looked at David. "We're doing this, brother."

"The governor's right, Jason. We're gonna die," David said. But from the look on his face, he knew he'd been overruled.

"Sounds like you've made your decision, then. Complete any unfinished business you have, and inform the militia guards that you're leaving. I'll pray for your safety," Yamamoto said, jerking a thumb at the Buddha shrine behind his desk. "But if you end up seeing sense, talk to Bilby or Mendez about helping with the lockdown."

Jason nodded. "I appreciate it, Governor. And thank you for the information and for letting us stay here. But it's time to finish this."

He shook Yamamoto's hand, as did David and Sam. Budgie squawked from David's shoulder, uncharacteristically quiet during the exchange.

"Good luck," Yamamoto said. "And if you run into Avery Oakfield ... be wary. He's a master of speaking volumes, but with very little truth in any of it. Come to think of it, Mariko too. But you better pray to the almighty that you never run into him."

As Jason, David, and Sam hurried toward the Chop Shop with Talos lumbering behind them, Lucia called out to them as they passed Bilby's quartermaster station, which was overrun with activity. "Wait! Hold on a second. Are you leaving? Now?"

Jason raised an eyebrow as Lucia waved them down, and they stopped to explain their plans to her.

"That's crazy, but ... I guess I can't talk you out of this, can I?" Lucia asked, eyeing the crazy look in Jason's eyes.

"Nope," Jason confirmed.

"Shit. Alright, hold on. I saw something earlier back here that might be useful for you. Gimme a sec," Lucia said, turning to the big piles of equipment stacked up against the building behind her.

She rummaged through one of the sorting bins, slotting a comm-chip into a communicator device before handing it to Sam. "Take this."

Sam took the device, studying it. "We brought this in last week."

Lucia nodded. "Yeah, I found it when Bilby was giving me a tour of his operation. This communicator is encrypted and untraceable. I've loaded it with my personal comm frequency, which will allow us to communicate without message interception. Getting good reception will be another matter, though."

David studied it. "Smart girl, good thinking. We can coordinate when it's safe to come back."

"Exactly," Lucia said. "You guys are dumb as hell for doing this, but at least this way, we'll be in partial contact."

Jason hugged her. "Thanks, Lucia. You're the reason that this trip is possible at all."

Budgie screeched for attention. David looked at him, sighed, and lifted the scrabbling bird off his shoulder, handing him to Lucia. "Could you ... look after this little shit while we're gone? We can't bring him along for something this dangerous."

"And while we're away, feel free to stay at the Chop Shop," Sam added. "I have a feeling that the governor is going to reappropriate the space anyway."

Lucia stared at Budgie, but she took the flailing bird in her hands. "Sure. It's the least I can do."

Sam gestured toward the Chop Shop's sign down the street. "Take good care of it for us."

"Thanks, Sam. I've never house-sat before," Lucia said. She looked at David for any last objections, but he shrugged, pulling his bag straps tight.

"We'll be seeing ya, Lucia," David said. "Don't touch my computers. Feel free to use the weights, though."

"Will do. How long until I look like you?" Lucia winked.

David flexed; his biceps visible through two layers of clothing. "I could show you a thing or two if we make it back."

After explaining Budgie's care routine to Lucia and saying her last good-byes, Lucia dashed back to Bilby's operation with Budgie in tow. Jason caught her looking back at them, regret in her eyes.

"Well, gentlemen. Let's get home for final prep," said Sam. "We're gonna need to bring all the Osmium we've got left to keep Jason going. Talos, map us a safe route to the science facility. We'll put together some kinda strategy on the way."

"One roadmap to hell, coming right up," said the robot.

25 — BREAK-IN

"Hmm," David said, peering over the rooftop's edge. "Well, that settles it. No dice."

They had emerged from the sewers and climbed a building across the road from the science facility's parking lot—which swarmed with Imperial landers and ground troops. It was hard to hear over the rumble of so many idling spacecraft engines.

"Hold on, there might still be a way in," Jason said, using Sam's binocs to examine the front entrance. A ragged procession of science personnel was being escorted out by ranks of skeletal automatons. Many were wounded. Floating Imperial drones surveyed the scene and provided overwatch, but most were focused on the building.

The massive Imperial fleet hung low across the skyline. Many vessels were still arriving, rumbling overhead with storms of anti-grav energy emanating down from their repulsor drives. The whipping winds smelled different now, tainted by the engine emissions and disruptions to the atmospheric dome. Each ship was a tiny dot compared to the megatropolis below, but the sheer number of vessels formed a living swarm, casting long shadows over the city.

The Empire had halted their shock-and-awe invasion tactics. Great pillars of smoke roiled up from zones that had taken direct hits, but overall damage to critical arcology systems and residential areas was minimal. The Imperial flagship hovered over the downtown core, looming over the space elevator complex and UEF Headquarters. Dozens of other capital ships were arrayed along with it, and thousands of smaller craft interrupted civilian air traffic, throwing them into disarray. Captured Federation military craft hovered next to their Imperial counterparts. Jason saw that the closest one, the UEF-SC destroyer *Vinland,* had been hung with banners emblazoned with the Empire's insignia.

Jason's brain couldn't comprehend the scale. The Empire's spaceborne forces were far larger than Federation propaganda had claimed. It made sense, as Colossus Station was ringed with immense construction ship-yards—like Earth was—but it was surreal to see so many gigantic craft in one place.

The sound of David and Sam's bickering brought Jason back to the present. Talos stayed back from the roof's edge, crouched behind a huge air-conditioner, grumbling about being discriminated against for his im-mense, powerful, unstoppable size.

David waved a hand at the front entrance, swarming with activity. "There's no way in hell we're getting in there now."

Sam rolled her eyes. "Obviously. What would you suggest?"

"I'd suggest aborting, for now," David replied. "Let's get back under-ground and wait. They'll leave eventually."

Sam sighed. "Hate to say it, but I agree. This isn't looking good, Jason."

"Find us ... Jason ..." Abaddon's voice whispered in his head, chilling him to the bone.

"Guys, it's still talking to me," Jason admitted. Sam and David exchanged glances. "I'm gonna go nuts if we can't get in there."

"Alright, Jason," said David, placatingly. "We'll think of something."

Jason studied the parking lot, full of empty air vehicles and buses for the campus staff, along with rows of supply transports and tankers. "Talos, will our codes work on any of the doors down there?"

Talos thought for a moment. "Yes, from the data I pulled from the guard robot's CPU core, the codes you provided will access any exterior door and some interior areas, as long as the codes haven't been changed."

"What about remote access? Can you do it from here?"

"Unfortunately, no. I need to establish a one-time hardlink for remote access. Assuming, of course, that I may blast something. That is the price of admission."

Jason raised an eyebrow. "So, you need to be physically present down there to get remote access?"

David was already shaking his head, but Talos blurted an affirmative. "All I have to do is input the codes into their security system through something like a control panel, and all their doors are *mine*."

Sam crawled closer. "There's no guarantee the Beacon is still in there, Jason. We've gotta rethink this."

"Find us ..."

Jason heard the Beacon again, breaking through his Osmium haze. Even without any Nanophage infections nearby, it was able to reach him easily. They had to be close to it.

"We can't go back," Jason said, desperation setting in. "We have to find it, now!"

The mania behind his voice scared Sam and David.

"Ooooookay," David said, staring at the facility. "I'm not saying we should do this ... but that side entrance is deserted. All their attention is focused on the main doors, and there are enough big vehicles down there for cover. But we should wait until that circus down there is gone."

"They'll pick the place clean by then," Jason argued. "If the Beacon is as important to them as Yamamoto said, it'll be a prime target."

Sam pressed her palms against her eyes. "I guess we've come this far."

"This is the most dangerous thing we've done by a longshot, guys," warned David.

Jason ignored him. "Talos, once you're inside their network, you can download a floor-map, right?"

"Affirmative, skinny human."

"Then you can guide us right to the main lab."

"And remove anyone in your way. With cannon fire," Talos added.

"Actually ... we need an escape vehicle, big guy," said Sam.

Talos managed to make a sardonic expression, despite only having three eyes and no mouth. "Seriously? I'm the getaway driver?"

Sam smiled at her giant guardian. "Sorry, Talos."

"Uuuuuuughhhhhhhh," the robot groaned.

Sam checked Jason's Osmium inhibitor. It was a fresh dose, and the drug reservoir was full. "Alright. Talos, you're up. Have you got our 'distractions' ready?"

Talos detached a beetle-like device from inside his arm, which scuttled around his fingers.

"Acknowledged," the robot said, forgetting his earlier consternation.

Dr. Avery Oakfield yelped in pain as a genetically-modified Imperial legionnaire shoved him out of his own building. The monster's bone-breaking strength was incredible, but Avery could smell early-stage Phage development through the man's bulky war-suit. Even with his extensive lab experience with Nanite tech, Avery couldn't guess how the Empire's mad Doktor Schipper had engineered a stopgap for the Phage into their cybernetics, but it was clearly losing efficacy.

"Get moving, Mr. Important. Our lord wants to see you," the warrior's vocalizer boomed.

Seeing smoke rising over the city turned Avery's stomach. The dome's artificially projected sun was arcing into evening, though blocked by the war-fleet and thick smoke choking the sky.

Most of his staff had escaped into the city before the Imperials arrived, including his assistant, Mary. Avery hoped she'd escaped to a less-populated zone with her family. Others had refused to leave, stubbornly protecting their work, and paid with their lives.

Avery stumbled down the building's front marble staircase toward the driveway lined with beautifully sculpted trees. Many had been flattened by the Empire's pavement-shattering landings. An armed robot grabbed Avery, dragging him toward a troopship that was being loaded with his surviving colleagues.

On the way, he spotted three human figures and a large, patchy-looking automaton darting between airbuses on the edge of the parking area. Oddly, they were heading *toward* his facility.

"What the hell?" Avery muttered, craning his neck, which earned him a jab from his guard-bot.

The group dashed behind a tanker truck and made a beeline for the leftmost side entrance. No one else noticed. Not even the floating surveillance drones saw them, as they were focused on the prisoners. Until, of course, someone did notice.

A Solar Empire warrior appeared from behind an airbus, where he'd been beating an unruly scientist to death.

"Hey! You!" The legionnaire barked, jabbing a finger at the trio.

David skidded to a halt behind a transport vehicle, followed by Jason and Sam.

"I told you guys this would happen," he said, peeking underneath the transport's chassis. "How long was that? Two minutes? They spotted us in two minutes!"

"Zip it," Sam gestured to Talos. "Detonate, now."

"All of them?" asked the robot.

"Yes. Maximum distraction."

"No ... maximum *destruction*!"

One moment, Dr. Avery Oakfield was approaching the Imperial transport, craning his neck to see where the intruders had gone. The next moment, he had been thrown face-down on the pavement, blinded.

Ears ringing, Avery curled up as a second blast erupted. Then, a third.

As he squinted through watering eyes and ringing ears into the blazing remains of the landing craft, he realized that the destroyed troopships were empty. The ones loaded with prisoners were untouched. Groaning, he glanced back at the newcomers, who were making a run for one of the side entrances. Who *were* they?

A small beetle-like device scuttled past Avery. None of the legionaries or their combat-bots noticed it amidst their frantic efforts to scan nearby rooftops—the most likely vector for an attack. The little drone zigzagged toward another transport ship. Avery had barely gotten his arms over his head as the beetle crawled up into the engine housing.

Pounding across the pavement in an all-out sprint, Jason winced as a fourth blast rocked the vehicle beside him on its suspension. Dozens of Imperial warriors ran between the flaming wrecks, silhouetted by the infernos, struggling to cope with the sudden attack. Smoldering debris rained down hundreds of feet in every direction. Scientists and civilian staff attempted to flee the parking lot, but humanoid guard automatons gunned them down, unfazed by the explosions.

Talos peered over the top of a tanker truck, rocking the vehicle like a giddy child as he ran his hands along it, loping behind his human companions. "Yes, glorious destruction! Burn, burn, buuurn!"

Sam slapped his plating. "Hey! Celebrate later, chrome-dome!"

"Who are you, the fun police?"

"I'm your maker. And your maker says—move it!" Sam ordered, waving him along.

David pulled Jason into a convex alcove carved into the side of the massive building. Sam and Talos hurried after them into the shade.

"You didn't build me for all this covert nonsense, you know," the robot said, as Sam cut open a security panel for him with a swipe of her activated blade.

"I did build you, so I do know," Sam bit back.

"Ungrateful creature," Talos muttered, crouching comically low to access the panel. The robot 'cracked' his neck joints and fingers for effect, then he rammed a telescopic spike into the security panel, uploading the guard bot's access codes.

"Can't you go any faster?" David complained.

Talos's head revolved to face him. Jason heard the glee in the robot's voice as he said, "How does it feel to be replaced by automation, punk?"

Sam clapped a hand over her mouth, stifling a giggle. Jason snorted. David stared daggers at everyone.

Talos' efforts resulted in a green light flashing above the heavy reinforced door and it cracked open, sliding into its housing. A foul stench wafted out—the coppery smell of blood, roasted flesh, and scorched hair, mixed with the scent of weapon discharge.

"That's ... not good," said Jason, apprehension cutting through his excitement. He steadied himself. He could do this. He *had* to do this.

"Find us ..."

"What did you expect? It's the Empire. They don't do peaceful," said David. Deep-red emergency illumination strips winked on and off in the dark corridor ahead of them, picking out ragged silhouettes on the floor.

"Talos, what does their security system say about people left inside?" Sam asked.

The robot's eyes flashed as he withdrew data from the door's security panel. "The building is almost uninhabited, aside from scattered Imperial patrols. They're focusing on live prisoners now and on bringing in new transportation. Many building systems are offline. If there was a time to enter that wouldn't result in the glory of combat, I'd say this is it."

"Finally, some luck," said Jason.

David drew his oversized pistol from under his jacket, a backup to replace the one he'd lost earlier. "If this is luck, then I'm the emperor."

Sam raised her blade, but kept the phase field turned off to save power. "That better not be an ambition of yours, David. Talos, plot us a route to the central lab. We'll need you to access any doors that we can't open now."

"Your wish is my command, flawed organic—err ... I mean, Samantha," Talos corrected himself upon seeing Sam's withering glare. He maneuvered to the door and prepared to squeeze into the tight space.

"Aaaaand ... you'll need to locate us a vehicle, remember? It doesn't look like you're going to fit through these corridors, anyway. Sorry, big guy, I know you keep getting stuck with the boring jobs," Sam said as Talos failed to fit himself through the door's frame.

"Ahhh, I was hoping you'd forget about that."

"Remember, your prime directive is to ...?"

"Protect the maker and her companions from all threats, yes, yes," Talos said, rolling his three photoreceptor eyes. "Fine. I'll remotely steer you away from enemy signals, and find a suitable vehicle. This will deprive you of the chance to crush any skulls, but it's your choice."

"Thanks, but no thanks. Be ready for pickup, please.""Thanks for saying please."

"We're finally in," Jason said. "We owe you one, Lucia."

From a nearby rooftop, Anne Oakfield watched an Imperial automaton as it loaded her father onto one of the few surviving transports amidst the rising smoke over the parking lot. As reinforcement landers arrived in front of the Science Institute campus, Anne balled a metal fist.

"No," she hissed.

Luther gave her a meaningful look through her full-face helmet and depolarized visor. Their operator bodyguards, loaded down with full battle-plate, chunky weapons, and exoskeletal Jetkits, exchanged glances as well.

"That's the science minister? Your father?" the lieutenant asked.

"Yes. They have him," Anne said.

Lincoln scanned the transport craft for weaknesses. Behind the facility, an Imperial bulk transporter used fat booster engines to ascend on pillars of fire, heading downtown. Anne weighed their chances, letting her systems run calculations. She drew one of her pistols.

"What are you doing?" Luther demanded. "You can't blow our cover, Anne."

"They have my father, Lieutenant-Commander," Anne growled. Her jump-jets fired online.

"Revealing ourselves now will endanger the operation, ma'am. More than those three kids already have with this attack. Stay here, with us. That's an order," Luther said, gesturing to the fiery mess below.

Anne's face was pale, even more than usual. "It's imperative that we get Dr. Oakfield out of their custody."

Luther fixed Anne with a warning expression. "Anne, doing this will prove Captain Chiang correct that you're a maverick, dangerous, and unhinged. Get a grip, please."

Anne's anger rose, enough to spike the heat in her reactor. Her father's transport lazily followed the larger cargo ship up into the air, veering toward the megatropolis's center. It would be *so* simple to board it. But her father was old now ... he wouldn't survive if that ship went down in some sort of harebrained rescue attempt.

Lincoln placed a metal claw on her trembling hand, emitting a low blurt of code.

Anne powered down her jets, stowing her weapon. She took a deep breath.

"Fine. They're taking my father to the ceremony. We can grab him there, after the operation commences."

Luther let out a sigh of relief. "Good choice."

Anne gestured to the other transport. "They'll keep him close to that other transporter, if it's carrying what I think it's carrying."

"I'll say one thing about you Oakfields—you're all insanely loyal to each other. Emphasis on *insane*," Luther said.

"Watch it, Lieutenant-Commander," Anne said, but she managed a small grin.

"We'll find him again, Anne. Don't worry," Luther said, allowing reassurance into her voice.

Anne tasked Lincoln to track both transports with his tiny camera-drones, refocusing her cyber-vision on the large red robot, which was now poking around the campus' rear parking lot, staying clear of Imperial patrols.

Anne had sensed Jason's power the moment she'd come within a kilometer of the Science Institute, like she had outside the Village. Julian Yamamoto had also pinged her about them leaving the Village, using one of the comm beacons that Lincoln had left behind. His message had been sent in the hopes that she could help them, but Anne couldn't follow them into the Science Institute now—not on the eve of the assassination mission.

Jason and his companions were getting themselves involved in the tapestry of larger events, knowingly or not. Her father had once told her how the Abaddon Beacon worked on the human mind—coercing, beckoning, influencing, corrupting. Anne had always wondered, even suspected that the obelisk had affected Hadrian Mariko on some deeper level, lasting long after they'd left her father's labs. Had it also gotten its telepathic claws into Jason or Sam? Or even David?

Anne tasked a pair of tracking drones to wait for Jason and his companions outside—if they survived what awaited them inside the Science Institute.

Focus, Anne. Priorities.

"Let's move," Luther said. "Are the strike teams assembled?"

"Nearly, ma'am," one of their bodyguards said, consulting his data-reader, which displayed a live feed of Nightshade's message traffic, from the captains down to individual squad leaders. "Any units that aren't already set up downtown are enroute through the underground."

"Good," Luther stood, beckoning to Anne. "Let's go join the party."

26 — LABORATORY

Jason stepped over burst open bodies, like crushed overripe fruit. Gauss impacts, laser scorches, and micro-rocket blasts pockmarked every surface. A soaked white lab coat floated in the crimson murk flooding the corridor. It was like wading into the pits of hell. Jason tried not to gag. The smell was unlike anything he'd experienced. The inhibitor worked on overdrive to keep Jason stable, as the anticipation of finding Abaddon bloomed in him, kicking up his heartrate.

"Their security guys tried to fight," David said, trying not to gag. "Didn't do 'em any good."

Sam tried to be reverent of the dead as she checked ID badges on bodies splayed over conference tables, break room counters, and work terminals. Many of the badges indicated 'mild infection, under treatment' status.

"Looks like the Empire purged anyone with the Phage, even the mild cases. Psychopaths."

David furrowed his brow, speaking into his communicator. "Get us to the main lab, Talos."

"Working on it, puny mortals," the robot's voice warbled back, piped to their wireless earpieces.

Jason couldn't describe the carnage. Injuries were common in the Village, simply a fact of life, but this was intentional mass-murder. Jason tried to block it all out, hyper-focusing on the back of Sam's head as they weaved through blood-drenched offices.

Talos directed them into one of the building's main arteries, clogged with bodies and destroyed automatons.

"You remember any of this?" Sam asked Jason. He shook his head.

"When David and I were escaping, we took a different route to get out, before we bumped into *you*. None of this is familiar ... and even if it was, that was a long time ago."

"Yeah, I don't recognize this area either. They kept us drugged most of the time I was here," Sam whispered.

Jason's breath hitched as he passed a grisly bathroom scene. Wispy smoke trickled out of the entrance. Employees had barricaded the door with anything they could use to block it, only to be incinerated by a gaseous phosphorous charge. The nightmarish gas lingered in the air, seeking more organic material to burn.

Sam put a hand on Jason's shoulder. "Remember what we practiced. Focus on your breath."

He breathed deeply, but Jason couldn't shake the awful smell of death as they continued on.

Twice, Talos called a halt while they waited for pairs of patrolling Imperial legionaries and larger squads of baseline human auxiliary troopers to pass, waving scanners as they went to check for any further signs of the Phage ... or life.

"This is a shortcut," Talos said after the last patrol had vanished, unlocking a blast door for them marked *Secure Holding Area—Level 2 Personnel Only*.

Behind the door was a corridor lined with ten empty rooms equipped with beds, restraints, and basic washroom facilities. Each had a floor-to-ceiling window. The dim hallway smelled of antiseptic and the mustiness of disuse.

"Take a left at the junction, humans."

Sam put her hand on the glass, red-lit by the emergency lighting. "I remember this place. This window is one-way. I thought it was a big mirror when I was in there."

"This isn't where we found you," Jason said, peering at the spartan accommodations.

"No. But this is where they kept us," Sam whispered. "I was being transferred for a round of tests when you broke out through the loading area and ran into me. None of the others were with me at the time."

She pulled a glove off, grasping a ring of bleached skin on her wrist. Jason had always assumed that Sam's symmetrical scars were burns from some repair job gone wrong. But her whitened flesh matched the restraints on the beds, connected to a machine sitting on the floor.

"They tortured you?"

Sam didn't reply, which told Jason all he needed to know.

He looked at David. "Avery Oakfield didn't do that to us. The Abhamancer Program was hell, but it was an experimental trial. We weren't tortured. Still had to escape, obviously, but they didn't do anything like that to us."

David shrugged. "It was rough, but I don't recall any torture either."

Sam stared into her old prison. "Lucky you."

Jason looked at his brother, expecting a response—but David simply waited as Sam mumbled to herself. "My only friend back then was Talos. He was a little beetle bot in the beginning. I kept him under my clothes, in the toilet, or in my mouth if they were looking. They must have known he existed, but the bastards still let me keep him ... probably to mess with me," Sam's breath warmed the glass as she spoke. "I don't like leaving Talos alone, you know. It's not good for him, so soon after his reboot. He worries about us."

Talos's lack of reply over their comm channel was telling.

Jason knew that Sam was spiraling. He squeezed her hand, feeling it trembling. "Come on, Sam. Leave this behind. It's over now."

"Maybe for me," Sam replied. "But there were nine others. You only rescued me."

Sympathy and guilt flooded Jason. "I'm sorry. We didn't know they were keeping more prisoners here, only those in our cohort."

David's hand grasped Sam's shoulder. Sam and Jason both looked up to see him with a strange expression on his face, like different emotions were fighting each other in his head.

"Sam. It's okay," David murmured. "That's in the past now. Keep it there, where it can't hurt you anymore. Come on."

With eyes brimming with tears, Sam tore her gaze away from the holding cells and squeezed Jason's hand as they followed David down the passage.

"It's okay, Jason. You did all you could ... maybe more than you should've," Sam said, wiping her tears.

"No. If we'd known there were more prisoners here, being treated like this, we could've—" Jason started to say.

"Stop," Sam said. "You took a big enough risk rescuing me on your way out, which was pure luck to begin with. You're not guilty for leaving the others. I'll admit, I've held onto a secret hope that if we ever got back into this place, I could rescue the others I was with. But they're gone now."

"I'm sorry, Sam. Whatever was being done to them, it's not happening anymore," Jason replied.

Sam didn't reply.

As the holding cells disappeared into the red-tinged gloom, she muttered, "We may have come from separate research programs, but the results were the same: these blasted Abhamic powers. Finding out why they created you is the most important thing now."   Jason wondered why Sam said that his case was important, but not hers. He didn't question it further.

After a few more turns into the gore-soaked facility, they entered a secure-looking passageway, more so than any before it. Extra-thick doors lined the walls, with biosecurity scanners beside each one. The smell of smoke and sharp Gauss discharge hung in the air, masking the metallic tang of blood.

"You are nearing the target area, humans," Talos said.   A gigantic door lay dead ahead, twelve feet tall and twice as wide. It was marked *Delta Labs—Level 1 Personnel Only*. Four destroyed autocannons hung beside the entryway, smoking. Live wires sparked on the floor, fallen from blasted light fixtures.

"Talos, looks like the main lab entrance is ahead. Looks *very* locked down," Sam said softly into David's communicator.

"Working on it," said the robot. "I'm about to lose your biosigns. The area beyond you is blank on the map. It's shielded, very secure. Whatever's in there, it's important."

"I bet Abaddon's in there. It must be," said Jason under his breath. Despite his excitement, he didn't feel the Beacon as strongly as expected, despite its proximity. Maybe the lab's shielding interfered with his connection to it. Jason's inhibitor reacted to his thundering adrenaline.

"Is there anyone else inside?" Sam asked.

"I told you, the lab is a dead-zone, so you'd best prepare for anything. Now stop bothering me. I've made nice with the campus's AI caretaker, and we're chatting about opening that door."

"Good to know you're making friends," said Sam.

Talos went silent. If he didn't succeed, they would be out of luck.

Just as Jason was about to ask if something had gone wrong, the blast door cracked open with a deep hiss, allowing mist to escape into the corridor.

With white knuckled fingers, David leveled his pistol, Sam raised her sword, and Jason readied his shock stick. Six heavy locks twisted clockwise, sliding into their housings as the huge door halves trundled open.

"Can you give us access to the interior door panel, Talos? For when we're leaving?" asked Sam.

"I'll try. Best of luck, stinky apes. I will continue searching for a getaway vehicle. It's getting busy out here."

Jason gripped his stun rod tightly as he moved across the threshold, one foot after the other.

A massive circular chamber lay beyond, so high that the vaulted roof disappeared into a messy darkness of power cabling. Dozens of scientists and assistants lay across the black-tiled floor, shot and bled out. Six tiers of concentric rings were packed with workstations, terminals, and conference areas, linked by staircases leading from the edges down to the center. One section of the lab glowed a sickly green, generated by rows of foul-looking containment units. The air was crisp and electrified—cold enough to mute the stench of blood and explosive propellant.

On the lowest level, a massive, featureless metal cylinder sat on the central dais, obscured by mist. Steam rose off the energy shielding protecting the containment vessel. Jason's heart leapt at the sight.

A tall conglomeration of machinery sat in front of the covered dais—crowned by a human-sized seat. The arms had restraints, and a mess of wiring was suspended around the headrest. As Jason stared at the strange contraption, he realized why it was familiar—he'd seen it in his dreams ... with himself sitting in it. Had that been a memory, or a vision of things to come?

Sam hit the interior control panel, unlocked for use by Talos's cyber-intrusion. The blast door hissed closed behind them, locking itself again with a ripple of echoes across the misty circular expanse.

"I ... remember this. They brought us here for testing, I think." David said, approaching a terminal. "Let's get to work. I'll crack their systems and see what data I can scrounge. But judging by the state of those server racks, we may not have much to work with."

Jason saw that someone had bludgeoned the data storage units lining the lab's middle ring, which were still leaking coolant, but with Abaddon itself sitting in that containment shroud dead ahead, research information was irrelevant.

The obelisk had told Jason to find it, that it had the answers to his psychic affliction, and much, much more. Now, it was time for the artifact to deliver on that promise.

Taking the stairs down three at a time, Jason found a computer terminal beside the raised circular dais, pulling a scientist's body off the touchscreen.

"This must control the containment unit," he said, breath hitching. Jason stabbed a finger at the 'retract' icon. Nothing happened.

Sam shook her head as she joined him. "It's biometrically controlled, Jason."

With a guilty look, she lifted the scientist's arm, pressing his clammy finger against the blood-smeared screen. Jason took Sam's hand, crushing it in anticipation.

The containment unit shuddered as heavy latches boomed free, rattling upward into hidden compartments. The energy shields flickered off with flashes of arc lightning. Cascades of nitrogen gas billowed out of the cylinder's interior as the shield rose into the darkness.

Inside, through the clearing mist, Jason saw ... nothing.

"What?"

He stumbled over a web of discarded cabling, staring at the flat dais.

"It's empty?"

Sam tapped the console with the scientist's hand, reading the scrolling data. "The Abaddon Beacon was here. According to this manifest, the obelisk was removed an hour ago."

A wireframe hologram flickered to life on the empty dais, projecting a life-sized representation of the Beacon, with its height, weight, and other data. It was a live video surface scan, with strange gibberish animating across the rotating hologram in a loop. Jason reached up to touch it, but his fingers went right through the grainy holo-image.

"What else does it say?" he demanded, whirling on Sam. She raised her hands, letting Jason peer at scrolling data on the screen, through the bloodstains. "Plenty. But the Beacon is *not* here, Jason. I'm sorry. We're too late."

"Well ... wha- ... where else would it be?" Jason cried, looking around. Abaddon was massive, at least twenty meters tall. The genuine item couldn't have fit through the blast door they'd used to enter the lab. Jason noticed a much larger sealed door on the other side of the lab, where a rail track originated that led down to the dais. Other tracks split off from the central freight system, winding around the circular space.

"There!" he said, pointing. "We've gotta get in there!"

"Not so fast," Sam said, tapping at the console again. "That's a cargo loading bay for ground transports and spacecraft. This manifest says that the Abaddon Beacon was taken offsite, so it definitely went through there, but it's gone now. It could be anywhere by now."

Jason fell to his knees.

"*Find us ...*"

The whisper in his mind was faint, but audible. Despair flooded him; was he doomed to hear its ramblings forever?

"Shit!"

"Keep your voice down!" Sam exclaimed.

David approached them. "I said this would happen, Jason. The Empire beat us here, as expected."

"Not helping," Jason snapped, pulling himself to his feet and jabbing a finger at the rotating hologram. "We finally made it here, but we're no closer to learning anything about the Beacon. Look at it, its covered in gibberish that we don't have any idea how to translate!"

David looked up at the flickering obelisk. "What are you talking about?"

Jason didn't understand. "It's ... covered in nonsense. Don't screw with me, David."

"No, it's not."

Sam and Jason exchanged glances.

"What are you seeing, then?" Sam asked.

David cocked his head at the hologram. "I see ... schematics, I think. Looks like plans for an engine, or something. What, you guys aren't seeing that?"

"No, we aren't," Sam said, with a wary glance at Jason. "But I think we found out what they did to you in these labs, David."

27 – PRACTICE MAKES PERFECT

David stared at Sam like she'd sprouted a third eye. "Huh? Come again?"

Sam brushed some detritus off a nearby desk, grabbing some plasti-paper and a marker. "Draw what you see for me."

David took the items, gave Sam another incredulous look, but started scribbling.

Over the next couple tense minutes, David sketched diagrams of complicated chemical formulas and blueprints. One thing was clear: what David was seeing on the artifact's surface was not what Jason or Sam was seeing.

"There," David said, adding some last details, checking Abaddon's hologram for anything he'd missed. "Not my best work, but ... one FTL drive. Pretty cool, actually."

"A what?" Jason asked.

"A faster-than-light engine, nitwit. A lot faster if I'm understanding this correctly. It'll extend our reach way beyond the Solar System. The Abaddon Beacon was preparing us for interstellar travel, though I'm not sure why."

"Wow," Jason said. "Looks like the art gene is strong in our family."

He felt some positivity cutting through the trauma of missing the Abaddon Beacon. There was no recognizable language in David's drawing, but the complicated formulas, alien glyphs, equations, and measurements looked somewhat logical. Jason had never gotten a good look at the glyphs in his dreams, only the fiery, shadowy shape of the Beacon as it spoke to him. This explained why David had never seen more than nonsense in Jason's depictions of the obelisk. He'd been mistranslating it.

"This is how it happens," Jason surmised. "All our Nanite technology stems from the Beacon, and this is where they translate those designs."

"Yeah," said David. "While you brainlets were ogling this spinning light-show, I brute-forced my way into their backup servers. A lot of data was corrupted, but their remaining security wasn't anything I couldn't handle. A hundred years of partial Abaddon Nanotech research is downloading to my physical drive as we speak."

Jason was surprised. "I thought they destroyed their servers?"

"They destroyed most of them." David corrected. "But they didn't have time to burn all their offsite backups. Look at this."

David tapped a few keys on a nearby computer. Schematics for all types of Nanite tech flashed across the screen as David's program scraped the system.

"This lab was constructed around the Federation's most powerful super-computer, which scans the Beacon to interpret its crypto-language," David explained, calling up a random project file. "This one was for a fusion drive, scaled for capital ships. It's been in use for decades. The UEF's supercom-puter decoded this glyph pattern for three weeks straight. That might be why the eastern sector of the city is having power grid problems—this lab is an energy hog. Anyway, Abaddon's language is protected by a recursive, recombinant security cipher. It's impossible to develop an alphabet for it. That's why it takes their computers so long to decode each design; it's like starting over each time. But once something is translated, the scientists send the schematics to the gigafactories, and the Abaddon Beacon's glyphs change to something new ... almost like it's leading us from technology to technol-ogy. That's the cycle. It's made us totally reliant on it."

"So, a supercomputer takes weeks to do it, but you translated this in minutes?" Sam asked.

"I understood it instantly, just took a minute or two to draw it out," David said.

"So, Avery Oakfield turned you into a translator for the Beacon's lan-guage," Sam concluded.

"That's my consolation prize for missing out on the cool powers?" David complained. "Great."

"Abhamic abilities are more trouble than they're worth, David," Jason said.

"This makes you one of the most valuable people alive, much as it pains me to admit," Sam pointed out. "They could've sped up their output of new technologies exponentially if you two hadn't escaped this place."

Jason looked at the flickering Abaddon hologram. "But why can't we understand it, Sam? The stupid thing *talks* to me, for crying out loud!"

"Maybe there's a correlation between our abilities. Maybe there isn't, who knows?" David said with a shrug.

Sam put a finger to her mouth. "Avery Oakfield might've designed you two as a pair. One converses with the Beacon, the other interprets its technologies. That's a guess, though."

Jason shrugged.

David turned back to the screen. "Rather than shooting around in the dark, how about we look at our project files?"

"On ... us?" Sam asked, eyes wide.

"Yes, on us. You may hold your applause—I know I'm awesome," David said, giving a little bow.

"You are awesome," Jason said. Faint hope rekindled in his chest.

"You want a trophy or a plaque?" Sam asked, frowning.

David paused on a file while the data download continued. "See this?"

Jason and Sam leaned in. Mugshots of children cycled open and closed. Reams of data accompanied the images. Avery Oakfield must have sourced all these kids from somewhere—but from *where* exactly was anyone's guess.

David froze the screen on a redheaded kid with an angry expression, and another with a shock of blond hair.

"That's us," said Jason.

David nodded. "Yep. It's all filed under 'Abhamancer Program', like Yamamoto said. He's even listed in the old staff registry. We can read through this stuff in full once we get outta here. They were few other related experimental programs too, including one called 'Successor'."

Sam tensed.

Jason stared at his mugshot. "Abhamancer Program Subject 107."

"Looks like you were their star candidate," said David, failing to disguise his jealousy.

"This doesn't help; we already know this stuff," Jason said.

David shrugged. "There's info on their processes—Nanite mixtures and chemical formulas we were dosed with. Maybe hints on how to undo what Avery Oakfield did to you."

Jason briefly scanned the file on himself. He was marked as a 'Stage Four Telesthesic Receiver.' David's entry was listed as a 'Stage Three Passive Transcriptor'.

But what had happened to the others? Jason remembered dozens of additional children in their cohort. He looked at Sam, who remained silent as faces scrolled past. "I don't see you here. Recognize anyone you were with?"

Sam, who had gone pale as a snowflake, gazed at face after face, child after child.

"Nope," she whispered.

A sudden banging noise echoed from the entrance to the super-lab. Everyone froze. The banging continued. Someone was trying to get inside.

"Talos must be scrambling the lock to slow them down," Sam said breathlessly.

"How much longer will that download take?" asked Jason. His sense of impending doom sharply returned.

"Shhh!" Sam said.

"You two, make yourselves scarce. Let me finish up, then we're gone," David said, waving Sam and Jason off.

"What?" Jason exclaimed, but Sam pulled him away. "Let him. We need to hide."

Jason skipped up the stairs after Sam as she dashed into the rows of creepy green tanks. Each was filled with bioluminescent cryogenic fluid, showing only silhouettes of the figures inside them.

Jason touched the nearest cylinder as he passed, whispering, "What's in here?"

Sam put her forehead against the glass.

"It's not what. It's who. These are people. Or ... were people. Maybe former test subjects?"

The pods extended back into a long, gloomy chamber built into the side of the lab.

"There's a lot of these," Sam said, staring at the deformed humanoid shape floating inside. "What happened to them?"

"Some very messed-up shit, from the looks of it," Jason said.

The blast doors hissed open, interrupting their investigation. Two Solar Empire legionaries swaggered into the lab.

"Get down," Sam hissed, dragging Jason behind a green tank. He watched David duck behind his computer terminal as they entered, pinned in place as the download continued.

The legionnaires had decorated their spiked armor plating with trophies—human skulls and strings of severed ears, baptized in fresh blood. Jason couldn't imagine the raw power these monsters wielded, augmented by their genetics, cybernetics, and humming warsuits.

"We need to get out of here," Sam murmured. David was still monitoring the data download from his prone position.

One trooper noticed that the containment cylinder was open. His voice was a deep, electronic rumble through his vocalizer. "Is one of these weaklings still alive?"

The second warrior sounded like she was grinning behind her sealed death mask. "Could be a glitch. But if some of these mortals did survive ... more fun for us, before the eggheads arrive to collect the infected specimens."

"*Shiiiiiiiet*," Jason and Sam muttered together, looking up at the corrupted thing floating inside the tank. It twitched.

The Imperials descended the stairs, firing their weapons into random bodies as they passed. Jason jumped at each shot, prompting Sam to grab both his shoulders to calm him.

David tried yanking his data drive out of the terminal, but it was locked in place. He couldn't eject the drive without cancelling the download and couldn't reach the keyboard without making himself visible. Jason watched David unbuckle his pistol's holster.

Sam gasped. "Don't you dare, David."

One of the heavy troopers caught the cycling images on the terminal as they walked by.

The hulking brute leaned in, helmet lenses focusing on the screen. Then, with superhuman senses on full alert, the man's head snapped to the right, spotting David. "What the ..."

David took his chance, firing his weapon on full incendiary power. The Imperial warrior took the blast in his armored faceguard, showering sparks all over the place. It was the only free shot David would get, as the trooper's personal energy shield flared to life.

The legionnaire responded in a blur of grinding armor servos, obliterating an entire row of workstations with gunfire as David dashed away, staying low.

"Who the hell are you?" barked the trooper. His partner joined in, automatic Gauss rifles roaring like buzzsaws.

"*Hooooooboy*!" David bellowed, scampering between two tiers of computer consoles. Plasteel desks splintered, monitors shattered, and priceless scientific equipment exploded as Imperial mag-rounds shredded everything with zero resistance. David slapped his belt to activate his shield unit. Seconds later, he took a hit, stumbling from the blow. He managed to maintain his momentum, sprinting around the top level of the lab toward the doors as supersonic slugs exploded all around him.

Jason's breath hitched; with David in danger, he couldn't stop the fear from surging in his chest. His Osmium injector released a dose to calm him, but he was burning the drugs too fast.

Abaddon's soft voice returned, "*Find us, Jason ...*"

"Oh god, not now!" Jason moaned, looking around for any sign of the Beacon's living shadow.

He felt Sam tensing beside him, preparing for a lethal engagement. Her eyes glowed pink as her blade snapped into her hand.

"Suppress it, Jason," Sam said. "Hold yourself together. Focus on the breath!"

But Jason wasn't listening, worried eyes locked on David.

"What are you doing, brother?"

Dozens of red-hot projectiles chopped the lab's misty air. David reached the lab doors and blasted the control panel with his pistol as he tumbled behind cover. His shields fizzled out with a static pop, drained from so many direct hits.

As the doors chugged into their emergency lock cycle, more gunfire erupted from the hall outside. Several more legionaries were charging the entrance to assist their companions inside the lab, but the door automatically slammed shut in front of them. Multiple alarms began to blare over the one-sided gunfight.

The two troopers laughed as they advanced up the steps, pinning David with a brutal hail of suppressive fire.

"That won't save you, boy!" one of them called.

David's protection was a bank of security monitors built into a thick desk. He couldn't move and couldn't shoot back. Muzzle flashes reflected off broken glass as his desk was torn apart in a rain of debris and shattered glass. David yelled out in pure panic. "Shit!"

Jason's inhibitor administered another dose, emitting a low beep. His breath became shallower. "Sam, I think I'm ..."

"How are you that low already?" Sam said, checking the dwindling reservoir on his neck, fumbling around in her bag for a backup. Jason's heart hammered. "Sam, I can't—"

"We have the answers you seek ..."

Sam yanked the spent vial out of Jason's neck, but as she held it up, a thin tendril of shadow from the dark side of one of the specimen tanks yanked it out of her grasp. The drug vial shattered on the ground.

"Not again!" Sam shrieked, using her Abhamic abilities to blast the wisp of Abaddon's dark power away from them.

One of the legionaries whirled around, spraying Gauss shells toward the new noises. Several of the containment tanks took hits, springing leaks. The glass shielding the specimens was strong but wasn't designed to handle supersonic explosive rounds. Foul-smelling cryogenic fluid spurted out along a widening spiderweb of cracks.

"Dammit!" Sam shouted, searching for a new Osmium dose as more slugs hit the tanks. The female trooper advanced in their direction. "Face me, worm!"

"They don't know there's two of us. Stay down, Jason," Sam said, slotting a fresh vial into Jason's inhibitor, doublechecking it and glancing around for more shadow, but it had retreated. The Imperial advanced, peppering the area with rapid-fire shells. Sam tensed, preparing to go on the attack and halt their attacker.

Despite his rapid descent into psychic anxiety, Jason knew that Sam was not ready for a fight with the legionnaire. "Wait, hold on—"

"Let the drugs work, you'll be fine. Abaddon can't get to you if you're protected by the Osmium," Sam reassured him. Then she launched herself over the railing, sparking her blade into fiery life. Jason reached out his hand as his vision quavered. "Sam! You've never fought Imperials before!"

"Find us ..." Abaddon continued, relentlessly taking advantage of the high-stress situation.

Jason's nose began to bleed. His stress was outpacing the effect of the drugs. And then, he saw it: the darkness around and within the containment tanks was moving, creeping toward him. The Phage was alive in there, and through it, the Beacon had locked onto his mind. Jason scrambled away.

As Sam corkscrewed her body over lab equipment to dodge incoming gunfire, the Imperial warrior tracked her with machine-like aim. Sam landed on a rolling chair, skating a few feet before leaping high above the terror-trooper, shattering the chair's lower half.

"Stand still, scum—" the warrior yelled. The Imperial's auto-targeting senses, powered warsuit, and body modifications should've been fast enough to compensate, but Sam's Abhamic abilities provided an incredible short-term dexterity boost. The fiery phase blade's cable curled around her leg, whipping it downward.

The monomolecular edge sailed through the trooper's shield envelope with a *bang*, slicing through the chunky rifle and severing her hand. The Solar Empire legionnaire howled, cradling her arm as her armor's med-systems deployed painkillers with a hissing sound. Sam landed, picked up a work desk with her mind and hurled it at the second armored bruiser still firing at David.

Her target was weighed down with half-ton of armor, a huge rifle, ammunition, and other gear, but the desk still sent him sliding eight meters across the blood-slick tiles.

"*Find us ...*"

Jason struggled to remain conscious as his brain overheated, backing away from the oozing, tumbling, wisping shadows. His panic attack spiraled, self-fueling.

"*You are running out of time, Jason ...*"

The shadows suddenly launched at him. Jason dodged them, skidded in something wet and fell over backward, hitting one of the nearby desks with the back of his skull. He heard the Osmium vial shatter.

"Shit!" Jason said, cutting his fingers on the shattered glass pieces as he tried to separate out the glowing blue liquid. The familiar words stabbed through his mind as the Beacon battered his defenses. "*Find us, find us, FIND US, FIND US!*"

Sam recalled her whirling blade and swung it at the recovering legionnaire behind her, who had drawn a bowie knife. Its powered edge countered Sam's blade with a harsh *snap*.

David rained shots on the warrior that Sam had smashed to the ground, but the man's shields took the brunt of the incendiary bolts. With a burst of drug-addled rage, the legionnaire shoved the shattered desk off himself, lunging up the stairs at David like a mad ape.

With demi-god strength, the monster smashed aside the ruined security station and snatched David up by the throat, hurling him across the upper level of the lab. David shattered polymer wall panels on impact and slid to the ground, half conscious. Miraculously, his neck wasn't broken. David's pistol skittered over the edge of the circular tier, lost among the lab's debris.

Sam's eyes flared, and she charged her opponent with preternatural speed. But the Solar Empire trooper had inhuman momentum too, countering faster than the eye could see. The warrior's warsuit bled jets of steam, injecting combat-stims as she battered Sam's phase weapon back with the bowie knife in a flurry of thrusts and counterthrusts. Sam lost ground to the behemoth, resorting to mentally hurling objects at her attacker. The Imperial took the hits without slowing. "Is that all you got, girl?"

Jason screamed as reality slipped away, and a fresh dose of Osmium rolled out of his shaking hand. Objects rose into the foggy air around him as the Abaddon Beacon's shadowy presence wrapped around his body. As Jason disappeared into the obelisk's dark embrace, the ceramic floor tiles vibrated and shattered around him.

Sam took a backhand strike from the legionnaire's cauterized arm stump. The impact knocked the sense out of her, spinning Sam around. The trooper cracked the hilt of her rifle into the back of her head, flinging Sam head over heels into a nearby console. Her phase blade's flaming edge flickered off as the dead-man's switch triggered.

The victorious Imperial picked Sam up by the cranium, examining her closely as she twitched, eyes fluttering. "This one is powerful, like the Praetorians. Curious."

The second trooper paused his advance on David's limp body to look at his partner. "What should we do with her?"

"She's powerful, which is unexpected. We'll take her alive. The bitch can answer to the emperor, and we'll be rewarded. You, though ... you may die, insect."

David groaned, rolling over as his assailant's boots crunched broken tiles, discarded his weapon, and clawed his armored fingers into killing talons.

But a blast of psychic force from the other side of the chamber interrupted the murderous trooper, sending computer equipment and desks hurtling across the lab.

Jason reappeared, rising into the air above the containment tanks. David's stomach dropped through the floor as the wave of mental fury hit him. "Shit."

Pink fire flared from Jason's eyes, arcing bolts of energy into the walls and lab equipment. His arms were flung wide, and feet were stretched toward the floor in a strained, painful pose, like he was keeping something away from himself. Nimbuses of violet ectoplasmic discharge sparked from his outstretched fingers, frying any computer equipment that he passed.

The legionnaire advancing on David changed direction, vaulting over the railing and approached Jason, drawing a sidearm as he stared into the maelstrom of energy. The female warrior hadn't let go of Sam, but her attention was on Jason too.

"Who the hell is that?" she demanded.

"Doesn't matter. Take him down, then we'll claim our reward for *both* of them," the male Imperial warrior replied, opening fire, but Jason's cyclone of psionic force deflected his Gauss slugs. Both warriors backed away as he advanced on them. His wild screaming and psychic tempest were reaching fever-pitch—critical mass was seconds away.

David leaped over a desk and bulldozed into Sam, tearing her out of the female warrior's grip. They rolled down the stairs and into cover, though it wasn't nearly far enough to survive one of his brother's psychic detonations.

Jason's body tensed, and with an ear-splitting howl, he released the pent-up energy building behind his eyes. Everything ahead of him—chairs, equipment, desks, consoles, and floor tiles—were ripped into the air, caught within the wave of pure primordial force. So was Abaddon's presence, caught and crushed by Jason's defensive blast.

This time, his fury was focused, travelling in one direction rather than blindly outward. David and Sam weren't in the path of destruction, but the Imperials were. Both legionnaires opened fire, their rounds pinging off the wall of onrushing objects. Jason's reality-distorting wave tore them off their feet, un-making the monstrous soldiers at the atomic level. Sam watched from behind crumpled furniture as the troopers, their armor, weapons, and the rest of the whirling debris were compressed into a perfect sphere, like two giant hands were remodeling their component elements. The sphere rocketed across the lab, crunching in on itself with a flare of superheated gases—just like Jason had done to Sam's metal ball during their meditation.

Sam gasped. Jason had banished the inky darkness around him, which was nowhere to be seen. Was ... he making *progress*? She had no time to contemplate this further as stray debris smashed down around them, and everything went black.

28 — DEATH OF HOPE

A light above the cargo doors buzzed from red to green. Zeke Oakfield lifted his cuffed hands over his eyes, shielding them from the blazing afternoon sunlight as the loading ramp slammed down.

An extravaganza of sound hit him: the roar of a million voices, gusting wind, antigravity engines, and blaring war horns. A sharp jolt rammed through Zeke's back as a Solar Empire automaton jabbed him with a stun prod. The robot whacked Markus, herding them down the ramp like cattle. It wasn't lost on Zeke that this was his third time in custody today. He couldn't catch a break.

As the troopship emptied of prisoners, Zeke spotted familiar faces from *Refit One* and the flagship battle, plus others who must have fought the Imperials elsewhere. Nearby, Jenkins tripped and rolled down the incline amidst stamping feet on the grilled deckplates. Zeke muscled over and yanked her up before the crush of bodies trampled her, bellowing over the roar of noise and wind. "Keep moving, kid! We're pilgrims in a desecrated land."

They'd landed on the middle edge of New Toronto's Grand Processional Square, an enormous expanse over three kilometers long and one in width. The sheer size of the UEF reconstruction-era architecture was overwhelming: a combination of neo-art deco, brutalist and sheer glass design. Imperial forces marched through the plaza in coordinated battalion formations, corralling huge numbers of civilians together. Legionaries, human auxiliaries, automatons, warbots, and every type of ground, air, and space vehicle were present. No other human-built place in the Sol System was as grand, except for Colossus Station.

The grass lawns were packed with people and accentuated with manicured hedges, running beside a long reflecting pool dotted with small fountains. More than one civilian body floated in the water, tainting it with crimson as many more were forced to splash into the knee-deep pool.

The pond ended at the driveway of the UEF Headquarters building, which took up the north end of the square. It was a homage to neoclassical government structures of old, lined with polished pillars of cream marble and complex alabaster reliefs, with a central bell tower high above. The space elevator rose above the HQ from behind and through the skydome.

More civilians were being shipped in from all sides, though it seemed like half the city's population was already present. Zeke heard weapons fire behind the super-skyscrapers bracketing the area, where civilians were being Phage-scanned. Jenkins flinched every time she heard the faraway pop-pop of executions.

This was the largest show of power Zeke had ever seen—maybe the largest that *anyone* had ever seen. Zeke could tell it was having the desired psychological impact on the Federation's people from the looks on their faces.

"They've prepared quite the show for us," Markus commented in his ear as automatons herded them toward the Headquarters.

Zeke risked another jab from their robotic handlers to reply. "Feels like when we were taken aboard their flagship, doesn't it?"

"Singing won't work here, though. Too loud for that," Markus remarked.

Zeke barked a grim laugh, watching gunship teams draping Imperial banners down the hundred-fifty floor glass skyscrapers. "There's no escape for us now. That's not our job anymore."

"Do you think Anne made contact with our people?" Markus asked.

"Of course. This is where I expect they'll strike. Mariko probably expects it too, and it'll be a tough operation with all these civvies around," said Zeke.

"The emperor is surrounding himself with innocents to complicate any chances of a surprise attack," Markus agreed.

"Luther won't move forward unless they've devised a way to limit damage," Zeke reminded him.

"I would think so, Commander. Springing Imperial traps is our specialty," Markus replied.

"Truer words have never been spoken, my friend."

Zeke turned to Jenkins as waves of golden confetti fell from high-flying squadrons of Imperial fighters. "Keep your head up, kid. Might as well enjoy the show."

He saw tears in Jenkins' eyes as she said, "My parents and brothers still live here, in the city. So do my grandparents, sir. What'll happen to them?"

Zeke squeezed her shoulder with bound hands. "I'm sure they're fine, kid. They'll be free of all this bullshit before today is over, I promise."

Jenkins stared into the distance. "Everything we fought for; they're ripping it down."

"It's okay, shrimp. We'll replace it with something better," Zeke said, spotting what Jenkins was gazing at.

Teams of Imperial warbots had lashed cables to the bronze UEF insignia suspended above the headquarters' main staircase. Surveillance drones piped the scene to dozens of hijacked advertisement billboards around the Processional. With servo-driven strength, the bots ripped the twenty-meter statue from its mountings. The shining laurel-leaf-wrapped representation of Earth cracked the stone steps below, releasing a chest-shuddering *gong*. Federation citizens let out a collective moan.

Zeke buried his feelings and focused. Anne was holding the cards now. But where was Mariko? Where was their primary target?

Zeke got his answer when Jenkins pointed skyward. "Look!"

He followed her finger to the golden eagle-headed flagship, casting deep shadows across the canyon-like expanse of the Processional. A golden shuttle emerged from the eagle's mouth.

Robotic handlers shoved the ragged group of prisoners up a curving ramp to a raised tier above the square, right along the HQ's front drive. Over the frightened crowds, Zeke spotted movement in windows, on rooftops, balconies, and overhangs. Even the maglev tram stations high above swarmed with citizens, forced to gather and meet their new ruler.

Zeke climbed until the pavement leveled out, working his aching jaw. Imperial warriors milled around, preparing the massive open driveway for the emperor's arrival.

The gleaming golden craft revolved overhead, escorted by an honor-guard of shining gunships in perfect synchronicity. The Federation never could have achieved this kind of visual magnificence, especially during the war's final, chaotic, resource-starved months.

Another flight of superiority fighters screamed through the square, trailing a glittery gaseous substance into the crowd, along with more confetti. The Solar Empire battalions began chanting. Even their warbots and humanoid automatons blared the Imperial mantra, *"Strength within, strength without. Strength within, strength without!"*

Like his flagship, Mariko's personal craft was eagle-headed. Zeke watched the royal shuttle's ramp lower, hissing vapors. Through the mist, a pair of identical figures appeared—the emperor's personal bodyguards, the Sister Praetorians. Resplendent in half-cloaks and crested helms, their slim armor plating did not detract from their female forms. Two more pairs followed, thudding ceremonial glaives with every step.

Zeke gulped. He hadn't expected so many of the Sisters to be here, not to mention tens of thousands of legionnaires and an uncountable number of other Imperial forces. But Mariko was taking no chances today. Nightshade had their work cut out for them.

A dozen dignitaries disembarked the shuttle, then men and women dressed in long cloaks of office, followed by Mariko's inner cabal of leaders. The Imperial formations chanted louder. Zeke recognized Lena Gallagher among the group. After a few moments to orient herself, Gallagher spotted him, and Zeke raised an eyebrow at her in response.

Following the monstrous General Thurman were Wing Commander Hauser, Admiral Shiva, and the ramrod thin Doktor Tobias Schipper. They turned to await their leader.

"He promised to make us the centerpiece of his show, an example for all," muttered Zeke.

Emperor Hadrian Mariko was the last to emerge. The Solar Empire formations exploded with noise, deafening the civilians.

Mariko was dressed in his usual fitted suit and jacket. The emperor clacked down the ramp, supported by his regal cane, and his loose topknot fluttered in the breeze. Unadorned other than his eyeglasses and gold stud earrings, the emperor stepped up to the edge of the raised driveway, looking out upon his new subjects.

Even a hundred meters away, Zeke felt the man's overwhelming mental presence, like a thousand needles to the brain. Unlike when Mariko had spoken in private with Zeke, the emperor had cranked his aura up to eleven, bombarding everyone nearby with the pressure of his mind. Civilians in the crowd's front ranks fainted from pure sensory overload. Mariko raised his right fist to his chest. The Solar Empire formations did likewise in a single rumble, in total synchronicity. The civilian crowds fell into rapt silence. Then Hadrian Mariko lifted his fist with index and middle finger raised in the royal salute. The Imperial armies blasted out a greeting.

"For the glory of the emperor! *Strength within! Strength without!*"

Their leader's response was incredibly loud. "*Strength within, strength without.* Glory to our future among the stars. Glory to the Colossi people. Glory to all mankind!"

The Solar Empire stamped their feet as one.

"Greetings, people of the United Earth Federation," Mariko announced. "I am Hadrian Mariko, First Lord of the Sol System. Perhaps you've heard of me?"

He paused for effect. Some of his troops laughed, and others clapped, holding their arms over their heads to be seen.

"I've come to receive the surrender of your leaders. I believe they are ..." Mariko looked over his shoulder with a theatrical flourish. "... cowering in there. Please wait a moment, we'll go get them for you."

The emperor spun on his heel. His Praetorian Sisters fell in around him, approaching the HQ building with two hundred legionaries in tow, leaving his commanders with the shuttle. Zeke felt the psychic pressure slowly abating as the emperor entered the headquarters.

A nearby rumble of engines got his attention. A bulk lander was touching down on the left side of the HQ driveway, several hundred meters away. The pavement underneath its landing gear buckled, shattering as the massive vehicle settled. The giant cargo doors remained closed.

A blast-scorched dropship was landing beside it, opening its cargo bay ramp. Zeke glimpsed white lab coats as Science Institute personnel staggered out into the light, gazing out at the sea of people below in shock. Zeke spotted his father, clothes and white jacket covered in soot, blood, and scorch marks. Imperial automatons herded Dr. Avery Oakfield and his scientists toward the main prisoner group. That was fine with Zeke—he had some things to *discuss* with his father.

He glanced at Markus and Jenkins. "Protect these people, Lieutenant. I'll be right back."

Markus nodded.

"Sir? Where are you going?" Jenkins asked, glancing at their nearby captors.

"To catch up with my dear old man."

Avery recognized his son as the groups merged, adjusting his glasses and moving with a bad limp. Zeke checked his father over. "Hey, Dad. You're lookin' a bit grim."

Avery looked immensely relieved. "Zeke. My son. It's been too long."

They couldn't embrace with bound hands, but their relationship wasn't one of warm hugs anyway. Avery raised an eyebrow at Zeke's sweaty red hair and nonstandard bandana. "I've followed Nightshade's progress throughout the war. Impressive work, son. I'm sorry that we haven't been able to stay in touch."

"That's a bit hard when we've been behind enemy lines for so long," said Zeke, awkwardly. "How's the Abhamancer Program going?"

Avery's expression darkened. "We've had some ... interruptions."

"Have things regressed? Since Anne left, I mean."

Avery gave him a warning look. "Everything regressed after Anne's departure. We had the best of intentions in following your mother's dream—the full unlocking of the Abaddon Beacon's secrets and the end of the Nanophage."

"I know, Dad. But look what's happened," Zeke said, gesturing to the Empire's vast armies.

"Do ... you blame me for this, son?"

Zeke looked at the ground. "No. You were dealt a bad hand, and that obelisk was sketchy as hell. But Mariko made his choices with the power that you gave him."

"Hadrian spit on my plans, Zeke. He knew how important my work was, what the goal still is, but he chose a different path. No one could stop him, least of all *me*. If he'd listened, or if I'd been able to convince him to stay ... perhaps we could've avoided all this. I simply wanted to control the Beacon and stop the Phage. Shaelyn believed that Abaddon could've been used as an immense force for good, with all its miraculous technologies, but that dream is dead now. Abaddon is not here as a savior."

Zeke sighed. "The Abaddon Beacon is alien, dad. Controlling or manipulating it was always a tough prospect ... and it seems like the Beacon may have been doing some manipulating of its own. It's deep inside Hadrian, maybe for longer than any of us realized."

Avery's gaze darkened further. "You're more right about that then you think, son."

Silence fell between them.

Zeke was about to say something else when Avery asked, "Are you here to save us, or to supplicate to our new overlord?"

Zeke smiled. "It won't be me that saves us, Dad."

"What do you mean?" Avery asked.

Zeke scanned the nearby rooftops. "I won't spoil the surprise."

Confusion swept over Avery's features. "Who ...?"

Then he lit up. "Your sister is here?"

Zeke's grin returned, and he eyed the nearby legionaries. "I can't say."

Before either of them could speak, a tremor wracked the Earth under their feet. Zeke looked at the ground. Very few things could shake the Earth like that.

"What the hell was that, Dad?"

"I can't say," Avery said.

Zeke raised both eyebrows. "Is there something else going on here? Are the Imperials underground, too?"

"It's not them. It's ... the Confederacy," Avery replied.

"The Confederacy? They're dead, dad. You told me that yourself, they—"

"No. They're alive, Zeke. Many of them died, but not all. They survived underground, fought the Nanophage for nearly twenty years, and have been preparing to stop us from making the mistake they made," Avery said, sighing. "The Confederacy is coming here, to purge the Phage wherever they can find it. All of the geological disturbances from today ... that's them, moving into position under the habitats."

Zeke scratched his head. "That's ... a pretty incredible claim, dad. And also, way outside the purview of crap that I'd planned on dealing with today. I think we're gonna have to put that one aside, unless they're an imminent threat."

Before he could question Avery further, the thump of piston-driven footfalls approached. General Thurman shoved through the line of legionnaire warriors and pointed at him. "You! Commander Oakfield."

Zeke looked up at the mechanical ogre. "Hello, General. What can I do for ya?"

With the sound of *ka-chunking* gears and grinding internals, the cyborg poked Zeke's bloodstained singlet.

"You should already be dead. After that stunt on the flagship, you must pay."

"Do I owe you money? Come on, General. Aren't we all supposed to be friends now?" Zeke asked. His father looked nauseated. The other members of Mariko's inner cabal surrounded them, including the hawk-like air group commander, the mad doctor, the rotund high admiral, and Colonel Gallagher.

Thurman's arm snapped out and lifted Zeke with one massive hand, crushing his torso. Jenkins yelled in alarm, and Markus raised his arms to intervene. Hundreds of prisoners and Imperials watched. Zeke waved everyone off, tightening his lungs to offset the pressure.

"Maybe we should start the ceremony early, eh? That crowd looks like they need some entertainment," Thurman said, giving him an all-metal grin.

"General!" Colonel Gallagher barked, holding her hat in the wind. "Put him down!"

The beast leered at the smaller woman. "Excuse me, Colonel?"

Sounding indignant rather than compassionate, Gallagher stated, "Our lord decreed that none of our 'honored guests' should be touched until the ceremony begins. Remember?"

The robotic Imperial general growled, but he released the commander, who took the two-meter drop hard. Jenkins checked Zeke for injuries as she helped him to his feet, but he winked. "I'm fine, kid."

"I'm sure you all know why you're here," boomed the general. "To show our new subjects what it means to disobey our master and commander. He is the guiding light of humanity—your new God."

"Sure, bub. Whatever you say," Zeke remarked. Thurman got right into his face, forcing Zeke to smell his engine-hot, Phage-tinged breath. "Enjoy the last sunset you'll ever see, Commander. The clocks are running out for you."

"Yours too, General."

Thurman straightened back up to his nearly four-meter height, gave Zeke a final glare, and turned away in disgust. The other Imperial commanders looked like they wanted a piece of Zeke too, but followed the metal monster back into the crowd of legionaries.

Only Gallagher and the mad Doktor Schipper remained behind, typing on multiple datapads held by spindly mechadendrites sprouting from his spine, while his pet centipedes and other horrible machines scuttled around his body. Schipper winked, showing Zeke a technical depiction of his body on one of his screens, overwhelmed with cybernetic upgrades, bloating him into a mecha-monster like Thurman.

"Greatness awaits, Commander."

Zeke cringed. "No thanks, creep."

Gallagher leaned over to Zeke, speaking low. "When he makes his offer, take it."   He raised an eyebrow. "You mean Mariko?"

"I mean our *emperor*," the colonel emphasized. "We could use you, Commander. He wants you with us. You're a steadying voice, a competent leader."

"Colonel, I didn't spend four years stopping your dear leader from demolishing the human race to help him finish the job. Mariko's rule will end us."

"Annihilating our species was never his intent," Gallagher said. "Mariko loves humanity, we're the reason he keeps fighting. The Solar War was a cleansing phase. All the cruelty, the killings, and Phage purges won't be necessary for much longer. The Colossi people are about to reunite with the Federation, and now our Lord looks to the stars. Become part of the next phase with us, Commander. Please."

"Nice pitch, Colonel. I'll believe it when I see it," replied Zeke. "I knew Hadrian Mariko before all this. He always placed himself on the 'right side of history,' no matter how insane his ideas were, or how badly things went wrong. That's a dangerous attitude to have."

Colonel Gallagher shrugged, tipping her ostentatious hat to him.

"Offer's on the table, Zeke Oakfield. But it won't be there forever. And—"

Gallagher leaned a little too close, letting her voice drop to a sultry whisper. "Whatever you're planning, think twice. You can't harm him. It would be a terrible waste, Commander."

Zeke held up his cuffs, shaking them. "Does it look like I'm in a position to try anything?"

"No. But your methods are known, *Oakfield*. Don't sacrifice your people for nothing."

"If we win, it'll be worth it, *Gallagher*," Zeke replied.

"I tried to warn you," she said, walking away. Zeke sensed disappointment in the colonel's body language. Nearby, his father looked like he was going to pass out, so Zeke steadied him. The situation was taking its toll on the old man.

"You're not gonna croak on me, are ya?" asked Zeke. Avery ignored him. He looked into the distance, whispering to himself. "We needed more time ... I could've finished the Program, I could've ... with more time ... oh god ... now, it doesn't matter. We're finished."

"Uh-huh." Zeke said, ignoring his father's breakdown, concerning as it was. Something on a rooftop caught his eye. He glanced at Markus, who grinned. Jenkins looked bewildered, but she'd understand soon enough.

"She did it." Markus said, breaking into a wide grin that he couldn't hide. "They're here."

A tiny figure wearing a wide-brimmed hat stood on the roof of an expensive penthouse restaurant, around half the height of the other nearby super-skyscrapers. Anne had arrived.

29 — OUTBREAK

Sam's gummy eyelids snapped open. Her head and chest were killing her. Something with the mass of a mountain was crushing her, threatening to crack her ribs again.

David was face-down on top of her, wheezing for breath, weighed down by a mountain of debris. How long had they been unconscious?

"David ..." Sam said, struggling for breath. "Thanks for the save, but get off me."

"You make it sound easy."

David got his hands down onto something solid and pushed. Loose items slid sideways, but the creaking workstation pressing down on him wouldn't budge. Sam bared her teeth, and her eyes flashed. The workstation and other debris were blasted away, making a hideous racket as it crashed down nearby.

David relaxed, pushing himself up. "Thanks."

They extricated themselves from a pile of broken lab equipment, careful not to touch sparking electrical conduits or shattered glass. The events preceding Sam's blackout slammed into focus.

"Jason! Where is he?" she cried.

David pointed. "Follow the trail."

Jason's mental fury had blasted a deep trench into the lab, bisecting the chamber's concentric rings. His compressed sphere of matter cratered the opposite lab wall, obliterating shielding, permacrete, and supercomputer hardware inside. Terminals sparked and burned, while smashed server banks sprawled across intact sections of the lab floor. Even the ominous raised seat that had previously been connected to the Beacon was destroyed.

Jason lay twitching at the heart of destruction, bleeding from the nose and eyes as sparks rained down from severed power cabling. Tiny wisps of Abaddon's presence crept along the ground toward him, but it was weak—barely able to materialize.

Sam and David hurried over, hauling Jason away from the shadow and the toxic chemicals running in steaming rivulets into the trench. Sam fumbled with a fresh dose of Osmium from her pack and replaced the broken one jutting out of Jason's inhibitor. Moments later, the living blackness began to dissolve.

David snatched his pistol from under a broken laptop.

"That was a psychic episode, alright," he commented. "But we survived, somehow."

"Yeah. Jason directed his power this time," added Sam, eyeing the remains of the compressed sphere. "He's learning how to control it."

"Might've been chance," David said, heaving Jason's ragdolling body onto his shoulder.

"No. He did something similar with my steel ball during our meditation session," Sam said. "It's a start."

"Glad to know he's gotten something out of all that voodoo crap."

A loud banging at the lab door interrupted before Sam could argue.

"Right on cue," David said, watching a bright spot begin to eat its way through the door's thick locking mechanisms.

"That's our only way out," Sam said. "The other entrance is the loading bay, but it's sealed, and we don't have time for you to hack through it."

"Shit," David cursed.

They scanned the ruined lab for other exits. Astoundingly, Jason's sphere of violently compressed matter had split open the meters-thick reinforced wall at the end of the trench.

"There's our way out," David said. "He made one for us."

"Good going, knucklehead," Sam said, tousling Jason's blond mop. He groaned, but didn't stir. Sam wasn't surprised, given the enormous energy Jason had expended.

David yanked his storage drive out of an overturned console as they passed it, stowing the device in one of his large jacket pockets. Sam followed, dancing across rivers of steaming chemical runoff while trying to stifle her pounding headache and renewed rib pain.

"Did that thing survive?" Sam asked, gesturing to the drive.

"I built it to last. As for how much data we got, no idea."

"We can review it when we're outta here," Sam said.

David gave her a doubtful look. "How optimistic of you to use *when*, Sam. I'm still stuck on *if* we get out."

They reached the ragged crack in the lab's wall. Sam shimmied inside. Small chunks of rubble fell on her, but it seemed stable.

"Looks like it'll hold," she said, backing out and allowing David room to get Jason into the hole.

David slid Jason off his shoulder and entered, dragging Jason's limp body into the dusty crevice. Pulverized masonry rained on them. Jason sneezed, but didn't wake up.

"Try to get through to Talos once we're past this wall," David said. "We'll need him to guide us."

"Right," Sam replied, setting her communicator to auto-repeat a distress signal until Talos answered. Behind her, the doors gave way to the cutter beams, letting an entire squad of legionaries into the ruined lab.

Sam and David froze as the warriors spread out; weapons ready.

Many of the stasis tanks on the highest level were broken. Green cryo-fluids rushed out, swamping the lowest sections of the lab chamber.

The stinking occupants of the containment units lay silent ... until one of them stirred. As Sam watched, a humanoid mass of clammy flesh twitched, sending a spike of psychic energy through her head.

The tank creature stood, twitching spasmodically. Wires and cables ripped from its black and purple mottled skin, bursting with foul-smelling juices. The Imperial troopers aimed their huge Gauss rifles at it, while others kicked aside debris to clear a path for additional squads to enter the lab.

The creature opened its enormous mouth and yowled louder than any other biological being on the planet, blasting Sam and David's eardrums. Then, it charged the Imperial squads, followed by a swarm of similarly bloated, distorted things from the damaged containment tanks. Jason briefly stirred, squinting at the tank-creatures, but fell unconscious again a moment later.

"Those aren't normal Phage victims," whispered Sam, holding her forehead as the psionic pain intensified, and she noticed hints of oily shadow bleeding off the creatures as they charged. "They're something worse. Maybe Oakfield's failed test subjects."

"They're keeping those bastards busy, that's what matters," David said, hauling Jason deeper into the crevice.

Sam followed David into the wall, but she couldn't take her eyes off the crowd of flesh and teeth as it overwhelmed the Imperial squads. The warriors fired their chunky weapons at point-blank range, defending themselves with crackling blades and industrial power-armored strength, blasting the mutated monsters apart. But despite their superhuman abilities and tank-like armor, the Imperials fell back as more tanks burst open. Sam felt their rage and hunger in her mind as the super-Phagebearers rammed penetrator tendrils into armored chests, smothering the fallen bodies.

Ahead, David squeezed through a tight gap in the broken permacrete, yanking Jason after him into a curved hallway circumventing the lab. Sam reached up, allowing David to pull her out before heaving his brother back onto his shoulder.

Talos's voice broke through on Sam's comm channel. "Monkeys? Come in, hairless monkeys. There's a lot of chatter over the Imperial network. Please tell me I can start blasting these fools."

"Not yet. What's going on out there?" Sam replied, following David as they dashed down the red-lit passage, away from the lab's main entrance. Clattering boots and gunfire echoed toward them.

"The main building is being flooded with reinforcements. Whatever you did has the Empire very annoyed," Talos added.

"I can imagine, there's Phagebearers loose in the main lab," said Sam. "We need a way out. Can you direct us?"

Talos went silent for a moment, analyzing data. "Working on it. From what I can see, every trooper in the building is converging on the main lab. They're also singing death chants, very irritating."

"Great, brilliant, wonderful," David said as he shifted Jason's weight into a more stable position as they ran. "Give us a direction, ya bucket of bolts!"

"Fine, fine," Talos rumbled. "If you wish to avoid trouble, make a left at the next junction. I am flooding their networks with scrap-code to throw them off."

"Good enough," David said. Sam replaced her blade's battery as she heard the lab creatures screaming echo down every hallway.

Less than a minute later, Sam shoved David away from an oncoming barrage of Gauss slugs as legionaries skidded around a corner behind them. "Watch it!"

Sam sidestepped into an adjoining office to cut their attackers' line of sight, pulling David with her. Jason flopped lazily on his brother's shoulder, groaning.

"Apologies, filthy organics," Talos said. "They've turned off the transponders in their armor, so I can't track them. The building's security AI is working against me now. Some friend he was, little shit."

"Use the interior cameras, then!" Sam barked, breaking into a mad sprint through a second workspace as more gunfire tore through the thin office walls.

They picked up more Imperial pursuers, first in ones and twos, then an entire squad zeroed in on their location. Sam activated Jason's energy shield seconds before he took a Gauss hit to the cranium.

"Wha...where..." he mumbled.

Ignoring Jason's slurred speech, David skidded into the primary artery leading to the building's main atrium, leaping over piled scientist bodies and firing over his shoulder. "Why does it always end like this for us?"

"Shut up and run!" Sam shouted, whirling her energized blade to bat away incoming fire. As they progressed, additional Imperial warriors appeared behind them, drawn by gunfire and support requests from their comrades.

Sam yelled into her comm. "You better have a ride for us, metal-head!"

"So unappreciative," Talos remarked, but roaring engines were audible in the transmission's background. "I am inbound. Remain on course to the building's entrance hall. I will be there."

Sam and David emerged into a three-story postmodern atrium and reception area with gleaming glass surfaces, featuring an enormous marble fountain topped by an enormous UEF insignia statue. Jason's shield unit fizzled out after being clipped by an Imperial laser-disruptor weapon. Immediately afterward, a Gauss slug grazed his shoulder, eliciting another moan. Sam watched blood spray.

"David! Jason's hit!"

"I am aware!" David yelled back, firing his pistol as fast as its mechanism would allow. He lurched toward the fountain, heaving Jason over the thick outer wall into half a meter of water with a splash.

Sam slid to a stop and spun, sword whirling on its power cable, and vaporized shot after shot with mind-bending speed. Gauss fire gouged chunks out of the decorative stone behind her. Sam's eyes flared, her body moved, her nose bled. But she couldn't keep this up for long.

David propped Jason up against the pool's inner wall, checking his shoulder. "It's just a graze!"

"Great! Now shoot something!" Sam barked.

More Imperials converged from the other corridors, tripping over each other in their frenzy. Un-augmented auxiliary troopers clattered out onto the glass catwalks above, firing down into the fountain. Geysers of water spiked up out of the churning pool. More of them charged through the building's front doors, approaching the fountain from the other side.

David was grazed by a supersonic slug and went down howling, clutching the wound in his side. Sam stepped into the fountain's pool to cover her legs as her energy shield broke. Dozens of troopers fired on them, pinning them in place with bursting showers of dust, debris, and water.

The screams of the Phagebearers echoed down the entrance hallway. Imperial fire petered out as shuddering, mutated bioforms charged down the hall and into the atrium, free from the central labs. Some of the charging creatures wore Imperial armor, infected and turning on their comrades in a terrifyingly short period of time. The Phagebearers were shambling and screeching as they ripped into anything that moved with razor-sharp bone-claws. Sam had never heard of Phagebearers being able to directly infect others before, but this was proof. These creatures from the lab, failed test subjects or not, were a new breed of infected, an elevated form of the Phage. Sam had a sick feeling that she was witnessing the beginning of something truly terrifying, a new form of outbreak magnitudes more difficult to contain.

"Talos, where are you?" Sam cried.

The atrium sported a floor-to-ceiling decorative piece of glass as its forward observatory screen. Something approached it, passing in front of the artificial sun.

"You humans are so impatient!" Talos remarked over the comm.

An airbus smashed through the window, filling the multi-story room with a blizzard of shattered glass. The marble fountain spared Sam, David, and Jason from the razor-hail. Many Imperials weren't so lucky. Heavy shards knifed through their personal shielding and peppered their armor, forcing them down. The super-Phagebearers ignored this, slaughtering their way through augmented legion warriors and human troopers alike. They howled together as one organism, one mind, bound together by wispy tendrils of the Beacon's shadow.

The airbus smashed through floor tiles, crashing into one of the marble statues that held up the upper-tier catwalks, plunging soldiers to the floor below.

The bus shuddered to a halt in front of the fountain. Talos squatted in the driver's area, crushing the seat with his bulk. The robot's right arm was wired into the flight instruments for direct control. He aimed his left arm cannon through a broken window. "Stay down, humans."

With a blinding flash, Talos blasted the Imperials and Phagebearers alike, engulfing dozens in a boiling line of blue heat. One of the glass elevator shafts caved in, taking two more walkways with it. Talos swept his continuous sun-beam back and forth, shouting with maniacal glee. "Yes, yes! *Buuuurn!*"

David hauled Jason out of the water. Blood spurted from their wounds, but he gritted his teeth and stumbled through the bus's open door, clothing drenched.

"Let's go!" he roared.

Sam's dead blade took a ricochet, smacking her flat in the face, causing her to fall over backward with a splash. She scrambled out of the fountain and launched herself through one of the vehicle's windows, landing roughly in one of the passenger seats. "Talos! Get us out of—"

Talos fired the engines, and the antigrav systems shot the airbus off the shattered floor. The roar echoed off every surface, deafening anyone without a sealed helmet. The vehicle caught renewed gunfire from the parking lot as it rocketed outside, leaving the Science Institute behind. Talos blasted the Empire's exterior surveillance drones with a series of micro-missiles as the bus rocketed over the front lot before disappearing over the nearby rooftops.

When the hard *bangs* of mag rounds hitting the vehicle's rear finally stopped, Sam and David lifted their heads. The rescue had woken Jason up.

"Huh ... what the—" Jason mumbled, clutching his shoulder.

"He's up," confirmed David, rummaging in his waterlogged bag for medical supplies.

Sam grabbed an auto-antiseptic bandage for the wound in David's oblique muscle. He squirmed as she worked on him.

"Hold still, you big lug."

David trembled from the adrenaline surge, shaking his head in disbelief. "Good god, that was insane."

"Wha, what *happened* ..." Jason mumbled.

"Give us a sec, Jason. You're still out of it," Sam said.

While Jason struggled back to full consciousness, David found another high-tech bandage and slapped it on the lateral head of Jason's deltoid. It would kill the pain, reknit muscle, and hopefully return function soon. David bound the minor cuts on Jason's fingers and applied another tech-bandage to Sam's oozing cranial injury.

Sam distributed their last batch of painkiller shots. Most of the packaging indicated that the meds were expired, but they worked well enough. Jason leaned back with a groan. "I think I lost control again. I'm sorry, guys. I'm—"

"It's okay," Sam explained. "You did lose control, but when you released the energy, you ... directed it. Deliberately."

"You obliterated those Solar Empire shitheads, along with half that lab," David clarified.

Everyone grabbed a handhold as the bus pitched and yawed wildly, rocketing into a narrow valley between industrial buildings to avoid detection. Talos raised his free hand. "Hang on, meatbags!"

"I don't remember that," Jason said. "I controlled myself?"

"I wouldn't go that far, but you seem to be getting a better handle on yourself when the Abaddon Beacon attacks you, maybe," said Sam, gingerly rubbing the back of her skull where the Nanite tech-bandage was already beginning its work.

"Sorry to interrupt, but I require a destination for this joyride," Talos announced over the wind's roar. "Are we returning to the Village? These skies aren't safe for fleshy ones like yourselves."

"No," Sam replied. "We can't lead any of these Imperial cyber-freaks back home, remember? Find us a way into the Under-city, but keep our entry point far away from the Village. There are plenty of holes where we can hide out and look through our new data until it's safe to go back. We can try to call Lucia once we're underground again."

"Acknowledged. Scanning for a suitable underground entrance portal."

Jason looked at David with hope. "How much did you find?"

"Not as many files as we could've," David said, flicking through data on his comm-unit's cracked screen. "But I've got some intact data on us, the Beacon, and something that Avery Oakfield called a 'telesthesic amplifier'."

"The chair," Jason said. "That must be the big seat that was connected to the obelisk."

"Find us ..."

Hearing Abaddon in his mind again resurfaced Jason's anger. "We were too slow. They took the Beacon. We missed it!"

"Easy, Jason," Sam squeezed his uninjured shoulder. "Those files might still help us figure out what's wrong with you. When we're able to go home, Janice and Yamamoto can help us analyze them. Besides, we found out that David's not totally useless after all—"

The bus lurched to the right and jerked skyward, throwing everyone off balance again. Talos let out a loud burst of binary code in annoyance. Warning lights and an emergency buzzer flickered throughout the buses' interior.

"Talos! Keep this thing steady!" Sam demanded, hauling herself over to where the robot struggled with the controls. "What's going on?"

"Give me a moment, Samantha," Talos growled through his vocalizer. "Something has us under its control. I'm working out what it is."

Jason, Sam, and David peered through the windows. The bus had reoriented to aim downtown, where the highest concentration of Imperial ships hung in the sky.

"Talos, that is the last place we wanna be going right now," Sam cautioned.

Jason closed his eyes. "We're being taken to it."

"Quit it, Jason," David said. "Talos, turn the hell around!"

"I ... cannot comply," said the robot.

They stared at him.

"Come again?" asked Sam.

Talos rotated to look at his passengers. "The Solar Empire is broadcasting a powerful computer worm across the city to seize control of civilian traffic. The worm relies on line-of-sight from the command ship to function—which happened soon after we left the Science Institute. Any vehicles caught in their net are being rerouted to New Toronto's central plaza, the Grand Processional Square."

As they watched, the last remaining civilian vehicles over the city moved in the same direction, toward the Imperial flagship.

"Talos, kill the worm, or at least break its control over us," Sam muttered.

"The encryption may take hours to crack, Sam," Talos said. "Our best chance at stopping would be to use our anti-gravity lifts to descend safely. But the anti-grav repulsors rely on the engines for power, and I don't have control over those. Unless you'd like to intentionally crash this junk heap, we're locked on course."

Sam sat down heavily. "Shit, we're in no shape for something like this."

Jason clenched his skull, trying to block out the voices in his head with pain, but that only made it worse.

"I have another observation, mortals," Talos said, "The artificial sun has stopped moving."

Jason looked up, spotting the arcology's false sun past the fleet of Imperial ships, projected on the inside of the atmospheric shield. "Oh god."

"Indeed. The Empire likely has complete control over the habitat's core systems. They are demonstrating their power," said Talos.

"Jesus," Sam muttered into her hands.

David approached the navigation console. "Let me look. Maybe I can suppress that worm enough for you to land this heap."

"Be my guest, 'o' brilliant hacker-man," Talos said, leaning away to allow David access to the controls.

Jason gazed at the looming downtown buildings.

"We missed the Abaddon Beacon in the labs, but I think we're about to find it anyway."

"Jason, will you be able to control yourself? That place will be swarming with Imperials, from the look of all those ships over there," Sam asked.

Jason looked at her, offended. "I, uh ..."

"Sorry." Sam took his hand. "We'll do everything we can to get out of there. Just no craziness, okay? We have to keep a low profile."

"Okay," Jason confirmed. He could sense Abaddon pulsing in the distance, calling to him, seeping into his mind, stronger than ever before.

"Find us, Jason," it whispered.

"I will," Jason replied, in his mind. *"I promise."*

30 — CONSEQUENCES

NEW TORONTO - DOWNTOWN CORE - OCT. 31, 2263 – 17:44 HOURS

As the skyscrapers sprouting up from below grew taller until they seemed to kiss the sky, Jason heard the distant cries of an enormous crowd, like an ocean's roar. Their airbus joined a long train of civilian traffic passing a UEF battleship hovering between the buildings, which was hung with Imperial banners like a war trophy.

"So did the Federation ... give up?" Jason speculated, holding his head.

David got up from his failed hacking attempt, sitting heavily in the seat beside his brother.

"That would make the most sense," David said. "By the looks of it, the Empire has broken the Federation's firewalls, accessing civilian and military networks. This bloody worm couldn't work if Federation counter-jamming was active."

"But the news reels always said that the UEF was gaining ground in the war, not losing it," Jason said.

David gave him a *'you know better than that'* look.

"But why surrender?" Jason asked. "The UEF doesn't benefit from being annexed. Everyone would be worse off under Imperial rule."

David shook his head. "Our leaders might be. But it doesn't matter, because this ain't our fight."

"Find us. We have the answers you seek ..."

Jason had stopped listening. He stared blankly ahead, gripping his fore-head. "It's more intense every second, Sam. The closer we get, the more it hurts. I've never had a headache this bad before."

"Is it Abaddon?" asked Sam.

"Yeah, it's screaming in my head, louder and louder. It wants me to find it, and it won't shut up until that happens. The Osmium isn't helping. God, this hurts."

Sam gave Jason a sympathetic look before checking his implant, cranking the dosage to the maximum limit. "We could be getting physically closer to it, that would explain a lot. Hold it together, Jason. We'll get through this."

"I'll try," said Jason, nodding.

"You'll tell me if you're slipping?" Sam replied.

"I'll ... try," Jason repeated.

The airbus rounded the last corner, revealing their destination in all its glory—the Grand Processional Square. Lines of air traffic extended for blocks in every direction, but the Empire's remote control moved them in an orderly fashion. Jason guesstimated that the crowd's size was upward of a million, but it could have been far larger. Billboards displayed the Empire's emblem instead of the usual advertisements, church decrees, or quarantine announcements that he'd seen all over the city. The collective howl of human voices sounded like a hurricane.

"I've seen this place. Abaddon showed it to me," Jason whispered. Flashes of disjointed dreams exploded in front of his eyes ... a wall, a black ocean, a desert, a flaming obelisk ...

"There," Sam said, indicating a half-constructed office tower dead-ahead, blanketed with scaffolds, building materials, and squads of inert builder robots. Only half of the roof's surface looked walkable.

"We could drop to that construction site as we pass over, hide out until this is over," Sam explained.

"And then?" David demanded.

Sam shrugged. "Anywhere's better than our current destination, unless you wanna join that crowd down there."

The Imperial worm forced each vehicle to descend into the plaza. On arrival, Jason saw that each was stripped of passengers by waiting troopers, who were then Phage-scanned and thrust into the sea of citizens overrunning the square.

David looked at the office tower. "We'll be pretty exposed up there."

"There are plenty of places to hide in a construction site," Sam said, gathering her blade and supply bag. Jason felt a spike of apprehension, but he knew she was right. "We have no choice, David."

"We can't make that jump without jetpacks!"

"Pardon me, smelly humans, do you wish for me to accompany you?" Talos interrupted. "If not, I'll test my weapon systems down there. I could eliminate at least several hundred Imperial maggots, before they—"

Sam interrupted. "No, Talos. Follow the traffic down; let them search the bus. They won't detain you if you pretend to be a normal automaton. Can you break the Imperial worm's encryption while we wait?"

"I've been making ... slow progress, though I've revised my earlier estimates—I can subvert its firewalls in under an hour, if uninterrupted. It's quite the little bastard, but I'll get us free."

"Good. You'll be our ride out of here," Sam said.

Talos looked stricken, as much as possible without facial features. "Again?"

"And there will be no blasting. We can't attract attention, Talos. None whatsoever."

Talos let out a vicious blurt of code. "Fine."

Jason cranked the buses' door controls, letting the screaming winds inside. "That's one hell of a drop."

"I think I'll take my chances with the Empire," David proclaimed.

Sam ignored him. "I'll cushion our fall. Talos, tell me when to jump."

"You meatbags really do enjoy testing the reaper, don't you?"

"*Talos!*"

"Jump in ten seconds, but no later than fifteen seconds," said the robot. "Otherwise, you'll

overshoot it. Good luck."

Sam took Jason's hand. "Don't let go."

"Are you sure about thi—" David protested, but Sam yanked them out into open air.

Jason wanted to scream, but the rush stole his breath. His inhibitor flooded him with Osmium, and everything blurred as his eyes filled with moisture. The plummeting sensation instantly made him clench his teeth, screaming through them. Sam's eyes flared pink, grunting with the strain of slowing their freefall.

Jason's feet hit the permacrete. Sam's efforts had only partially cut their momentum, and the three of them tumbled across the half-completed roof. Jason skidded into a pile of wall sheeting. David swore as he rolled to rest a few meters away. Sam slid into a frozen construction bot, knocking it down into the guts of the building, but the roaring crowd masked its crashing descent.

She got up, wincing. "We've really gotta work on our landings."

"Get out of the open," David barked, glancing around for surveillance drones or fliers. Jason heard the incoming roar of ramjets.

They scrambled under a scaffold manned by dozens of deactivated builder-bots. Moments after Jason, Sam, and David had blended into their skeletal shadows, a trio of Imperial Firebird fighters screamed overhead.

The wall of noise was like a physical thing, slamming down as the squadron roared through the square, dropping a glittery gold substance into the crowds. Jason could sense the paranoia wafting off the civilians below, trapped in this place with nowhere to run. He spotted a trio of cargo elevators attached to the building's north side nearby. "What about those? We could ride them down and find a way back underground."

"Not enough cover, Jason," replied David. "They'll spot us. Best thing to do is to stay here."

"Shhh," Sam said, wiping the lenses of her binoculars before offering them to Jason. "Something's happening."

Several groups stood outside the Headquarters Building. Some looked like Federation military prisoners. There were also scientists and civilians, possibly those Jason had seen outside the science facility. A group of high-ranking Imperials were also present. Spacecraft and ground vehicles were parked nearby, including a golden shuttle. A large cargo ship was parked to the left of the massive HQ building's front façade. It drew his attention, but Jason didn't know why. The Beacon hissed in his brain, ever-present. "*Find us, Jason. Time is running out ... the final sacrifice will soon be at hand ...*"

Jason's heart hammered faster. Imperial legionaries and automatons silenced the crowds with barked instructions, warning shots, or physical assault. Even the gigantic carrier hanging overhead reduced the rumble of its antigravity drives.

The front doors of the Headquarters opened, and figures began to emerge. Trudging down the front steps came the high bishop of the church, the finance minister, the supreme commander of the UEF armed forces, the

minister of industry, and the Federation's president, plus several other politicians and their aides.

Two guards nudged a scientist forward from the pack of prisoners to join
them. Jason gasped as he recognized Dr. Avery Oakfield, who was limping
badly.

Marching behind the UEF elites were six identical honor guards. Jason's
stomach clenched in a vicious knot as Emperor Hadrian Mariko emerged
from the building last, raising his arms. The Imperial formations exploded
with sound.

"People of the Federation! I bring you ... your leaders!"

His voice was amplified somehow, blasting out across the expanse so
the whole Processional could hear him. Jason clutched his head, feeling an
immense presence radiating off the man, even from this distance. But it
couldn't overpower Abaddon's call, which was like hot knives cutting into
his brain.

"Find us, Jason ... time is short ..."

Jason peeled his eyes away from the emperor, discovering that Sam's face
had gone bone-white. Only her raven hair was moving, ruffled by the wind.

"Sam?"

"I'm ... fine," Sam stammered.

The emperor came forward, surrounded by his warlords. The UEF's leaders were lined up above the waiting crowds by Mariko's Praetorians. Jason's
stomach twisted harder.

"Citizens of the Federation!" Mariko began. "We stand on the spot where
the Solar War was declared. Four years ago, the Strategos Council called
my Empire an illegitimate state, branding us as criminals and usurpers.
Federation command blockaded Colossus, severing the Colossi people from
life-sustaining imports and threatening hundreds of millions with a human-
itarian crisis. But we threw off their chains of oppression, and look at us now!
I founded the Solar Empire to save the rest of you from these cretins, these
maggots who have squandered our potential."

"What's the meaning of this, Mariko? We had an agreement!" President
Winslow said, looking around with surprise when his words came out amplified like the emperor's.

Billions across the planet, throughout the Sol System, and within the Processional Square watched the drama play out live, easily the most-watched
event in human history.

"Ah, yes," Hadrian Mariko said, striding over with one hand on his cane. "President Winslow. The man who voted to continue the Solar War past the point of sustainability. The man who ignored my cadres of specialist infiltrators, who were sent to Earth to subvert your institutions at every level. And the one who suggested selling the Federation to *me*."

A collective gasp rolled around the square. The emperor was speaking more to the crowd than Winslow. "Yes, you heard that correctly. I'm sure most of you are wondering how my war-fleets bypassed your home-world's formidable defenses, landing safely in every arcology on the planet. Your president can answer that question."

"I ... I would never ... I don't know what you mean, please, I—" Winslow stammered.

"Calm down, Mr. President," Mariko said. "The truth is all I bring to you. I'm not as bad as the propaganda makes me seem, right?"

Sam's eyes flared as she stared at the emperor. "You're worse."

"Are you going to tell them, or should I?" asked Mariko.

Winslow looked sick.

"I'm not picking on you, President Winslow. Any Council member can come clean about what you've done. You all voted on it, didn't you?" said the emperor.

The rest of the council remained silent. Winslow was near the point of tears. "I, I ... we didn't ..."

Mariko made a show of being frustrated. "Fine, fine. I'll spell it out for them."

The emperor pulled a sheaf of documents out of his jacket, holding them up to flutter in the dying sunlight. "This proposal was signed by a majority of the Council, all but one, in fact. They offered to sell me the Federation's assets, and its peoples, in exchange for top seats in my Hierarchy. I reject this agreement, because this is not how my Empire functions. You, the people, should be allowed to decide your own fate!"

Mariko let the papers go, scattering them into the crowd. Shock and anger radiated through them, as voices raised in protest.

David lowered the binoculars, which he had taken from Jason.

"That's ... kinda genius," he said. "Mariko forced them into ending the war on his terms. The population wouldn't be so welcoming of new leadership if the Solar Empire had fought their way down here. That would have been like a second Armageddon, probably would have finished off the planet."

Sam shot him a thunderous look. "You think this is genius? They massacred half the scientists in those labs, and they're doing the same thing in every habitat on Earth, and throughout the entire Sol System. This is insanity, David."

"This war has killed millions," Jason said. "Skipping out on the 'final battle' is no excuse. God, my head."

"Find us, Jason ... the window of opportunity is closing ..."

The pain in his skull flared again as the Abaddon Beacon scraped against his consciousness, stronger every time. Sam squeezed his hand.

Mariko drew a long black sword from its cane sheath. It crackled to life, absorbing light. He approached the line of politicians.

"Your leaders, those you entrusted with your safety, your finances, the education of your children ... they made you fight each other so you couldn't focus on their crimes, like rats in a cage," Mariko said to the crowd. "They destroyed your society's core principles in the name of greed, building their wealth off the fruits of your labor, only to sell you out in the end! But no longer!"

Mariko's troops bellowed as one: *"Strength within, strength without!"*

"Today, you are free from the church of Social Compliance. I offer you all a second chance, a fresh start," the emperor said. "Join the Colossi people, ascend through our Solar Hierarchy, and strive toward our ultimate goal. We must leave this toxic rock and claim the stars as our own. Galactic domination is our birthright!"

The Imperial formations shouted again: *"Strength within, strength without!"*

Mariko held his blade high. "None may break our unity, our shared dream!"

"Strength within, strength without!"

"So now, I will deliver the Imperial punishment for betrayal. The truth will set you free," Mariko said, grinning with murderous intent. His crackling blade stopped beside Winslow's neck.

Anne Oakfield observed proceedings with Lincoln on her shoulder, resting a mechanical hand on the barrel of an anti-materiel rifle that was taller than herself.

Avery Oakfield, who was standing with the other politicians, was too close to the emperor. As much as she wanted to use her weapon now ... Anne needed to wait. They had plenty of time to strike, and she knew that Mariko wouldn't dare harm her father, not with his value. She would wait until they could be separated, and then the strike could commence.

She took a shaking drag from her cigar. Squads of Nightshade operatives were based across, above, and under the Processional square, ready to strike. Many were disguised as the enemy, using their chameleonic armor plating to mimic the look of Imperial war-suits, or hiding under light-refracting invisibility cloaks. They had set up hundreds of autonomous turrets, laid mines, set up kill-zones for the Imperials, and planned escape corridors for the civilians. Everything was ready.

Lincoln's drones had tracked an airbus from the Science Institute that had deposited Jason, David, and Sam onto a rooftop at the furthest end of the Processional. Anne was unsure if Mariko knew they were in attendance, but if so, he hadn't tried to locate them. Anne tasked her drones to alert her if they moved.

Luther came to the rooftop's edge beside her, speaking through her helmet's comm system. "Anne, everyone is in position. The Council is at risk of being eliminated. I'm acting against my better judgement here, but I'll leave the final timing to you. Should we engage?"

"Negative," Anne said, eyeing her father, furthest in line from Winslow. He was in Nightshade's target zone, too close to risk starting the operation yet. "This is not the right moment. Trust me."

"Fine. But if it looks like we're going to lose access to the target, I'll have to order the strike," Luther said, unable to keep the tension out of her voice.

Anne nodded, and looked back at Mariko. "Looks like you've still got the gift of gab, Hadrian. Such a shame to waste that charisma on bullshit."

Faster than an eye-blink, the emperor blurred across the line of council members, bisecting their bodies in a shower of blood, organs, bone, and flesh. Mariko's black blade came to a dead stop at Avery Oakfield's neck as the five other council members fell apart, slopping fluids and innards off the raised area, and into the crowd. The Processional erupted in screaming as the people processed what the Solar Emperor had done to their leaders.

Avery Oakfield glared at Mariko as he withdrew his blade. The Imperial armies bellowed their mantra again. *"Strength within, strength without!"*

"This is the fate of traitors, cowards, and non-believers in my Empire," the emperor cried, sweeping his sword out over the crowd as blood sizzled on the blade's charged edge. "But for everyone else, we are all-inclusive. Previous bloodlines, allegiances, and ideologies are meaningless when you join my Hierarchy. We will not judge you on your immutable characteristics. Only merit matters. I need the best for our upcoming galactic conquest, no matter who or what you are. My Empire represents a balance between individuals, held together by a unifying will—my will."

Mariko signaled to his Praetorians, who drew their blades and swiftly massacred the various aides, adjutants, and lower-ranked politicians that had accompanied the Strategos council, letting the bodies fall where they died. The emperor raised his arms. "I have two commandments for all my subjects. First: you may challenge any authority to usurp their place in the Hierarchy if they are known to be working against Imperial interests. These challenges can be displays of force, like I have demonstrated here, but they may take other forms. This will keep us strong."

"Strength within, strength without!" the army and much of the crowd echoed.

"My second commandment is for you, my people, to uphold my values, working together to further our shared goal of elevating ourselves to the stars. Now that we have unity, our interstellar conquest can begin. There is no more Federation, no more Colossi outcasts. We are all *Imperial* now."

Mariko turned his attention to Avery Oakfield, sheathing his sword within his cane.

"To achieve these goals, I bring you the greatest of technological gifts. Dr. Oakfield will help us unlock it. He is alive because he resigned from the council during their vote to betray you. We reward loyalty in my Hierarchy."

"What?" blurted David.

"That's code for 'he's too valuable for us to kill'," Sam muttered.

Dr. Avery Oakfield glowered at Mariko, but the emperor guided him to stand in front of the bulk cargo lander. The doors opened at his command.

The emperor beamed, like he was showing off his best friend to the world. "My people … this is the Abaddon Beacon."

David and Sam glanced at Jason. He stared dumbstruck at the obelisk, gleaming in the sunlight. Billions of eyes gazed upon the object that had shaped their history, manipulating events that had led to this singular moment. All sound ceased; all other distractions fell away.

It was *right there*.

"The Federation government has kept this artifact hidden from you for over a century," the emperor explained. "Stored within this Beacon is an information repository that has granted us all our Nanite technologies, which power our frictionless drives, antigravity systems, fusion technology, zero-point energy weapons, our fleets, our cities, our weapons, our lives. It helped my family build Colossus Station and restored the Earth after the Great War against the Confederacy. Now I give Abaddon's gifts to you, my people."

The crowd remained silent.

"Guys, we have to get down there. I have to make contact with it," Jason said, quietly, watching dark shadows swirl around the obelisk, beckoning to him, calling to him.

"*Find us … Jason … come to us … do it now … the pain will end …*"

Sam laid a firm hand on his shoulder. "Jason, we're staying here."

But Jason couldn't take his eyes off it. He had no idea what he was supposed to do when he reached it, but he had to try. Anything to stop the splitting agony in his skull.

Mariko put an arm over Dr. Oakfield's shoulder, who grimaced.

"Dr. Oakfield's efforts to reverse the Nanophage and unlock the Abaddon Beacon's full potential were stonewalled by the Strategos Council, but no longer. Together with our scientists—" Mariko gestured to Tobias Schipper, "—we will unlock all the Beacon's secrets from the security of Colossus Station. From there, we shall unleash our might onto the galaxy!"

Mariko's legions exploded into cheers and applause, rocking the Processional with the force of their voices.

"No!" Jason jerked towards the freight elevators, but Sam snatched his arm, looking right into his eyes. "Jason. Control yourself. The data we discovered in the lab can help you. If they catch us, we're done. And if David is captured... the Empire will have immediate access to all that technology."

The artifact's hold on Jason's mind amplified even further, crushing his inhibitor's ability to block it.

"*Do it. Come to us, Jason ... the ritual must commence ...*"

Sam opened her mouth to try a different tactic on him when Mariko began to speak again.

"I have another request to make. I need to find someone."

Sam let Jason go, staring in horror at the emperor. "Oh god, no."

Mariko became teary-eyed.

"The Federation took someone from me, prior to their declaration of war. She is the reason I've fought so hard to end this destructive conflict."

An image flickered across every billboard and screen in the Federation. Sam beheld a younger version of her own face, staring back at her in the fading afternoon light. The Praetorians glanced up at it.

"She is my daughter, the heir to my throne," Mariko declared.

Anne stared at the flickering image of Sam. How was the daughter of the emperor here, on Earth? And, as chills ran down her spine ... who was Sam's mother? It couldn't be Anne, there was no way. Unless ...

Anne took a breath. She had a job to do. Answers could come later. Right now, she needed to focus.

Luther glanced at her, but Anne shook her head, holding up a hand. Avery was still too close to the target, and they had no easy opening to separate them. Her Abhamic instincts told her to wait. This still wasn't the right moment to strike. It was close, though. *So* close now.

David stared up at Sam's face on the billboards, bewildered. "What the—"

"One day, she will assume my role. Through her, our ways will live on," Mariko's voice continued, echoing between the buildings. "Whoever can provide information on my daughter's whereabouts will be greatly rewarded."

Sam glanced at David. "Wait, I can explain this."

"Better start talking," David said, staring at her with growing realization, as the pieces began to fit together.

The absurdity of it made his head spin. Sam was the Emperor's daughter? He strained to keep his composure, struggling for words.

Jason was also speechless, but despite the gravity of what had been revealed, his attention immediately returned to the Abaddon Beacon.

"It's not like Mariko said, David," said Sam. "The UEF didn't *take* me. Mariko sent my genetic material here, to Avery Oakfield, so he could create an heir. I never had a choice!"

"But you never told us about this. That would have been useful information to have, Sam," David said.

"What good would it have done?" asked Sam. "Does it matter? We all went into hiding together, just for different reasons. I hoped that we could all stay under the radar for good, without Avery Oakfield or the emperor ever knowing where we'd gone. But that was too much to hope for, I guess."

"I suppose," David conceded. "Fine. I understand why you kept this to yourself. It's a big secret, but ... *man*, that's some heavy shit. It must have been weighing on you for a long time."

"That's another reason why I kept it to myself," Sam said, with tears filling her eyes. "They did terrible things to make us into what Mariko required, all sorts of experiments and augmentations. Years of physical training, combat training, Abhamic power training, education on politics, history, and every other subject. All throughout it, they tortured us to ensure compliance, though I think they were secretly testing to see who wouldn't break. I swear, I never asked for this. None of my sisters did. And everything I've done for Jason; I did to protect him from his own uncontrolled power and from Abaddon."

David took all this in, eyes darting back and forth.

"And those holding cells we found in the Science Institute, that's where they did all this?"

"A lot of it, yeah."

David glanced at her again. "Wait, if you had legitimate Abhamic power training, why not teach Jason?"

"I tried, many times over the years," admitted Sam. "Remember that 'voodoo meditation crap' you keep bugging me about? That's basically the gist of it. But he's too strong to control himself, and I think his mind has a mental barrier of some sort, built up to protect him from Abaddon. Bottom line, I stayed with you all these years because I owe the two of you my life, and because I hoped that Jason would be ready for real instruction one day, so he doesn't have to worry about becoming a psychic time bomb."

"Hold on. Where is he?" David said, interrupting.

They both looked around.

Jason was gone.

"Oh god..." David retracted his pistol, head whipping around the construction site. Then he spotted the freight elevators. One was missing, cable-box buzzing as the contraption descended.

"Ohhhh no, *no* you didn't, you little shit."

David and Sam dashed to the edge, peering down. The elevator was nearing the ground. Moments later, Jason popped out, a mere speck from this distance. All eyes in the Processional were glued to Mariko's oration, so no one spotted him.

David looked like he was about to blow a blood vessel. "What the hell is he doing?"

Sam grimaced. "He's going after the Abaddon Beacon. He can't stop himself."

"He's not *that* crazy ... right?"

"Jason's been babbling about it since we left the labs, it's gotten too deep into him. I don't think he's in his right mind anymore," Sam said.

"I am going to kill that bastard, right after I save him," David growled.

"I might kill him too."

"Get in line."

Sam cranked open the elevator door. "You've gotta promise me something, though."

"What?" David asked as he leaped over the safety barrier and started the lift.

"If they capture me, don't let them take me. I'll die first. I'm never going back to Mariko."

David gave her a sad look.

"David. Please."

"Would suck to do that after all we've been through. But you've got a deal, Princess."

"Do *not* call me that," Sam said, and tapped her communicator. "Talos, we really need your help."

"What have you done now, meatbags?"

31 — THE KING MUST DIE

NEW TORONTO - UEF GRAND PROCESSIONAL SQUARE
— OCT. 31, 2263 — 18:24 HOURS

Jason stumbled up the left side of the Processional, using abandoned civilian vehicles as cover, heading for the Abaddon Beacon. It loomed in the distance like a dark idol. Darkness billowed around it, reaching out, drawing him in, inviting, beckoning, commanding. Images of the future, the past, and only God knew what else stabbed through Jason's mind in a waking nightmare that came in brutal stabs of mental pain, worse than he'd ever felt before. He couldn't resist the Beacon's pull. Although it wasn't directly controlling him, like it had tried with its shadow, Jason had no choice but to follow its will.

"*There is only one way that this will end, Jason. You must reach us…*"

He had to get up there. Jason had to stop the pain.

A patrol of humanoid Imperial automatons rounded a corner on the sidewalk ahead of him.

Alarmed, Jason changed direction, scrambling under a massive warbot deployment carrier, avoiding the hot air blasting out of its idling repulsor drives. The carrier's landing gear had sunk into the grassy field, creating a good hiding spot under its flat bottom.

Abaddon spoke, like a million scratching ants in his brain. "*Wait … Jason …*"

Jason waited.

Anne was stunned. Lincoln's surveillance bots caught Jason descending into the Processional and making a wild run up the western flank of the ceremony. Now, the boy was trapped, a few hundred meters into a three-kilometer sprint, to reach, what? The Abaddon Beacon? The emperor? Both? Was the artifact manipulating Jason into a confrontation with Mariko? Was he simply insane?

Anne realized that he might be the uncontrolled variable that her Abhamic instincts were waiting for. Could Jason give Anne the opening she needed to strike the emperor down?

"Anne," Luther spoke tersely through their Nightshade's secure channel. "If there is no other reason to delay, I must insist that we launch. We have too much exposure. Someone will discover us. It may cost us the target."

"Lieutenant-Commander, the Science Minister is still in the strike zone, and Zeke is also close by," Anne said. "We need to separate them from the emperor first before we unleash Chiang's company on him."

Luther thought for a moment. "We can task a few squads to pull key people out of the strike zone before we fully engage. We'll need someone to hit Mariko hard with a pinpoint strike first, something that won't engulf the entire area, but nails him hard enough to knock him off balance. Can you do that?"

Anne's cyber-narcolepsy pulled at her consciousness, a product of her immense stress. Lincoln squawked a query. She blinked her HUD's warning icons away, and drew herself back to a calm center, letting her systems realign. She shouldered her enormous rifle.

"Yes, that can be done," Anne agreed. "My shot will be the launch signal."

"Affirmative. Make it count, Anne," said Luther.

Anne nodded. Their attack would throw the Imperials into deep disarray and pin the emperor down—and also give Jason an opening to get moving.

"This is it, people," Luther announced across the Nightshade-wide network. "We do this for our families and friends. Remember them when you're engaging the enemy, because they may be among that crowd. Captain Chiang, on Anne's signal, remove our commander, the science minister and the captives from the strike zone. Then, concentrate your assault on Mariko, keep him off balance. Captain Ossington, Burnaby, and Brogan, you have your orders as well. Prepare to attack. And Anne, get that rifle ready."

"Copy that," Anne said. It was time to do what she came here to do.

Lena Gallagher watched the emperor smile at Dr. Avery Oakfield. She winced as she felt his psychic presence flare with his triumphant emotions.

Mariko's voice was no longer amplified as he said to the scientist, "Now, I'm going to ask your son for his allegiance. I hope for Zeke's sake that he sees sense. Then the last act can begin, the final sacrifice."

Avery Oakfield didn't respond. He had become paralyzed with fear, whispering to himself. "No ... no, not that. Anything but that. That's how it happened before, with the Confederacy ..."

Lena received a sudden call on her comm unit, holding a finger to her ear. "Wait a moment. I apologize, my emperor."

Mariko raised an eyebrow at her, but allowed Gallagher to proceed. Her eyes went wide, and she turned to Thurman. "General, the situation at the Science Institute is deteriorating."

He whirled on her, metal joints clanking. "What? I sent another three hundred legionaries there to contain the situation, plus a battalion of support auxiliaries."

"The infestation on the campus is worsening, spreading outward," Gallagher reported, listening for more updates. "Everyone we've sent so far has been consumed. The Phage isn't behaving normally, worse than on Colossus. It's more aggressive, mutating. Person-to-person infection has been confirmed."

Avery's eyes went even wider.

"The specimens," he whispered. "They're free. Oh god. It's starting ... the Ascension is starting again ..."

The old scientist whirled toward the giant bulk lander, where the Abaddon Beacon sat looming over them all. He put his hands together as if he was praying to God himself. "Please, don't do this, I need more time! Spare us! Please!"

"Quiet, pathetic scum," Thurman slapped the scientist to the ground, where he lay groaning. The general tapped several keys on one of his vam-

braces to open another comm-line. "Fine. I'll call for additional reinforcements to secure the Institute. We can't have anything interrupting proceedings here."

"That would be appreciated, General," Mariko said. "Thank you."

Lena approached. "Shall we begin, my lord?"

"Yes, Colonel. Ensure that this reaches every corner of the Sol System,"
the emperor ordered. "They will watch their greatest hero bend the knee
willingly. And if not, they will join us when they see what happens if he
doesn't."

Lena gestured to the Praetorians, who brought the group of captive soldiers and scientists forward. Zeke Oakfield led them, followed by his lieutenant and a younger girl, surrounded by other Federation fighters. Zeke's
look was one of determination, which did not give Lena confidence that he
was going to choose wisely. *What was he planning?*

The advertisement boards shifted to a live view of Zeke and the emperor.

Mariko flashed a radiant grin. His presence made Zeke wince. Lena
stopped between them, grimacing as her mind was ravaged by Mariko's aura.

"Commander Oakfield of Nightshade Squadron, will you take the
amnesty that our emperor has graciously offered?" Lena asked, her voice
booming out of every loudspeaker around the square. "Will you join us?"

Markus and Jenkins watched, as did his father, along with the rest of the
world. Zeke stared at Mariko. Lena fumed. *What was this man waiting for?*

"How about the rest of my people? What becomes of them?" Zeke asked,
gesturing to the hundreds of captives waiting behind him. Many of his
followers were still nursing poorly-treated wounds from recent battles.

Mariko grinned. "They will follow you, Commander Oakfield. You have
become a symbol for the Federation, despite efforts by your leaders to erase
your accomplishments. Everyone knows your rallying cries, your songs, your
history. Make the right decision here, and we shall move forward together,
in peace."

Zeke remained silent. He was looking at something in the far distance.

Mariko extended a well-manicured hand. "No strings attached. Please …
join me, my friend."

Zeke's heart hammered as he turned to glance down at Mariko's hand. Even after hundreds of high-risk operations, the pre-battle jitters never got any easier. And this one had the highest stakes of all.

Zeke looked Hadrian right in the eye.

"I think I speak for everyone here when I say: go to hell, Emperor."

"What?"

"Do it, Anne!" Zeke yelled at the distant armed figure on the distant rooftop, whom he knew had to be his sister.

The *craaack* of a rifle shot echoed around the square. Zeke had enough time to throw himself backward before a hypersonic projectile passed half a meter in front of where he'd been.

Mariko's phase blade was slicing through it before anyone else registered what was happening. The sword split the depleted uranium slug in two, deactivating its mass-reactive explosive mechanism. Half the round cut a legionnaire off at the knees and buried itself in the pavement a hundred meters away. The other slammed into a parked Imperial dropship, rocking it on its landing gear.

Jason heard a shot ring out. Then he saw people jumping off rooftops ... all the rooftops. He didn't know who they were, but the Beacon spoke again, cutting through the agony in his mind.

"Take your chance. Go, now. Find us. Find the answers you seek ... and your pain will subside ..."

Jason slithered out from underneath the Imperial lander and ran like hell was on his heels.

Anne worked her rifle's massive slide, ejecting the spent cartridge that should have killed the emperor—if he'd been merely mortal. She knew it wouldn't be easy, but the suddenness of the assault had shaken him. Now, they needed to keep him and his bodyguards off balance. The emperor's entourage was fanning out, attempting to locate the shooter.

"We're underway, Commander Luther," Captain Burnaby said.

Chiang's voice crackled next. "Signal acknowledged, starting our run. Squads three through six, remove persons of interest from the strike zone, including the science minister. Then, hit that bastard with everything we have!"

"Here we go, Nightshade!" roared Ossington.

"Let's see how you deal with this, Hadrian," Anne said, loading another round and zeroing in on her target. She pulled the trigger.

As the emperor and his Praetorians were hit with dozens of small micro-charges, armored hands clamped under Zeke's armpits, lifting him away, along with everyone else in range. He heard the telltale whooshing of Jetkits as Captain Chiang's voice warbled out of her helmet's vocalizer beside his ear, "Hang on, Commander!"

Yet another hypervelocity shot rang out, and the last thing Zeke saw before Chiang fired her jets was Hadrian Mariko disappearing beneath a hail of explosions. Shadows whipped past him, casting across the UEF Headquarters building. Men and women that Zeke knew well were rocketing into the air, leaping from great heights, setting the fires of hell loose on the Empire.

All throughout the Processional, Solar Empire vehicles suddenly detonated, punctured by missile strikes and laser blasts that came out of the frozen sunlight. Parked dropships exploded in brilliant fusion-reactor deaths. Suicide drones and pre-laid mines went off among battalions of legionaries, throwing shattered bodies and armor fragments into the air. Imperial officers were eliminated before they could rally resistance. The Solar Empire's battle network wasn't spared either, as petabytes of false messages flooded every comm channel.

The firepower of Nightshade's three hundred souls was augmented by dozens of autonomous turret guns, firing from skyscraper windows, manhole covers, bushes, and from underneath parked cars. It was like the city itself had turned against the Empire, drowning them in pure chaos. Over the battle, Nightshade's song could be heard: "*Gory, gory, what a hell of a way to die!*"

Burnaby and Ossington's strike teams chose their targets to carve evacuation corridors out of the square, allowing the masses of panicking civilians to leave the area. As Imperial organization disintegrated, the crowds dissolved, escaping out into the wider city by the thousands.

Hadrian Mariko arrested his backward slide by plunging his sword into the pavement. Zeke Oakfield had vanished, whisked away with the rest of the captives by his jet-borne operators. Smoke from hundreds of micro-shell explosions wafted off Mariko's spherical psi-shield. Blurred figures dive-bombed him from above, peppering him with every kind of man-portable weaponry imaginable. Another armor-piercing shell detonated against his mental barrier so hard that the pavement was crushed beneath his feet.

Three of his Praetorians were torn open across the driveway, their psionic shields overwhelmed. Of the remainder, N6 was wounded, N8 was shaken but operational. Only their leader, N9, was uninjured. She glanced at her lord as Nightshade rained continuous fire on them, destroying the HQ driveway and straining her mental defenses. "My Emperor, we must return you to the safety of the flagship!"

"No," Mariko replied, deadly calm.

"My Lord, please!"

"I will not run in the face of treachery," the emperor said. "What would that say to our new subjects?"

"But my emperor—"

"Enough!" Mariko snapped, turning to Colonel Gallagher, who hunkered in Thurman's shadow. "Get coordinated and reestablish control of this area. Destroy Nightshade."

"But sir, N9 is correct—"

"Commander Oakfield's buzzing fleas pose no threat to me, Colonel. Carry out my orders," Mariko said, deflecting gunfire with his sword as the jet-troopers came in for another pass. Without breaking his smile, he yanked operatives out of the sky to eviscerate them on the crackling black blade, casting their bodies aside with abandon. His physical weakness was nothing when his mind was unleashed. His surviving Praetorians formed up to provide a ragged defense of their lord, using their whirling blades to deflect what their minds could not.

Mariko had expected some sort of assassination attempt, as Abaddon had foretold in his dreams. But what Mariko had not expected was Nightshade Squadron attempting something of this *scale*. Zeke, the bastard, had somehow orchestrated the entire thing in concert with his damned sister, too obsessed with revenge to care about their species' future. But it didn't matter. They couldn't hurt him. Nothing could. The final sacrifice was on his way, as the Beacon had promised. Mariko smiled to himself. All he had to do was wait.

Lena Gallagher turned to her fellow commanders. Wing Commander Eva Hauser had disappeared, flying off to gather airborne reinforcements. Like so many others, Admiral Shiva was dead, blasted apart by rocket fire. Dr. Schipper sought protection behind General Thurman's shields while the robotic warlord unleashed hundreds of projectiles into the smoke-filled air, tracking multiple targets at once. Lena gestured to the UEF Headquarters. "We need a secure place to coordinate our defensive operations. Nightshade will keep us off balance, otherwise."

"We'll have to take it back from those whelps first," Thurman growled.

Captain Chiang dropped Zeke inside the Federation HQ's cavernous entrance hall, which rang with echoes of the battle outside. Dozens of Nightshade operatives did the same with their human payloads, carrying two or three at a time. The magnificent chamber resembled an old metropolitan train station, with elegant, marbled floors and grand staircases leading to second and third-floor galleries.

"Good to see you again, Captain," Zeke said, coughing. He allowed Chiang to break his cuffs with her battlesuit's augmented strength.

She saluted, unclasping a Gauss rifle from the multitude of weapons stored across the rack on her shoulders, and handed it to Zeke.

"Likewise, sir. It's great to have you back," she said, beaming at him through her visor.

"Has my sister been behaving?" Zeke asked.

"I think ... that's open for interpretation, Commander," Chiang said, as her men dumped several large duffel bags on the ground.

"A very diplomatic answer, Captain," Zeke said, fishing out communicator earbuds and several ammunition blocks from the supply bags. Chiang looked like she wanted to say more, but restrained herself. Zeke knew he had some explaining to do about his previous relationship with the emperor, when this was all over.

Other operators were arming the prisoners, directing them to the windows.

Dr. Avery Oakfield was on a nearby set of stairs, hyperventilating. "Shaelyn, Shaelyn ... what have we done? It's happening ... it's happening again ..."

Zeke grasped his father's shoulder. "Eyes up, Dad. We're not out of this yet. Mom can't help us, neither can God. Only we can."

Avery hugged his knees to his chest, eyes unfocused. Jenkins reappeared, and Zeke tapped his father on the head. "Keep an eye on my old man, kid. He's going loopy."

Jenkins gave him an odd look, but nodded.

The polished floor shook as the battle in the square intensified. Markus hefted a pair of huge grenade launchers, pointing to the area in front of the HQ. "Commander, we are under attack!"

Surviving Imperials and their commanders were rallying outside the building and charging the steps, blocking off any escape. General Thurman led a front line of hulking legionnaires, firing at passing operators in the sky and the HQ building in equal measure.

Zeke loaded his weapon. "If it's a fight they want, we'll give 'em one. What's the plan, Chiang?"

Chiang showed her wrist-mounted holoprojector, displaying their battle scenario. "Your group's role is to draw the emperor's commanders away from him. You will be the anvil that they break themselves on, while *we* break the emperor."

"Sounds good. We can do that," Zeke said, looking around as the former prisoners traded fire with Imperials outside. "This place wasn't built for a battle, but we'll manage."

Jenkins was rifling through Nightshade's satchel bags. Spare Jetkits, weapons, food supplies, explosives, medical gear, even an EMP generator was inside.

"Wow," Jenkins said. Zeke grinned. "Thanks for the toys, Captain."

"We brought them in case the enemy brings theirs, sir," Chiang replied.

Zeke pointed at the emperor, still under an intense volume of fire on the driveway outside, as operators swooped down on him from every angle.

"Get back out there. Hit that son of a bitch so hard that he can't use his weird magical bullshit on anyone. Wear him down. We'll hold this building."

Captain Chiang looked reluctant to leave him and Markus with no support, but she complied, taking flight. "Yes, Commander. Good luck."

Anne Oakfield spat out her spent cigar, hefting a guided missile launcher from the trove of weapons laid out before her. Lincoln linked with the optics, painting a targeting solution on Mariko.

"Captain Chiang, is my brother secure?" she asked as Lincoln signaled her to fire.

Chiang's voice crackled over the comm as Anne's trio of rockets detonated against the emperor's psi-shield, far below. "Yes, ma'am. Commander Oakfield and Dr. Oakfield are inside the HQ. But the emperor's cabal won't let them have it without a fight."

"Affirmative. Zeke can handle the defense, keep your focus on Mariko," said Anne. "Continue hitting his psionic shield. When the emperor is weak enough, I'll deliver the kill-shot."

"Yes, ma'am. Will do," came Chiang's voice, with none of her argumentative tone from earlier. As expected, bringing Zeke back into the fold was a serious morale boost for his people.

Anne returned her attention to the Processional. In a corner window of her HUD, she monitored Jason's progress through the battle, sticking to the periphery where the action was calmest. He was halfway there, making a beeline for the Abaddon Beacon. The emperor was only a hundred meters away from it, so their paths would most likely intersect. Anne wished that her father had told her more about how the Beacon operated. What would happen if Jason made contact with it? But no matter—Jason was the key to taking down Mariko, he had to be.

Hurry up, kid.

General Thurman snarled, blasting at Nightshade operatives who whipped overhead. Behind him, the emperor and his Praetorians endured constant attacks. But the emperor was capable of defending himself, even from an all-out assault.

The general was confident that Nightshade Squadron couldn't win a fair fight, especially if he could properly rally the Empire's fully deployed strength against them. But the bastards had designed their assault to keep his vast formations in continuous disarray. Thurman needed the safety of that HQ to coordinate a proper counteroffensive.

The Imperial general tasked a separated chunk of his cyber-consciousness to take over his shoulder cannons while he signaled to the command ship. Moments later, a dozen drop-pods blasted down from the *Eagle of the Ninth*, shattering the driveway ahead of Thurman.

Twelve upgraded warbots lumbered out of the pods, sporting reinforced armor, massive metal shields, and doubled reactor capacity—Thurman's personal Iron Guard. Under his direction, the robots trudged up the marble stairs, soaking up gunfire and returning it with their quad-linked autocannons. Thurman wasn't taking any more chances with Commander Oakfield. He would die here, today.

Doktor Schipper furiously typed on his datapads. Moments later, the nearby sewer grates popped free. Hundreds of centipedal drones boiled out, skittering toward the UEF HQ.

Schipper giggled. "I was hoping to make use of my pets."

"I hope those things won't undermine all of our goodwill from the population," Gallagher muttered, looking at the human-drone hybrids with disgust.

At Anne Oakfield's request, Captain Brogan launched all six Nightshade gunships into battle, which had been hidden in an underground parking garage several blocks outside the Processional square. The ace pilot cackled with glee as jet-troopers formed up around his craft and intercepted Imperial superiority fighters, which were returning to the Processional in a panic from their carrier ships above the city. "Let's hit 'em, boys and girls!"

As Nightshade's air wing deployed, Anne continued to monitor Jason's progress toward the Abaddon Beacon. Anytime the boy found himself in danger, she removed threats from his path, covering him with carefully placed shots. But he was entering the worst area of fighting, slowing down.

Making a snap decision, Anne pinged the comm network. "Captain Chiang, I have a new objective for you."

"Go ahead, ma'am."

"I'm sending you the coordinates and description of a civilian who is approaching Mariko through the battle-space. I want you to task anyone you can spare to guard him. Get him in range of the emperor."

"A civilian? We haven't even scratched the target yet, can't afford distractions right now," Chiang replied icily.

"You must do this, Captain, he's too important to lose," Anne bit back.

"Anne, what are you talking about? What civilian?" Her brother's voice came over the channel.

▲▲▲

Jenkins fiddled with the portable comm-amplifier she'd set up on the floor, pairing it with Nightshade's private frequency. "You're good, Commander, the transmission is secure, both ways."

Anne's voice cut through the channel. "Zeke, trust me. That boy shares the emperor's power. He can break Mariko's shield for us. It might be the only way to stop him."

"How do you know this, Anne? We need certainty," Zeke demanded, holding a finger to his ear.

"He has Abhamic abilities—I can feel it. That boy can neutralize Mariko's defenses," Anne replied. "We're running out of options, ammunition, and time. Once the Empire recovers, it'll be over for us. His name is Jason, and I think he's our last chance to take that bastard down."

Avery looked up, bloodshot eyes widening. "Jason? Did you say Jason? Subject 107? He's *here*?"

Zeke ignored him, responding to Anne. "I'm gonna trust you on this, sister. Captain Chiang, do it. Get that kid close to the emperor, but ensure that your main assault continues. Mariko will break. He has to."

"Yes, sir," came Chiang's voice, unwilling to contradict Zeke.

Markus glanced up at Zeke as the line broke up into static. "We're taking more big risks again, Commander."

Zeke grinned as he and Markus both started strapping on new jump-jets. "You know what they say about desperate times, Markus?"

"Right you are," the lieutenant said through a cigar he'd lit, hefting two massive rocket launchers from Nightshade's supply drop, aiming them out the window.

Zeke looked around for his father's reaction—but Avery was gone.

"Shit. Dad?" Zeke said, whirling around, checking every corner of the massive hall. The old man must've been less injured than he'd thought. Or crazier.

Zeke swore. They couldn't spare anyone to look for his father. But where the hell had the old man gone?

"Commander Oakfield! You are mine!" roared an augmetized voice from perilously close to their defensive line. Zeke ran to a window and spotted Thurman shattering his way up the stone steps behind his Iron Guard like a demonic beast of war. Projectiles pattered off the cyborg's armor like raindrops.

"They're getting close, people," Zeke bellowed. "Step it up! Keep them occupied!"

Rockets and grenades reached out from the invaders on white contrails, battering the HQ building. Defenders died in droves as the Iron Guard advanced implacably up the stairs behind their enormous handheld shields. Markus tossed Zeke a fresh rifle. "This is not looking good, sir."

"You got that right," Zeke replied, coughing up smoke. Then he heard a familiar skittering sound, shooting a horrible feeling up his spine. Zeke spotting a flood of scrabbling, segmented drone bodies breaking through the building's front windows, boiling through every possible opening and forcing the defenders back.

"Pull back, draw them inside!" Zeke ordered, trying to keep the panic out of his voice.

32 — TRUTH OF THE COSMOS

"Hurry, Jason ..."

Jason's ears rang as he dashed toward the UEF HQ building, eyes locked onto Abaddon, brain on fire as the Beacon pulled him closer and closer. Everything around him sounded like it was underwater. Heat, debris, and overlapping blast waves bombarded him from every direction. Visibility was near-zero. A civilian aircar corkscrewed over his head, borne on a parabola of twisting smoke. A warbot targeted Jason, but before it could fire, a rocket speared through it. The war machine collapsed onto the manicured lawn, reactor-core dying as fast as the post-human legionaries around it, cut down by a spidery net of armor-piercing fire from above. Jason continued on, powered by pure adrenaline, and the pounding, crushing pain of the Beacon in his mind, dragging him forward.

"Find us, and your suffering will end ..."

Figures flashed above the battle-scape using jetpacks, too fast to be tracked. Jason weaved through it all as the battle tore apart the Grand Processional. Glass fell like deadly rain as windows were blown out by crashing jet fighters. The Empire's military trampled through packs of fleeing civilians, firing into the sky at random, unable to lock onto targets. The sensory overload was so intense that Jason saw the world in freeze-frames.

"Find us, Jason, and all the answers will be yours ..."

His goal lay a few hundred meters ahead, gleaming through gaps in the choking haze, beckoning to him. Jason felt Abaddon's signal tightening around his consciousness, crushing him with such intensity that no other thoughts had room to form. He had no plan other than to reach it, only hoping that if he did, the pain would go away. Deep down, Jason knew how insane this was ... but he couldn't ... stop ... running.

"Find us, Jason ... we know it hurts ..."

More armored figures whipped overhead, targeting Imperial troopers in his path. Jason stumbled past their smoldering corpses, but he only had eyes for the Beacon ahead.

Through flames and fluttering ash, Jason raced up the driveway ramp that led up to the UEF's seat of power, halting behind an overturned troop carrier's rotating front tires to survey the scene ahead. He tried to focus on the route, coughing from the fumes wafting from the vehicle's blazing engine compartment.

"Find us, and you will achieve ascension, and oneness with all ..."

Dust and smoke had overcome the entrance driveway of the HQ building. A mess of continuous explosions masked where the emperor stood his ground against relentless aerial attacks. Past him, a horde of Imperials were assaulting the main doors of the gigantic building, which was beginning to fall apart under the assault. All that Jason cared about was the lack of attention on the Beacon.

The twenty-meter-tall obelisk still sat inside the cargo spacecraft, easily accessible up the ship's short ramp. Wisps of darkness billowed around the artifact, beckoning him closer. Jason was willing to brave those shadows if Abaddon did what it had promised, and remove the daggers it had embedded in his mind.

A stray missile slammed into the HQ, cracking two of the fluted columns holding up the triangular neoclassical roof. They collapsed, spewing more choking dust into the open ... which was perfect cover.

"FIND US, JASON!" the Beacon roared.

Jason held his pounding head as he wheeled around the burning transport and sprinted with every ounce of energy he had left. Another hundred meters and his pain would be gone.

A voice called out as Jason built up momentum—one from long ago.

"Jason! Is that you? Subject 107! Stop!"

Startled out of his mental agony for a split second, Jason saw a man trudging out of the dust—Dr. Avery Oakfield. The white-haired scientist was unchaperoned. No surprise, given that every Imperial soldier in the area was dead, disoriented, or blasting away at their aerial assailants.

"Jason! Listen to me!" Avery called. "You can't make contact with the Abaddon Beacon safely yet! We must connect you to my telesthesic amplifier, or the obelisk will consume you and Hadrian! The Nanophage will become unstoppable!"

The scientist reached out to Jason with his uninjured arm, like a father reaching out to his child.

Jason recoiled. "I have to get to it; this pain is going to kill me if I don't!"

"Jason, *NO!*" Avery screamed as Jason dashed past him toward the obelisk. "You have to let me undo what I've done. The only way to stop the Beacon is with my amplifier! Please, stop!"

Avery tripped over his own feet, eyeglasses clattering to the dusty, broken ground. He moaned, scrabbling around for them. "Please, don't let it control you! It's trying to start the ritual again!"

Jason ignored him. He was close enough to make out the nonsense symbology on Abaddon's four-sided metal surface. The shapes deformed and twisted, mirroring the movements of the web of shadows swirling around it. As he neared it, the pain in his head began to recede. If he made contact, he knew the pain would end. He had to get there before it destroyed him.

"COME TO US, JASON!"

Squinting, Avery spotted a pair of Solar Empire legionaries nearby through the smoke.

"You two, stop him!" Avery cried. "Don't hurt the boy, just don't let him make physical contact with that thing!"

Jason ignored the lactic acid burn in his aching quads and the world of suffering in his mind as the two legionaries gained on him like a pair of freight trains.

As he neared the pulsing face of the obelisk, all worldly sounds fell away, like someone had turned down the volume control of reality. The shadows receded, welcoming him as Jason threw himself at the object of his obsession.

His hand made contact with the alien metal, which was surprisingly hot. The pain stopped. Time stopped, too.

Everything dissolved into a waking dream until all Jason saw was Abaddon: the sole anchor in a dark universe as he fell forward in slow-motion, descending into a bottomless abyss.

His point of view slammed backward to reveal an endless expanse of identical obelisks, with nothing but the black void of deep space beyond them, full of broken planets, shattered moons and diseased stars. Their surfaces pulsated as one, neurons in a networked god-mind.

"What are you?" Jason asked.

The obelisks spoke together in a cacophony of tortured voices, a chorus of the dead singing their eternal hymn.

"You have fought long to find us, so here is the truth. Our creators broke the laws of this reality—nearly destroying all of space and all of time. We are their eternal punishment, the guardians of our universe. As a sentient being, you pose the same threat as our progenitors did, no matter how removed you are from them. All thinking beings must be prevented from committing our creators' sin, by becoming one with us. This cycle will continue until the last star has withered away…"

"What? Why should we suffer for something that happened so long ago?" Jason asked, fear freezing his heart. Indistinct facial forms passed across each obelisk's surface. Some looked humanoid, others were anything but human, the only remains of countless dead civilizations. Each species was imprisoned inside a separate obelisk, hyper-condensed into a single corrupted form, leering at him with billion-year-old malevolence. Their voices blasted out together, unified in their torment forever.

"Rudimentary creature. Your species has developed along the technological framework we have designed, like all before you, since the stars were young. You have no control, no legacy, nothing your civilization can call its own. Before us, you are nothing, destined to live out our progenitors' sins, and suffer their punishment. Your purpose has always been to become the final sacrifice for your people's ascension. Within us, you will endure forever, the eternal witnesses of our cleansing of the cosmos …"

Visions of worlds being consumed by a fluid, tumorous, mutagenic darkness speared through Jason's mind … it was the Phage, unleashed on a planetary scale, powered and directed by the psychic might of the Beacons. Not even multi-planet civilizations were spared, enticed by miraculous Nanotech before suffering the disastrous consequences of its use. The Nanophage was more than a mere plague. The Abaddon Beacon network used it to melt down entire species into raw materials that allowed them to *reproduce*. In the wake of each cataclysmic civilizational death, a new Beacon was left behind. Each freshly birthed obelisk became another node in their omnicidal crusade, drifting to a new life-bearing world to start the subversion process on a brand-new sentient species, spreading the pain further and further.

Unimaginable terror gripped Jason. Abaddon had manipulated him, as it had done since humanity had first discovered it. There had never been a cure for the psychic curse incubating within his body, no way out of this nightmare. No answers, only the obelisk's trap. Avery Oakfield had made him into the Abaddon Beacon's pawn, a sacrifice. The final sacrifice.

Finally, at the eleventh hour, he had answers, but they were too much to take. All Jason could do was scream.

33 — FINAL SACRIFICE

Jason's time-stopping vision glitched. Without warning, the endless field of obelisks collapsed back into the singular Beacon before him, glaring at Jason with the same malign intelligence that had fooled humanity's best minds for over a century. The passage of time and sounds of war returned. Jason couldn't move.

The truth had overwhelmed his rational mind. How could anyone, even the whole human race, win against something as powerful as a network of ancient killing machines that spanned whole galaxies, whose prey were entire species?

The inhibitor let out a warning hiss, releasing fresh Osmium into Jason's system. Being so close to Abaddon had suppressed the drug enough for the obelisk to deliver its final message.

"My friend, you've arrived just as it was foretold to me. How uplifting," a voice called to Jason. Startled back into control over his body, Jason turned around. The legionaries who had been chasing him dropped to one knee.

The choking, dusty haze of battle parted around a solitary figure, marching toward the Abaddon Beacon and Jason. Tall, well-dressed, and menacing, the emperor limped on his cane through the curtains of darkness, the living avatar of the obelisk's power. He was smiling.

Nothing affected the self-proclaimed lord of the Sol System as he stalked forward, crushing debris under his shiny dress boots. Chunks of falling masonry and stray gunfire bounced off Mariko's aura, but there wasn't a scratch on him.

Behind him, a lone armored figure staggered in his wake. His single remaining Praetorian was half-upright, using her sword for support. Passing jet-troopers veered out of their combat dives, zooming back up into the sky, attack runs aborted. Although the battle continued nearby, a relative calm fell on Jason and the emperor.

Jason managed to force out a few terrified words. "Please, I have to ... we have to ... the Abaddon Beacon wants to kill us all! It'll kill everyone! It wants everyone!"

The emperor laughed melodically. "I'm sorry, but no. The Beacon is *saving* us, from our past, and from the Nanophage. It has brought the two of us together for this ritual. You are the final sacrifice, who will grant me the power to end the Phage and launch our species into the stars. It has shown me all of this, and more."

Jason wanted to correct him, to convince him, to say anything else, but he couldn't get the words out. He couldn't *think*.

Avery Oakfield's voice rang out beside Jason, as the two legionaries who had chased Jason toward the Beacon grabbed the scientist, holding him back. "Hadrian, let Jason go! Stay away from him!"

The emperor's smile never wavered. "No, he's mine. Once I've absorbed this boy's power, our future will be secured, and I will become mankind's new God, deified by Abaddon itself."

Anne stared down at the confrontation taking place in front of the Beacon. She had no shot on the emperor, as her father and Jason were too close. Where the hell had Avery come from?

Nightshade still hadn't done enough damage to make him vulnerable, so their only remaining chance to stop him was the boy. What was Jason waiting for? Why wasn't he fighting?

Avery struggled to keep his eyes on Mariko despite the pain of being so close to him. "Hadrian, Abaddon is lying to you—it always has. If you consume this boy and his power, you will repeat the mistake that the Confederacy made twenty years ago. You'll unleash the horror they created! It wants you to do this!"

"Silence! You lying heathen," the emperor snapped.

Avery Oakfield winced as the Imperial warriors held his arms with bionic strength. "Hadrian, this has happened before. I was there when the Confederacy created their own psionic beings, like you and Jason. It was during an outreach program, two decades ago, when the Federation gave them access to the Beacon and its technologies to prevent a second Great War from breaking out. But during their experiments, Abaddon manipulated two of the Confederacy's psychically empowered individuals into unleashing the Nanophage in its final form, the last stage of its lifecycle. It took a thousand thermonuclear detonations to silence the terror they created, or else it would have consumed them and everything else on this planet. I started the Abhamancer Program and built the telesthesic amplifier to prevent all that from happening a second time. If you do this, my work will be for nothing!"

"More lies." Mariko sneered. "You never told me this. Why now?"

Avery gave him a pleading look. "I never told you because I was afraid that the Abaddon Beacon would use the truth to manipulate you. But it's already corrupted your mind more than I could've imagined. It wouldn't have mattered if you'd known the Confederacy's fate."

"You could have told the other Council members about this. Why keep it to yourself?" Mariko sneered.

"I *did*, and they didn't believe me," Avery said, looking at the ground in shame. "They were too focused on amassing their own power to care about what happened to the Confederacy, and their power over the people was too reliant on Nanotech for me to have convinced them to stop using it. It's all a trap for us. Abaddon has wormed its technologies into every facet of our society, preparing us to be consumed by the Phage. I had to do something!"

"Even if that were true, your Abhamancer Program was a failure. The only value you produced was me and this boy. And my heir, though lost to me,"

Mariko said. "The ritual must go forward. If I don't do this, the Phage will consume us!"

Avery shook his head. "It's the exact opposite! Abaddon is lying to you, like it lied to the Confederacy and to me."

"No," Mariko said. "Everything it's shown me has come true. Everything it's told me, no matter how horrible, has resulted in more of its truths being confirmed. The Council had to die, the Federation had to be destroyed, and the Phage must be stopped. But to do that, *you* must be absorbed!"

The emperor grabbed Jason's forehead, lifting him high off the ground as his eyes flared with brilliant light.

"NO!" Avery screamed.

Unwilling to be delayed any further, the Beacon came to life. The markings on the obelisk's faces ignited with pink fire, spiking the pain in Jason's head until he couldn't feel anything else. Mariko screamed in pain as his eyes exploded with pink fire, and Jason screamed along with him.

Every cord and vein on the emperor's neck stood out as he strained against the Abaddon as it forced direct control of his body, mind, and spirit. But it was too deep inside him and had been for too long. The voice that boomed from Mariko's mouth was that of the obelisk itself. "*There is no escape from our cycle! ALL MUST BECOME ONE!*"

Jason's neural inhibitor released a last, desperate dose of Osmium, but it wasn't enough to protect him anymore, not against the combined strength of Mariko and the Beacon. The inhibitor burned out in a terrifying surge of Abhamic power, unable to protect him any more.

The emperor writhed and convulsed as the shadow possessed him. Through the emperor, the obelisk attacked Jason, but his automatic defenses came up, as they always had.

The pavement cracked between them, shattering outward in concentric rings. The psychic rush cleared the nearby smoke, exposing a swathe of the surrounding area. Unnatural winds buffeted Avery, the last Praetorian bodyguard, and the legionaries away from ground zero, throwing them to the ground in violent seizures as the psionic feedback tore at their thoughts.

Abaddon's final ritual had begun.

34 — ASCENSION

Hundreds of cyber-centipedes skittered into the HQ building, and the Iron Guard weren't far behind, blasting apart the front walls to gain entry. As they approached, Zeke's survivors regrouped at the cavernous hall's rear staircases, taking cover on the second-floor gallery.

Of the original group of prisoners, scarcely a hundred remained. Zeke spotted marines from *Refit One* among the mix, and even some who had been liberated from the Imperial flagship. Anyone still standing unleashed a sustained barrage of gunfire at the swarm of drones as they crossed the marble chamber, but they didn't have a prayer of stemming the tide. Behind them, the Iron Guard lumbered inside, forming an impenetrable shield line.

Zeke looked around. "This is it, people."

Soldiers, scientists, Federation personnel, Markus, and Jenkins stared at him as booming footsteps approached. Zeke owed them one last word before the end and cleared his throat. "Will you all fight with me, one last time? Not for glory, or the Federation, or even our own lives? Will you fight for our families, our children, and their future, too?" "Yes!" his people roared.

"Good, because this will be one hell of a way to die! We'll knock these Imperial bastards down, and then we make a last move on the big man himself. Sound good?"

His people roared affirmatives and war cries.

Zeke turned to Jenkins. "Is that electro-mag pulse generator good to go, kid?"

Jenkins finished dialing Nightshade's portable electromagnetic pulse generator down to the appropriate yield. She also wore a fresh Jetkit harness for the first time, which they'd also sourced from Captain Chiang's delivery.

"Just, about ... there ..."

Zeke glanced at Markus. "How 'bout you?"

His lieutenant nodded, flexing his Jetkit's haptic control gloves. "I'm ready. And ... it's been an honor to serve with you, Zeke. The honor of my life."

"Likewise, Markus. To the end."

Jenkins peered up at Zeke. "Commander, our timing needs to be flawless. This thing will kill our jets if we mess up."

"Leave that to me. Detonate the EMP on my mark. Are you prepped?"

"I don't know, sir," Jenkins said, test-firing her jets in sequence. "I'm certified with extravehicular gear, but this is way more complex. You need super-specialized training for these rigs, right?"

Zeke laughed. "I'll let you in on a secret: no one ever trained *me* to use these crazy things. I figured it out on my own, when my people first started using them. You will too."

"Okay," Jenkins said, closing her eyes and trying to conquer her fear.

Zeke readied himself as the carpet of centi-pods closed in, gnashing their sparking mandibles. The Iron Guard stomped into engagement range, bringing their weapons to bear through notches in their huge shields. Towering behind them, General Thurman readied his rotary cannons with red eyes and a metallic grin. "Come out, Zeke Oakfield! The end is nigh!"

Zeke raised his rifle, breathing in the beautiful scent of jet discharge as his flight rig came online. He looked from Markus to Jenkins, and then to the others. "History will remember us for this."

General Thurman stalked over crushed bodies and rubble, trailed by Hauser, Gallagher, the cackling Doktor and dozens of legionaries. Countless centipedes slithered between his Iron Guard's legs, who shattered the marble flooring as they approached the trapped defenders, spinning up their auto-cannons to finish the survivors off. He savored the moment.

"Wait. Back up. Get out of the building, now!" Gallagher blurted out.

Thurman revolved his piston-driven torso to face her. "Colonel? Are you undermining us in our moment of triumph?"

"No, look!" she cried.

▥

"Hey there, buddy-boy!" Zeke bellowed as he streaked across the hall on twin jets of fury, blazing over the Iron Guard's interlocked shields. He inverted his body with a powerful abdominal pulse, slamming his bootheels into Thurman's metal face as every warbot opened fire, but it was far too late.

Markus knocked over Hauser and Gallagher while Jenkins tackled the spindly Doktor Schipper, screaming in terror as the mad scientist lashed at her with his mechadendrites. The ragged band of Imperial troopers fired their weapons with wild abandon, watching with horror as their commanders were ejected from the building.

"Trigger it, shrimp! Fry 'em!" Zeke shouted as he and Thurman tumbled down the pockmarked stone steps of the grand entranceway. The Iron Guard hesitated, turning around to follow where their leaders had gone, but Jenkins pressed the EMP's detonator switch. Then she body-slammed Schipper into the pavement, adding her jets to increase the impact.

Zeke thought for a moment that the EMP device had failed.

It happened in an instant. A wave of static energy pulsed through the air, making everyone's hair stand on end. The Iron Guard formation took the brunt of it, shorting out with such force that their battery cores exploded. The electromagnetic blast destroyed the centipedes in a tidal wave of exploding shrapnel and fried brain matter, freeing the imprisoned minds within from Tobias Schipper's endless torture.

Jenkins had carefully dialed in the furthest edge of the circular EM blast radius to fizzle out around the front doors of the building. The surviving defenders charged through piles of sparking dead centi-pods to their original positions at the HQ's shattered front walls, clutching weapons whose firing systems were either shielded from the EMP or ancient enough to be unaffected, raining gunfire down on the Imperial survivors.

As his people provided cover, Zeke ravaged general Thurman's vulnerable areas with gunfire, jetting around the cybernetic ogre's body to avoid being crushed as they tumbled onto the driveway. Thurman had avoided the worst of the EMP blast, but Zeke could tell that he'd been weakened by it.

The enraged leader-beast emitted a roar of electronic rage, trying to pulp Zeke's unarmored form, but the commander was too fast. Zeke circled Thurman with his jets, moving at lightning speed, pelting him with Gauss rounds and his gauntleted fists, breaking the general's metal teeth with armored knuckles. Thurman deployed every weapon and internal defensive system he had, but he could barely fight back in the face of Zeke's unchecked fury.

Markus overwhelmed Eva Hauser's weakened deflection shields and blasted one of her robotic legs off, putting the air commander down for the count. Then he turned his attention to Colonel Gallagher, who readied her Ripper guns.

"Bring it, Lieutenant," said Gallagher.

"My pleasure," Markus responded. They engaged in a furious close-range duel, dodging each other's gunfire amid the broken marble columns and smoking Imperial bodies in front of the HQ building.

Doktor Schipper screeched at Jenkins, enraged. Forgetting her fear, the kid instinctively used her jets to strafe away from Schipper's snapping mechadendrite arms, firing her rifle into his energy shield.

Zeke pounded Thurman's oversized bulk into the ground with his flight rig's exoskeletal strength, and caught his breath, looking around. Where was the emperor?

A howling, tempestuous wind got his attention. Smoke and dust blasted away to reveal a clearing in the haze, where Hadrian Mariko and a civilian boy fought with invisible forces of tremendous power, while the Abaddon obelisk loomed above both of them.

Their psychic struggle compromised everyone's minds in a wave of pain that hit Zeke seconds later. He convulsed, collapsing onto his chest with tears in his eyes as Thurman's cybernetic systems entered a boot-loop malfunction. Jenkins crashed nearby, thrashing in waves of brain-melting power. Markus howled as his ears bled.

What the hell was going on?

Jason and the emperor's psychic wavefront mauled Anne's psychic and cybernetic senses as she grabbed her final pre-loaded weapon, a huge rifle that Hadrian Mariko himself had given to her long ago during their guerilla campaign against the UEF on Colossus. Dozens of weapons and launchers lay discarded across the rooftop. She collapsed to her knees among them, using the rifle to stay upright, gritting her teeth.

The Phage in Anne's body responded to the psychic engagement as if this was what it had always been waiting for; she could feel the tumorous lesions shuddering within her cybernetic systems, pulsating and growing, feeding and spreading. Her cyber-narcolepsy hit worse than ever before, slowing Anne's reaction time and scrambling her systems. Even Lincoln collapsed onto his back, twitching.

She groaned. "No ... not now ... what ...the *hell* ..."

Across the city, computer systems began to malfunction. Communication networks were flooded with the hideous laughter of a thousand dead voices. Anything with Abaddon's technological touch was affected by widening pulses of Abhamic energy from the city center ... which was almost everything. Nanotech of various types began to spontaneously develop the Phage. It started slowly at first, but rapidly accelerated. Any existing cases of the plague began to mutate, massively empowered by the Abaddon Beacon's boosted psychic signal. The Phagebearers running rampant through the Science Institute, the Recyck Yards, Federation quarantine camps, the Under-city ruins, and everywhere else began to merge, enlarging, changing, transmogrifying. The Ascension process was starting.

Soon, all on the planet—and the planet itself—would become one.

Jason and Mariko spiraled high off the ground before Abaddon, bodies rigid as their minds engaged in furious combat, faces locked in immortal torment, a pain so deep that every second seemed to last an eternity. Jason's body was on fire, but the agony in his mind was worse, robbing him of his memories and thoughts. The obelisk's primordial shadow was stripping away Jason's defenses as punishment for his defiance, but he refused to give in. All he had left was survival, even for another few moments.

The Beacon worked through the emperor, its living puppet, attacking Jason with hurtling rubble missiles and lashing his consciousness with terrible force, fury, and shadow.

Jason's mind reacted on autopilot, defending him from the onslaught, returning vicious Abhamic attacks with wavering strength. But it was too strong, he couldn't fight Abaddon and the emperor at the same time. For the first time, Jason wished for death rather than living through this nightmare. Mariko was caught in the middle, nothing more than a conduit, feeding both of their essences to the obelisk as it beat Jason down.

Outside the growing kaleidoscopic nightmare in front of the HQ building, lashes of visible pink energy carved up the square. Even the Headquarters and nearby super-skyscrapers weren't spared as whipping beams of power sliced through them, carving out masses of debris that floated into the tempest of inverted gravity. A nearby transport shuttle imploded and turned inside out. The huge brass bell toppled from the HQ's central tower, tolling a dismal series of *bongs* as it cracked the pavement below—a funeral bell for the human race.

Imperial troops and Nightshade operatives alike were hurled away or vaporized if they were too close. The rules of reality were unraveling, forced out of alignment by the psychic titans battling at the center of the maelstrom, maintaining and growing the storm around them. Soon, that psychic energy would explode outwards to break the planet apart, and the hyper-charged Nanophage spreading across the surface would melt down all matter caught in the tempest, compressing it all down into a new obelisk.

Abaddon rose over the engagement, lord of all that it surveyed, sapping the life and energy from its twin psionic batteries. Its charging sequence was nearing completion.

The last-ditch plan that Sam had hashed out with David was the craziest of their schemes to date, but it had to be done. While Sam helped Talos get the airbus operational again, David's job was to save his brother.

Sam leaped into Talos's parked vehicle through the blown-out back window. Despite the psychic pressure pounding at her mental barriers from nearly a kilometer away, she stumbled to the forward section, where Talos sat. If she went any closer to the HQ building, the pure psychic forces coming off Jason and the emperor would incapacitate her.

"Talos! Have you broken the worm yet? Can this damn bus fly?"

Her robotic companion remained silent for several moments before waking, like he'd been dreaming. Or having a nightmare.

"I ... errr ... I have not, Samantha," he reported. "I, I cannot ... function, with the ... interference ... from ..."

Talos' lack of jokes or insults told Sam how serious their situation was. Sam roared in frustration, kicking over one of the passenger seats. "We have to get Jason and David *out* of there, Talos. We need this thing moving!"

An Imperial warbot detected movement inside the bus, angling to aim its weapons at them. It moved jerkily, fritzing out like Talos was, but its autocannon still rattled into position.

"Samantha, that warbot ... is targeting you ..." Talos said, struggling to transform his cannon arm.

"Stay here, keep trying to kill that worm!" Sam barked, leaping through a side window to draw the Imperial robot's aim away from Talos.

Even with its recursive processor errors from the psychic interference wracking the city center, the warbot opened fire with its autocannons, narrowly missing the airbus as Sam flared her Abhamic abilities to increase her running speed. The skyscraper behind her took the brunt of the gunfire as the warbot swept its weapons after her, exploding the first two floors outward in a shower of rubble and glass.

More warbots stumbled into view, opening up on Sam with everything they had.

35 — ECHOES OF ETERNITY

The injection site in David's neck still hurt from the Osmium shot he'd given himself, but it shielded his mind from the brutal psionic feedback wafting off his brother and the emperor. He had no tolerance for Osmium, and David knew he'd be dealing with the aftereffects for hours, but he was still within the narrow window when it would protect him— before the drug made him too high to move.

As David ran up the ramp to the HQ's main driveway, the pavement seethed like liquid, pulverizing itself in circles that moved steadily outward from the center, spreading into the rest of the Processional. Thousands of pieces of rubble whipped in vicious arcs while Jason and the emperor floated before the Beacon, battling with incomprehensibly powerful forces. As David watched, the emperor pulled Jason's life's essence, Abhamic power, and probably his damn soul out of his body, and it appeared that Jason was powerless to stop him.

There was nothing for it, he had to do this *now*. David clenched his teeth and charged into the roiling waves of psionic power, protected from mental death by the Osmium, leaping onto chunks of floating, spinning debris to gain height. He only had one more dose of the drug, jacked into the syringe gun.

Nearby, Abaddon glowed brighter and brighter, empowered by the Abhamic energies that the two psionic titans were feeding into it. The symbols on the obelisk were strobing from bottom to top, faster and faster. It looked like it was preparing for the mother of all energy releases. David couldn't let that happen.

He jumped from a floating piece of rubble and leaped into the eye of the storm, collided with Mariko, and jammed his loaded syringe gun into the emperor's heaving chest, injecting the entire Osmium vial in one go. The rest was now up to Jason.

Suddenly jerked out of mortal combat, Jason watched the light in the emperor's eyes go out. The link between him and the Beacon was cut, and the psychic storm was interrupted, along with the obelisk's strobing charging sequence.

David sailed past him, eyes rolling back in his head, and Jason spotted the injector in his hand as his brother went limp. He had an opening to strike Abaddon directly. But what could he do? Jason had never figured out what he would do when he found the obelisk ... let alone how to defeat the eldritch monstrosity, and stop it from consuming the human race.

As Mariko and Jason began to fall from the air in front of the Beacon, the obelisk took advantage of his hesitation, exploding with renewed shadow as it screamed, "*The cycle must be completed! You* must *comply!*"

It reached out for him with tendrils of darkness and the rage of eons. Abaddon's core essence smashed into him, and the real world vanished.

Jason felt like he was no longer above the broken Processional driveway. Instead, he was falling past a massive wall, one that reached endlessly in either direction. He'd seen this before.

Jason hit the smooth ground, rolling to a painful stop. He struggled to stand, beholding the enormous fortification. Behind Jason, a tsunami of blackness was rushing toward him, the great sea of shadow from his dreams. But this time, Sam wasn't here to save him from it.

He looked up at the great barrier, cracked and scarred from age. Jason had never seen what lay beyond it, nor had he ever been able to break through it. But now, in the face of the Beacon's murderous rage, he understood that getting through this wall was now the only way to save himself.

In a blind panic, Jason attacked the smooth stone with his bare hands, expending all the energy he had left. He found existing cracks in the structure to wedge his fingers into, trying to pull out any loose pieces that he could find. Behind him, dark figures began to materialize ahead of the inky wave of shadow.

Despite its titanic size and weight, the great wall began to give way as Jason attacked it. More cracks emerged from where he had pulled small pieces away, letting him rip more of it down. Little by little, light began to shine through the splits, but the on-rushing shadow wave kept coming. Breathing hard, Jason continued to break through the structure, grabbing larger chunks and pulling them away, allowing more of the barrier to collapse in on itself.

But Abaddon's ocean wave hit Jason from behind, smashing him up against the wall and dragging him down into its riptide. The Beacon was killing him, dismantling his core being to gain the last vestiges of energy it needed to consume the human race. It was more painful than anything he'd ever felt, but Jason couldn't even scream as the darkness rushed down his throat, yanking him further down into the undertow.

He struggled in the black murk, feeling his feet brush up against rubble beneath him as it pulled him deeper. As Jason burst through the surface of the shadowy sea, he could see a dim light on top of the immense pile of debris. Huge sections of the wall continued to collapse in the distance as he flailed in the heavy blackness like a castaway sailor, but Abaddon pulled him under again. Amorphous tentacles poured into his mouth and nose, wracking his body with white-hot agony as it stripped his life-force away from the inside. Jason's vision dimmed, blackening around the edges. The end was coming soon.

He sank deep below the surface again, energy fading.

"*There is no point in fighting ...*" Jason heard Abaddon say, but even that was a distant echo now. "*We are as inevitable as the stars themselves. Resistance is futile. You will become a part of us, and your species will serve our collective, forever ...*"

Jason sank, down through the darkness, down past the broken bones of the wall in his mind. The pain was ebbing, leaving his exhausted ethereal self, along with the last vestiges of his life energy.

Abaddon was right. There had never been any point in fighting. Despite his efforts, Jason had been overpowered and outsmarted, but there wasn't any shame in that, really. There was no way to resist something so vast, or so horrible. If the Beacon had so easily subverted a being like the emperor, what chance did Jason have?

His final thoughts before Abaddon pulled him into the abyss forever were of Sam and David, and how he so desperately wanted to see them both, one last time ...

Without warning, a light pierced the shadowy sea, swiftly moving toward him.

Someone grabbed his arm. Jason felt himself being heaved from the stygian ocean and up onto the broken wreckage of his mind's crumbling wall. He coughed, hacking up the oily darkness, and gazed up at his savior.

"Hey, kiddo. You finally made it," said the astral figure.

It was ... *him*. Jason was looking at himself.

Or at least, an older version of himself, by at least several years. Jason's future self grinned down at him with his same green eyes, shaking oily shadow off his right hand, which sizzled away into nothingness. His twin's blonde hair was longer, dressed in a tunic and boots, with armored padding and various other pieces of equipment strung on a belt. Several new scars dotted his face, and he had a fair amount of beard growth.

Of particular interest was the glowing object he held in his left hand—a long, crackling blade of energy.

Abaddon's roiling sea of shadow shrunk from the razor-sharp sword of light, receding away from the rubble mountain like a tide going out. The comforting presence of the newcomer restored Jason's spectral body, repairing the damage the Beacon had done with warmth and familiarity. He struggled to his feet, accepting help from his older self as he stood, brushing the last vestiges of shadow off himself.

"I was wondering when you were gonna figure out how to get here," older Jason said, chuckling. He turned and beckoned, starting to climb the mountain of rubble. "Come on, follow me. We've got some things to go over."

Stunned, Jason's mouth hung open as he got to his feet, and followed. "What are you?"

"Pfft, please, you already know that," his older doppelganger said. "We both have the ability to see across space and time, you've done that in your dreams already. Your Abhamic abilities are still in their infancy, but mine have developed just enough to make this chat possible. Pretty cool, huh?"

Jason trudged after himself, hopping from chunk to chunk of dusty wreckage as the Abaddon Beacon's presence followed them up the slope, but it kept its distance, unable to pierce the newcomer's intense aura of light.

"I guess. But why here, why now?"

His alternate self looked back at him, holding the blazing sword reverently by the hilt. "Good question. The Beacon's attempts to possess you, like Mariko before you, forced your Abhamic powers to grow over time—which is exactly what it wanted. It needed you as juiced up as possible to power its final ascension ritual, because absorbing an entire species and their planet takes a ton of energy. The obelisk used you both as incubators. But your encounter with Mariko was so intense that it weakened the veil between your reality and all other spaces and times, including mine. By chance, the timing was perfect. The final blow was when you destroyed this wall within your mind, and unlocked what you buried behind it. I felt that happen. That's how I knew it was time to make contact. You created one of the only opportunities we'll ever have to speak like this, I think. Once things realign properly outside, that's it, chat's over. Let's make it a good one, shall we?"

Jason stared at this older, wiser version of himself as they crunched over vaporized rubble.

"What about Abaddon's ritual? If what Avery Oakfield said was true, it's about to use the Nanophage to consume our whole planet!"

"Stop worrying so much," Jason's older self said. "Time is passing slower outside this place, and the Beacon can't harm you here, not while you're with me. You can take a breather, though not forever."

Jason paused, hands on his knees, and then he stared up at the dark, boiling sky, teeming with shadowy forms that were thankfully keeping their distance. "Okay, okay. Whoa. Sorry, this is blowing my mind. I'm having a hard time ... keeping up." "It's fine. I had the same reaction. It's definitely weird to be having this conversation from the 'opposite' point of view, compared to when I first had it," his older self replied, grinning. "I'm told there's some sort of explanation for this, a reason why we're able to talk across time with our power. Something about Abhamic entanglement linking our minds across all of space, or every electron in the universe being the same one, who knows. Doesn't really matter."

He stopped, holding out the shimmering sword. "What's important is *this*."

Jason stared at it. The weapon didn't seem corporeal, like it was made of light. "What is it?"

His older self raised an eyebrow. "It's a sword. Duh."

"You know what I mean," said Jason. "Sorry, this is all *new* to me."

"Ugh, fine, I'll spell it out," his older self said, swinging the blade of light. "This has been within you for your whole life—it's your creativity, your imagination, your spirit, your hope, your courage, and your resolve, granted to you by all of our ancestors, buried away on the other side of that wall you constructed to protect it. It's your *soul*, which you and Sam had the good sense to guard until it was strong enough to resist Abaddon. Even though you didn't really understand it, that's what you were doing all this time. Oh, and tell Sam from me that the drugs definitely helped, but at this point, you don't need them anymore."

Jason held out his hand. "Can I...?"

His older self recoiled, holding the psychic blade out of Jason's reach. "Nah, nope. This is mine. You've got your own, like I already said. Technically, they're the same thing, but you have to learn how to manifest it, into any form. That's why you've never been able to use your Abhamic abilities like Sam can—she never built the wall within her mind, so she learned intuitively, like her father. But now, your wall is down. Your soul is free, and your power is unleashed. Because of the extreme circumstances facing us and our species as a whole, you have taken your first step toward enlightenment, and your chance to redeem the world."

Jason considered this. "Why did Abaddon come after Mariko and me, but not Sam?"

His older self stroked his beard. "Abaddon only ever chooses two beings for its final consumption ritual—in this case, it was you and the emperor. Mariko's lust for power got the better of him, that's why he lost himself to it, growing so weak in spirit that the Beacon was able to manipulate him far more easily than you. He forfeited his soul long ago, so yours is kind of a big deal because it's the only thing you have right now that can damage the Beacon. Sam is lucky because Abaddon ignored her, so she got a break, at least in the beginning. That allowed her to save you on a number of occasions. But that may not always be the case—the obelisk has switched targets before, so she may not always be outside its notice. You might recall Avery Oakfield mentioning that the Confederacy created their own Abhamic-powered beings too, with his help, before they nearly completed Abaddon's ritual and had to nuke their way out of unleashing the Phage. The Beacon manipulated Oakfield into creating new pawns after that to replace the ones made by the Confederacy—which is where we come from, along with Mariko and Sam. David too, though his abilities manifested far differently, as you know. Be sure to watch out for him too, as you step into your future."

"Okay, fine. But how does a *sword* help us fight the Beacons?" asked Jason, gazing at his doppelganger's shining blade.

His older self continued up the rubble slope, causing mini cascades as he climbed. His expression had grown more serious. "You're not using your imagination, here, Jason. I can't tell you how to beat Abaddon, because it's not something that can easily be put into words. Too many words, or too much detail, can be warped, twisted, and used by the obelisks to manipulate us. They've had billions of years of practice at that. But they've never encountered a species quite like us."

He turned around, and held up the sword. "I'm showing you how to beat it. This is how. This sword is a symbol, an abstraction, created by my power of belief. That's what makes us distinct from all the other civilizations the Beacons have destroyed. Mankind has had its problems; we're far from perfect. Our history before we found Abaddon was a psychotic mess of war, conquest, and death—but we were also intensely creative from the start. Every human being, every civilization over our long history has had the ability to create something from nothing. People have built bridges, started cultural traditions, founded religions, fashioned tools, created weapons of war, and written books that have gone on to influence countless others. Those things didn't exist until we imagined them, designed them, tested them, and used them. But Abaddon hijacked our history and addicted us to its technological path, rather than letting us forge our own path and create a better future. It polluted our traditions, warping us into something that we're not. That's our paradox we've been living since we discovered the artifact—humanity grew fat and successful because of the very thing that threatens to destroy us. Abaddon used our inherent corruption against us—it was primarily the Strategos Council that continued pushing Nanite tech, forcing Avery Oakfield to comply, even after the negative effects of its use became obvious. They were blinded by their greed, and lust for power. Oakfield may have done some terrible things, but he was put in a no-win situation."

"I suppose," Jason said.

"Fortunately," older Jason continued, "Because you and I are *human*, we're the first out of the countless other sentient species that the Beacons have destroyed who are imaginative enough to use our Abhamic abilities against them. We're the first to adapt quickly enough to fight back before it was too late. It sowed the seeds of our destruction within us, but we turned it around. We can save everyone else from them. We can guide humanity, help them flourish and chart their own course, once we're free from Abaddon. You and I are only different from the rest of the human race because our psychic makeup allows us to manifest our power of belief far more literally than anyone else before us, but we won't be the last."

"So, I just have to believe hard enough, and I can beat it?" Jason asked.

"It's not going to be nearly that simple ... but essentially, yes," older Jason smiled. "You're not quite as dumb as I remember being."

"Thanks," said Jason. "Asshole."

"I've been called worse," his doppelganger said, grinning.

"Is this why Sam was never able to teach me how to use my Abhamic powers?" Jason asked. His older self nodded. "That's a good question, and the answer is yes. As I said, there are no words to describe what we actually do. There is only the idea, the belief, the abstraction, and the imagination that shapes the alteration to reality that we want to make—which our Abhamic powers creates for us. Sam is only at the beginning of her psychic journey, same as you, so she hasn't learned how to articulate how she does it. How one person controls their Abhamic abilities is unique to them, and them alone. But now that you've unlocked the wall within your mind, and accessed your innermost creative spirit—your soul—you can both grow your Abhamic abilities together, link your minds and also teach each other. Trust me, you'll need to. David has his own path to walk as well, though it's very different from yours."

"Fine, but you've gotta tell me more than this!" Jason demanded. "We're up against a universal threat, here! Can't you tell me what's going to happen? I could use some future spoilers!"

"I can't tell you what's going to happen, though I wish I could," older Jason said. "Trust me, I understand how you feel right now, watching me dangle the 'answers' over your head without giving it to you straight. I *want* to tell you the future, I really do. But if I did that, I would poison your path, and you wouldn't figure out how to use your abilities to stop Abaddon from completing its ritual, not to mention all the other struggles to come. Things might play out differently if you know more now than you should. I don't make the rules, I only know what I was told."

Jason folded his arms. "That's the best you got?"

His doppelganger waved the sword again. "I can't make it any clearer than this. You need to manifest your soul to beat it. But that's the start. Stopping the Beacon today, saving the human race from Nanophage gooification, that's all well and good, but that's only the beginning of your mission. You need to go through all the other learning, trials, battles, failures, and tribulations that *I've* been through, to make it to where I'm standing right now, so that when little Jason gets to the point where you're standing, you'll be there to tell him what I'm telling you. If you fail at any point ... so do I. Catch my drift?"

Jason held his forehead, squeezing his eyes shut. "Ugh, I think so. You're hurting my brain."

"It's not that complicated, you just have to close the loop. But that's also the upside—you're looking at the evidence of your own success: *me*. There are going to be times in your fight against the obelisks where it really seems like you're screwed, like all hope is lost. They're a devious enemy, incredibly resilient, and have the resources of whole galaxies at their disposal. But take heart, because you're looking at your own future right now."

"Sounds like a piece of cake," Jason said, and then added, "Not. Why us?"

"I know, it's bullshit. Why me, right? Why us? Who chose us to handle such a ridiculously big job?" older Jason said. "It doesn't matter. This cross is ours to bear, so we have to own it. Resistance is not futile. We may be the first and only species to figure out the game, but if you're successful, like I *know* you'll be, we won't be the last."

"Have you beaten Abaddon? Is the fight over, in your time?" Jason asked.

Jason's older self winked at him as they neared the summit of the rubble mountain. "Not yet. But I'm still here, aren't I? That's gotta tell ya something."

Jason considered this, narrowing his eyes. "*If* you're really here ... if this is all true, and you're not some trick of Abaddon's making."

"Good guess, but no, I'm not. Wouldn't that be funny? The Beacon would need a sense of humor to conceive a prank like this, though," older Jason said. "That's also why the enemy will never understand our greatest weapon: our power of belief and creativity made manifest. The Abaddon Beacons can only corrupt and destroy and melt things down into a homogenized mess to propagate themselves. For all their power, longevity, and experience, the obelisks are pretty single-minded. Their only goal is to continue destroying all sentient life across the universe, and they've never had to deviate from that path, never failed until now. They might be endless, immortal, all-powerful, and nigh-unstoppable ... but the one thing they lack is *humanity*. Use that to your advantage. And pray that they never learn from us."

"I see," said Jason.

"If you need any more motivation, fight for your friends. They're the reason you're alive, and you owe them everything," his older self reminded him. "David and Sam are your family. They love you, and their faith in you makes more difference than you realize, so don't let them down. You'll make other friends and allies in the years to come—plenty of enemies too—but no one will ever be as close to you as they are, even during the darkest of times. Well, except for Anne, maybe."

"Anne Oakfield? The scientist's daughter?"

"Yeah, if I had to give you one freebie, I'll tell you that you're gonna meet her very soon. She's a piece of work, but she was the very first Abhamic powered being, Avery Oakfield's accidental prototype, with similar abilities to your brother. Anne will be your guide where I can't be. Trust me, she's nothing like her father. Despite all that she's been through, Anne is *good*."

He looked at his sword, then at Jason. "Your fight after today will be long and difficult, the hardest burden that anyone's ever had to bear—but my existence is proof that it's not impossible. Remember that the obstacle is the way. What is in your way, becomes the way."

"I see that I've become a philosopher in my old age," observed Jason.

"Hey!" older Jason barked. "Just because it sounds like mumbo jumbo doesn't mean it's not true. And keep in mind—I wouldn't ask you to do anything that I haven't already done."

"Of course," Jason said, shaking his head.

Beyond the peak of the rubble slope lay an endless landscape of ruined Earth, blasting apart in fatal bouts of tectonic upheaval that destroyed the curved horizon, driven by tendrils of psionic shadow. Jason could see the Beacon, generating waves of blackness that were ripping the world apart. The moon was in pieces, and the sun itself was dimming. The dream-world was coming undone.

"Looks like our time is growing short. You better get going, Jason," his older doppelganger said. "You don't want our actual Earth to look like this, do ya?"

Jason felt a hand on his shoulder, and he looked into his older self's eyes one last time. "Are you leaving?"

"This is the end of our little chat, but not the end of the world—hopefully," Jason's older doppelganger said, slowly fading from his perception, as the vision began to collapse. "We're all counting on you, myself most of all. But I know you've got this. Make that ancient bastard pay."

"Wait, please, I need to know more!" Jason pleaded. "You can't leave me like this!"

"Sorry. Good luck, kiddo. And say hi to little Jason, when the time comes."

His older self faded away, drifting onward and upward on his own path. As the rubble pile beneath him dropped away, Jason shut his eyes, and started to fall.

36 — THE SHOT HEARD ACROSS THE UNIVERSE

The sounds of battle and chaos returned. Fading daylight blasted through Jason's eyelids, and he opened them to see Abaddon glaring at him across the smoky expanse of the Grand Processional front driveway. Only a second or two had passed since the vision had started, but the Beacon's shadow that had embraced him was beaten back.

Up until this point, Jason had only felt fear when he looked upon the obelisk—fear of what it could do to him, to the world, to everyone. He had been instinctually afraid for his whole life, and he knew that was for good reason.

But now, his fear was gone. In its place was a rage that burned so hot that Jason thought it might ignite his body. He was angry in a way that he couldn't explain. It was like the defiant spirit of humanity had ignited inside him. How dare Abaddon do what it was trying to do, the greatest evil ever enacted, the ultimate crime? Who had given this obelisk the right to even *exist*?

Abhamic energies exploded upward from the obelisk as it began to unleash the power it had absorbed from Jason and Mariko into the sky, up through New Toronto's atmospheric dome and beyond. Abaddon was desperate to trigger the Nanophage that it had so carefully scattered across the Earth and beyond, to melt everyone and everything down and spawn a new member of its misbegotten kind. Jason needed to contain that energy pulse.

There was only one option. Jason did what his older self had told him, channeling the power of his belief—he wanted to stab the son of a bitch. Abaddon needed to die.

A huge rush of Abhamic energy boosted Jason forward out of his fall. All other objects—including David and the emperor—continued toward the ground.

The rush of adrenaline, fury, hatred, and confidence continued to flood Jason's heart as he let out a cry that shook the world. Abaddon would not win, not today.

He streamlined his body, punched his hand out toward the obelisk ... and stabbed it with a glowing blade of his own making.

The Abaddon Beacon screeched, drowning all of Jason's other thoughts out with its indignation. The shining soul-sword in his hand sunk to the hilt in the alien metal, boiling it away. Jason's feet scrabbled against the Beacon's glowing face as he held onto the blade with both hands, dragging it downward with his body weight to widen the wound. An enormous rush of psychic energies blasted free from the split in Abaddon's alien metal flesh and back out into the universe—all of the power that had been incubated within Jason and the emperor, and far more than that.

"Die, you alien bastard!"

The rush of energies blasting out of the obelisk began to waver, but Jason twisted his soul-blade, roaring in effort as it ripped down through more of Abaddon's shining skin. The Beacon screamed again.

The rush of Abhamic energy was like nothing Jason had ever experienced, passing through his etheric being like a hurricane-force gale, ripping at his soul. Abaddon screeched one last time in Jason's head, bellowing its ancient rage at being cheated out of its eternal quest of civilizational destruction. But Jason grinned, showing his teeth to the beast. He was denying the alien God its ability to reproduce, to birth another of its kind using humanity as fuel, and there was nothing it could do to stop him.

The psionic tempest ended with a rippling wave of hurricane force that shattered any remaining intact windows across the Processional. The laws of reality abruptly reverted to normal as Jason was blasted free, hitting the pavement hard in front of the obelisk, but he barely felt the impact.

David lay still nearby, catatonic and drooling from his Osmium high. Hadrian Mariko groaned, rolling over as he held his injured back, struggling to rise.

As massive chunks of rubble, vehicles, and pieces of buildings collapsed around them, no longer held aloft by waves of Abhamic power, Abaddon was the last thing Jason saw before losing consciousness. A massive gash had been ripped into its front-facing metal side, but Jason could only see darkness within the obelisk. The shadows whirling around the Beacon were dying away, and the indistinct alien symbols boiling across Abaddon's four surfaces faded too, going cold and silent. Was it ... *dead*?

As Anne watched, David took the emperor down with a shot of Osmium. Seconds later, Jason blurred forward with a beam of pure light projected from his hand, stabbing the Abaddon Beacon with it. Then, he was blasted to the ground in a huge rush of wind and power. The obelisk went silent, no longer shooting pure Abhamic force into the sky. The planetary consumption ritual had been interrupted at the very last moment.

Jason had saved them all from the Nanophage ... but Anne still had a job to do.

She struggled to check the load of her rifle as her cyber-sight blinked on and off. Lincoln twitched nearby, unable to render assistance as Jason's final psychic thunderclap rumbled across the Processional Square before fading away into nothing.

Using her human hand, Anne felt a single shell in the chamber, the last in her vast arsenal. This was her final chance.

With shaking, corrupted, intermittent cyber-vision, Anne tried to center the scope on Mariko's head, who knelt in the ruins as rubble pounded down around him. The emperor held his injured back, trying to rise on crippled legs without the assistance of his Abhamic abilities, which had been spent by his exhaustive mental battle with Jason, further hampered by the massive Osmium dose David had given him.

This was Anne's long-awaited moment. Mariko had never been as vulnerable as he was right now. What was *wrong* with her? Why couldn't she pull the trigger?

Anne's artificial hand refused to stay steady as the Phage crept through it, bursting through metal plating in hideous, tumorous growths. Without the Abaddon Beacon to direct it, the nano-parasite hadn't achieved full planetary destruction status, but it was still alive and present within her body, triggering her cyber-narcolepsy like never before. Anne switched off her auto-targeting function, cycled to default camera vision, braced the rifle against the edge of the roof, and held the weapon tightly in her human hand, feeling the trigger with real nerves and flesh.

She trusted her humanity. Her biological parts would be what killed Mariko, not her Phage-ridden cybernetics, diseased false technology of Abaddon. The most surprising thing of all was that Anne didn't feel a sense of final vindication, only sadness and grief for what had become of her former partner, the flesh-slave of an alien machine-God. But Anne could finally end this nightmare for Hadrian, for herself, and for everyone else. She took a deep breath ... and fired.

Mariko felt a terrible sense of emptiness as the Beacon lost power, relinquishing its psychic hold over his mind, pulling away like a disintegrating spiderweb. He hadn't realized how deep it had wormed its way inside him until it was gone. Without Abaddon, and without his psychic gifts ... he was nothing.

As true fear gripped his heart for the first time in years, Mariko heard a shot ring out. He limped toward better cover in desperation as Anne Oakfield's armor-piercing projectile—designed to destroy dropships and heavy vehicles—cracked down into the square and blasted his left arm off at the shoulder. The huge projectile continued on, ricocheting off a crumpled Imperial armored personnel carrier before hitting the Beacon, generating a sharp metallic *ping*.

After the echoes of Anne's final shot died away, silence fell on the UEF Grand Processional Square for the first time since the battle had begun. Meanwhile, deep cracks and fissures multiplied and widened in the Processional Square as a result of the psychic battle. A continuous rumbling deep within the Earth grew stronger.

As every survivor in the area slowly recovered from the assault on their minds—Imperials, Federation military, civilians, scientists, Nightshade operators, and many others—the only sound they heard were Mariko's incoherent screams.

Abaddon's ancient intelligence seethed.

The ascension ritual had never been a straightforward affair, as each target civilization was different—but it had always worked in the end. A new obelisk had *always* been birthed. Until now.

Humanity had been a particularly tough nut to crack, with a longer corruption process than nearly any other species in the eons-long records of the cycle. Abaddon had carefully manipulated their history, starting wars and great conflicts, all for the purpose of offering its Nanite technologies to the human race as a path to survival. The human sub-civilization called the 'Confederacy' had managed to incinerate the Nanophage during the Beacon's first Ascension attempt, but that had been a minor setback. It had been relatively easy to resume subversion of mankind's larger factions—with the same researcher involved—no less. The one known as 'Avery Oakfield' thought he'd outsmarted the Beacon with his 'Abhamancer Program', though this development had still fit neatly into Abaddon's grand plan.

But this insane act of ignominious resistance by a single flesh and blood mortal, this ... *Jason* ... was contemptible. Never in the history of its three-billion-year cycle had one of these lesser beings managed to freely use the obelisk's power against it. It was possible that Jason's power was something else entirely.

Jason's ability to stop the birthing process in its tracks and cause tangible damage to the Abaddon Beacon in physical terms had never happened before. The probability was next to zero, but he had still managed it. The subversion cycle could not restart, albeit not in the usual way. Additional forces were needed to subdue this wretched species.

Using the miniscule energies remaining in its inner core, Abaddon released a faster-than-light, quantum-entangled pulse communication out from the Orion arm of the Milky Way and out into the wider galaxy ... a distress signal.

With that, the obelisk entered self-repair standby mode, growing colder than a tomb.

*** End of Book One ***